Praise for *Marked for Death*, the first book in the Lost Mark trilogy . . .

"A rousing action-packed science-fiction/fantasy novel, full of unknown and wondrous creatures . . . sword fights, flying ships, magical creatures, and magic that left me wondering what was going to happen next."

The Arbiter

Three thousand years ago, the first dragonmarks— elaborate patterns on the skin—appeared among the races of Eberron, granting the bearers access to the arcane energies that fill the world.

Twelve dragonmarks have existed for millennia. With the powers granted by the dragonmarks, their chosen few bearers have wrought many wonders in the world, forging a society like none ever seen before.

But tales survive of a thirteenth dragonmark, lost for thousands of years—the feared Mark of Death. For generations, it has been lost, its power gone from the world. . . .

Until now.

EBERRON

THE LOST MARK
BY MATT FORBECK

Book One
MARKED FOR DEATH

Book Two
THE ROAD TO DEATH

Book Three
THE QUEEN OF DEATH
December 2006

THE ROAD TO DEATH

THE LOST MARK   BOOK 2

MATT FORBECK

THE ROAD TO DEATH

The Lost Mark · Book 2

©2006 Wizards of the Coast, Inc.

Cover art by Adam Rex
Map by Rob Lazzaretti
First Printing: January 2006
Library of Congress Catalog Card Number: 2005928111

9 8 7 6 5 4 3 2 1

ISBN-10: 0-7869-3987-7
ISBN-13: 978-0-7869-3987-9
620-95469740-001-EN

U.S., CANADA,
ASIA, PACIFIC, & LATIN AMERICA
Wizards of the Coast, Inc.
P.O. Box 707
Renton, WA 98057-0707
+1-800-324-6496

EUROPEAN HEADQUARTERS
Hasbro UK Ltd
Caswell Way
Newport, Gwent NP9 0YH
GREAT BRITAIN
Save this address for your records.

Visit our web site at www.wizards.com

DEDICATION

For my grandparents: Ken and Angie Forbeck and
Ray and Berenice Fink.

They raised great kids.

Special thanks to Mark Sehestedt, Peter Archer,
Christopher Perkins, and Keith Baker.

CHAPTER

1

The chill breeze blew through Esprë's body like a gust of knives and stabbed her awake. Her head aching and swimming, she first thought she might be back in Mardakine, the town on the edge of the shrouded waste known as the Mournland that she and her stepfather Kandler called home. Sometimes an icy wind came whistling from that barren, time-stopped place that loomed over their house and down through the window of her bedroom, shattering her restless sleep.

Esprë hadn't slept well for weeks. Since the strange mark had appeared on her back—the dragonmark known as the Mark of Death, she now knew—images of wailing souls had assaulted her dreams, screaming at her to free them, to help them slip this mortal flesh and find peace in Dolurrh, the Realm of the Dead. Then the people around her, people from Mardakine whom she'd known for years—since the birth of the young town—started dying, and the dreams got worse.

Not wanting to think more about the horrible images swimming in her brain, Esprë wrenched her eyes open. The overcast sky above her was a dead-white color. She'd never seen it anywhere else. She was in the Mournland.

The young elf shivered, this time not from the cold, and brought her hand to her forehead. "Ow!" she said, wincing in pain at the bruise she found swelling there, just under the hairline of her long, blond locks. She sat up to hold her head in her hands and saw that she was on the deck of a ship. No, not the deck. She spotted the wheel there in front of her. She was on the bridge.

Memories gushed through her mind. This was the airship, the one that Kandler and Burch had stolen from that crazy elf in her cloud-shrouded tower, the lady with the papery skin and the dead-leaf laugh. They'd escaped there with Sallah, the pretty knight with the long, red hair.

After the rescue, Esprë had thought it was all over, no more vampires kidnapping her in the middle of the night. The insane, deathless elf—Majeeda was her name—had made sure of that, no more changelings posing as a long-lost aunt.

Then they'd gone after the rest of the knights, and the changeling had come and stolen her away again. Images of a horrible battle flashed through Esprë's mind. Kandler and the others had come after her, chased her to that walking city of warforged—living golems fashioned as soldiers for the Last War—and become embroiled in a fight for her life, for all of their lives.

Esprë remembered flying the airship over the battle, using it to crush the warforged leader, to kill him, she'd hoped, but that was all. Her memories ended there.

"Hey," a soft voice said from behind Esprë. "How are you feeling?"

Esprë knew that voice, but the throbbing in her forehead kept her from admitting that to herself. She turned slowly, unable to resist the urge.

There, leaning over the young elf, stood Te'oma, one hand on the airship's wheel. A slight woman, with pale skin the color of the Mournland sky, her all-white eyes narrowed at the girl as she evaluated her injuries. The wind whipped her white-blonde hair around her soft-featured face, and a hesitant, half-finished smile played across her mouth, which sat like a sharp cut between her chin and nose.

The changeling.

Te'oma reached out toward Esprë's forehead with a long-fingered hand, and the girl let loose an ear-splitting scream. She scrambled backward, away from the changeling, as fast as her feet could push her along the bridge, until she slammed her back into the railing along the starboard side. Then she drew a breath and screamed again.

The changeling stayed frozen where she was, her arm still reaching toward the girl, and grimaced. "It can't hurt that bad, can it?" she said.

"Where are we?" Esprë demanded. She was hurt and cold, and she just couldn't take any more of this. She'd rammed the ship into the warforged leader so she could save Kandler. It wasn't supposed to happen like this.

Te'oma looked up at the overcast sky then back at the girl. "We're still in the Mournland," she said, "but we're on our way out. This is no place for a young girl."

"You brought me here!" Esprë pointed out.

Te'oma frowned. "I never wanted to. That was Tan Du's idea. He thought the blanket of mists here would protect him from the sun. It did, but even so I argued against it." She glanced up at the sky again. "I'd rather have taken the long way around."

"Where's Kandler?" Esprë asked. She tried to hide the desperation in her voice, but even she could hear it there.

Te'oma's frown deepened as she rose to her feet, still keeping one hand on the ship's wheel. She said nothing, just shook her head. As she did, her features shifted, and Esprë found herself staring up at her stepfather's mournful, dark-eyed gaze under his short-cropped hair the color of polished wood. It was the same look he'd worn when he'd come to tell her that her mother had died on the Day of Mourning, the horrible event that had created the Mournland from the fair nation of Cyre and killed everyone within its bounds.

"No," the young elf whispered to herself as her soul threatened to freeze solid inside of her. "Burch?"

Kandler disappeared, and the shifter replaced him. Burch was shorter than his old friend and much darker. The blood of werecreatures flooded his veins, lending him a feral, almost animalistic look. Jet-black hair covered his deep-tanned skin almost everywhere but his face, tumbling down in knots past his shoulders and sweeping down from his forearms and the backs of his legs. The nostrils of his wide, flat nose flared as he looked down at the girl. A tear welled in his eye, something Esprë had never seen in the real shifter's face.

"S-sallah?"

Burch disappeared, and a beautiful, red-haired woman took his place. Her green eyes shone back at Esprë with more than a hint of sadness. A fat tear welled up in one emerald orb and rolled down her soft, pink cheek.

Esprë almost had to remind herself that this was Te'oma looking at her, not the woman who'd fought so hard alongside Kandler and Burch to rescue her. The fact that Te'oma's clothes remained the same helped. Only the person in them seemed to change.

"Brendis?"

A black-haired young man now kneeled where the fake Sallah had once stood. The tears flowed more freely from his gray eyes.

Esprë began to cry too. "Even Xalt?" she said. She found herself sitting next to the changeling and realized that she'd been inching her way closer to her throughout the transformations.

The mourning youth vanished as Te'oma let the façade fall from her natural form. She knelt there in front of Esprë

4

and reached out a hand to wipe the girl's tears away, nodding sadly.

"I can't make myself look like a warforged," Te'oma apologized. "They're just too different."

Esprë buried her face in her hands and wept. The knot on her forehead throbbed as she did. When she was finally able to speak again, she peered up at the changeling and whispered, "They're all dead? All of them?"

Te'oma nodded. She brushed Esprë's golden hair back from her face, streaking trails of tears along behind it.

"Say it!" Esprë said. "I want to hear you say it!"

"Yes, dear," Te'oma said. She swallowed once before continuing. "They're all dead, every one of them."

Esprë just stared at the changeling, not wanting to believe her.

"The warforged—there were just too many of them. Once the airship broke free from the stadium, they came rushing back in. If not for my bloodwings," the changeling shrugged her shoulders, and her bat-colored cloak rustled to life for a moment before falling limp once again. "Well, I would have been trapped there too."

"What happened?" Esprë asked. "The last thing I remember is aiming the ship for that huge warforged." She rubbed her forehead. "What happened?"

Te'oma put her arm around the girl. Esprë tensed and considered pushing the changeling away, but she needed someone now. Anyone.

"The airship bounced off the arena's floor, and you hit your head," Te'oma said. "It knocked you unconscious. When I realized what had happened, I flew after you to save you."

"And the others?" Esprë looked up into the changeling's all-white eyes, trying to keep even a shred of hope from her voice.

"By the time I got control of the ship and turned it

around, it was too late. Warforged soldiers had swarmed into the arena."

"Maybe they took them prisoner," Esprë said, hope forcing its way out of her despite her best efforts to suppress it. "Maybe they're still alive."

Te'oma shook her head and held the girl closer. "I flew over the arena." Her voice choked for a moment. "I'm just glad you didn't have to see it."

"Did I . . . ?" Esprë started. "Did I kill him, that warforged leader?"

"Bastard?" Te'oma said. She sighed. "No, you missed him. You're *not* a killer."

Esprë buried her head in Te'oma's chest and wept bitter tears. She knew how much those words were lies.

Chapter

2

"Damn, boss," Burch said as he chewed a strip of raw horseflesh between his sharp, pointed teeth. "That was one bone breaker of a fight. Thought we were dead for sure."

Kandler nodded in agreement from atop the horse that rode alongside the shifter's steed. It wasn't the short, shaggy *lupallo* the shifter normally mounted. He perched awkwardly on it, even as he continued to marvel at their escape from Construct, the mobile city founded by the Lord of Blades, the leader of the warforged castoffs who'd congregated in this forsaken land.

Sallah rode behind them, trying to sit tall in her saddle while Brendis slumped against her back. The young knight's wounds from the fight in Construct had nearly proven fatal. Sallah had used her powers as a Knight of the Silver Flame to heal him as best she could, but she'd only been able to do so much.

"It would be best if we didn't move him," Sallah had said to Kandler that morning as the first hints of the daylong false dawn of the Mournland broke against the distant eastern horizon. There hadn't been a choice though, and she'd known it.

They all hurt, some worse than others. Burch was the best off, just bruised a bit from when the warforged titan had taken down the wall of the arena on which he'd been perched. Consequently, the shifter was in the best mood of them all, flashing Kandler a bloody smile now and then as he shredded bits of the freshly killed horse in his mouth.

Kandler had almost bled to death during the mad gallop away from Construct. Only a scant mile away from the place, Burch had insisted on stopping to tend the justicar's wounds. The shifter had bound them up tight, calling on his long experiences on both the battlefield and the trail, then Sallah had relieved his pain by laying her hands upon the worst of his wounds.

It had been enough that he could get back on his stolen horse and ride until the night fell so hard it had been impossible to see. Even so, Kandler had argued they should go on, fearing they'd lose any trace of Esprë's path through the Mournland's sky.

"We'll catch her, boss," the shifter said. "Just like tracking a wounded bird."

Kandler knew that Burch's cavalier attitude masked his deep concern for Esprë's fate. Years spent in the shifter's company had taught him that his friend was as serious as a blade through the chest when it came to those he loved. He was just trying to keep Kandler's own spirits up. The justicar appreciated it, although he couldn't manage to admit it to his friend. He suspected Burch knew anyhow.

Maybe his own injuries kept him from that. One of his eyes was swollen shut. The skin on his knuckles was shredded, and he thought he might have broken his left hand. He had a stab wound in the back of his left calf and another in his right shoulder. Pain lanced through him with his mount's every step, but he ignored it the best he could. He knew that Sallah would tend to him again as soon as she could, but taking care of Brendis had exhausted her for now.

Sallah had barely taken the time to help herself. Bastard, the warforged juggernaut who ran Construct, had stabbed her twice in the chest and once in her upper arm. She'd lost a lot of blood and had scarcely been able to gallop away from the warforged city with the others.

Despite being short half a hand, Xalt had carried Brendis on his horse. The warforged artificer had more than proved his loyalty to the others long before then, but Kandler was continually impressed with the creature and his sympathetic ways. While the steel-faced Xalt had been created as a soldier—as had all of the warforged manufactured in the final years of the Last War—he displayed more caring than most "breathers" Kandler had ever known.

The warforged had been injured in the battle as well. Leaping off of the deck of an airship could put a dent in the toughest hides. Still, he bore all his troubles without complaint.

When they'd left Mardakine only—damn, was it only days ago? It seemed like a lifetime had passed. In fact, several had.

When Kandler and Burch had led the knights out of Mardakine to rescue Esprë from the vampires and the changeling who had kidnapped her, there had been seven of them: Kandler, Burch, Sallah, Brendis, Levritt, Gweir, and Deothen. Now three of the knights were dead, and another was hammering on death's door.

"We've had better weeks," Kandler said, more to himself than anyone else.

Burch cocked his head at his friend. "I don't know," the shifter said. "It's not every week we got fresh horsemeat in Mardakine."

"I can't believe you eat that raw," Sallah called from behind, barely disguising her disgust.

Burch rolled his yellow eyes at Kandler before responding over his shoulder. "Horse was as good as dead. We got no food. Easy choice."

9

Xalt spoke up from where he trotted along next to Sallah. "I have never been more glad that I do not need to eat." Kandler thought he heard a hint of a smile in the warforged's voice, but since the creature's face couldn't flex like that—apparently his builders hadn't considered such a skill worth working into his design—the justicar could only guess.

The tireless warforged kept pace with his mounted friends easily, never breathing hard or showing any sign of exertion. Perhaps, Kandler thought, it was because Xalt didn't need to breathe. He apparently only bothered with it so he could talk.

It had been Xalt's horse that had fallen lame as they raced away from Construct with what seemed like three score of well-armed warforged following them on foot. The creatures couldn't keep up with a horse at a dead gallop, so Kandler and the others had pushed their stolen mounts as hard as they could to put some distance between themselves and the wounded city smoking behind them.

Thankfully, Construct no longer moved. The city itself—or at least dozens of the golem legs on which the thing marched—had been wounded in the battle with Bastard and his titans in the place's arena. It would be mobile again soon, Kandler was sure, but by then they would be long gone. In the meantime, they just needed to keep ahead of the warforged who were sure to still be chasing them.

Kandler, Sallah, and Burch had been riding hard all night. When Xalt's mount went down, they'd just moved Brendis up behind Sallah and kept going. They'd slowed since, hoping to prevent the same thing from happening to their own steeds, and they'd stopped long enough for Burch to butcher the fallen beast.

Kandler hadn't wanted to do it. He'd pressed to keep moving on, chasing after Esprë and Te'oma on that airship on which they'd escaped the battle, even though they'd been out of sight for endless hours. The ship was damaged, and from the holes torn in the hull, Kandler guessed that it had no supplies left on it either. Eventually, it would have to stop someplace, and he planned to reach it when it did.

Burch had pointed out—wisely, Kandler had to admit—that they weren't likely to find food elsewhere in this blasted waste. Few creatures made their home in the Mournland, and those that did were usually too tough to be edible. It was hard to sink your teeth into a living ball of fire that exploded anytime you got too close, for instance.

"Think they're still following us?" Kandler asked.

"I would guess not," said Sallah. "Leaving Construct in flames gave us a substantial lead. They must give up the chase eventually, right?" No one responded, and she added, more uncertainly this time, "Right?"

Xalt cleared his throat. "My apologies, but I don't believe that. The people of Construct are as dedicated as they are tireless. They will pursue us until we leave their domain."

"How far does that extend?" Kandler asked, dreading the answer.

"The whole of the Mournland."

Burch turned around in his saddle and peered back at the horizon. The gray, dead grass on the rolling hills behind them stood frozen in the grave-still air of the land. "Leaving a trail like a battle wagon," he growled.

Kandler didn't need to look back. He'd already seen it. Even Esprë would have been able to track the riders through here. The hoofprints of their steeds stood out as if they were trotting along fresh-fallen snow. He stared forward instead.

That's when he saw it: a line of gray stones running from east to west, across the horizon.

"Is that what I think it is?" Kandler asked.

The shifter swiveled in his saddle and peered in the same direction as Kandler. A thin smile spread across the shifter's feral face.

"What is it?" Sallah asked, trying to keep any tone of hope from entering her voice.

"Maybe our ticket out of here," said Burch.

CHAPTER

3

When the riders reached the line of stones, Kandler saw that they stretched in both directions as far as the eye could see. They were perfectly round, at least the parts that weren't resting in the earth, and spaced just far enough apart that he could not touch two of them at once.

"What are these?" Xalt asked. The warforged ran his hand along one of them as a parent might caress a child's cheek. As he did, bluish arcs of electricity followed his touch, arcing across the stone's smooth surface like lightning trapped in granite.

"Does that hurt?" Sallah asked.

She still sat on her horse, Brendis propped up behind her. The young knight had groaned when they came to a halt at the line of stones, but he had been horribly silent since.

The horses snorted loudly as they rested for a moment. The riders had pushed them hard to get this far so fast, and they were happy to stop now, even if only for a few minutes.

"It . . ." Xalt's voice trailed off as he searched for words that would not come. "I've never felt anything like it before. It's like something light and feathery dancing along my plates. It . . . it makes me want to laugh."

"It tickles?" Kandler arched an eyebrow at the warforged.

Xalt stared back at the justicar with his unblinking ebony eyes. A noise that sounded something like a giggle escaped from his open mouth. "I suppose that's right." He bent his head to stare at his hand running over the stone again. "Warforged aren't ticklish though. It wasn't a necessary part of our design."

Burch snorted as he leaped atop one of the stones. "First time for everything."

"It's the lightning rail line," Kandler said, answering Xalt's earlier question.

"I've heard of these," Xalt said. "Placed next to each other, they form a repellent field that can carry strings of connected coaches along them as fast as an airship can fly. Aren't they supposed to glow all over?"

"I used to ride this line a lot," Kandler said. "The Day of Mourning put an end to all that."

Burch nodded as he crouched like a frog, his legs splayed wide, and peered down to examine the stone. No electricity leaped from the stone to tickle his feet. "Killed Cyre and the rail line too."

"Where does it lead?" Sallah asked, peering off toward the east. The line of stones drove straight across the wasted plains until it disappeared from view.

"Metrol," Kandler said, "but it doesn't follow our path. We need to head north too."

Burch shook his head. "Follow it, boss. Airship could be anywhere."

Kandler squinted at his old friend. "It was headed northeast. If we don't go that way, we could miss it."

"Nothing says it kept northeast," said Burch. "Changeling's smart, she hightails it out of here first. We're smart, we do the same."

Kandler ground his teeth. What the shifter said made sense, he knew, but he didn't want to admit it. If they started questioning the idea that the airship had gone northeast, where would the doubts end?

"We can follow the line straight into Metrol and through the mists," Burch said.

A miles-thick border of dead-gray mist surrounded the Mournland and had ever since the Day of Mourning. It sealed the place off from the rest of the continent of Khorvaire and all of its former enemies.

No one fought over the Mournland anymore. It would be like fighting over a graveyard.

"Can't you just find your way through it like you did outside of Mardakine?" Sallah asked.

Burch shook his head. "Maybe. I know Mardakine. Been through the mists there lots of times. Never been this far into the Mournland."

"Following the stones would be simple," Xalt said. "Even I could lead us through the mists by doing that."

"Is that why you never left here?" Sallah asked the warforged. "Were you trapped?"

Xalt cocked his steel-plated head at her. "Warforged don't need to sleep, breathe, eat, or drink," he said. "I was thinking of you and the others."

"Burch is right," Kandler said wearily. "We can't help Esprë if we end up lost in the mists. Back in Mardakine, we saw more than one group of fortune hunters get turned back that way. Those were the lucky ones, most times."

"What happened to the others?" Sallah asked.

"The Mournland," Burch said with a humorless laugh.

Kandler ignored him. "Some never got out of the mists. They just wandered around until they ran out of food and water. Others made it through but ran into one kind of predator or another."

"Warforged," Sallah breathed. As she did, she noticed Xalt looking at her, and she blushed a bright red. "You're not *all* bad," she said sheepishly.

"Thanks," Xalt said without a trace of irony in his voice.

"Not just warforged," Burch said. "Carcass crabs, living spells, things worse."

"Worse than a—what kind of crab?"

"Carcass crab." The shifter bared his teeth. "Giant crab likes to bury itself under bodies on a battlefield. Corpses stick to its shell when it moves."

Kandler nodded. "That was my first thought when those warforged attacked back near the monument."

"Wouldn't have been the first time," Burch said.

Sallah shuddered despite herself. As she did, she noticed Kandler watching her, and her eyes turned steely in response.

"What's worse than a carcass crab?" she asked.

"People," said Kandler. "There aren't too many of them here in the Mournland, but those few are usually up to no good."

"We're here."

"We destroyed a good chunk of Construct and killed some of the most powerful warforged that lived there."

Sallah lowered her eyes. "Point taken."

"The worst of them are the scavengers, people who pick through the corpses hunting for things to steal. Some parts of the Mournland are thick with them. The worst of them is Ikar the Black and his crew. They'd kill you for your hair."

One of Sallah's hands absently stroked her long, red curls. "You can't be serious."

Kandler gazed at her warmly. "It's beautiful hair."

"Ikar sometimes works out of Metrol," Burch said, shattering the moment between Kandler and Sallah.

The justicar found himself more drawn to the young lady knight every passing day. He hadn't been with another woman since Esprë's mother had died on the Day of Mourning. He'd been too busy helping carve out Mardakine and protecting its people from threat after threat—including that of Ikar the Black. Love hadn't ever entered his mind.

This wasn't love, though, he told himself. He barely knew the woman, and she certainly knew little enough about him.

He was going to have to change that.

"All right," Kandler said. "Let's head for Metrol. Once we make it to the Talenta Plains we can head north for Karrnath. I'm afraid that might be where this changeling is headed."

"Wouldn't it be easier for her to just head north then?" Xalt asked. He grew uncomfortable for a moment as all eyes turned toward him. "I follow geography," he said with a shrug.

"Maybe," Kandler said. "Maybe the changeling doesn't even know where she's headed. Remember she barged into Mardakine with at least a score of those Karrnathi zombies, not to mention that bloodsucker Tan Du and his vampire spawn. With them all gone, she's probably desperate. It's hard to tell what she might do."

"You breathers never cease to amaze me," Xalt said. "A warforged would consider the girl lost and go back home."

Kandler fought an urge to rip off the creature's tin-plated head. "Esprë *is* my home," he said instead. "There's nothing for me back in Mardakine."

"Why don't you leave us and return home then, Xalt?" Sallah asked, transparently doing her best to turn Kandler's mind from mayhem.

"We just about destroyed my home," the warforged said. "I don't think I'd be welcomed back with open arms. I'm sure," he said, focusing on Sallah, "that you would be welcomed in Flamekeep."

Sallah smirked. "The Knights of the Silver Flame do forgive those who repent their sins," she said, "but for me to fail in my mission would be a disaster of the highest order. The Mark of Death that Esprë carries has the potential to alter the face of the planet. She cannot be allowed to fall into evil hands."

"So much for that," Burch said evenly.

"Enough!" said Kandler, giving his steed his heels and steering the beast to follow the line of stones to the east. The others quickly fell into line behind him. "East for now and then north," he called back as he urged his mount to a steady trot. "I won't give up hope for her—ever!"

CHAPTER

4

The next afternoon, when the riders and Xalt reached the top of a tall hill, Kandler called a halt. They'd ridden hard since the first suggestion of dawn in the east, and they were all tired, thirsty, and sore. From the hilltop, they could see for miles around in any direction.

"Good place," Burch said as he leaped to the ground from the back of his horse, which shivered as he moved off, seemingly glad to be rid of him. "See anyone coming from forever away." He paused. "Course, they can see us too."

Kandler dismounted, then cracked his neck. "No fires," he said, "just like before. Don't want to draw any more attention than we have to."

The justicar stretched his legs as he approached Sallah's horse. He and Xalt helped the lady knight bring Brendis down from behind her. The dark-haired young knight was finally conscious, due to Sallah's ministrations that morning. Once awake, he'd personally tended to his own battered flesh.

"The magical powers the Silver Flame grants its finest adherents do not reach into the Mournland," Sallah had explained to Kandler. "As knights of the Flame, though, we have some power of our own, and the pall that hangs over this land has not diminished that. It is but a candle compared to the Silver Flame, but it still can light the way."

Even so, every movement caused Brendis pain. He winced as his feet touched the ground, nodding his thanks to Kandler and Xalt even so.

Sallah was beside her fellow knight in an instant, putting herself under his shoulder, letting him lean on her as they made their way toward where Burch sat. Already fishing around in his pack, the shifter pulled out a well-wrapped bit of still-bloody horseflesh and offered it to the knights. Sallah accepted it for them as she helped Brendis sit on the withered, gray grass, but neither of them opened it yet.

Kandler sat down next to Sallah and favored her with a wry smile. She smiled back at him softly.

"Is there no way we can cook this?" the lady knight asked, holding up the package Burch had handed her.

"Only if we want every creature in these parts to know we're here," Burch said. "Warforged patrols probably still on our trail."

"Do you really think so?" Sallah asked. "Construct must be hundreds of miles behind us by now."

"Not far enough," the shifter spat.

"He's right," Xalt said. The warforged stood on the south side of the hill, peering back the way they'd come. He had no need for food and little for company. The crucible the group had found themselves in over the past few days had cemented them together, but Kandler didn't doubt that the creature still felt a bit like an outsider sometimes. Whether or not that bothered him, the justicar couldn't tell.

"There they are," Xalt said, pointing behind them with a thick finger, the only one left on that hand.

Kandler squinted in the direction the warforged indicated. There, just on the edge of the horizon, he spotted a scattering of dark dots. He couldn't tell if they were moving.

"Are you sure?" he asked the warforged. "That's leagues away."

Xalt nodded. "I've been watching for them ever since we topped that rise they're on now. When we broke camp this morning, I feared that they might have gained ground on us. I am sad I was right.

Kandler cursed then looked over at Burch. "Get a fire going, would you?" he said.

"Why not?" The shifter shrugged. "They already know we're here, and we're still hours ahead of them. Might as well have full bellies."

Within minutes, Burch was roasting bits of horsemeat over a crackling fire made mostly of the Mournland's gray-green grasses and a stunted shrub that looked like it had died years ago but just never knew to fall over from it.

As the others gorged themselves on the fresh-cooked food, Kandler wandered off to the eastern edge of the hill and gazed out into the distance. There, on the horizon, he saw a smudge of gray that was darker than that of the grass or the sky, poking up from the surrounding land.

Metrol, or what was left of it.

Beyond it, the mists that covered the sky of this forsaken land cascaded down to the earth, forming a backdrop between the city's battered skyline, which he'd once known so well, and the Cyre River, which he thought must be sparkling in the rays of the unseen sun.

Kandler heard Sallah coming up behind him before she spoke. Her step was firm yet light, unlike Burch's scamper, Brendis's heavy limp, or Xalt's thudding stroll. Her hand fell on his shoulder in the same way, and he reached his own hand up to hold hers in place.

"We'll find her," Sallah said. "She'll be all right." Her tone was as soothing as her words, although they did little to ease his worries.

"You can't know that," Kandler said. "For all we know,

she's already dead." He tried to keep the bitterness from his voice, but it echoed there anyhow.

"If you believed that, you wouldn't still be on this path, chasing after her so hard. Revenge can always wait."

Kandler bowed his head. It was a moment before he spoke, and Sallah let the silence lie between them easily. He liked that, and he liked her.

"I used to live in Metrol," he said. "That's where I met Esprë's mother. She was one of the king's elite battle sorcerers, working in Cyre at the behest of her family in Aerenal."

"I didn't know she hailed from the elf homeland," Sallah said.

"Esprina had more class than anyone I'd ever met before. I'd known elves, but they mostly left me cold. People who live ten times as long as you don't ever seem to have the same set of problems.

"She was different, though. Her father said her time in Khorvaire had tainted her, made her too 'human.' Maybe that's so. She was two hundred years older than me, but that never seemed to make a difference."

Sallah dropped her hand from Kandler's shoulder and moved up next to him. He put his arm around her. The warmth of their bodies together pressed back a chill in the air that, up until that point, he hadn't known was there.

"How did you meet her? Metrol is a long way from Sharn."

"In more ways than one," Kandler said. "I came to Metrol in the secret employ of King Boranel."

Sallah cocked her head up at the slightly taller man. "You were a spy?"

"I preferred the term 'elite agent of the Citadel.' "

Sallah looked out at the city in the distance. "Did she know?"

Kandler squinted at the Metrol skyline a moment before answering. "Eventually."

He looked down at Sallah and saw her gazing up at him.

Her green eyes seemed to shine even under this dead-dull sky.

"She was one of my assignments. I was supposed to get close to her and learn everything she knew, then report back to Sharn."

Sallah glanced away. "Did you?"

"I got close to her, all right. Closer than I've ever been to anyone."

Sallah nodded. "But did you report back to Sharn?"

Kandler held the woman closer. "Burch and I were on our way back to Sharn with Esprë when we ran into Argonth and hailed it for a ride.

"Argonth? The floating fortress?"

Kandler nodded. "We figured it would get us to Sharn eventually, and despite our orders we weren't in much of a hurry. Better to get there safe than fast, we told the captain."

"The captain?"

"Captain Alain ir'Ranek, the commander of Argonth. While our excuses still echoed in the general's quarters, he informed us that Breland was mounting a massive offensive against Cyre. Argonth had already unleashed an army of thousands to stab deep into Cyran territory. We were to sit tight until the operation was complete, then follow the troops in to report on our efforts."

"You had a child with you," Sallah frowned, confused.

"We were all going to move to Sharn. Esprina had a few details to work out, she told me, but she promised to follow as soon as she could. Just one more mission for Cyre, she said, then she'd be free to leave her adopted country for another."

Sallah shuddered against Kandler's side. As she did, the justicar remembered how they'd passed by a monument to the dead when they'd first entered the Mournland. Esprina was buried there, he'd told Sallah then, killed on the Day of Mourning.

"Did you know she'd be part of that battle?" Sallah asked, her voice soft and low.

"I left Esprë with Burch and commandeered the fastest horse I could find. I rode hard in the wake of the army, following its trail of trampled land, until I reached the borders of Cyre.

"As I got closer, I saw a long bank of clouds settled along the ground before me: the dead-gray mists that surround the entire nation, although I didn't know that at the time. All I knew was that Esprina was in there somewhere, possibly in the middle of a vicious battle, maybe dead."

Sallah closed her eyes and held Kandler tight around his broad chest. "What did you do?" she asked.

"What I had to," he answered. "I gave my horse its head and galloped straight in.

"I rode hard into the cloud bank for a while, hoping I'd just dash right through and into the sunlight beyond. After a minute, I realized that something was wrong. The mists swirled about me like a tornado, but I felt no wind. They blotted out the sky. It was impossible for me to tell which way was east. I almost couldn't tell up from down.

"I stopped for a moment, lost. I thought I suspected the worst. I was wrong, but only because I couldn't have imagined how bad things would be.

"I spurred my horse on and rode through the mists for what seemed like days, although it could only have been hours. I got turned around though, and I found myself back outside the mists as the sun set over Breland, painting the sky crimson red.

"I knew that I would soon not be able to see, so I uncapped an everburning torch and held it high. The heatless flames didn't do anything to burn away the mists that curled out at me from the edge of the cloudbank, almost as if trying to draw me back into their embrace.

"The only thing I knew for sure was that I couldn't go

back. I couldn't face Esprë without some sort of news about her mother, and I couldn't face myself without knowing what had happened to Esprina. I turned that horse right back around and dove into the mists again.

"I wandered about in there for I don't know how long. Eventually, I emerged from the mists again. For a moment, I thought I'd just come back out into Breland again. It was darkest night, and it's impossible to tell one side of the border from the other around there—or at least it was. Then I looked up and saw that there were no stars. What I'd thought was a cloudbank reached up into the sky and covered the entire land beyond.

"I wandered through darkness so thick it almost seemed solid, my magical torch the only thing shedding light as far as the eye could see. As I rode, the sky began to grow lighter, but never bright, like an overcast winter's day. It was then that I finally saw it.

"Saw 'them,' I should say, what was left of the battle from the day before.

"I later heard reports that it was a three-way affair, with Cyre and Breland skirmishing for a bit before the goblins of Darguun swept in, unable to control their bloodlust at the sight of such a hard-fought conflict. There were no goblins in the part of the battle I stumbled upon, just a sea of dead people, mostly human.

"I knew there was at least one elf floating in there though.

"The carnage seemed to stretch on forever. I've been in battle before, seen more fights than I care to remember, killed more people than I can count. I'd never seen anything like that. It was as if everyone on the battlefield had been dropped in their tracks, all at once.

"I looked for the standards from Cyre. It was easy to pick out the golden crown on the bright green field. Those flags seemed to shine as if they could still see the sun hidden overhead.

"I spent the better part of the day picking my way through the bodies and the wreckage. As I did, one thing struck me: there was no smell.

"Bodies that lay out in the weather begin to turn fairly soon, but these looked freshly dead, as if they'd all been breathing just a moment ago.

"Few of them looked like they had any reason not to be walking around. Some had fallen in the battle that had been going on when the Mourning happened, but most were unscathed. All of those had one thing in common though: their eyes and mouths were frozen wide in absolute terror."

Kandler felt Sallah shudder against him, and he fell silent.

"Go on," she said quietly. "I didn't mean . . ."

"It's all right," he said. He took a moment before he started again. He felt all the long-buried emotions welling up in his chest once more. It had been more than four years since that horrible day, but it still ate at him.

"I got there before anyone else. Over the years, scavengers have started to strip the place. There's so much of it though, so many bodies, it's hard to imagine how long it might take before they're done."

"Did you ever find your wife?"

Kandler bowed his head. "I looked for three days. Most people would have given up, but I knew what her unit's standard looked like. I had some hope. Besides, I knew that getting back through the mists again would be chancy at best.

"On the morning of the third day, I found her. It was in that spot near that black stream, right where Burch and I and the rest of Mardakine raised that monument after the Last War ended, right where Gweir was killed."

Sallah wiped her eyes at this. Kandler could tell she'd been thinking of her fellow knight already, before he'd mentioned the young man's name. He'd been the first of the knights they'd lost on this mad chase through the Mournland trying to save his daughter or, in the case of the knights, to keep her from permanently falling into the wrong hands.

"I found her collapsed near her unit's green and gold standard, face down in the turf. It looked like she'd been trying to run toward Breland, where she knew Esprë and I waited for her.

"I don't know if she made it more than a few steps. She had the same horrified look on her face as everyone else, although on her I saw the tracks of the tears that had fallen from her eyes.

"I buried her right there next to that foul, awful stream. I recognized some of the others in her unit, and I thought about burying them too. When I looked out across the swath of bodies, though, I knew if I started down that path I wouldn't be able to stop.

"Instead, I lay Esprina to rest by herself. I said a few words as I knelt over her fresh grave, and I left her there to rot."

"Only nothing ever rots in the Mournland, does it?" Sallah said.

Kandler shook his head. "I couldn't leave her lying out in the open like that," he said. "I wanted to give her back some of the dignity she'd had so much of in life.

"That's one of the things I hate about this place," Kandler said as he gazed out over the low hills that separated them from the deserted city of Metrol in the distance. "The whole land is an insult to everyone who ever lived here. It's bad enough they're all dead. There's no one left to bury them."

Kandler fell silent. He hadn't ever said so much about that fateful day, not even to Burch. He stood there holding Sallah to him.

He hadn't been with a woman since Esprina. Until the end of the Last War, two full years after the Day of Mourning. He'd been too busy. The time since then was, if anything, more of a blur than those first two years: helping found Mardakine, building a town in that forsaken crater; trying to maintain some semblance of law in a new place on a merciless border; trying to raise Esprë the way he thought his wife would want, knowing that the elf girl would barely be an adult by the time he was a doddering old fool.

Now, though, he couldn't stop thinking about Sallah. He hadn't known a woman like her since Esprina: strong-willed, beautiful, powerful.

When Kandler had first met the lady knight, he'd chalked her off as just another religious fanatic. The intense time they'd spent together showed him that she was much more. She was devout, to be sure, but she didn't let her faith define her so much as she lived within it. He didn't know everything about her, yet, but he knew that he wanted to know more.

Kandler turned to Sallah, and she raised her face to meet his, their eyes locking together, saying more than their words could ever. He leaned in to kiss her, and she lowered her head so that his lips met her forehead.

"My apologies," he whispered to her. "I thought you might want that too."

Sallah nodded, Kandler's lips still on her brow. "I do," she said softly. "I do. You are an amazing man, the kind of man I could give my heart to."

"But?" Kandler's heart fell into his stomach. He desperately wanted to hear this answer—needed to—but it terrified him.

"But I need someone who's not still in love with his wife."

With that, Sallah turned and walked back to the fire that Burch had set. The fast-blazing, grass-fed thing was already starting to die.

Kandler watched her for a moment, then turned back and stared out at distant Metrol once more.

CHAPTER

5

Walking through Metrol as night fell over its silent streets was like wandering through a mausoleum, only the bodies still lay out in the open rather than encased safely and respectfully away in their graves. The riders, with Xalt loping along behind, had yet to enter any of the buildings in the place, but Kandler was sure that the mayhem inside was if anything worse than that without.

Parts of the city seemed almost untouched, apart from all the bodies, almost as if everyone in them had simply fallen asleep and was trapped in an eternal dream. Some moments, Kandler felt that a simple spell would cause the people to climb to their feet and resume their interrupted lives as if nothing had ever happened.

Other parts of the city, though, looked as if they'd been trampled by a pack of iron-booted giants. Buildings lay toppled against each other like felled trees in a forest of cut stone and treated timbers. Stacks of cobblestones crunched up out of streets as if the land itself had tried to vomit upward in the aftermath of the horror. Large, deep holes occupied what had once been thriving neighborhoods.

"This must have been a magnificent city," Xalt said as

he trotted alongside Kandler's horse.

"It was," the justicar nodded, then shook his head in a mixture of wrath and despair. "The crime committed here . . ." He couldn't finish the thought, much less the sentence.

"Better find a place to hole up for the night," Burch said.

Kandler glanced at his old friend and saw the hairs on the backs of the shifter's arms standing on end. He could sense that something was wrong here. He might not be able to give voice to his concerns, but they were tangible even so.

"True," Sallah said. "We could run into scavengers or worse."

"We could take them," Brendis said. The young knight was healthy again finally. He seemed embarrassed by how badly he'd been hurt, now determined to show through false bravado that he would never be laid so low again. "How many of them could there be?"

Kandler knew that Brendis was deluding himself, but he decided not to do anything about it. If the young knight needed to believe he was invulnerable to get through the coming days, he wasn't about to disagree with him. False bravado was better than nothing at all.

Sallah, though, wouldn't let the younger knight get away with it. "We are not here to do battle with the ghosts of Metrol," she said. "We are passing through as quickly as possible on our way to rescue Esprë. Keep your focus."

"Yes, Lady Sallah," Brendis replied. Although Kandler didn't turn around to look at the young man's face, he could hear the tension in his voice.

Kandler looked up at the sky overhead. Although the Mournland's ever-present mists still smothered the place, the rushing in of the dusk almost made it possible to ignore the mysterious overcast, as if it were little more than the thick cloud cover of a wintry day. Kandler had spent many a night in Metrol under just such a sky, wishing for a glimpse of even one of the moons that danced through the heavens on a clear night. Now, though, the break in the clouds he longed for—a sign of an encroaching spring—might never come.

Off in the distance, an unearthly howl broke the eerie silence that engulfed the city.

"By the Silver Flame," Brendis said, his voice quivering, "what was that?"

Kandler craned his neck around to where the sound had come from off behind them. The vacant buildings lining the wide street stared back at him blankly, their doors and windows void of life. He shot a look at Burch, but the shifter just shrugged.

"No animal I ever heard," Burch said, sniffing at the air. "Nothing but death around here."

The horses whickered nervously. Kandler kicked his along a little faster. "Let's keep moving," he said. "Whatever that was, I'd rather it didn't catch up with us."

"Indeed," Sallah said, making the sign of the Flame by touching her forehead and drawing her fingers down to touch her heart with a flourish.

The horses' hooves on the cobblestone street rang like a dozen crude bells, drowning out any sounds for a moment. Kandler remembered Metrol as a city always filled with noises, even in the dead of night, and the way the clatter of the hooves echoed along the street made him wonder if they could be heard anywhere in the city.

Something loosed another howl into the night, this time from somewhere off to the left.

Xalt, who had been trotting alongside the horses, slid to a halt. "It sounds like a wolf being turned inside out," he said.

Kandler tried to ignore the image that leaped into his head. "Just keep moving," he said. "We stay in one spot, they'll get us for sure."

31

"Do you know what's making that noise?" Sallah said. "If so, don't keep it to yourself. We must know whatever it is we face."

Kandler frowned. "It's the reason I haven't been back to Metrol before."

"Other than the whole of the Mournland between it and Mardakine," Burch said.

"Other than that," Kandler agreed, "but mostly it's the ghostbeasts."

The justicar reached down and pulled Xalt up to sit behind him. The horse was too scared by the noises to protest. The two riders would be too heavy for the beast to carry for long, but Kandler suspected it soon wouldn't matter.

"What are these?" Sallah asked Kandler as he spurred his horse forward to lead the others ahead.

"I don't know," he said. "Maybe no one does. Some say they're the ghosts of the dead of Metrol. Others think they're the remnants of whatever it was that murdered Cyre. They might be something else."

"Less talk, more speed," Burch said.

The shifter had naturally taken up the rearguard as the line of three horses trotted through the vacant city. As if to punctuate his words, a wail like the sound of a bear in mourning ripped through the night behind them. It was so loud it seemed like it echoed off the clouds, which now seemed so low that someone might be able to reach up and touch them from the top of Metrol's highest towers.

These stone structures were nothing like the network of spires that covered Kandler's hometown of Sharn, the legendary City of Towers, but their proximity to the blanket of mists made them seem as if they held up the sky.

The tallest of the towers—the Prime Pillar, as Kandler remembered—stabbed out of the cityscape before the riders as they cantered down from higher ground toward the docks on the Cyre River, the wide track of water that separated what had once been Cyre from the lands beyond. When Kandler had lived here, he had used the Pillar as a navigational point any time he'd gone wandering throughout the city. As long as he could see the Pillar, he always knew roughly where he was.

Another howl—more of a wail than a growl—erupted from just ahead and to the right. Kandler scanned the rooftops for any sign of whatever had made the noise.

There, silhouetted against the dark, blotted sky, something raced along the rooftops, trying to match the riders' speed but failing. Kandler struggled to get a good look at it, but it was impossible. It was only outlines of strange shapes flickering in and out of view.

When the riders reached an intersection, Kandler plunged straight through it. As he did, he looked back to see the creature leap across the gap in the rooftops, and he finally saw it whole.

The thing's arms and legs—two of each—splayed out as it crossed the space, framed for a moment between the two rooftops. It was shaped like a human, with a head, limbs, and torso all in the right places, but no person Kandler had ever seen looked so strange. He could see its grayish bones and muscles right through its skin, as if it were some strange golem made of random bits of flesh wrapped together in liquid glass. Strangest of all, the thing's entire body—perhaps its translucent skin, maybe its spoiled-meat interior—glowed with an unearthly light.

The creature's gray-green eyes, something akin to the color of the Mournland's grass, fixed on Kandler with an unholy rage. As the thing landed on the next rooftop, continuing its relentless pursuit, it unleashed another wailing growl. The horse beneath Kandler's legs bolted at the sound, bursting into a full-out gallop in a desperate effort to leave the horrible thing far behind.

CHAPTER

6

Another howl pierced the Mournland night, closer this time, but this one came from ahead, not behind. Kandler bent low over the neck of his mount and spurred it on harder. Now that he knew what to look for, he spotted a glow limning the edge of a rooftop ahead on the left. Peering into the darkness below, he saw other glowing shapes moving across the roofs of the city.

Some sprinted like men. Others ran on all fours, more like wolves. One thing was clear, though. They were working together, speaking to each other somehow through their horrendous wails. Like a pack of hunting dogs, they quickly converged on their prey: the five riders on three horses, stampeding toward the shore of the Cyre River below.

"Can't make it!" Burch shouted as he bounced along atop his horse. "River's too far!"

As the only mount with a single rider, his beast champed at its bit, ready to charge into the lead. The shifter kept a tight hold on its reins with one hand, hauling the horse in behind the others. With his free hand, he reached for the crossbow strapped across his back.

Kandler knew the shifter was right. The ghostbeasts

would catch them long before they reached safety. A roar right behind him told him that.

The justicar slung his blade from its scabbard. It was notched in three spots from his battle with Bastard, but he knew its edge could still bite. He'd had to pull it from where it was wedged into the floor of the arena in Construct, stabbed through one of the warforged leader's arms.

He'd been the lucky one. Sallah's sacred blade, a sword that burned with the power of the Silver Flame on command, had been destroyed in that same battle. She still carried a short knife with her, but it was a poor substitute.

Brendis had offered his sword to Sallah as a replacement, but she'd declined. "It was my blade," she said. "I used it well, and I cannot take yours in its stead."

"You used it to save my life," Brendis pointed out.

Sallah had been unmoved.

Now, though, as Kandler glanced back at the woman urging her steed forward with all her might, he saw that she felt the lack of the blade. Brendis, thankfully, already had drawn his own sword. Silver flames crawled along the length of the blade like a living thing, hungry for righteous battle.

Kandler looked up past the young knight and saw that his sword was about to have its chance. Before he could shout a warning, the nearest ghostbeast leaped from the rooftop straight at Brendis's back.

The young knight slashed out at the creature, his sword cutting a blinding arc through the dusk and slicing across the predator's chest. Glowing blood splattered in a trail after the tip of the blade, and the ghostbeast unleashed a sound that made Kandler want to plug his ears.

The creature lashed out with its glowing claws, seeking a way to get past not only Brendis's flashing blade but his gleaming armor too. Kandler knew that it was only a matter of time before it succeeded. Perched atop the back of the terrified horse, it was too close for the knight to strike at it again.

A wire twanged from behind the ghostbeast, and the creature tumbled off Brendis's back. Burch's mount trampled the monster beneath its hooves as the shifter slammed another bolt home into his crossbow. His wide, toothy smile stood out starkly in the dimness.

"I'm all right!" Brendis announced as he turned to face forward, glowing fluid splashed across his face and arm.

Kandler wanted to be relieved, but he knew that this was just the first attack of many to come if they didn't get to safety soon. He scanned the road ahead, looking for some sort of shelter, someplace they could hide both themselves and preferably their mounts.

Dozens of open doors and windows gaped at him like welcoming mouths, beckoning him to dare their dark embraces. Any of them might have been the right place to go, to hole up until the ghostbeasts lost interest or the sun lightened the overcast sky again. They might just be openings into dead ends, indefensible spaces that could only serve as open graves.

Then Kandler spotted something off in the distance. At first he thought it might be another of the ghostbeasts glowing in the darkness, but the hue of the faint light spilling from the top of the Prime Pillar burned with a warmth he suspected the ghostbeasts would never know.

"There!" he shouted to the others, stabbing a finger at the rapidly approaching Pillar. "There's someone there!"

"It could be a trap!" Burch said, his eyes searching the rooftops for another attacker, another target.

"If it gets us away from these things," Brendis said, "that's one trap I'll leap right into."

As the riders galloped closer and closer to the Pillar, Kandler realized that the light he'd seen must have been a signal of some sort, but to whom and from whom he could not tell. He just hoped they could reach the Great Circle, the open plaza that surrounded the Pillar, before the ghostbeasts could catch them.

A pair of the glowing creatures emerged from across the street ahead of the riders. They crouched low, ready to spring at the riders. A pair of wails that set up a disturbing harmony echoed in Kandler's ears, and he felt Xalt cling to his waist tighter.

A bolt from behind Kandler sailed wide over the head of the creature on the right, and he heard Burch curse. The shifter wasn't used to loosing his crossbow from horseback, and the constant jolting had spoiled his aim. Still, Kandler thought he might be able to take advantage of the effort, missed or not.

The errant bolt caused the ghostbeast on the right to dodge closer to the other, just where Kandler wanted them. He drove his horse straight at the creature on the left and swung his sword down at the other as it steeled itself for an attack at him as he passed.

Kandler felt one monster go down beneath his mount's hooves as he drove the point of his sword forward like a lance, using the horse's momentum to impale the ghostbeast on its tip. The dying creature slid forward along the length of the blade that ran it through until it smashed into the sword's hilt, nearly tearing it from Kandler's grasp. The thing was close enough that the justicar could smell its breath, like steel hot from the forge.

The ghostbeast hung there for a moment, clutching at its wound before trying to claw Kandler's eyes out. The justicar let the tip of his blade fall toward the ground, and the monster slid off the sword with a gut-wrenching wail that lasted until Sallah's steed trampled it into the pavement.

More howls reverberated throughout the city. Kandler felt like the sound alone might cause him to fall to his knees were he not clinging to the top of a horse spooked even worse by the songs of that unholy chorus. Instead, he just held on to the horse with one hand and to his sword with the other as they careened toward the Great Circle.

Kandler started to breathe easier as they raced closer to their goal. The legendary plaza opened slowly before them as they sprinted recklessly toward it. The light in the top of the tower grew brighter, and Kandler imagined that he heard the shouts of men over the thunder of the riders' hooves. He didn't know to whom they belonged, but they had to be better to deal with than the howling ghostbeasts.

Just before the riders reached the Great Circle, the road opened up into a small square that let out into the main plaza. As Kandler's steed crossed into that space, something slammed into him and his mount, knocking him and Xalt from their saddle.

Kandler tucked himself into a ball around his sword as he hit the ground and rolled to a painful stop against an abandoned shop. As he scrambled to his feet, his sword out in front of him, ready to taste whatever the ghostbeasts used for blood, he saw that Sallah and Burch had reined their horses in and turned around to come back for Xalt and him.

"Keep moving!" he roared at them.

As he spoke, he turned to see the ghostbeast that attacked him tear open his horse's throat, the hapless beast's blood fountaining everywhere, blotting out the monster's glowing form with blackness where it splashed against it.

"I think we're in trouble," Xalt said from behind the justicar.

CHAPTER

7

M ove!" Kandler yelled, pushing Xalt after the others.
As the warforged scrambled away, Kandler shuffled backward
after him, keeping the tip of his sword pointed at the glowing
creature goring his mount.

The dying horse tried to kick its assailant away, but the beast
was already in too close, tearing away at the steed's soft belly
with its claws. As the horse collapsed, dead already, the glowing,
blood-drenched creature rose from behind the still-hot corpse
and unleashed a horrific noise from deep within its throat,
something that seemed like it could only have been trapped in
the belly of a demon, festering for centuries untold.

Kandler's eyes locked with the creature, which was
strangely human for all its unearthly ways. Madness danced
in those pale glowing eyes, madness and a driving hunger to
quench the fires of life in all it faced.

The justicar turned and sprinted away.

Kandler knew that the ghostbeast could outrun him. It
and its ilk had kept pace with a galloping horse, and he wasn't
nearly so fast. All he wanted, though, was to put some distance
between himself and the creature, just enough for Burch to
get a clear angle.

As Kandler sprinted for the Great Circle, memories of the square he ran through came flooding into his mind. Over there, under a black awning, sat a Brelish pub—Ginty's—at which he and Burch had shared many a drink. Esprina had come to find him there the evening after their first meeting, a happy surprise in many ways, as he'd supposed she'd be after his head.

"Duck!" Burch shouted.

Kandler dove forward, just ahead of the sound of the blood-gorged ghostbeast slavering on his heels. The shifter's crossbow twanged, and a bolt hissed overhead. The creature tumbled to the ground, the claws on its dead hands feebly scraping the back of Kandler's boots.

The justicar raced up to the others. "I thought I told you to keep moving," he said, feeling angrier about it than he should.

"You're welcome." Burch smirked down at his old friend as he offered him a hand up onto his mount. "Don't waste time."

Kandler shook his head. "Two horses for five riders won't do it," he said.

"I can follow on foot," Xalt volunteered.

Kandler clapped the warforged on the back. "No one gets left behind."

Xalt shot a wary glance at the dead ghostbeast bleeding into a glowing, pale pool. "Perhaps they don't eat warforged," he said hopefully.

Kandler wasn't having any of it. "We need to make a stand here."

A series of howls, none too far away, punctuated the statement.

"Ginty's it is," Burch said as he pushed his steed across the square. Sallah's horse followed close behind, with Kandler and Xalt hard on their heels.

The pub had no name on it, no sign flapping from a

chain, only the red boar's head of the Brelish coat of arms emblazoned across the center of the black awning that hung over the high, tight windows and the brightly painted red door. The boar's head was enough to identify it as a Brelish establishment to anyone who'd ever been near Breland, and that had been enough for the founder—Old Ginty himself—and the dozen generations of descendants who'd had the place handed down to them.

In the lead, Burch leaped from the back of his horse and landed in front of the door, then wrenched it open. It was dark inside, just as it was in every part of the town.

Kandler wondered about that, why the everburning lights used throughout the city had all burnt out. He guessed it had something to do with how the Mourning had altered the land, making magic work strangely here if at all. Perhaps the lights had blazed for months after the disaster, or maybe scavengers had made off with them all. He was sure he'd never know.

Burch threw the door wide and stepped into the darkness beyond. Sallah and Brendis followed right behind, the flames on the young knight's sword bringing some much-needed light into the place. Kandler pushed Xalt on ahead of him, doing his best to watch their back, his blade at the ready.

Just as Kandler reached for the door, another excruciating wail sounded out, this one far too close for comfort. Then the awning next to the justicar was torn to pieces as a glowing figure fell through it, shredding the fabric with its long, sharp claws as it went.

Kandler turned to face the creature, even as Burch called for him.

"Get your ass in here!" the shifter shouted.

Kandler brandished his blade at the beast. If he went for the door, the monster was close enough that it might be able to tear into him or wedge a part of itself across the threshold, keeping it open long enough for its friends to work their way in. He wasn't prepared to let that happen.

The creature stared at Kandler for a moment before screeching at him. Close enough that the thing's spittle landed on his arm, Kandler could see that the thing had once been human. Its glowing skin was so thin now, though, that he could see through it to the muscles and bones beneath. Where it had once had fingernails, it now had six-inch claws made of the same translucent material as its flesh. Its teeth were longer and sharper than he could have thought possible in a living creature, but perhaps it wasn't living.

Before Kandler could react to the ghostbeast's challenge, Sallah stepped in front of him, holding up a small silver charm fashioned in the form of a blazing flame, the icon of her religion's mysterious, burning god.

"Get back, you unholy beast!" the lady knight said, holding the holy symbol before her as if it were a shield.

The creature stared at the wrought silver flame for a moment, then threw back its glowing head and laughed, exposing all of its terrifying teeth. It hauled back into a crouch so that it could leap at Sallah and rip her flame-haired head from her shoulders.

As the thing made its move, Kandler shifted to a two-handed grip on his blade and brought it slicing down at the creature. The edge cleaved through the creature's shoulder and chest, knocking it wide of Sallah. It landed next to Ginty's façade instead, its glowing blood pumping from it as it expired.

Two more screams sounded from the far side of the square as a pair of the dying thing's kin leaped down from the rooftops, ready for mayhem. Kandler swung around his sword, dripping with luminescent fluids, ready to take them on too. Other wails sounded nearby, far too many.

"Get in here!" Sallah said. She grabbed Kandler by the arm and hauled him into the pub after her.

Burch slammed the door shut as Kandler tumbled into the place, then threw fast a thick, oaken bar behind it.

Ginty's was just as Kandler had remembered it, although he'd rarely seen it as empty as this. The dark polished paneling and tables reminded him of some of his favorite haunts back home, places he'd practically grown up in. Ginty's had always been authentic, importing Brelish ales, stouts, and whiskies by the keg and cask, brought in weekly by lightning rail, and serving lousy Brelish meals to go with them.

One thing that struck Kandler was the lack of bodies. He'd seen them throughout the Mournland and even throughout Metrol. When the Mourning happened, hundreds of thousands of people died right where they stood. With the thick mists surrounding the place, keeping most people out, there had been precious few people to deal with the corpses littering the landscape. Even fewer of those had bothered to try. The task was just too monumental. In a sense, the Mournland's mists formed the grave in which all of those people were buried.

Kandler had seen fewer bodies in Metrol than he'd expected. He suspected that scavengers and creatures like the ghostbeasts had moved many of them out of the way or even eaten them. Here in Ginty's, though, he didn't see a trace of a single body, nor even the patina of dust that should have been there.

He had no time to think more on that.

"The back door!" Kandler said.

"Xalt's on it," Burch said. "Brendis has the windows."

The young knight had already shuttered three of the four sets of small, glazed panes. As he reached for the fourth, a frantic, glowing figure hurled itself through the wood and glass, sending it and Brendis flying back into the pub. The thing caught halfway into the pub, the shards of glass left in the window frame stabbing into its gut. It wailed in pain and anger.

Trapped within the cozy confines of the pub's main room, the sound hurt Kandler's ears worse than ever. He gritted his teeth and stabbed his sword straight into the screeching thing's face as it flailed about. The blade caught it below its chin and slid into the thing's chest, catching on its spine.

With another push, Kandler shoved the dead creature back out of the window, blood spurting after it as it cascaded to the cobblestone square outside. Sallah and Burch slammed the shutters closed and barred them, sealing the place tight.

Outside, a chorus of frustrated wails railed against Ginty's façade.

Xalt came stomping up from the back room. "The rear is secured," he said plainly.

"What do we do now?" Sallah asked. She flexed her hands in frustration, and Kandler could tell she ached to fill them with a sword.

Kandler glanced about the place, then walked over and sat on the same barstool he'd used a hundred times before. That had been in another life, one lived in the dying days of the Last War, before anyone had ever conceived of something like the Mournland, before Kandler had taken an elf wife and become a father to her daughter too.

Forever ago, he thought, looking deep into Sallah's emerald eyes.

"Now," he said, "we wait."

CHAPTER

8

Esprë had long since dried her eyes. Now she was just burning mad and aching to do something about it. Over the years of her life—as yet short in the eyes of an elf—she had lost her father, her mother, and now her stepfather as well. She was as alone in this world as she had ever been, and she needed to do something to change that now.

The delicate, blue-eyed waif of an elf strode to the bridge of the ship, her long, blond tresses snapping in the wind behind her like a war banner. Te'oma stood before her at the wheel, gazing out into the distance. Now that they were above the mists of the Mournland, the changeling spent much of her time searching for any sign of an end to the miles of rolling dead-gray clouds that sprawled off beneath them in every direction.

Esprë had no idea how high up they were. There was literally nothing around by which she could judge. It was cold, though, chilly enough that she spent much of her time close to the ring of fire that propelled the battered airship through the sky.

She was amazed that the ship was still together. The thought that the whole thing might fall to pieces beneath her kept her up at night.

This was no idle wandering of her imagination. On the few times that Esprë had taken the ship's wheel since she'd awoken here in Te'oma's care, she could feel the harnessed elemental creature of fire that was bound up in the ring gloating to itself. Even it believed it was only a matter of time before it was freed in a spectacular explosion that might consume everything—and everyone—on the ship long before its remains hit the ground.

Now, though, that was the last thing on her mind. She wanted something more than just her feet on solid ground. She wanted answers.

"Where are we going?"

The changeling turned slowly at the young elf's words, almost as if she'd been expecting them. Esprë supposed that was possible. Te'oma was a telepath, after all, gifted by fate with strange powers of the mind that let her peer into a subject's soul and do gods knew what else. Esprë had felt Te'oma rummaging around through her brain before, though, and she didn't detect the changeling's presence in there now. She wondered, though, if she would always know it if she did.

A strange smile splayed across the changeling's thin, pale lips, somehow caught between sadness and mirth. Te'oma hadn't bothered with taking a better-formed aspect since they had left Construct far behind. Esprë suspected the changeling felt more comfortable in her natural state

"Where would you like to go?" Te'oma said slowly, carefully.

"Home," Esprë said flatly. She was ready for an argument with the changeling, who had kidnapped her in the first place.

"Where is that?" The changeling's eyebrows—so thin and pale they were more of a suggestion—rose as she spoke.

Esprë stopped for a moment. She hadn't thought this through entirely. All she knew for sure was that she didn't trust the changeling and wasn't willing to go with her anywhere. She didn't know how she would get away from her, but she knew she had to try.

"Mardakine?" Te'oma asked. "There's not much of it left now, is there? How do you suppose the people there will react when they learn it was you who killed all their friends and family in the middle of the night?"

Esprë recoiled in horror. "How do you—?" She cut herself off before finishing the question. The answer was too obvious.

"I couldn't control it," Esprë said, her voice little more than a whisper that barely carried over the crackling of the airship's ring of fire. "I didn't mean . . . It's not my fault."

"Oh, I know," Te'oma said, putting a comforting hand on the young elf's shoulder. "There wasn't a thing you could have done to stop it, but do you think the people of Mardakine will see it that way?"

Esprë hung her head low. She couldn't face going back to Mardakine. The thought of facing her friend Norra, knowing that she'd killed her mother, stopped her breath. Besides, with Kandler gone, there was little else for her there now. She was just a young elf wandering alone in the world. Perhaps any one place would be as good as another.

"There's Aerenal," Esprë said as the thought struck her.

"The elf homeland?" Te'oma frowned. "Do you think they'd welcome you back there? How old were you when you left?"

"Too young to remember it, but I have grandparents there, probably some other family too. They would take me in. They wouldn't abandon me."

Te'oma shook her head sagely. "Have you forgotten about your dragonmark? The Mark of Death?"

The changeling bent her neck to peer into Esprë's downcast eyes. "The last time someone bore the Mark of Death, the dragons and elves put an end to their centuries-long war to eradicate her and everyone else in the House of Vol."

Esprë's eyes widened. "They killed the whole of an extended family? Why?"

"The bearer was a mixed breed of elf and dragon blood. Her parents thought that their love, given life in the form of their daughter, would show the elves and dragons how to put an end to their perennial conflict. In a sense, it did that, but only because it provided both sides with a common foe.

"Both the dragons and elves saw the very existence of this lady of Vol as an abomination, and they determined to put an end to her and anyone who sympathized with her at once."

Te'oma pulled back the collar of Esprë's shirt, exposing the pattern of her raw-edged dragonmark beneath. "The blood of House Vol must run through your veins. Just think what they'd do to you."

Esprë shrugged free from the changeling's grasp. "Those people who helped you kidnap me," she said. "They were members of the Blood of Vol, a cult that bears that lost house's name."

Te'oma nodded. "The legend of House Vol lives on in the cult and its fascination with blood. It's no coincidence that it has vampires in its ranks."

Esprë raised her eyes to look into the changeling's pearly, blank orbs. "You talk as if you are not a member."

Te'oma grinned softly. "Smart girl," she said. "I believe in no gods, only in myself. It's cost me dearly, but it's who I am."

"Do you think yourself to be a god?"

"If I was, this trip would have been a great deal easier."

Esprë narrowed her eyes at the changeling. "Where are we going?" she asked again.

Te'oma measured the girl carefully before answering. "To find some people who desperately want to meet you."

"What if I don't want to go?" Esprë pouted at the changeling defiantly, trying her best not to look like a little girl. She was probably older than Te'oma—much older—but her long youth betrayed her still.

Te'oma reached out and caressed Esprë's soft cheek with one of her pale, barely formed hands. "That doesn't really matter."

With that, Te'oma stared past Esprë and off into the distance. As the young elf strolled toward the ship's prow, she did the same. On the horizon, she thought she saw a dark line, an end to the rolling mists they'd scudded over for so long. They would leave the Mournland soon. From there, it might only be a short while before Te'oma turned her over to her compatriots. If Esprë wished to act to save herself, it would have to be soon.

Only one answer came to her mind as she peered out from the prow. She would have to kill Te'oma and take control of the ship. She could figure out what to do from there.

Esprë knew she had the power in her to murder the changeling. She'd felt it growing in her for the past few months. So far, the dragonmark's power had only randomly taken innocents. As horrible as that had been—even before Esprë realized she had been unwittingly behind it—she had no memories of it beyond a few fragments of dreams.

This would be the first time Esprë would use her dragonmark consciously, purposefully, to take a life.

The young elf stared down at her hands and began to weep.

CHAPTER

9

Although Esprë had never killed anyone before intentionally, she'd seen death before, and not just in the strange dreams her dragonmark thrust upon her. When she was little more than a toddler, her mother had brought her to Khorvaire to look for a new life away from the stultifying elf society of Aerenal. They had made the ocean voyage on a large passenger ship that docked at Pylas Maradal, the largest of the port cities in Valenar, the elf colony-nation on the southern coast.

Soon after Esprë and her mother arrived, brigands had accosted them, determined to rob them and leave them for dead. Esprina had been traveling incognito, and the thieves hadn't realized the power the sorcerer wielded. Within moments, three of them lay dead in the road and the others had fled.

"Don't look, darling," Esprina had said. She'd wanted to protect her daughter from the horrors of violent death, something that few elves worried about.

In the Aerenal culture, most elves looked forward to death rather than fearing it. In Khorvaire, though, Esprë had learned to fear death. She had few memories of her homeland, and most of them featured her mother arguing with her grandparents about things she didn't really understand. There, in Aerenal, death had seemed a distant dream someone else was having.

It was almost like adulthood. Esprë knew that she'd grow up someday, and she could see what it was like, but in her gut she never expected it to happen. It was too far off.

Here, in Khorvaire—especially right now—death lurked around every corner. The Priests of Transition were an ocean away, and all a fallen elf had to look forward to was an eternity of oblivion.

All these thoughts and feelings coalesced into a sick feeling in Esprë's gut as she strolled nonchalantly—perhaps too much so, she feared—toward where Te'oma stood on the bridge. The changeling looked relaxed, hopeful even, her hands held loosely on the airship's wheel as she coaxed the ship toward the northeast again. Her blank eyes stayed fixed on the horizon as they sped toward it, never once flicking toward Esprë as she approached.

"I can't wait to put the Mournland behind us," Te'oma said breezily, as if they'd met on the street and were talking about the weather.

Esprë nodded, trying to appear happy about the change. "I hope to never see it again."

The two fell silent then, as they had for the past day. They had little to say to each other. Every now and then, Te'oma would comment on something, and Esprë would usually just nod in agreement.

As they reached the edge of the Mournland, though, the unspoken tension between the two had grown. To Esprë, at least, it had almost become unbearable, although Te'oma showed few signs she was aware of it. If the young elf had learned one thing in her time in the changeling's company, though, it was that she could not read Te'oma's emotions at all.

"You can see the Talenta Plains," the changeling said,

pointing a thin, pale finger off to the east. There, past the miles of roiling mists that still rolled out before them, she could see a strip of golden green that stretched all the way to where the land met the sky.

"Nomadic halflings, right?" Esprë said, pretending to be interested.

The changeling favored her with a smile, still not turning to look at her. "That's right. You know much for a child."

"I'll bet I'm older than you." The young elf could not keep the edge from her voice.

This time, Te'oma did look at her with her blank eyes. "I suppose that's true," she said. "It must have been strange having a human for a stepfather, born before him and sure to outlive him."

Esprë frowned. "I never thought about it much."

She felt the dragonmark on her back start to itch and then burn, as if it had a life of its own. Did it want her to use it? Did it suffer from a thirst that only lives could quench? Or was that how she really felt instead?

The dragonmark burned not hot, but cold, like an icicle lancing through her skin. The chill crept along her shoulders and down her arms until it reached the fingers of her hands. There it pulsated, throbbed, waiting to be set loose.

"So," Te'oma said, staring out at the horizon once again, "you've finally come to kill me."

Esprë's breath caught in her throat. The look on her face must have betrayed her. How had Te'oma known?

The changeling narrowed her eyes at the young elf. "I don't have to be a telepath to know what's on your mind. Here we are at the edge of the Mournland, and I'm taking you off to Vol knows where. It's time for you to make your move."

Esprë flexed her hands in and out of fists to ease the throbbing cold in them. "I thought you weren't a part of that cult."

"I'm not," Te'oma said. With that, she threw herself away

from Esprë and over the railing that separated the bridge from the lower deck.

Esprë lunged at the changeling, but she was too late. Te'oma fell away, inches from the young elf's outstretched hand, and then she was gone, the railing standing like a fence between them.

The ship pitched forward madly and careened toward the world below. Esprë reached out and grabbed the wheel as she fell against it. She could feel the airship's elemental striving against her, doing its best to resist her control, but she steeled her mind against it and bent its will to her own. Soon the ship leveled off and flew straight again.

Esprë leaned out over the wheel and cursed at the changeling. The words, she knew, were more for herself than her captor. If she'd only been smarter or faster or . . . better.

"Would your mother want to hear you speak like that?" Te'oma said. "I think that justicar has been a poor influence on you."

Esprë let loose a raging stream of obscenities now, finishing up with, " . . . and the bitch cursed to bear you." The changeling's face pinked at the words, which pleased the young elf to no end.

"If Kandler had spent more time teaching you to fight and less filling your head with filthy words, you'd have killed me by now."

"He also taught me patience," Esprë said, squinting at the changeling. Her voice shook with the anger she'd let take control of her for a moment. "It's a small ship," she said. "You can't avoid me forever."

Something foreign stabbed into Esprë's brain like a knife through her left temple. The right side of her body started to go numb, but she held onto the wheel and glared down at the changeling who stared at her with murderous intent.

"Get out of my head!" Esprë screamed. "I fought you off once. I can do it again."

Pain lanced through her right temple this time, and the young elf felt her knees give way. She collapsed onto the wheel, struggling to force her limbs to obey.

"You can't do this!" Esprë screeched herself hoarse as she wept hot, bitter tears that washed away the dragonmark's chilly hunger. "I'll *kill* you!"

The world spun around her as if she was suddenly the center of the universe. She fought it with all her might, but it was like trying to swim out of a whirlpool that was sucking her down. Just as everything swirled to black, she heard Te'oma say one thing to her.

"Sweet dreams."

CHAPTER

10

Something large, heavy, and angry slammed into the leftmost of Ginty's shutters again. The sound made Kandler wince, even though he'd already heard it a dozen times before.

"The shutters are starting to give," said Xalt, who stood before the window where the coverings had just bent inward a bit. The warforged seemed to be playing a game in which he tried to guess which window the creatures outside the pub would attack next. So far, Kandler noted, he'd been right more often than wrong.

"They'll hold," Kandler said. "The door and shutters are magically reinforced." Something smashed into the shutters again, and Kandler eyed them warily. "Of course, the thick bands of iron around them don't hurt either."

"Is there anything in a Brelish pub worth breaking down the door for?" Brendis asked. The young knight sat slumped on a barstool near Kandler. He jumped every time something hit the front of the place, ready to hurl himself into battle.

"Depends how much you like your drink," Burch said.

The shifter slid a pair of small, low glasses—filled with a dark, pungent fluid—toward Brendis and Kandler. Then he turned back to pour others for Sallah, Xalt, and himself from a black-painted bottle bearing a Cyran seal.

Kandler handed his glass to Sallah and waited for Burch to fill all their hands. When they were ready, he raised his three fingers of brandy to offer a toast. "To Cyre," he said. "May she someday rise again."

The five friends clinked their glasses together and drank—except for Xalt who sniffed the liquor's strong bouquet instead. As they did, another creature slammed into one of the sets of shutters again.

Brendis, who'd only managed to choke down half his strong drink, dropped his glass at the noise. It shattered on the slate floor.

Burch shook his head as he reached for a fresh glass for the young knight. "Waste of good drink," the shifter said sadly.

Xalt hummed to himself for having missed another chance to guess which window would be hit, and he moved in front of the shutters nearest the door. A moment later, a creature smashed into that set and fell back. The warforged clicked his tongue and stayed right where he was.

Kandler savored a mouthful of brandy as he looked into Sallah's eyes. The smell of the place, though muted, brought back a flood of memories—that and the taste of the liquor. It had been over a year since he'd had a taste of such spirits, and he hadn't realized how much he'd missed it.

Still, it felt good—felt right—to be here, sharing a drink with a beautiful young woman again. He could almost forget that Metrol was as dead as his beloved wife, and that only an inch of good, ironbound wood separated them from the pack of glowing, howling monsters that wanted their blood.

"This is good," Sallah said, allowing a sly smile to dance across her lips.

"Better than it has any right to be," Kandler agreed.

"Got that right," Burch said as he held his pint up to his eyes and examined it curiously. "After two years in an opened bottle, this shouldn't be much more than dirty water. It ain't natural."

"What *is* in the Mournland?" Kandler said as another beast slammed into the window in front of Xalt. The warforged stayed where he was again. "Nothing decays here. Magic doesn't work so well." He looked directly into Sallah's emerald eyes. "What can you trust?"

"You are correct," Xalt announced, looking back from the window at Kandler.

"Damn right," Kandler said, taking another swig of his drink. "What are you talking about?"

"Magic here doesn't work how it should."

"True," Burch said, pointing a claw-tipped finger at Kandler. "Remember those living fireballs wandering around the crater before we threw up Mardakine there? Now those were—"

Kandler held up a hand to cut the shifter off. He called over to the warforged. "What did you mean, Xalt?"

The warforged pointed a thick, stubby finger at the shutters. "The magic that once held these fast is weak. Perhaps even gone."

Kandler emptied his glass and set it down on the bar, then put his hand on the hilt of his sword. "What are you trying to say?"

Xalt turned to look at the justicar. "The ghostbeasts have figured this out. They've also decided to focus their efforts on this shutter in an effort to weaken it quickly. Once they break it down, they will come streaming through to join us here." At this, the warforged glanced at each of the others in turn. "To kill us."

A massive weight slammed into the shutters in front of Xalt again. This time, Kandler heard the wood crack. Xalt was right. The ghostbeasts would beat their way into the pub. It was only a matter of time.

Kandler fell in next to Xalt, his blade raised and ready.

Burch leaped up to kneel atop the bar, his crossbow in his hands loaded and ready, trained on the shutters before Xalt. Brendis gulped down the rest of his drink before taking up his flaming sword and standing to Kandler's left.

"By the flame," said Sallah, staring at her empty hands. "What I wouldn't give for a good blade right now."

Kandler nodded at Burch. "Give it to her," he said.

Without a word of acknowledgement, the shifter reached into his quiver of bolts and extracted a long knife with a blade so black it seemed to soak up the light around it. He reversed the handle and pitched it over to the lady knight.

Sallah caught the knife by its grip and turned it over in her hand, staring at it. "This belonged to the changeling," she said. "You took it after the battle in Construct?"

"You're welcome," the shifter said before returning his attention to the battered shutters.

As he did, they bent inward far enough for Kandler to see an inch or two of glowing flesh framed between the shutters' halves. Near the top, a wide eye with tiny, constricted pupils glared through the gap at them.

Burch loosed a bolt at the creature, and it zipped straight through the small opening. The glowing monster fell back, howling more bitterly than ever.

"That'll teach them to come knocking on our door," Kandler said with a spare grin for his friend.

Silence fell over the room for a full minute. Outside, Kandler thought he could hear the creatures shuffling around, but he couldn't be sure.

"Do you think they're gone?" Brendis asked.

"No," Xalt said quietly. "I think they're learning from Burch's lesson."

"What's that supposed to mean?" the young knight said, unable to conceal the irritation in his voice. Kandler didn't blame Brendis for his frayed nerves. They were all on edge, and for good reason.

Before Xalt could reply, a heavy mass slammed into all four of the sets of shutters at once.

Sallah screamed in surprise. Brendis leaped back and nearly dropped his sword. Kandler dropped back toward the bar and swept his sword back and forth at all four covered windows.

The creatures smashed into the windows again. And again.

The justicar adjusted his grip on his sword. Soon the creatures would break through, maybe in four different places at once, and they would be fighting for their lives.

Kandler gritted his teeth in rage. This wasn't the sort of thing he needed to deal with right now. He had to find Esprë, and every delay like this was lost time, another hour or more that the changeling could get his daughter farther away from him in their stolen airship.

He found that he wanted the creatures to break through and to do it now—the faster, the better. He couldn't stand being holed up here any more anyhow. He was ready to kill his way to Esprë's side or die trying.

It was then that Kandler realized that the creatures had stopped battering the shutters. Instead, a horrible howl went up from the square outside, a cacophonous choir of wails that spoke of anger, hatred, and eternal frustration. Some of the screeches ended abruptly. Others transformed into cries of pain.

A whooping noise erupted in the square and quickly turned to a cheer. Then there were voices, chattering something in the common tongue of the land.

"Trap?" Burch said.

"Either way, we hold tight," Kandler said.

"What choice do we have?" Sallah said.

After a long moment, Kandler heard someone outside shuffling up to the door. He checked to see that Burch had him covered, then moved to stand an arm's length away from the door, his sword pointed straight at it.

A meaty hand pounded on the door, followed by a voice as deep as a canyon. "Whoever you are in there, you can come out now," it said. "The ghostbeasts are gone."

Kandler frowned. "We're just fine in here, thanks," he said.

"You are strangers here in Metrol," the voice said. "The boss insists."

"He's not our boss."

The voice laughed low and evil. "In Metrol, everyone answers to Ikar the Black."

Kandler's stomach flipped. Ikar and his band of scavengers—"salvage experts," as they liked to be called—were the landed equivalent to pirates of the worst kind. He'd dealt with some of them in Mardakine before. Then he'd had a few dozen well-armed villagers backing him up. Now he would be entirely at the mercy of these black-hearted thieves.

"Hey, boss," Burch said. "Ask him if we can have the ghostbeasts back instead."

CHAPTER

11

We can't let Ikar take us," Kandler said. "We don't have the time to deal with him. Esprë gets farther away from us every minute."

"We should take the battle to them," Sallah said. "If we charge straight at them, we might be able to break through their lines before they can stop us."

"Might work," Burch said from where he perched on a table jammed up under one of the shuttered windows, peeking through the gap a ghostbeast had battered there. "If they *had* a line."

"How many of them are out there?" Brendis asked, apparently not caring anymore if anyone could hear the tremor in his voice.

Burch bared his teeth as he peered at what he could see of the square. "A score, at least," he said. "Maybe more."

"What about the horses?" Xalt said. Kandler had seen the warforged cringe at having to leave the trusty mounts to the nonexistent mercies of the ghostbeasts who had chased them in here.

"Gone. Dead or stolen, but gone just the same."

"What are we going to do?" The words came from

Brendis, but they echoed the thoughts in everyone's head, Kandler knew. The others' eyes all fell on him.

"Out back," he said, already leading the way through the rear rooms of the pub. "They might not have covered it yet."

Kandler threaded his way through the dark hallways like a cat in the night. Although it was pitch black, except for Brendis's sword far behind him, he'd spent enough nights in the place that it was still like walking through his own home.

When he reached the back door, he gestured for the others to stay back. Then he reached up and undid the latch that Xalt had fastened just moments ago. It slid back on well-oiled rails.

Kandler cracked the door open a hair and peeked out. The alley led straight away from Ginty's back door. It was empty, so he opened the door some more.

Litter flittered around the place on a stiff night breeze. Bags of garbage sat piled high along one wall, much higher than Kandler ever remembered them.

"Looks clear," he said, stepping through the door and motioning for the others to follow him. They filed out right behind him as he prowled toward the open end of the alley, a few dozen yards ahead.

Somewhere, a bird called.

Kandler swore. No birds lived in the Mournland.

"Trap!" Burch shouted. The shifter leaped back toward Ginty's rear door, but he hauled up short when a load of bricks smashed into the pavement before it, sealing it shut.

Glancing up, Kandler spotted a cackling figure peering over the roof, surveying his handiwork. Others no doubt crouched near the two other doors that opened into the alley, ready with heavy loads of their own. Holding his sword before him, the justicar sprinted toward the free end of the street. Before he covered half the distance, though, a swath of bodies swept in and blocked off the exit.

"Surrender!" a deep-throated voice growled from the center of that mass.

Kandler could see the speaker in the light of an ever-burning torch a nearby lackey carried. He stood a foot taller than the justicar, or any of those near him, with a chest like a barrel and arms strapped with corded muscles. A black, spiky crest of hair fell back from a low, mean brow that shaded his beady, ebony eyes. He showed all his jagged, yellow teeth in a savage smile that stood out sharply against his wart-crusted, dark gray skin.

"Hello, Ikar," Kandler said.

The half-orc opened his mouth to reply, then stopped. He grinned at those surrounding him, a malignant pack of muscle as coarse and ugly as the band's leader. The crew hunkered around him, instinctively protecting him from a bolt from Burch's crossbow or some other assault.

"My fame precedes me," Ikar said, clearly pleased. "Then you should know what I want from you."

"What's that?" Xalt said earnestly.

"Everything, of course."

Kandler considered charging straight into battle, perhaps before the bandits were ready, but he suspected it was already too late for that. They'd corralled Kandler and his friends in this alley like rats, and they'd taken the time to plug all the holes.

The justicar didn't see that he had a choice here. He strode straight up to Ikar and his crew. Without looking back, he knew that Burch would sweep the others forward behind him, keeping them all together in case everything went wrong.

Of course, Kandler couldn't see any way for it to go right.

"I haven't got time for this," Kandler said as he stepped into the bandits' torchlight. "I'm on a mission for King Boranel. I need transport across the Cyre River. Now."

Ikar glared down at Kandler for a moment. The Brelander could almost hear the gears whirring in the half-orc's brain. Then a smile split Ikar's mug.

"Not even a 'thank you' for saving you from the ghost-beasts?" Ikar rumbled, bemused. "That hardly seems polite, justicar. Although after the reception you gave us the last time we were in Mardakine, I don't suppose I should expect any better."

"I don't recall that," Kandler lied. "I spend so much time running ghouls like you and your crew out of town that they all blend together."

"Well," Ikar said with an evil smirk, "you're in *my* town now."

Kandler sighed. "Look," he said, "we're both professionals here. Let's do this the easy way. Let us go on our way, and we'll be out of your hair for good."

Ikar raised an eyebrow. "You mean to say there won't be any problems for us in Mardakine too?"

Kandler shook his head. "Not from me, or Burch either— or any of the rest of us. We have no business here. We're just passing through."

Ikar scratched at the scruffy goatee that stuck out from his chin. Then he nodded. "All right," he said. "I can wrap my head around that."

"Thank the Flame," Sallah said solemnly.

Kandler didn't relax though. He knew that Ikar wasn't done yet.

"Of course . . ." the half-orc started. His thugs sniggered at his offhand tone. "Those who pass through Metrol and enjoy the security that we offer them must return the favor with some sort of recompense."

"What are you talking about?" Sallah said, stepping up beside Kandler and pushing aside the hand he put out to keep her calm. "Speak plainly."

"A tax," Ikar said, mischief dancing in his eyes.

"You mean to rob us?" Sallah said, glaring up into the half-orc's sharklike eyes.

Ikar shook his head sadly at Sallah. "I prefer to call it a toll." He glanced at Kandler. "I thought you wanted to handle this professionally."

Kandler put a hand on Sallah's shoulder to pull her back, but she shrugged it away. When she spoke to Ikar next, she held her tone even.

"How much?" she said. "We have little to spare."

"Not much," the half-orc said, his eyes wandering over Sallah and the others like a starving man in a butcher shop. His gaze fell on the blazing sword in Brendis's hand. "Just all of your blades."

"Never!" Brendis said, clutching the blade close enough to himself that Kandler could see the young knight starting to sweat. "The sword of a Knight of the Silver Flame is sacred! The twain are not to be parted."

Ikar nodded, then looked at Sallah with a wolfish grin. "What happened to yours?" The crew around him cackled.

"It's a long story," Kandler said.

"Why bargain with these curs?" Brendis said, rattled. "We should cut them down and be done with it."

Ikar's lips curled into a sneer. "Look all around you, little knight," he said cruelly. "Then, if you think you have it in you, do give it your best effort."

Brendis stared at the half-orc for a moment, then swiveled his neck about. Kandler heard a gasp as the young knight finally spotted the archers stationed around the edges of the roofs overlooking the alley. There had to be a dozen of them at least.

"There were another dozen warriors in the square too," Xalt said softly.

Brendis flushed red. "My blade will only leave my grasp when the Flame has taken my soul."

"Don't tempt them," Kandler said.

Ikar loosed a throaty laugh. "Fear not, little knight," he said. "Keep your burning trinket. I'm more interested in something else you have. Hand it over, and I'll consider it a fair price for escorting you lot from this blasted land."

"What's that?" Kandler asked, dreading the answer.

Ikar's eyes blazed with greed as he spoke. "Why, your warforged there, of course."

CHAPTER

12

"Done!"

Kandler pivoted to goggle at Xalt, unable to believe the warforged had given in to the bandit leader's demands so quickly.

"No," he said to Xalt. "If anyone should give himself up for the rest, it should be me."

Ikar snorted. "I don't want you, justicar. I want the warforged."

Xalt stepped forward and put his hand on Kandler's shoulder. One of his wide fingers was missing, lost when the warforged had first stood up for Kandler and his friends. "You need to move on," he said. "Fast. You don't need me."

"We don't leave friends behind," Sallah said over Xalt's shoulder.

The warforged huffed in pained happiness. "To think that I might have friends." He fixed Kandler in his ebony eyes. "I will be all right. I can make a new life here. Go."

"Don't press your luck," Ikar hissed at Kandler's ear. "The warforged wants to stay with us. You get to move on. Everybody's happy."

Kandler stared into Xalt's eyes, wishing that the warforged

could somehow wink at him or give him another sort of signal that everything here would be all right. Maybe the warforged didn't dare risk it with Ikar watching like a hawk, but the justicar felt that Xalt had something in mind other than making himself into the bandits' slave.

"All right," he said to Ikar, never taking his eyes off Xalt. "It's a deal."

The warforged stared back at him like a statue. Kandler thought he saw him incline his head at him ever so slightly, but it could have just been a trick of the torches' flickering light.

"Unless you have pressing business here in Metrol, then, I suggest we get moving," said Ikar. "It's not safe to be out in Metrol by night."

"You don't say," Burch said.

The half-orc narrowed his eyes at the shifter. "Had you not stirred up the ghostbeasts so well, we'd have already been safe on the other side of the river. You're fortunate we let our curiosity get the better of us. Otherwise, they'd be feasting on your souls."

"Lucky us."

Despite Ikar's warnings, the streets of Metrol stretched out wide and empty all the way to the shores of the Cyre River. The bandits took the straightest route possible, sticking to the widest roads with the most space around them. They kept their new guests surrounded at all times.

Kandler wondered for a moment why Ikar hadn't bothered to disarm the lot of them, but when he saw how many bandits there were, his consternation faded. They outnumbered him and his friends at least five to one. If they'd tried to fight their way through them, they'd have been slaughtered.

The river seemed to sneak up on Kandler. One moment, he strolled along wondering when he might see it through the mists that seemed to thicken as they worked their way to the east. The next, they turned a corner, and the mighty river lay there, rolling silently past its banks as it had for millennia.

"We're not heading for a pier?" Kandler asked.

Ikar snorted. "If you think the ghostbeasts are bad, you should see what waits beneath the surface of the river. The beasties like to congregate around the piers where they think they might find fresh prey. We moor our boats in a new place every day."

The half-orc pointed to a long, low ship tied up near the water's edge. It resembled a large cutter in shape and size. Green and gold paint limned its sides, and the polished wood of the deck gleamed in the flickering torchlight. The name *Salvation* spanned the stern in gold-leaf letters.

As Kandler took in the handsome ship though, he noticed there was something odd about it, although it took him a moment to place just what. Then it hit him: the ship had no sails. It had no rigging and no oars, nor any other visible means of moving through the Cyre's murky, mist-shrouded waters.

"She's a beauty, isn't she?" Ikar said proudly. "She takes us up and down the river as fast as an airship, in any kind of weather. We liberated her from the King's Pier shortly after the Mourning."

"It—it's a sprayship," said Xalt. "It's amazing."

Burch smacked the warforged on the shoulder with the back of his hand, then looked at the startled Xalt and jerked his head at the watercraft.

"Ah, yes," the warforged said. "This is a magically powered craft. It works something like the—um, like an airship. Instead of harnessing a fire elemental, this craft uses a water elemental bound into the aft of the ship. At a command from the person at the tiller, the creature spins rapidly, spraying itself into the water and then spinning back up into the air to do so again."

Xalt gestured toward a large wooden box that spilled over the ship's stern. Arcane runes covered its surface, carved deeply into the wood and illuminated with red and gold paints. "The water shoots out of the holding box like it was cascading from a waterfall. The force pushes the ship forward at amazing speeds."

"Well put," Ikar said, slapping Xalt on the back hard enough to rattle the warforged's iron carapace. "I can tell right now you're going to be an excellent addition to my crew."

Something grated deep down in Xalt's chest before he spoke. "I'm sure I'll make a large impact on your efficiency very soon." Then, with a saluted touch to his forehead at Kandler and the others he left behind, the warforged crawled on to *Salvation*'s polished deck.

Sallah squeezed Kandler's arm. "We can't let them take him," she whispered in his ear, low enough that he hoped Ikar, who was busy directing *Salvation*'s launch, couldn't hear.

"Patience," Kandler murmured back to her. "This hasn't had a chance to play itself out yet."

Many of Ikar's scavengers scrambled after the warforged and on to *Salvation*. At the touch of a green-skinned orc who wore a rune-covered poncho, the ship leaped to life, water flowing slowly out of the end of the box where it spilled into the river's surface.

"Where do we ride?" Kandler asked as he scanned the length of the ship, looking for the most strategic place to sit.

Ikar and his crew would be at their most vulnerable during the crossing, and the justicar hoped to come up with some means of exploiting that. A full-scale attack in the middle of the river seemed foolhardy, but he refused to rule it out. Once they reached the other side of the river, he feared that Ikar might change his mind about letting the four of them go. He hoped to figure a way to bring Xalt along with them, but making sure he didn't lose any ground to the bandit leader came first.

Ikar cackled low and loud as he pointed to a small dinghy floating in the water behind *Salvation*. Kandler hadn't even seen the low, dark boat in the dim light. Now that he could, it looked as if it might roll over at any second and let the river's powerful current suck it under and away.

"Special guests like yourselves get your own private accommodations," Ikar said. "Careful not to tip her when you climb in, and be sure to hold on tight once we get going. At speed, the nose lifts right out of the water."

"I'll sit on the bow," Burch said.

Ikar laughed again. "The last time someone tried that, the whole boat got dragged straight down to the bottom. Just sit in the middle as best you can and enjoy the ride. If we see anything unusual happening back there as we cross the river, we'll be forced to cut you loose." As he spoke, the half-orc stared out into the swirling dead-gray mists that threatened to engulf the shore at any moment. "It's a long, hard row across—assuming you make it."

Within minutes, they were underway. Kandler, Burch, Sallah, and Brendis rode in the leaky dinghy, clutching the creaking sides for dear life as the thing skipped across the waves like a stone thrown by a giant. Ahead of them, towing them along, *Salvation* sliced through the water, Ikar the Black at the bow, barely visible through the Mournland's border mists, more like a suggestion of himself than the actual bandit.

Kandler whispered to the others. "As soon as we get in the middle of the water, we're cutting the tow rope."

"Are you mad?" Brendis asked. "We'll be trapped in the mists."

"I'll take my chances with them instead of Ikar," Kandler said, fishing a pair of rickety oars out of the bottom of the boat and fixing them in place. "For all I know, he wants us to do it rather than force him to deal with us in front of his entire camp. If we show up in his headquarters, I don't think we can expect mercy, no matter what kinds of deals we think we've cut."

"What about Xalt?" Sallah said. "We can't just leave him with them."

"They can't treat him worse than that warforged patrol we found him with," Burch said. "This'll be a step up for him."

Sallah ignored the shifter, focusing her emerald eyes on Kandler. "You told him. You said, 'No one gets left behind.' Were those just words?"

Kandler growled in frustration. "We can't do him any good if we're dead. Unless you think you can walk along this towline like a tightrope, we can't get to that ship until we reach the shore, and—"

"Hold it," Burch said, holding up a hand. "Something's wrong."

A cry went up from *Salvation*, and a loud crack followed it. Peering into the mists, Kandler saw Xalt stand up next to the elemental restraining box at the ship's stern.

"By the Flame," Sallah said, "what is Xalt doing?"

With another crack, Xalt tore a rune-covered plank from the restraining box. The ship shuddered violently and began pitching left and right as it raced blindly through the mists. Kandler heard a pair of splashes as two of Ikar's crew pitched off the edge of the fast ship.

A sharp voice started to bark out something in an unnatural tongue, but the boat's pilot stopped short when Xalt slammed into him. The warforged knocked him back into the restraining box, splintering it even worse.

Ikar roared as the ship bucked up and down. "You'll pay for this, you tin-plated traitor!" He stumbled back toward Xalt, but the deck fell out from under him, sweeping him off his feet.

"Cut the line!" Xalt shouted. "Now!"

Kandler didn't pause to question the order. His blade

came out and sliced through the taut, waterlogged towrope with a single, powerful blow.

The dinghy skittered across the surface of the river for a moment before slowly sliding to a rest. Before it sloshed to a stop, a pillar of water exploded somewhere in front of the leaky boat. Dozens of people cried out in the mist-shrouded darkness before their splash into the water cut them off.

A moment later, some of the voices restarted, renewing their earlier complaints. As Kandler listened, he could hear the current pulling the disaster's survivors farther and farther away into the mists. Even if he'd felt inclined to save some of them, the idea of wandering around lost in the mists for hours with them would have put an end to those thoughts.

"May the Flame take those poor souls," Sallah breathed.

"Kandler!" Ikar's voice rang out in the darkness. It seemed to echo in the mists, making it hard to tell from which direction it came. "Kandler, you low-down, sleazy carrion crawler! You'll pay for this! If I ever get my hands on you, you'll pay!"

"Flame save us," Brendis said. "What—what do we do now?"

Burch handed the young knight an oar.

CHAPTER

13

When Esprë awakened, the stabbing pain in her head still threatened to send her reeling back into unconsciousness. For a moment, she hoped the darkness would take her again, that she could fall back into the peace of oblivion. Perhaps her head had hurt as badly while she slept—she didn't feel rested at all—but at least she hadn't known the suffering so well.

The sun shone down warm and welcome on her face. She felt her skin pinking in its heat, and she wondered how long she'd been asleep, and what had woken her up. She peeled open her eyes and found herself lying on the airship's bridge, unprotected from the sun.

Then she heard the screaming again and recognized it as the sound that had dragged her from her troubled dreams. She tried to get up to see who—or what—could make such a miserable sound, but she discovered her hands were bound to the ship's railing, making it impossible for her to rise past her knees.

Still, as she got to her knees, she spied Te'oma slumped over the ship's wheel. The changeling's shoulders shook as she sobbed into the polished wood.

"What?" Esprë said. "Did you run out of homeless orphans to torture?"

The changeling's head snapped up, and she glared at the young elf, her blank, white eyes tainted with veins of red. For an instant, Esprë thought the telepath would mentally hammer her back into unconsciousness. Although she'd hoped for such a fate just a moment ago, she gritted her teeth and steeled herself to fight the changeling's invasions again. She might want peace, but she refused to let the changeling get the better of her once more.

Te'oma just looked at the young elf though, her eyes locking with Esprë's sparkling blue orbs. Then she bowed her head to weep again, her screams fading to heartbreaking wails.

Esprë let the changeling wallow in her sorrow. Although the young elf's first instinct was to reach out to help comfort anyone in such pain, she hardened her heart to the noise. She hated Te'oma for everything she'd done to her. She had no sympathy for her.

At least, that's what she wanted to believe.

"What?" Esprë said after the changeling refused to stop weeping. "What, what, what?" She didn't bother hiding the irritation in her voice.

Te'oma let loose one last, hideous scream, this one rooted more in frustration than despair, then snarled out at the young elf. "You couldn't understand."

Esprë winced at the noise, shook her head, then shrugged. "I don't really want to. My head hurts—which is your fault too—and you're hurting my ears. If you have to cry, just please be quiet about it."

Te'oma pushed herself out of her slouch and wiped away her tears with the sleeves of her outfit, which Esprë noticed now was the same color as the clouds that coated the Mournland sky. The changeling spoke, her voice worn raw with emotion.

"I should just toss you overboard and be done with it," she

said, weary misery etched into every syllable. "It's hopeless anyhow. Hopeless."

Esprë wanted to roll her eyes, but she feared the gesture might set the changeling off. With Te'oma clearly staggering along the edge of sanity, the young elf kept her own anger in check.

"It's not that bad," Esprë said. As the words left her lips, she heard them ring hollow. She wanted to fill them with more feeling, empathy even, but she didn't know how.

"You know *nothing!*" Te'oma said, her voice rising to a scream again. "It's worse than you could possibly imagine."

Esprë jerked her head at the bonds chafing her wrists. "You still have me."

Te'oma goggled for a moment, then she started to laugh, hard. She laughed until tears flowed down her face again.

"Thanks," the changeling said when she could breathe straight again. "I needed that. You don't know how funny that is."

"Glad I could help," Esprë said. "Now, if you could return the favor by setting me free . . ."

Te'oma giggled. Esprë wished she could stuff the sound down the changeling's throat. Instead, she kept her face like stone.

"I'm afraid I can't do that," Te'oma said. "You have proven yourself too dangerous, child."

Esprë tried a confident smile, hoping that the changeling couldn't see through it. "What makes you think I need to touch you to kill you?"

Te'oma laughed again, but this time there was no humor in it. "Your bluffs grow more desperate."

"Think about all those people who died in Mardakine," Esprë said, letting her anger leak menace into her tone. "I wasn't even in the same place with them when they—" Esprë found she had to swallow here before she could correct herself. "When I killed them."

Te'oma wiped her face dry again. "If you could manage it," she said, "I'd already be dead."

The young elf noticed that the changeling had positioned herself well away from even Esprë's feet, keeping a good amount of space between the two.

"Your dragonmark is still fresh on your skin," Te'oma said. "The mark itself represents the control you have over the power that courses deep within you. Right now, it's still small, no wider than a hand's span. With time, it will grow, as will your control over your power.

"Right now, though," Te'oma said with a bitter smile, "you're no threat to me or anyone else."

"Unless I happen to find you in my dreams."

"I'm willing to chance that."

Esprë shifted about on her knees, trying to get some blood flowing back into her arms, which had fallen numb as she slept. She suspected the changeling had tied her like this on purpose. Even if she managed to get free, her arms would be next to useless until her blood pumped through them again.

"So why all the tears?" Esprë said, hoping to change the subject.

"You don't want to know."

Esprë found that she did, despite her hate for the changeling. Perhaps the answer to her question would give her some sort of leverage over Te'oma. At the moment, no other path promised better.

"Tell me," she said.

Te'oma's lower lip quivered, and Esprë thought the changeling might burst into tears again. She'd never thought of Te'oma as weak before, but something had shaken her to her core.

"My—my employer," Te'oma said. "She's done something horrible."

"You are the company you keep," Esprë said before she

could consider what she was saying. "That's what my mother used to say," she added, embarrassed at her lapse.

"She is not my 'company,' " Te'oma snarled. "Had I a choice, I'd never have crossed paths with her. She is a merciless mistress, her cruelty matched only by her power."

"So why do you work for her?"

Te'oma grimaced. "That, my little elf, is the question at the heart of the matter, isn't it? I once prided myself on having no ties to bind me to anyone. The life of a changeling is change." She narrowed her eyes at Esprë and spat cold words like darts. "At least, that's what my mother used to say."

Esprë ignored the crack. "What changed that?"

Te'oma used the long, pale fingers of one hand to brush the hair from Esprë's eyes. As she did, the young elf tried to reach out with her powers to strike the changeling dead. She imagined Te'oma falling to her knees, screaming, then collapsing in a lifeless heap. She felt the dragonmark on her back, square between her shoulder blades, burn. It ached with hunger for the changeling's life, but nothing happened.

"I got pregnant," Te'oma said. "He left me, of course, when he found out. No changeling likes to be tied down for long. Fathers never stay. Mothers often leave their children on the doorstep of a church or a kindly stranger."

"Did you?" Esprë noticed tears welling up in Te'oma's red-blotched eyes.

The changeling nodded, mute for a moment until she regained what little control she had. She reached out to caress the young elf's soft, round cheek, then drew her shaking hand back.

"She was about your age—or at least the age you seem—when I last saw her."

"Was?" A fist of dread clenched in Esprë's gut.

"My . . ." Te'oma struggled to put her anguish into words. "I just spoke with my employer telepathically."

Esprë resisted the urge to prompt the changeling to continue. Instead, she watched Te'oma struggle for a moment against the tears filling in her eyes before they spilled hot and unimpeded down her cheeks again.

"My daughter is dead—and her body's been destroyed."

Esprë's heart went out to the changeling despite her anger at her. The elf had lost many people in her young life, including Kandler just days ago. Her eyes blurred, and the tears she hadn't let herself cry for so long came rushing out as if through a broken dam.

"How?" she said. "What happened?"

Te'oma looked as if she wanted nothing more than to throw her arms around Esprë's neck and weep into the young elf's bloodstained shirt. Instead, she collapsed atop the wheel again and wrapped her arms around its wooden span. Between sobs, she eked out an answer. "She—she did it.

"My employer.

"She destroyed her."

CHAPTER

14

Kandler couldn't remember the last time he'd enjoyed a sunrise so much. He hadn't seen the sun for over a week, and the way it rose out of the tall, endless grasses of the Talenta Plains as he, Sallah, Burch, and Brendis rested on the Cyre River's eastern shore made his heart feel lighter than it had in weeks. Rosy hues painted the distant wisps of clouds in glowing orange and pink, pushing the blackness of the western sky toward a deep and vibrant blue.

The justicar breathed in deep through his nose, smelling the damp, black earth that lay all around. His mouth watered as he caught the scent of the breakfast Burch cooked over an open fire the shifter had built out of the branches of a dead shrub he'd found on the river's edge. He'd been at it for a while, and Kandler and the others had long since eaten their fill.

"Gotta cook it all," Burch said. "Eat as much as you can. Outside the Mournland, meat killed there turns fast."

Kandler rubbed his full stomach and waved the shifter off. "As soon as you're done with that, we get moving."

"Where are we going?" Sallah asked. Her tone told Kandler that she was trying not to anger him, and that annoyed him even more.

"After Esprë," he said, daring her to ask the questions for which he had no good answers.

He should have known better than to dare a Knight of the Silver Flame. Still, Sallah hesitated for a moment, and Brendis stepped into the breach.

"On foot, we chase after a wounded airship we haven't seen in days. We might as well search for poor Xalt at the bottom of the river." The young knight stared into Kandler's eyes, measuring the justicar's reaction, ready to defend himself should Kandler lunge at him. "This is madness."

Kandler spat into Burch's fire. "We're trying to save my daughter and maybe the whole of Khorvaire while we're at it. I thought your child prophet gave you marching orders to bring Esprë in, to 'save' her from everyone else."

"Watch your blasphemous tongue," Brendis said. "As Knights of the Silver Flame, we do our duty as best we can in whatever way we see fit. The changeling has swept the girl off to only the Flame knows where. We have lost over half of our number since we left Flamekeep, including our glorious and honorable Sir Deothen. We have failed."

The young knight shot a sidelong glace at Sallah, who bowed her head in momentary grief at the mention of her father. Kandler hadn't known the man was Sallah's sire until after Bastard had killed him. That spoke volumes about the kind of relationship the father and daughter had—distant at best—but the justicar knew that Sallah had loved him still. Despite that, she hadn't stopped to grieve for him yet. There hadn't been time.

"What would you like me to do?" Kandler said, offering Brendis an open hand. "Give up? Forget about my daughter?" He shook his head, anger and frustration burning in his eyes. "That's not going to happen."

"We should go back to Thrane," Brendis said. "There we can consult with the Voice of the Flame. She may be able to divine the elf-maid's location, and we can construct a new plan from there. We need information that only the light of the Flame can provide. Otherwise, we wander lost in the darkness."

"Even on fast horses it would take more than a week to reach Thrane. We'd have to either go back through the Mournland or go around through Karrnath, and then we'd have to come back." Kandler spoke through gritted teeth. "Esprë might be dead."

Brendis looked up at Kandler with mournful eyes. "Likely she already is."

Before Kandler even realized what he was doing, his fist lashed out and smashed into Brendis's chin. The blow knocked the young knight back on his rump.

Kandler took one step toward Brendis but stopped dead as Sallah slipped between them. He glared past her at the young knight, who sat on the turf rubbing his bruised chin. Then he spun on his heel and stalked away toward the shore.

"Kid," Burch said loud enough for the justicar to hear, "you're just lucky he hit you before I could."

Kandler sat steaming by the river, gazing out at the dead-gray mists that separated the Mournland from the living world. He was mad, not at Brendis but at himself. He'd let himself lose his temper, not because the young knight was out of line but because Kandler feared he was right.

The justicar held his head between his knees. It felt like it might burst at any moment. When he felt a soft hand on his shoulder, though, instead of pricking the veneer holding him together like an overfull wineskin, it deflated him. He kept his eyes locked straight ahead as Sallah knelt next to him and slipped one of her slender arms around his shoulders.

"You didn't have to do that, you know," she said softly.

Kandler stuck out his jaw as he bit back one bitter response after another.

"No," Sallah said. "I mean, you didn't have to worry about what Brendis said. He's not the senior knight here. I am."

Kandler kept staring into the mist. "What would you have me do?"

"Go after your daughter, of course," Sallah said. "I may have only known you for a week, but it's clear that there is no other path for you."

Kandler hung his head. "I know," he said, "trying to find Esprë at this point is a fool's errand." He looked up into Sallah's emerald eyes, and her beauty stopped his tongue for a moment. He had to turn his head again before he could speak.

"If you and Brendis want to go back to Flamekeep for reinforcements or advice or whatever else, then go. I won't try to stop you, but I'm going after her the best I can. Now."

Sallah leaned against Kandler and gave him a squeeze. "Of course."

"And you?" he asked.

"I will not leave your side until Esprë is safe," she said into his ear.

Kandler turned his head. His lips hovered only an inch from hers. He could taste her breath on his tongue. She waited there for him, not moving forward, not pulling away. He could feel his heart pounding against his chest, and for a moment, the beat froze him like a chorus of drums in the darkest jungle.

Then he leaned toward her, and their lips met in a soft, supple kiss.

If anything, Kandler's heart raced faster, but in delight rather than dread. They held the kiss for an eternal moment before parting again. He looked into her face, and her smile told him everything he wanted—needed—to know.

"Then," he said, "everything will be all right." He leaned in to taste her full, round lips again, but before they met, something came splashing up at them out of the river.

Kandler leaped to his feet, his blade already in his hand. Sallah stood beside him, her knife at the ready. In that instant, the way they reacted together, as one, as if they'd fought alongside each other in a thousand battles, felt as right as that sweet kiss that still lingered on Kandler's lips.

"Something in the mist," Burch whispered from behind the duo. Even without looking back, Kandler knew the shifter would be kneeling there to one side, his crossbow loaded and ready, hunting for prey for its hungry bolt. "In the river. There!"

Kandler stared at the shape coalescing out of the swirling mists, a dark form that grew darker and more solid with every splashing step. The justicar felt the heat of Brendis's blade approach as the young knight dashed up behind him. Even though he'd hit the man, Brendis still had his back, and the thought made Kandler smile.

"Hello!" the figure said in a familiar, metallic voice. "Hello! I hoped you hadn't gone too far yet. I've been search-ing the shore for you."

"Xalt?" Burch said, recognizing the warforged first. The shifter let out a little war whoop of delight.

"By the Flame," Brendis said as Xalt trundled out of the water and into his friends' embrace, "I had not dared hold out hope."

Kandler grinned. "Oh ye of little faith," he said.

Sallah slapped the justicar on the shoulder, a wide smile on her face. "You claim your faith is stronger than his?"

Kandler rubbed the top of the warforged's head. "Not my faith. I *knew* Xalt would make it."

"How?" Brendis asked the warforged. "When that boat sank, I thought for sure you would go down with it. Are you not too heavy to swim?"

Xalt nodded. "I did not try. Warforged do not need to breathe. I fill my lungs only so I can talk."

"You sank to the bottom of the river and then . . . ?" Brendis could not complete the thought on his own.

"I walked east until I found the shore. Once I did, I kept

to the mists for fear of running into more of Ikar's bandits, but I kept my ears open for your voices. It was only a matter of time until I found you—or so I hoped."

"Lucky," Burch said.

Kandler shook his head at the shifter. "Why do you think I let you take so damn long cooking that meat?"

Xalt put a hand on Kandler's shoulder. "You have my thanks," he said.

"For your bravery in dismantling Ikar's ship," Sallah said, "you have ours."

CHAPTER

15

"You can't leave me here," Esprë said, "not bound like this. I can't feel my arms."

The changeling looked down at the young elf from the airship's bridge. "I'm sorry about that. I truly am, but I can't worry about that right now."

Esprë sighed. "Honestly," she said. "I can't feel my arms at all anymore. I think they might fall off. I thought you were supposed to bring me to your employer in one piece."

Te'oma glared down at the young elf. "Whatever made you think that?"

Esprë tried to shrug but only succeed in moving her chest up an inch. Her arms hung loosely from her bonds. "If you could take me in 'dead or alive,' I'm sure I'd be dead by now."

Te'oma growled as she stormed off the bridge toward Esprë. "You're not quite that annoying." She stood over the girl and glared down at her. "Not quite. My employer isn't as picky about your condition as you might think. She just wants you brought to her. If you're dead, it's just a bit more complicated is all."

Esprë nodded. "I see, but can't you at least tie me up some-place with my hands lower than this? It really hurts."

"I thought you said you can't feel anything."

"What I can feel hurts really bad."

The changeling looked down at Esprë, suspicion etched on her blank face in simple lines.

"Please?" Esprë did everything she could to look innocent, short of batting her eyes. She didn't want to overdo it.

Te'oma snorted in annoyance. "Oh, all right," she said, "but you have to promise to be good."

Esprë flashed her sunniest smile. "You have my word."

The changeling reached down with one hand and undid the knots that held Esprë's arms fast to the ship's rail. As the ropes came off, the young elf let her arms fall into her lap and breathed a grateful sigh.

"Thank you," she said as she tried to rub some life into her limbs.

"Stand up," Te'oma said. "Stretch your legs."

As young as she was, Esprë's joints creaked as she struggled to stand. Her arms had hurt so much she'd ignored how stiff her legs and back had become. She groaned as she stretched her arms up over her head and flexed to force the lethargy from her muscles.

She turned to look out over the railing to which she'd been attached. Grassy plains of amber stretched out before her as far as she could see. The mist-shrouded Mournland still lay off to the west, but she ignored it. There was nothing to see there, and she hoped never to enter the place again. Instead, she stared out toward the distant horizon, watching the wind thrum through the plain, ruffling its surface like the waters of a vast, open sea.

"What's that?" she asked, stabbing a finger toward a dark block squatting on the horizon.

"Karrnath," Te'oma said. The changeling stood farther along the railing, out of arm's reach. "That's one of the forts they established to keep the halflings who roam these plains from invading their land."

"Do they work?"

Te'oma chuckled. "Not as well as Karrnath would like. The halflings do not covet any lands but their own. If they wished, they could run right past the forts and strike deep into their neighboring lands before anyone would be able to stop them. The forts only serve to remind the halflings where their boundaries lie—the nomads are notorious for not caring about such things—and what penalties there might be for crossing them."

Esprë shuddered as she remembered the vampires that kidnapped her had hailed from Karrnath. "Is that where you're taking me?"

"No," Te'oma said. "Our destination is much farther north and east of here. We have no business in Fort Bones."

Esprë gave the changeling a sideways look. "Why would they call it something so horrible?"

"The soldiers there are mostly Karrnathi skeletons, savage undead creatures that follow their master's orders to the letter and need no sustenance or sleep."

Esprë shuddered again. "It sounds dreadful."

"It's not an inn," the changeling said. "It's not meant to be inviting."

Esprë's arms tingled as the blood rushed back into them. The feeling in her fingers started coming back. It stung now, but she knew it would soon pass. Now that she could move her arms again, she had to take matters into her own recovering hands.

She concentrated as hard as she could and felt the drag-onmark on her back begin to burn. She had only seen the thing once in the mirror in her home in Mardakine, and the angle kept her from getting a good look at it. Still, the intricate pattern it weaved over her skin leaped into her mind as if she could see it on a page. She traced the edges of it with her thoughts and watched them leap from her skin with the dark red glow of dying embers. As she ran over them again and again, the edges started brightening, growing hotter and hotter, as if a bellows forced the latent fire back to life.

Esprë felt the power creep down from between her shoulders and along her arms like an army of fire ants marching along her skin. It crawled past her elbows and into her hands, where it pooled like a dammed river, pressing against the tips of her fingers, begging for permission to burst out.

She peered at Te'oma out of the corner of her eye. The changeling seemed lost in thought, as if the vast expanse of land that stretched out before them absorbed her whole.

Esprë rubbed her hands together. The heat from the friction forced away the tingling, but the invisible power still seemed to crackle between her fingers.

"No," Te'oma said, her voice distant, "my employer's home is far from here yet, across the frigid waters of the Bitter Sea. I've only been there once, but it is a nasty place suited only to the dead. You—" The changeling noticed Esprë staring at her now, holding her hands out in front of her.

"I'm sorry." Esprë reached out toward her captor with her right hand.

"No," Te'oma said, trying to move away, "wait."

Before the last word left the changeling's lips, the palm of Esprë's hand landed on her thin, pale cheek. She had more to say, but the words froze in her throat.

With a tender caress from Esprë's hand, Te'oma's body locked up as if every joint froze at once, a sort of instant rigor mortis. The young elf felt the power within her dive into the changeling's skin, devouring her life force and leaving nothing in its wake. The pressure in her hands, her arms, her back flooded from her, whom it could not hurt, and left Te'oma struggling near death.

The changeling held her awkward pose for a moment, her face frozen in surprise and terror. Then she collapsed to the deck in a heap, every muscle in her gone limp.

The airship started to pitch immediately, but Esprë reached out and grabbed the wheel with one hand. As she did, she stared down at the changeling for a moment, watching a line of saliva drool out of her mouth and onto the deck. She'd expected something more terrifying, screams perhaps, but this silent sloughing off this mortal coil disturbed her even more. To have it be so easy, as if she'd simply and kindly put an end to a suffering creature's every trouble—that scared her.

She wanted to do it again. That scared her even more.

Esprë reached down with her free hand and rearranged Te'oma's body into a more restful pose, straightening her head and limbs and folding her hands across her chest. The changeling looked like she was just sleeping, although Esprë knew it would be a rest from which she would never awaken.

The young elf wondered when the tears would come. Perhaps the shock of using her dragonmark willfully for the first time had killed her emotions, or maybe she really was a cold-hearted killer who felt nothing for those she murdered.

Esprë rested her hands on the airship's wheel and felt the mind of the craft's elemental there, anxious and ready to strike out in a new direction, but where?

Esprë considered going back to Mardakine, but there was nothing for her there. Perhaps she would try Sharn instead, which lay even farther on the other side of the Mournland. She wondered if the airship could take her back to Aerenal, the eternal homeland of the elves. She hadn't been there since shortly after her birth. She wondered if her grandparents would recognize her, much less take her in.

The young elf had no home. With Kandler gone, she was alone in the world.

The tears started then.

Esprë still wept when something that felt like a jagged, razor-tipped knife stabbed into her brain. She screeched in terror as she fought to shove back against the telepathic attack, but its sharp point sliced through her mental shields. If not for her savage grip on the airship's wheel, she would have fallen into a pile of bones on the bridge.

The young elf summoned every bit of her determination to haul herself up by her arms. As she did, she glared down and saw Te'oma struggling to her knees. "There's your first lesson as a killer," the changeling rasped, her pale skin faded to skeletal white. "Always make sure your victim is dead."

Esprë didn't waste any effort on words. She knew that this was the end. Either she or the changeling would die here. She wouldn't have it any other way.

"Hold very still," Te'oma said, in the tone of a mother scolding an errant child. "I'm going to bind you hand and foot this time. That's the penalty for breaking your word."

Esprë ignored the telepath's patter. Instead, she cleared her mind and reached out to the elemental trapped in the ring of fire that wreathed the airship like a golden ring around a tattered scroll.

The ship lunged forward and down, and Te'oma flipped straight over the bridge's console, then slid along the main deck toward the bow, screaming the entire way. Only the railing at the ship's prow kept her from sailing right over the edge and into the open sky below.

Then the ship leaned forward farther, and Te'oma tumbled right over the railing and disappeared.

Esprë reached out for the leather strap hanging from the ship's console and bound herself to the wheel. She knew the changeling wouldn't be gone for long. She grabbed the wheel and coaxed the elemental into charging toward the ground with every bit of speed it could muster.

"No!" Te'oma screamed as she swung in behind the ship's stern on the leathery, batlike wings of her magic cloak.

The changeling dove down at the young elf, her arms spread wide, her brain lashing out at Esprë's tender mind. "I won't let you do this," she said. "You can't!"

The pain in Esprë's head blinded her for a moment, and she thought she might pass out. She slumped over the wheel, feeling the wind blasting through her hair as the ship plummeted to the ground like a blazing stone.

"Stop it!" Te'oma screamed as she wrapped her arms around Esprë, trying to grab for the wheel, to wrest control from the young elf and pull the airship up before it was too late. "I said *stop it!*"

A melancholy grin appeared on Esprë's face as she looked over her shoulder at the changeling who was trying to save her life. "I'm not trying to kill myself," she shouted over the roaring wind, or maybe the ring of fire that seemed to be cackling with glee. She reached back with a hand and slapped the changeling across the cheek.

"I'm trying to kill *you!*"

Esprë's head exploded in an excruciating show of pain and light. As darkness swept over her in an undeniable black wave, she saw Te'oma's eyes roll back into her head.

The last thing she knew was her own bitter smile.

CHAPTER

16

What do you mean 'thunder lizards'?" Kandler said to Burch.

The shifter pointed down at the large pile of fresh dung in front of him. "Step in it once, you never forget it."

Kandler, Burch, Sallah, Brendis, and Xalt had been walking northeast for the better part of the day. "Better to get away from the Cyre," Burch had said, "and Ikar's bandits."

The plan was to march until their path crossed that of the north-south lightning rail line that ran through the nation of the Talenta Plains, from the capital of Gatherhold in the south up toward the Karrnathi capital Korth.

"Unless the changeling can navigate by the stars, she's probably just guessing which way to fly that ship," Burch had said. "With luck, she'll follow the rail line north until she spots something she recognizes."

"Do we have any prayer of catching her?" Brendis had asked.

"Prayer's your solution." The shifter twitched his nose at the knight as he picked up his pace, forcing Brendis to trot after him to keep up. "Not mine."

Burch had smelled the dung long before Kandler saw it.

The waving grasses stood high in the plains, past the justicar's waist, which made spotting something lying on the ground difficult. The shifter had signaled for Kandler and Sallah to stop but let Brendis step right into the smelly mess.

While the young knight tried to scrape his boots clean, Sallah asked Burch the question burning in Kandler's mind. "What size of thunder lizards are you talking about?"

Burch screwed up his face. "Spoor's not too big."

"It covered my foot to the ankle!" Brendis said, dragging his foot through the long grass in a wide circle around the others.

"Small, for a thunder lizard," Burch said. "Probably a clawfoot, about as big as a *lupallo*. Good fighters too. Got a toe claw you could use to harvest wheat. Halflings around here ride them to war."

Sallah blew out a deep breath. "I've heard of such things, but they seemed mere fodder for stories, tales told to scare children."

Burch smirked. "They're real enough. Just ask Brendis."

"How many?" Kandler asked.

A few yards to the north, Brendis slipped in something soft and disappeared in the grass. "The Flame take this whole place!" he cursed as he scrambled to his feet, dragging his leg behind him, trying to wipe it clean.

"At least two," Burch said, laughing softly at the young knight, his mouth drawn wide and baring his rows of sharp, pointed teeth. "Keep hopping around," he called to Brendis. "You'll find them all."

"Is this trouble?" Kandler asked.

Burch shrugged. "Wild clawfeet hunt in packs. They can devour a bull in a matter of minutes. If they're tame, well, it depends on who's riding them, don't it?"

"The halflings of the plains are peaceable folk," Brendis said as he gave up on getting himself any cleaner. As he walked back to the others, Kandler wondered if the horrible stench that followed the knight would draw the clawfeet to them or drive them away.

"Ever met any?" Burch asked.

Brendis shook his head.

"The Plains aren't a nation like you'd think of it— more a collection of tribes. If Cyre and Karrnath hadn't kept bugging them during the Last War, they'd have stayed that way. Only a common threat like that brought them all together."

"So they stand united," said Brendis, "civilized by their interactions with the other nations."

"If you can call defending yourselves 'interaction,' then sure, but the war's over. They're sure to revert to their old ways."

"Which were?"

The shifter gazed at the young knight with his wide, yellow eyes. "Nomadic hunting and gathering, punctuated by deadly arguments between tribes."

"We have nothing to do with their disagreements," Sallah said. "Perhaps they will let us pass unmolested."

"It's a strange world," Burch said, his tone betraying his true feelings on the matter. "Anything could happen." He stalked off to the northeast again, letting the others trail in his wake, each of them watching their footing as much as him.

"So," Kandler said, trotting to catch up with the shifter, "have you ever been this way before?"

"More than once," Burch said. "Not since the end of the war." He stared out at the horizon before them. "Lot's changed."

"How so?"

The shifter jerked his head off to the right. "I don't remember seeing such a large hunting party before."

Kandler looked south. There, just on the crest of a low hill, he saw a section of especially tall grass waving in the wind. At first, that didn't seem unusual, but then he realized that the wind was blowing from the west. He shaded his eyes with his hand and squinted at the hill.

The extra tall grass turned out to be harvested tufts of the stuff used to camouflage something large moving beneath it—or several somethings. Kandler counted at least ten different sections of independent grass roaming their way toward them. At the rate they moved, they'd overtake the walkers in a matter of minutes.

Kandler looked around, but there was nothing to see in any direction but rolling hills covered with the same, sun-blasted grass.

Burch caught his eye as he motioned for the knights and Xalt to join them. "No chance," he said.

Before the shifter could explain things to the others, a dozen creatures tossed off their grassy covers and sprinted toward them, their tiny riders letting loose a spine-tingling war whoop as they came. The large lizards—clawfoots, just like Burch had guessed—stood about six feet tall and easily massed over two hundred pounds. They were long, lean, and muscular, covered with thick amber scales above, with splashes of emerald green on their chests. Their arms were thin and stunted but ended in vicious claws that looked like they could pry open a man's chest in seconds. They raced about on long, thick-muscled legs that propelled them on a sharp, fast gait no mammal could mimic. Their heads appeared to be mostly rows of razor-sharp teeth.

Brendis drew his sword, which burst into silvery flames as it leapt from his scabbard. Kandler put a hand on the young knight's shoulder and said, "Put it away."

"Are you mad?" Brendis said. "We are under attack."

"We don't know that yet," Kandler said, "and even if we are, do you think we can stand against a dozen clawfoots and their well-armed riders?"

"With faith in the Flame, all things are possible."

"Put that damn thing out before you start a fire!" Burch growled.

"But that is the symbol of our faith," the young knight said.

Sallah lay a hand on Brendis's sword arm. "Then rely on your faith rather than its symbol."

Chastened, Brendis extinguished the flames but still held his blade before him, ready to defend himself and his compatriots to his last breath.

By this time, the clawfoots had the walkers surrounded. Each of them bore a rider on a reptile-skin saddle on its back and had a bit jammed into its mouth. They stared at the walkers with their slit yellow eyes, straining at their bits, hoping for a chance at the fresh meat standing before them.

None of the people riding the clawfoots could have been more than half Kandler's height. Despite their size, they exuded danger. They wore dark tattoos and red war paint in aggressive patterns over their sun-bronzed skin. No city halflings, these nomads were wiry and strong, used to living an entire life on the trail, never stopping for more than a week to settle down—and often much less.

"Wrong place for you," one of the halflings said. This one, with his long golden hair held back in a thick braid, rode the largest of the clawfoots, a creature that strained against its bridle with every step.

"We're on a rescue mission," Kandler said, speaking straight at the leader. "We're trying to rescue my daughter."

The halfling glanced at his fellows and laughed. "Long way from home."

"We come from Breland. We followed her kidnapper through the Mournland to here."

"Those not Brelish." The halfling pointed at Xalt and the two knights with his spear. The stone tip had been worked to a vicious edge with a barbed head behind it. Three red feathers dangled from its other end.

"Our friends joined us in our quest to get my daughter back," Kandler said, walking closer to the leader. "In such desperate times, nationalities matter little."

The halfling jabbed out at the justicar with his spear, forcing the man back. "Countries mean nothing to us—or the dead."

At this, Burch stepped forward. "I've not been here for a few years, but is this how the hunters of Talenta treat all their guests?"

The halfling nodded as he considered this. "We hunt no food. We spot a ship in the sky three days past."

"The airship!" Kandler stepped toward the leader again, and the halfling loosed his reins enough for his clawfoot to bite down at the justicar, its teeth snapping empty air only inches from Kandler's face.

"You know it?" the leader said, spitting on the ground. "Here, we kill spies."

"No," said Kandler. "That's the ship that took my daughter from me. Which way did it go?"

The leader shook his war-painted head. "We don't share secrets with spies," he said.

"Let's go," Burch said. The shifter walked straight between two of the clawfoots and off to the northeast again. As he sauntered away, a spear from one of the leader's lieutenants slammed into the ground before him and stuck.

"Another step, and the next one will be through your heart," the leader called.

Burch turned on the halflings and glared at each of them in turn. "You're a bunch of cowards," he said. "You're not going to hurt us, so if you're not going to help, then get out of our way."

"You dare talk—"

"He dares," said Kandler, following his old friend's lead. He glanced at the others. Brendis looked horrified by the turn of events. Even Xalt stood open-mouthed. Sallah just smiled at him and waited for him to speak to the halflings again, which he did, gazing into her eyes. "I dare. We all dare."

Eleven spears stretched toward Kandler and the others still in the circle. Not for the first time, Kandler wondered if he and Burch had made a terrible mistake.

CHAPTER

17

Esprë couldn't remember ever feeling so bad. Her head hurt where she had banged it on the airship's wheel—again—and pain lanced through her left arm every time she tried to move it. And it was hot, hotter than a sun-savaged desert. She licked her cracked lips and winced. She raised her right hand to her face, and it came back slicked with blood.

She couldn't find the changeling, and the thought that Te'oma might come back to kill her sent her heart racing. She shoved off from the bridge's console with her feet but realized she was still strapped to the wheel. As her right hand moved to release herself—she tucked her left into her waistband to offer it some support—she wondered why everything looked hazy, like she was caught in the mists of the Mournland again.

Then the smell of smoke set her coughing, something the mysterious border of that damned land had never done. Was the ship burning?

Esprë glanced up and saw the ring of fire still spinning around the ship, crackling with power that strove to shatter its mystical harness. She spied cracks in the upper binding arc, a long curve of polished, rune-crusted wood, and she wondered if the lower arc still clung to the ship.

The smoke spiraled up around the ship, past the arc, and into the sky beyond. Esprë stumbled away from the airship's wheel, the ship pitched forward at a steep angle that threatened to pull her toward the splintered bow, but she clawed her way with her one good arm to the bridge's aft railing and surveyed the damage.

The airship sprawled in a shallow valley surrounded by easy, rolling hills on all sides. Pieces of it lay strewn in the wake it had cut through the tall grasses of the plains as it skidded to a halt. It sat in the center of a wide circle of ash, black and gray remnants of the tall grasses that had done nothing to cushion its landing. On the edges of the circle, gouts of flame fed on fresh, dry grass, surrounding the ship in an ever-growing nimbus of fire.

Esprë gasped at the sight, then choked on the smoke that collected in her lungs. She spun about and slid back down to the airship's wheel, desperate to move the battered thing up and away from the fire. She wondered for a moment why the fire hadn't consumed the entire ship, made of wood as it was. Then she thought of the ring of fire that propelled the ship through the air and knew that part of the magic that bound the fiery being into the ring must also protect the ship from its heat.

She wrapped her right hand around the wheel and reached out for the elemental with her mind. Most times, she enjoyed piloting the ship. The thrill of having such a large boat driven by such a powerful creature respond to her will never got old. Now, though, the ship ignored her. Instead of the grudging pliancy she expected from the elemental, it seemed to laugh at her efforts. The crackling of the fiery ring intensified as she tried to push the creature harder, filling her ears with its mean-hearted mirth. The elemental sensed that the ship would soon fall apart and it would be free.

Esprë brought her injured arm up so she could grab the wheel with both hands, and she concentrated on getting the elemental to move the ship with all her might. She willed it to pull free from the earth that dragged it down, to slough off gravity's greedy bonds and soar high once more through the clean, fresh skies. Sweat beaded on her scorched brow as she changed from ordering the ship to move to pleading with it.

Nothing worked. The ship stayed mired in the soft land in which it had crashed—in which she had crashed it.

Just as Esprë gave up on the ship, she heard a groan from the other side of the console. She peered over and saw Te'oma there, her body draped across the remains of the hatch that led into the ship's hold. Back in the city of Construct, a warforged titan had torn through the hull, demolished the hold, and smashed the lid from the hatch, but its frame still squatted there in the cracked decking.

The changeling must have been flung from the bridge in the crash and caught there, Esprë guessed. Otherwise, she would have skittered along the deck and fallen into the fire that had devoured the surrounding landscape.

It stunned Esprë that Te'oma still lived. She'd tried to use the dragonmark to kill her twice and failed each time. Was it that she couldn't bring herself to kill anyone? Or did the changeling have some kind of special hold on her, perhaps a mental block she'd telepathically placed in her head? Or perhaps Esprë just needed to try harder.

The young elf stared down at the changeling and wondered how she could make it down to her without hurting herself. Her injured arm would make navigating the deck difficult.

If she reached the changeling, what would she do? Should she kill her on the spot, finish what she'd started? Perhaps she should take Te'oma's knife and cut her throat, but she didn't know if she could bring herself to do it. Mustering the resolve to use the power of her dragonmark—something that was a part of her, a twisted birthright of some sort, whether she liked it or not—had taken all her resolve. To stick a blade into someone's neck and twist it around until she died seemed impossible.

Before Esprë could even figure out how she could get off the bridge, the sound of clanking armor rang out from the crest of a nearby hill. She snapped her head around to see a handful of figures rising up on the other side of the flames, their forms silhouetted in black through the bright, hungry wall of blazing tongues.

The young elf held her breath as she watched the figures march closer to the fire and then straight through it. They emerged from the conflagration, their blackened, spike-riddled armor rattling loose on their limbs, their helmets perched on their heads at awkward angles, each with a scimitar clutched in its fist.

Esprë peered at them with their strange gaits. Who could they be, and how could they ignore the fire like that? A regular soldier would have been cooked alive in his armor.

When she got a good look at the closest one's face, her gut twisted inside her. Empty eye sockets stared back at her from a skinless, sun-bleached skull, and the soldier's grim, lipless rictus grinned up at her.

The young elf screamed.

Below her, on the deck, Te'oma raised her head long enough to see the creatures marching toward them with their relentless strides. As Esprë watched, she tried to struggle to her knees, but she only succeeded in dislodging herself from the hatch's frame. She moaned in pain and despair as she slid down the pitched deck and landed in a crumpled heap where the bow crashed into the scorched earth. The ashes puffed up around her and settled on her pale skin, and she did not stir.

The closest of the soldiers reached Te'oma and walked right over her. It clambered up onto the ship's broken bow and climbed up toward the bridge, using the spindles in the ship's railing as a makeshift ladder. Another soldier climbed after it, then another, the last taking the railing on the port side instead. Within moments, they would be on her.

Esprë shoved back from the wheel and scrambled up the few feet of the bridge's decking to where the ship's aft rail had stood before the battle in Construct had demolished it. She considered jumping down to the ash-covered ground, but it looked so far away she feared she'd break a leg in the attempt. Still, as the creatures climbed closer, it seemed the only way for her to get free.

Then another of the soldiers stalked around from the ship's bow and stationed itself straight under the bridge. It saw her leaning over the empty space and spread its arms wide like a parent encouraging a scared child to leap down from climbing a tree.

Esprë huffed in frustration then turned to see the other soldiers closing in on her. She looked down past the bridge, thinking of leaping past them, sliding along the deck to the ground and then seeing if she could outrun them, even if it meant somehow dashing through the fire, but a fifth soldier stood where she would have landed, right over Te'oma's body.

Frustrated to the breaking point, Esprë sat down in the space behind the canted console on the bridge and caressed the ship's wheel as she wept.

CHAPTER

18

Kandler grunted in pain as the clawfoot beneath him leaped over a rivulet and came crashing down on the other side. Bound as he was with his hands around the creature's neck, he had no way to cushion the impact other than to hold his breath and grit his teeth every time the creature bounded into the air. It did this often as it ran in a straight line over what Kandler could only guess was the same damn stream that kept meandering back and forth across their path.

The halfling riding behind Kandler—a scrappy, deep-tanned hunter who wore little more than a loincloth and an eagle's feather braided into his hair—laughed every time the justicar hurt. Kandler would have thought he'd have gotten tired of it by now, but the small hunter never seemed to tire of the joke.

Kandler glanced to his right at Burch, who lay strapped to the mount of the halfling riding alongside him. The shifter looked like he might try to take a bite out of the scaly hide of the creature in front of him, just from sheer spite. He watched Burch's claws extend from the tips of his fingers and start to worry away at the fibrous rope binding his wrists.

Kandler did not doubt the shifter would be free soon,

although Burch would choose to reveal this fact in his own time. The thought of the resulting mayhem to come put a smile on Kandler's face, and he felt glad that the halfling behind him couldn't see it.

The justicar shifted his head to the left and spied Sallah atop the clawfoot racing along on that side. He marveled at the creature's raw power and grace. For a moment, their surrender stopped galling him. If they'd tried to fight the Talentans, their mounts would have torn them apart. Having a giant carnivorous lizard feasting on his liver was not how Kandler wanted to go.

Sallah scowled at him. She and Brendis—especially Brendis—had been all for fighting to the last, but Kandler and Burch had overruled her by giving up on their own. When Xalt had followed suit, the two knights had no choice. Even they weren't foolhardy enough to try six-to-one odds against the hunters and their deadly clawfoots.

"Where are they taking us?" Sallah shouted over the pounding of clawed feet.

Kandler noticed that the creatures' vicious middle claws on each foot dug into the ground as they ran, making them as sure-footed as any warm-blooded mount. They also tended to spit out dirt behind them as they ran, which explained why the hunters moved in a wide-swept line rather than single file.

"Why don't you ask them?" Burch said.

The one astride Kandler responded in a grave voice and a thick accent. "You'll find out soon enough." Then he rattled out a long set of orders in what Kandler recognized as the native halfling tongue. The riders all dug their heels into their clawfoots' sides, and the massive lizards sprinted on even faster.

"What did he say?" Xalt called from the other side of Burch.

The clawfoot he was strapped to labored hardest of all.

Not only did the warforged weigh more than anyone else, but his rider was the pudgiest of the halflings too. Their nomadic life made most of the hunters into lean, muscular mites, but this one seemed softer than the others in every way.

Burch bared his teeth. "Literally? You don't want to know."

"I do not fear their words."

Burch chuckled. "Halflings like to hear themselves talk. They use a dozen words where one'll do."

"So what did he say?" The warforged's curiosity would not be denied.

" 'Hustle!' "

The halfling riding behind Burch smacked him in the back of the head.

"I don't know," Kandler said. "Seems that one prefers action."

"We are taking your soft, worthless hides to the Wandering Inn," the halfling behind Kandler said. "There, we and our elders shall determine what fate shall befall you each."

"The wandering what?" Kandler asked. He stretched his neck around to see the halfling sneering down at him. The hunter jerked his chin out before him as they topped a large hill.

"The curious can see for themselves," the halfling said.

Kandler craned his neck around the clawfoot and saw a small city of colorful tents sprawled out in the plain before him. They came in all colors and sizes, from a green and gold specimen large enough to house a platoon of soldiers all the way down to tattered brown sleepers that even a halfling couldn't stand up in.

From high up on the hill, Kandler could pick out some sort of order to the place. Paths wove their way through the tents, some wider than others but none of them straight enough to let a rider stampede through the place unimpeded. The largest tents collected in the central part of the town, clustered around a large open space that served as a public square. Farther from there, the tents grew progressively smaller until they reached a series of eight tall, thin tents that surrounded the town in a rough circle. A halfling warrior stood on each of these, facing outward, scanning the horizon and the sky for friend and foe.

Overhead, a flight of leather-winged, long-headed lizards circled in the sky, riding thermal updrafts like living kites that might never decide to come down. Kandler spotted tiny heads peeking out over the edges of those wings, prodding the creatures to greater heights. Then one of them spun out of the formation in an acrobatic swoop that brought it gliding down to land in front of the green and gold tent that faced the main square. Kandler guessed the rider had to be strapped in or would have fallen to an untimely death.

As the clawfoot riders neared the camp, the halfling on the nearest lookout post sounded three long blasts on a horn that looked like it had been taken from the skull of a massive beast. Halflings of all sorts poked their heads out of their tents, looking south toward the riders, to see who or what approached their homes.

When the clawfoots reached the edge of the tent city, the riders brought their mounts to a canter and fell into single file behind the mount on which Kandler rode. Many halflings stood along their path and stared up at the hunters and the newcomers. Most of them wore the same nomadic clothes as the hunters, but some of the fatter ones were dressed in more civilized garb.

The clawfoots threaded their way through the tents until they reached the main square. A phalanx of halflings awaited them there, standing before the largest tent. The ones in the center wore fine clothes: pants, shirts, and waistcoats, most in the same emerald hues as the tent. Lean, shirtless, sun-baked warriors flanked them to either side, each holding a sharp-tipped spear as tall as themselves.

"Greetings, Lath Berlun," the gray-haired halfling in the center of the line said, a wide and easy smile creasing his chubby face. "What sort of prizes have you brought us today?"

"Larger and livelier sorts than we usually find in the plains, Baronet Walsley, although not, I'm sure, nearly so tasty." With that, he cut Kandler's bonds with a small knife and pushed the justicar off his mount.

Kandler landed on his feet and saw that the others managed the same. Burch hit the ground first, as he didn't have to wait for his bonds to be severed.

"Welcome to the Wandering Inn," Walsley said, spreading his arms wide and exposing his bulging belly. "Please enjoy your stay with us as our honored guests. I am Baronet Walsley of House Ghallanda, your humble host."

"I am Lady Sallah of the Knights of the Silver Flame," the red-haired knight said, her eyes flashing with anger. "I am accustomed to better treatment from those who deign to call themselves my host."

"My apologies, my lady. Our warriors are charged with the sacred duty of ensuring the safety of all who visit the Wandering Inn and who reside here." Walsley raised a bushy eyebrow at the one he'd called Berlun. "The lath here can be a bit overzealous at times, but I assure you it's all in the best interests of those we serve, especially in the case of such illustrious company as we find ourselves in today."

Burch spoke, stepping forward and flexing his claws, a steely glint in his dark eyes. "What's your guest's name?"

The baronet stepped backward a half step, and the warriors on either flank of the line brought their weapons to the ready. Kandler put his hand on the hilt of his blade, but Burch waved him off with a quick flick of his hand.

"Wait a minute!" a deep, gravelly voice called out from inside the tent. "Is that a no-good, yellow-bellied son of a wereskunk I hear out there?"

The baronet cleared his throat before responding, eyeing Burch's still-popped claws as he did. "Ah, yes. A shifter has accompanied Lath Berlun back from his latest patrol, sire."

A broad- and bare-chested halfling stepped out through the tent's front flaps and squinted into the sunlight. He stood two hands taller than any of his fellows and looked to Kandler like he could wrestle one of the clawfoots to the ground all by himself. A few gray hairs wound through his black, rough-cut mane, and crow's-feet clustered in the dark-tanned skin around his sparkling blue eyes, but all of the halflings took a step back out of deference when he entered their presence. He squinted up at the visitors, his sharp gaze landing on Burch.

"The lath of laths, the most powerful of our great leaders, Lathon Halpum," the baronet said by way of introduction.

The lathon waved off the civilized halfling's patter. "People either know who I am or don't care." He stepped forward and stuck his hand out toward Burch.

"You shifty old shifter," he said with a wide, winning grin, "how in all of Khyber are you?"

CHAPTER

19

Esprë gasped to find herself lying in a bed lined with fresh sheets when she awoke. She hadn't known such luxuries since she'd been taken from Mardakine, and she had begun to despair that she would ever find a place again in which she could sleep undisturbed and awaken refreshed.

For a moment, she thought she was back home in Mardakine, in her bedroom in Kandler's house, warm and cozy. When it struck her, though, that she didn't recognize the ceiling, that hope shattered.

She glanced around and saw that she lay in a modest feather-stuffed bed in a high-ceilinged room with rough-hewn wooden walls. Late afternoon light streamed in through a pair of shutterless windows, catching dust motes dancing in the air. Somewhere outside, birds chirped at the encroaching dusk.

Three other beds stretched along the walls of the modest room. Two stood empty, but someone lay snoring softly in the third, farthest away from Esprë.

The young elf half sat up and stretched her neck to spy a pale-skinned figure nestled among the ivory sheets on the opposite bed: Te'oma. Dark circles dragged under the changeling's eyes, and a long gash on her forehead bore a neat line of black stitches.

As Esprë sat up straight in her bed, she heard someone shuffling about in an adjoining room. "Hello," she called. "Is someone there? Can you tell me where I am?"

Fear and gratitude warred in the young elf's head. Kandler had drilled into her head that anything too good to be true almost always was, especially when it came from strangers, and she didn't know anyone so far from home, she was sure.

A polished white skeleton in an ivory tunic stepped through a curtain that hung across the room's only door, a silver cup clutched in its bare, skinless fingers, the sun glinting on its hollow skull, reaching into the shadowy emptiness inside.

Esprë scrambled backward until she smacked into the wall behind her and let loose a piercing scream that started in her toes and rang out through her head.

The skeleton ignored the noise, and Esprë wondered if—how—the thing could hear without any ears. She pressed herself into the corner near the head of her bed as hard as she could as its feet clacked across the wooden floor. It placed the cup down on a table near the bed, then looked up at her.

Esprë saw right through the vacant eye sockets to the rear of the creature's skull, and she froze in fear. It cocked its head at her for a moment, an all-too-human gesture she somehow found comforting. Then it turned and left the way it came.

Esprë glanced over at Te'oma and saw that her outburst hadn't caused the changeling to stir a muscle. She sat there, still splayed out against the wall behind her, panting in panic, trying to catch her breath.

Just as the young elf felt her heart start beating again, footsteps—the heavy footfalls of boots rather than bare bones—sounded in the space beyond the curtained doorway. A meaty hand reached through and shoved the curtain aside, and a lady dwarf dressed in blackened chainmail, a double-bladed battle-axe hanging from her belt, stormed into the room.

"You're awake," the dwarf said. She had a good, honest face, broad and plain, with a button of a nose, something unusual in a dwarf, as was her white-blond hair she kept pulled back into a long, flowing ponytail. "You were unconscious for days. I thought you might have taken in too much smoke."

"Where am I?" Esprë said.

"That's gratitude for you." The dwarf allowed herself a brief smile. "Welcome to Fort Bones, young elf. I hope your stay with us will be short and pleasant."

Esprë stared at the dwarf, her eyes as wide as moons. "What am I doing here?"

"Healing," the dwarf said with a quick glance at Te'oma. "One of my patrols rescued you and your friend over there from a crashed airship. I daresay they saved your lives."

Esprë stabbed a shaking finger at the changeling's oblivious form. "She is *not* my friend. She kidnapped me, stole me from my home."

Concern creased the dwarf's wide brow as she rubbed her cleft chin with a thick-fingered hand. "The mystery of our visitors deepens. I wondered where a pair like you might come from. Your ship bears no Karrnathi markings."

"We're in Karrnath?"

Dread filled Esprë's heart. Her mother and Kandler had both fought against Karrnath in the Last War, and their tales of the undead-infested place had always terrified her. To the elves of Aerenal, the land in which she'd been born, undeath represented the worst of the fates that could befall a mortal soul, and any nation that relied on the services of the undead could only be evil at its core.

"It's not so bad," the dwarf said, compassion warming her voice. She started toward Esprë but stopped when the young elf tried to press her body through the wall behind her. "My name is Berre Stonefist, the Captain of Bones." She held her open hand up before her. "You have my word that no harm will come to you while you are here."

"I don't know you," Esprë said. "How can I trust you?"

Berre glanced over at the sleeping changeling. "My poor girl," she said, "do you have much of a choice?"

Esprë considered these words for a moment, then shook her head, a pout on her lips.

"Where are you—? Pardon me. With so few of the living under my command these days, I sometimes forget my manners. How are you called?"

"My name is Esprë."

"That's Elvish for 'hope,' isn't it?"

Esprë nodded.

"Your parents must have high hopes for you."

"They're dead."

Berre frowned and glanced at Te'oma.

"No," Esprë said. "They died years ago. I never knew my father. My mother died on the Day of Mourning."

"Ah," Berre said, understanding dawning on her face. "You're Cyran?"

Esprë nodded again.

"You don't live in the Mournland."

"Mardakine. It's right on the western edge."

"You crossed the Mournland in your airship?"

"Mostly." Esprë's face brightened into half a smile. "It's complicated."

"I look forward to hearing the tale."

Esprë steeled herself. There was a question she had to ask, although she dreaded the answer. "What will happen to me?"

Berre looked around the walls of the room. "This is no place for a child—for anyone who doesn't have to be here, really. Once you're well enough to travel, I'll arrange for transport to the court of King Kaius III in Korth. His majesty will be interested in your tale, too, no doubt. Your fate will be up to him, although I see no reason why he wouldn't arrange for an escort to return you to your home."

Esprë's face fell at those words.

"Do you have a home anymore?"

"I . . . I don't know."

"Kaius is a good and wise king. He will help you find your way."

Esprë liked how sincere the dwarf seemed. She wanted to believe her, but it still seemed too wonderful to wrap her heart around it. She glanced at Te'oma and shivered.

"Don't worry about your un-friend there," Berre said. "We shouldn't move her until she awakens, but I'll post a guard in here with you around the clock. Ibrido!" the captain called at the curtained doorway.

A moment later, the most handsome man Esprë had ever seen slunk into the room. Tall and lean, he had the refined features of an elf, but rounded ears and wide, dark eyes marked him as human. His black, wavy hair fell to his shoulders, framing a strong face anchored by a sharp jaw.

"Yes, captain?" Ibrido said, his eyes fixed unblinking on Esprë as if they could see straight through her and the wall behind her too. His voice was deep and resonant, although it carried no trace of warmth.

"It seems the changeling is a kidnapper and our elfling here was her latest victim. Post a guard between them and report to me the moment the changeling awakes."

"Yes, captain." Ibrido's gaze never wavered from Esprë.

"Her name is Te'oma," Esprë said.

Ibrido's eyes flickered to the changeling for a moment before returning to Esprë, but his expression never changed. "Te'oma shall not harm you," he said to her. "On that you may rely."

"Very good," Berre said, turning to leave. As she reached

the doorway, she looked back and said, "Get some rest, young Esprë. You've had a long journey, but there is hope for you yet." With that, she left.

Esprë looked up at Ibrido, who stood staring at her like a statue. She couldn't even tell if he was breathing. With a repressed shiver, she lowered herself into the bed and pulled the covers up to her chin, then closed her eyes and tried to go back to sleep.

After a while, she opened her eyes again, and he stood there still as ever. She turned over on her side, putting her back to him, somehow sure that Ibrido's gaze never wavered.

CHAPTER

20

"Tell me," Kandler asked Lathon Halpum, after relating the tale of how he and his companions had come to be in the halfling leader's grace, "how do you know Burch?"

The halfling leader put down his massive flagon of ale and wiped the foam from his mouth with the back of hand. "Now that is a story worth telling, my friend."

The other conversations around the massive dining table all ground to a halt at the sound of the lathon's voice. Until now, he'd spent most of the meal chatting with Burch like brothers, but their conversation had been private. Kandler had been fine with that for a while, but he couldn't contain his curiosity any longer. He'd known Burch for years, and the shifter rarely spoke of his time in the Talenta Plains, much less any friendship with the most powerful of the halfling chiefs.

"You and me, we met in Cyre," Burch said to Kandler, a savage smile on his face, "but I had a life before that."

The shifter seemed, well, happy. Kandler didn't think he'd seen him so relaxed since they'd left Metrol for Sharn over four years ago. The Day of Mourning weighed on Burch as much as on Kandler, and the shifter had never felt at peace in Mardakine, Kandler knew. He sympathized with his friend. Since that fateful day, he hadn't much been himself either.

"I'd like to hear *that* story," Sallah said, mischief glinting in her shamrock-green eyes.

"Later," Kandler said, trying to avoid the subject. That tale involved Esprina too, and Kandler wanted to steer Sallah's thoughts away from his dead wife. He felt a pang of guilt at that. He'd always been a faithful husband, and since her death he'd dedicated himself to founding Mardakine and taking care of Esprë. Thoughts of romance had not crossed his mind for years, and they seemed so alien that he felt like a schoolboy again, both giddy and nervous. "We'll have plenty of time on the road tomorrow."

Sallah's smile set Kandler's heart beating. He turned back toward the lathon, who took one last slug from his beer before launching into his story.

"I was a young lath. I'd earned my rank only three seasons before, and I was still eager to prove myself at every chance. My tribe, the Red Wolves, wandered the eastern part of the plains in those days, on the edge of the Blade Desert, in the long shadows of the Endworld Mountains. We traded sometimes with the yuan-ti of Krezent. The tribe of serpent people there mastered growing succulent desert fruits we coveted, and they enjoyed the pelts we could provide them.

"Just after a visit to Krezent, we began to lose people from our tribe. The first two were old, past their prime, and we assumed that they had gotten careless and fallen victim to some predator of the plains. Then my daughter Monja went missing. She was just shy of coming of age then, already a promising student of Balinor, the god of the hunt. If she had disappeared, then something terrible was wrong.

"I led the search party that went looking for Monja. Seven moons spun in the sky that night. Barrakas, the largest, rode low and full, the perfect, silvery hunter's lamp."

Burch interrupted at this point, and the lathon let him take over the story with a smile.

"Me, I'd been hunting all sorts of werecreatures for years at that point, and I was hot on the trail of one I'd been chasing for days. I'd tracked him over the Endworld Mountains from Q'barra, where he'd been terrorizing the people of Whitecliff. I think he'd been part of the black-scale lizardfolk who live around Haka'torvhak, home of the dragon-god Rhashaak.

"That's one nasty group of souls there, and his was blacker than any of the rest. Gigantic, too, even for a yuan-ti. After he'd eaten a dozen of his own kind, more or less alive, they forced him out into the wider world so he could torture inno-cent folks instead.

"His name was Ss'lange, or at least it had been back when he'd had a mind of his own. After the lycanthropy took him over, most of his conversations started and ended with him tearing out someone's throat. He needed putting down. That's where I came in."

"This Ss'lange," the lathon said, taking over the narrative again, "came over the mountains looking for fresh prey, and he found it in our tribe. When he took Monja from us, I knew we only had a matter of hours before he killed her. He liked to terrify his prey before killing them. He thought it made their blood taste better.

"From the fact that the killings had started with the fill-ing of the moons, I figured that some sort of werebeast was using us for its larder. I just didn't know what kind, so when this monster comes barging out of the darkness," the lathon chucked Burch in the shoulder with a rocky fist at this point, "you can guess what we thought."

Burch flashed a toothy smile. "I was trying to warn them about Ss'lange, and they filled me with arrows instead. Luck-ily, halflings only loose toothpicks, or I might have been hurt."

As the two spoke, Kandler noticed a young halfling enter the room and slip into a darkened corner. Her golden, sun-bleached hair was tied back in a loose braid woven through with stalks of grass and a single red ribbon no thicker than a child's thumb. Her wide, blue eyes danced along with the torchlight in the tent, like sapphires set in her wide, merry, well-tanned face. She wore a short, simple tunic made of the dappled skin of a thunder lizard, a knife belted at her waist. She carried a short, plain-carved staff in one hand. A wolf's red-haired tail hung from its tip.

The lathon smacked Burch harder this time, and the shifter laughed. "You howled loud enough when you took one of mine in your shoulder," the halfling leader said.

"That was me trying to warn you about Ss'lange," Burch said, laughing harder. "Halflings can't tell one kind of howl from another."

"Anyhow," the lathon said, "one of his howls happens to come out in something that sounds almost like Halfling, and he's saying, 'Don't hurt me!' Well, no werebeast I ever met stopped to chat with me before, so I figure it's worth giving him his say."

"I'm in the middle of explaining to these runts who I'm after when this creature comes out of nowhere and attacks us. We made such a ruckus, it wasn't like it had to hunt too hard for us."

"I'd never seen anything like it before," the lathon said, spreading his arms wide as he spoke. "Huge, with fangs as long as your arm, and covered all over with scales."

"Huge for you, you mean," said Burch. "Truth was, it wasn't any bigger than me."

"You said Ss'lange was gigantic," Brendis said.

"Hey, the boy's listening," the lathon said, waving for a server carrying a pitcher of ale to come over. "Be sure to top off his glass," he said, pointing at the young knight. "He's far too clearheaded."

"Here's the kicker, kid," Burch said. "This critter wasn't Ss'lange. I'd been tracking him through the region for about a week, and it turns out he'd gone and infected one of his surviving victims—on purpose. He figured it might throw me off the scent. Nothing else he'd tried up until then had worked.

"I've seen him before though. Fought him once, even. I can tell right away that this critter's nothing like him, and I figure out what's happened, so I do what I have to.

"What's that?" asked Sallah from the edge of her seat.

"I smack it once, hard, to get its attention, to get it to chase me away from the others. Thought they might have blown all their arrows on me. Once I had it to myself, I beat it half to death."

"Of course, as he's doing that, we spread out to look for him. Just then Ss'lange pops up out of the grass and tears into us. He was a cunning hunter, waiting for us to get far enough apart he could take us on one at a time.

"I've hunted dozens of different breeds of thunder lizards, but this weresnake was something else. He gutted two of us and ripped the throat out of a third before we realized there were two of them running around with us in the night—three if you count Burch. He came after me next, but I made him pay for it. I gashed open his chest with my spear."

"About then, I showed up to save the day," said Burch.

Halpum threw an arm around the shifter and pointed at him. "This crazed shifter launches himself at Ss'lange so hard and fast I thought it was a rabid clawfoot."

"Clawfoots get rabies?" Burch asked.

"I don't know," the lathon said with a laugh. "It's a strange world. Who can tell?

"So there we are with two of these monstrous critters trying to claw each other to death right in front of us. The smart thing to do is run, but we're too thickheaded for that. I figure the furry one hasn't done us any harm yet, so I call for a charge, and we all stab our spears into the scaly one, who's got his coils all wrapped around Burch by then, crushing the wind out of him."

"This doesn't do much good," Burch says. "Ss'lange cleaned his fangs on bigger sticks."

"But it gets Ss'lange's attention."

"Which is all I need." The shifter grabbed his neck with a ripping motion. "Next thing, the weresnake's on the ground, missing a throat."

Halpum nodded, smiling. "Fight over." He paused for a moment. "Course, that's not the end of it."

Burch shook his head. "There was still his daughter to find. Plus the fact Ss'lange gored my shoulder with his fangs before he went down."

"You're still here," Brendis said.

"Barely," Halpum said. "He spent the better part of a month with us, recovering. It wasn't the wound so much as the poison."

"And the girl?" Kandler asked. Esprë weighed heavy on his mind as he spoke.

"Ask her yourself," the lathon said, jerking his head toward the young halfling who had entered the room earlier.

Burch leaped across the table before Kandler could even turn his head. The shifter landed in front of the newcomer, sweeping her up into his arms like a long-lost child.

"I thought I scented you," he said. "It's been a long time. Too long."

Monja giggled as he held her out away from him at arm's length to get a better look at her. "Children do grow," she said.

Burch hugged the halfling to him before setting her back on her feet and kneeling down next to her. Then he stopped marveling at her and reached up to caress the wolf's tail hanging from her staff. His black eyes grew wide.

"You're the clan shaman now?" he said. "I'm getting older than I thought."

Monja shook her head. "Wodager is still with us. I'm next in line."

Burch grinned, showing all his long, sharp teeth. "That's a proud line." He rubbed his shoulder, where Kandler guessed the scars from Ss'lange's fangs rested under the shifter's thick fur.

"I didn't call for you for a reunion, daughter," Halpum said from the other side of the table, "no matter how happy it may be. Our friends here, new and old, can't stay long. Kandler there, a kidnapper races north with his girl. To Karrnath at least, maybe beyond."

Monja stepped forward to where Kandler sat on the ground, his legs folded under the low table at which he ate. She put her hand on his shoulder. "I am with you, then, until we find her. Your cause is mine."

Kandler started to protest, but the words caught on his tongue. He turned to Halpum and forced them through. "I cannot risk your daughter to save mine."

Monja grabbed Kandler's chin and turned his head to look at her. "I am no child. I am likely older than you."

The justicar started to open his mouth again, but the halfling shushed him. "Don't look to him." She stepped closer, near enough he could taste her breath. It smelled of anise. "I've known the terror of a kidnapped child. Your cause is mine."

CHAPTER

21

When the plates were cleared and the flagons topped off, Monja spoke to Kandler again. A dazzling presence in the lathon's tent, all eyes stayed centered on her as she slipped into a space cleared between Burch and her father without a needed word. She chatted with them both, taking up with the shifter as if not a day had passed since they'd last met.

Her exuberance reminded Kandler of Esprë in her brighter moments, in the days before the Mourning, before her mother had been lost to them both. Since then, a cloud had always hovered over the young elf, casting even her best days in shadow. Living in Mardakine, nestled up against the horror of the Mournland, hadn't helped. More than once, Kandler had thought to give up on dead Cyre, but neither he nor Esprë could find the strength to tear themselves away from the place and head for more pleasant climes.

Circumstances had done that for them.

It took the justicar a moment to realize that someone had called his name.

"Kandler?" Monja said, the lilt now gone from her voice. "Are you with us?"

The justicar nodded.

"I asked if you had anything of your daughter's with you."

Kandler lowered his eyes for a moment, then shook his head. "Burch knows her scent. We never thought we'd have to track her through the air."

"Nothing?" Monja's face fell. "Not even a small token she might have given you? A birthday gift?"

Kandler and Esprë had never gone in for such sentimentality. Esprina had been the most pragmatic elf Kandler had ever met—one of the many things he'd found attractive about her—and she'd passed that trait on to her daughter. Living as nomads in wartime too—and then in barren Mardakine—necessities had crowded out much else.

"Why?" he asked.

Monja's grimace creased her childlike face, and Kandler saw her for her true age. Wisdom lurked behind those youthful eyes.

"By means of my magic, I can spy upon those far away, but I must know something about them for the spell to work. I've not met your daughter, so having something she once owned would be the next best thing. Without that even, I have little to go on, nothing for my magic to latch on to." She cursed in an unchildlike way.

"Wait," Sallah said. "I have something."

Kandler turned to look at the lady knight, hope rising in his chest. He quashed it back down right away. "You have something of my daughter's?" He failed to keep the disbelief from his voice.

"I didn't say that." Sallah reached for her belt and drew out the black blade that had once belonged to Te'oma. She'd carried it with her since the battle in Construct. Now she tossed it onto the table, where it slid and spun until coming to a rest in front of Monja.

"This was the changeling's," the lady knight said. "If we find her, we may find Esprë too."

A smile spread across Monja's face, exposing her small,

pearly teeth as she handled the knife. The flickering light of the everburning torches danced across the surface of its polished, ebony blade. "This will do just fine," she said.

With a sharp gesture from Monja, the flap at the front of the tent opened, and a handful of halflings trotted in, carrying a large, brassy basin filled with smoky water. They hauled it up and set it on the table before Monja, then she dismissed them with a curt wave.

Monja stood on the seat of her chair so that she could look down into the basin from above. Burch motioned for the others to come nearer, and soon Kandler, Brendis, Xalt, Sallah, and Halpum surrounded the basin too, craning their necks to stare into the murky fluid inside.

Monja chanted something low and soft, words that seemed to slip in and out of Kandler's ears without stopping to mean anything in between. As she spoke, she held the changeling's black dagger out in front of her and used it to stir the waters with a flourish. As the waters swirled, Monja kept chanting, and the cloudy concoction in the basin became pale and clear.

An image began to form on the water's spinning surface. Monja slowed her stirring bit by bit until the dagger didn't move at all, and the water seemed as flat and smooth as a mirror.

A wooden ceiling appeared in the water, and for a moment Kandler thought it was just a reflection. Then he remembered he stood in a tent.

Monja tilted the tip of the dagger, and the image in the water moved, panning about until it revealed an open window set in a wooden wall. Through the window, Kandler could see torches guttering in the night air. One of them moved from right to left before disappearing from view, and he thought he could make out the form of a sentry in the glow of the distant light.

Monja moved the dagger again, and the vision in the

water rotated about the room, taking it in one piece at a time. A lantern burned in one corner, casting sharp shadows throughout the place. A number of beds were crammed into the room, but only two seemed occupied, long lumps resting in them beneath thin blankets.

The image in the basin rotated up and looked down on the form in the nearest bed. Kandler heard Sallah gasp as the sleeping face of the changeling spun into view.

"She's hurt," Xalt said, his voice betraying more concern for the changeling than Kandler thought he could have mustered.

"Not bad enough," Burch growled. Kandler looked over to see the shifter flexing his hands, popping his claws.

"Try the other bed," Kandler said.

Monja dragged the tip of the dagger an inch across the water, and the image panned straight over the other sleeping form. Esprë lay there below them, a purplish bruise across the bridge of her nose spread out to blacken both her eyes. Her breath came soft and even, though, and she seemed peaceful despite her location.

Kandler felt his heart clench in his chest. He wanted to reach out through the image to touch her, to stroke her golden hair, to whisper that everything would be all right, but he feared it would break the spell and steal her from him forever.

"It's some kind of sick room," Sallah said.

"I wonder what happened to the airship," said Brendis. The young knight had been the last of them to fly the craft.

Not for the first time, Kandler wondered if the knight felt responsible for it getting away from them and thereby Esprë too. Brendis couldn't have done a thing to prevent it, but Kandler knew that knights like him often let guilt eat at them. Such feelings motivated some of them to make amends, to repair any damage done. In others, though, the emotion festered, always open and raw.

"Where are they?" Kandler said.

Monja shook her head. "The spell only shows me the person I'm looking for, not her location on a map."

"Can you move the image out through the window? Just looking around a room doesn't tell me enough."

"The vision centers on the changeling. If she moves, I can follow her. Otherwise . . . perhaps we can try again in the morning."

"No need," Halpum said. "I recognize that place. Spurbin—one of my best hunters spent a long week there once."

All eyes locked on the lathon.

"It's the infirmary of a Karrnathi outpost far to the north of here on the border between our land and that of King Kaius. We were hunting a swordtooth titan, a big lizard, tall as a dozen halflings put together. They rarely wander so far from the central lands, but this one was hungry and mad with pain. It lost one of its spindly upper arms in a fight, along with a double armload of its yard-long teeth.

"Even wounded, the beast was dangerous, maybe worse than ever. It rampaged through one of our hunting camps, killing a dozen good halflings before we ran it off. We tracked it from there, following it north."

"Like following a herd of cattle, right?" Burch said. "The tail alone on a thing like that's wider than a wagon."

Halpum nodded. "Crazed as it was, it ran fast and hard but wandered all over the place as it went. We kept a good distance from it, wary of it scenting us and turning to attack. I figured it would run itself out soon enough, then we could put it down. A kill like that is worth a little risk.

"Instead, the dumb beast ran right at that Karrnathi fort. Fort Bones, they call it. Stuck inside those wooden walls, the soldiers had nowhere to run, and it tore through their defenses like they were kindling.

"Of course, it didn't help that most of the soldiers there aren't more than bones either, tools some necromancer raised from peaceful graves to serve in the Karrnathi army until the moons all fall from the sky."

"We met some of their friends in Mardakine the night Esprë was kidnapped," Kandler said.

"More meat on those bones," Burch said. "Stinking zombies."

Halpum shook his head. "Karrnath's always liked recycling their dead soldiers. You don't have to feed them, and they always follow orders. They're dumber than a clawfoot, but you can't have everything.

"Fort Bones uses only skeletons for its operation. Fort Zombie sits forty leagues to its west, closer to the Mournland. You can guess what kind of guards they have there."

Sallah nodded. "It seems that our changeling may have friends in Kaius's court at Korth."

"I always hated Karrnath." Kandler fought the urge to spit. As an agent of the Citadel, he'd been to the northern nation many times, and he'd come to dislike its leaders, whom he found as cold and merciless as one of their brutal winters.

"The Karrn aren't all bad," Halpum said. "After we helped them bring down that big lizard, they invited us in for a feast. All that lizard meat and only a handful of living Karrn to share it with. We stayed a week, until Spurbin could move again. He nearly lost an arm to the thing. Just lucky it bit him with one of the gaps in its teeth."

"Fort Bones, you say," Kandler said. As he spoke, he looked down into the basin. The waters had clouded through again. "How far north is this?"

"About seventy leagues," Halpum said. "You can leave at first light."

CHAPTER

22

"How long do you plan to keep us here?" Te'oma demanded.

The changeling had awakened in the Fort Bones infirmary only minutes ago, the sun streaming in through the window, burning the sleep from her brain. She didn't know how long she'd lain in that straw-ticked bed under its bleached white sheets. It amazed her that she was still alive. When the girl had crashed the airship into the ground, she'd been sure she would die.

In some ways, Te'oma wished she had died. It would be so much simpler that way. No more working for her shadowy masters, no more mourning for her dead child, no more hoping that she could somehow find a way to bring that child back to life. It would finally all be over.

Instead, she'd woken up in this strange room, guarded by a pair of fleshless skeletons draped in Karrnathi armor who'd immediately sounded an alarm. When she'd tried to get up, they'd sat on her chest. Weak as a blood-drained cat, she couldn't summon the strength to resist them, and she'd lay pinned there until the dwarf—Berre Stonefist, the Captain of Bones—entered the room to interrogate her.

The skeletons still pressing into her with their uncushioned bones, Te'oma had thrashed about, looking for any way out. Her eyes fell on the elf girl. As they did, Esprë leaped back as if stabbed, a tiny scream escaping from her lips before she covered them with a delicate hand.

"Help me!" Te'oma had said. "They'll kill us both."

The young elf had turned her back on her, huddling in the corner, trying to make herself as small as possible in some vain hope that Te'oma might then ignore her. Esprë had apparently heard enough of Te'oma's lies.

Her body trapped, the changeling had probed around with her mind. Mentally, the skeletons were empty holes. She might as well have tried to telepathically approach her bedding instead.

Esprë's mind shone out like a beacon, tempting Te'oma to attack it, almost daring her to dominate her. The changeling couldn't muster the effort to break down the young elf's defenses though. The mere effort wasted what little energy she had, and she sank farther into the bedding, giving up beneath the skeletons' weight.

Then the dwarf walked in.

"How long do you plan to keep us here?" Te'oma demanded.

"Us?" Berre said. "You're being a bit generous in your collection of others to your side." She gestured toward Esprë. "I don't think our young elf here cares for your extension of the word 'us' to include her. A better question would be, 'How long do you plan to keep *me* here?' I'd think."

"Let me rephrase," Te'oma snarled. "Am I your prisoner?"

A grin crept across the dwarf's lips. "The bony beasties on your chest weren't clue enough?"

"Why?" Te'oma said. "I've done nothing wrong."

"Ah." Berre flashed a frown. "Then it seems we have a wee difference of opinion. This lass," she jerked a thumb at Esprë, "claims you kidnapped her from her stepfather's home on the other side of the Mournland and dragged her out here for the Host knows what reason."

"Lies," Te'oma said. "She's my ward. She must have been hit on the head in the crash. She doesn't know what she's talking about."

"Is that so?" Berre raised her eyebrows at Te'oma. "You expect me to take the word of a changeling wearing the symbol of the Blood of Vol—a vile cult that's been outlawed here in the fair land of Karrnath—over that of an innocent elf maiden?"

The dwarf leaned forward and whispered to the changeling. "Perhaps it's you who's been hit on the head."

Desperate, Te'oma used her fear and her fury to reach down deep into her mind and hurl a mental blast at the Captain of Bones. If she could reach into the dwarf's mind, twist it until Berre saw things her way, she might be able to get out of here yet. She stabbed forward blindly into the dwarf's brain, hoping to strike something vital.

Berre fell forward, landing on her knees with a grunt. As she did, the two skeletons sitting on Te'oma reached down and began to pummel her in the face. Her concentration smashed, along with her nose, the changeling felt her assault against the dwarf melt like a sharp-tipped icicle in a hot forge.

Berre clambered back to her feet, wiping at a bit of blood trickling from her nose. "You damn yourself with your own actions," she said. "Friendly folk don't try to fry my brains."

The Captain of Bones looked at the two skeletons still sitting atop the changeling. "If she tries to escape, if she tries to harm the girl—mentally or physically—then kill her."

Then she turned her attention to the battered Te'oma. "Don't worry yourself," she said, menace dripping from every word. "You'll be relieved of our hospitality soon enough. We're due an airship with new supplies here shortly. Its captain will be only too happy to take you along with him back where he came."

"Where is that?" Te'oma murmured between her busted lips.

"Korth," Berre said. "I'm sure Kaius will get a charge out of you."

Night had fallen when Te'oma awoke again, a rough hand on her shoulder. The light of a single lamp cast the room in sharp shadows, and for a moment she couldn't see the face of the person looming over her.

"Back to torture me again?" she asked, assuming it was Berre who stood over her, framed in the lamplight. Then, as the effects of her long sleep sloughed from her mind, she realized that this person was twice the dwarf's size.

"Your friends from Fort Zombie send their greetings," the figure's voice rasped. "It's a pity you didn't crash a bit farther to the west. You might have saved yourself a great deal of trouble."

"Who are you?" the changeling asked.

The tension left her as she realized that this was the mole from the Blood of Vol that the Captain of Corpses had told Tan Du about as they'd passed through the Karrnathi border on their way to Mardakine so many weeks ago.

"Here, I am called Ibrido," the figure said. As he spoke, he backed up into the light, and Te'oma saw a man dressed in a Karrnathi officer's uniform. His dark eyes stared at her in the lamplight, never blinking once. "That doesn't matter, though. What happened to your leader and the others, the vampires? We didn't expect to find you wandering about with a single wisp of an elf."

Te'oma thought back to how the people of Mardakine had made quick work of the Karrnathi zombies she and Tan Du had brought with them. They'd thought to overrun the tiny town fast, but they hadn't realized that everyone of age in the place was a battle-hardened veteran of the Last War. They'd even lost part of Tan Du's coven of vampire spawn before they'd managed to grab the girl and escape.

Then Kandler, Burch, and the knights had killed all but Tan Du and herself as they raced through the Mournland. Still, they might have been able to get away had they not encountered Majeeda, a mad elf who had slain the too-rude Tan Du with little more than a gesture. Te'oma had been lucky to escape with her life and even luckier to manage to capture Esprë again. It seemed her luck was still holding.

"It doesn't matter," she said, waving off Ibrido's concerns. "I have the bearer of the Lost Mark, and I'm on my way to bring her in."

"You seek to reach the court of Vol herself?" the Karrn said. "Illmarrow Castle is a long way from here, and the Lich Queen is not patient."

Te'oma thought of her daughter's frigid corpse. "I know that as well as anyone, but I am determined to see this through. Can you find me passage out of here? For me and the girl?"

"*She* is the bearer?" Ibrido stared at the sleeping elf who lay sprawled in the corner. "I expected someone more . . . impressive."

"Can you get us out of here?"

Ibrido hesitated for but a moment before nodding. "It will take time, but it can happen. Our best way out of here is an airship. Our crew is repairing the one you came in on, but it will not be completed soon. We will wait for the next one to come in later this week. Then we can commandeer it and take to the skies, leaving this pit of a place far behind."

"You seem eager to go."

Ibrido crept over to where Esprë slept and stared down at her. "With a prize like this," he said, "I'll let nothing stand in my way."

CHAPTER

23

"This is madness," Sallah said as Kandler reached down to help her up the last rungs of the ladder and onto the wooden platform that swayed high above the Wandering Inn. Looking down at the whole of the nomadic village splayed out below them in the soft light of the breaking dawn, he had to agree.

Few of the halflings had roused yet, but those who had rushed about the place as if Halpum had set fire to their loincloths. To the east, a massive threehorn lizard, already yoked to an even larger wagon, lowed soft and mournful, as if it yearned to charge free through the grassy, open plains. A pack of bridled clawfoots scratched at the hard-packed earth just beyond it, eager to be off. The Wandering Inn never stayed in one place for long, and already these beasts could sense it was time to go.

"How does this work again?" Xalt asked.

Kandler thought he detected a hint of fear in the warforged's voice as he peered over the unrailed edge of the platform to where the ground spun fifty feet below. Even to the justicar, the set of long, thin poles that held them in the air seemed like they might snap like lengths of straw at any moment and send them tumbling to the unforgiving earth.

A westerly wind carrying the faint scent of the Mournland on it—the stale smell of a fresh-dug grave—swept through them, and the platform wavered again.

Brendis fell to his knees and clutched the wood beneath them, finding purchase on a leather strap nailed there for that purpose. "Humans aren't meant to fly," he said. "The airship was bad enough, but at least it was a ship. This," he stared at the winged lizards waddling about at the platform's northern edge, their leather collars lashed to it by short lengths of a rope so thin it only suggested that the creatures stay in place. "This is insane."

"Fastest way to go," Burch said. "Clawfoots might take three days to make Fort Bones. Glidewings can do it in one." The shifter smiled at the discomfort of the others. "Just like riding a horse. Hold on tight. Don't fall off."

"It's a bit more of a drop," said Sallah.

"Hold on tighter."

Burch busied himself helping Monja check the riggings on the massive creatures: long leather straps that ran over their shoulders and met other straps coming around their middles, holding in place a thin, molded saddle that rode just above where the wings met the body. One of the lizards stretched out its leathery wings, displaying a stunning wing-span that could have hidden a family of halflings beneath. It opened its long beaklike mouth, exposing rows of tiny, sharp teeth, and squawked at Monja as she tightened its harness.

"It's all right, Swoop," she said. "They're not *that* big." She turned to the others to explain. "They sense your fear. It makes them nervous."

Brendis gulped but did not let go of his strap yet. Sallah steeled herself, resting her hand on the pommel of her new sword. It wasn't one of the sacred, blazing blades of the Knights of the Silver Flame, but it beat out that black dagger of Te'oma's, which rode on the lady knight's other hip.

Halpum had outfitted Burch and his friends with all the

food, drink, and weapons they could need. Despite his protests, Sallah had insisted on paying him with Thranite gold.

"Consider it my contribution to your cause," he had said to her.

"This money comes not from your friends but from the coffers of the Silver Flame," she said, pressing it into his hand.

"Well," the lathon said with a smile as he accepted the gold, "why didn't you say so?"

Kandler's stomach warmed at the thought of not having to subsist on smoked horsemeat for the rest of the journey. He and the others had eaten well that morning, joining the lathon once more. Now it was time to go.

The justicar strode across the platform, feeling it sway under his feet, something like the way a ship moved in the ocean, or so he tried to tell himself. He stood next to Monja and waited for her to finish.

"You are ready?" she asked when she was finished checking over the last of the riggings.

"More than."

The halfling shaman smiled and gestured for Kandler to climb onto the glidewing she had called Swoop. "Riding a glidewing is not quite like riding a horse," she said, showing him the stirrups for his feet and the straps for his hands. "If you rode it sitting up, the winds might lift you right off its back. Instead, you must lean forward, lying on your face in the saddle."

Kandler followed Monja's instructions and ended up hugging Swoop from behind. His feet trailed behind him in the stirrups, and his hands wound into the straps atop the massive creature's shoulders.

Even perched on the edge of the platform, Swoop stood taller than Kandler. As the justicar wrapped himself around the glidewing's back, he realized that any creature he could ride would be able to snatch him right out of the plains if it wanted and carry him away to feast on his heart. He held the beast tighter. It had none of the warmth of a horse. In fact, its scales felt cool to his touch yet strong, like the grip of a good blade. He almost wondered if the thing was alive or perhaps some kind of magical construct like Xalt. Then he felt it breathe—like a cold bellows gobbling air and then blasting it back out. The sensation startled him but comforted him at the same time. If he had to risk his life in the air, he wanted to be on the back of a living thing.

"Why do we need to take off from here?" Kandler asked as Monja helped the others into their riggings one by one. "With wings like these, can't the glidewings just flap into the air?"

"If they had to," Monja said as she returned to tighten a safety strap around Kandler's middle, lashing him to Swoop's back. "Glidewings aren't meant to carry people, especially ones as big as you. They normally take off by waddling down a hill until they get enough air under them to catch some sky. From there, they're the most graceful things you've ever seen. On the ground, though, they're worse than hobbled ducks."

The shaman patted the back of Kandler's hand. "Once you're in the air, you use these to steer. Pull left to go left, and right to go right. Pull back to go up, and push forward to go down. If the glidewing starts fighting you, trust it. It knows how to fly much better than you."

"Once we're in the air?" Xalt asked from atop his own glidewing. The thing squawked as he squeezed it a bit too hard. "How do we get 'in the air'?"

Monja smiled. "With luck, you'll find out in a moment."

The others secured to her satisfaction, the young shaman climbed atop the last of the glidewings. This one seemed to know her, reaching back to nuzzle her cheek with the top of its long, pointed head as she mounted it. As she rubbed its beak, Kandler noticed that she hadn't bothered to strap herself to the creature. She perched in her saddle light and easy, looking as if she'd been born to ride such a beast. Perhaps she had.

"Just hold on and follow me," she called to the others as her mount waddled up to the edge of the platform, its long talons scratching deep scars into the wood.

"Do we have a choice?" Kandler asked.

"Not unless you want to die," Monja said.

Her glidewing leaped about a foot into the air and a couple of feet forward, not quite enough to clear the platform. It smacked its tail on the edge, slapping the platform back a couple of feet, and then it disappeared as it plummeted toward the earth far below. For a half-second, Kandler thought the platform would tip over and dump all of them onto the ground with it, but it righted itself soon after.

As the justicar clutched Swoop's scaly, muscled neck, the breath rushing in and out of it like air through a blowgun, Monja's winged reptile flung itself high into the air. Its long-stretched wings caught the air and sunlight in them and rode them both higher and higher into the sky.

Kandler watched for a moment, his own breath stopped cold in his chest. Then he gasped as the flying lizard rolled all the way around to the right until Monja—who'd been dangling free and unstrapped from its back, high over the Wandering Inn and the open plains beyond—sat upright in its saddle again, the western winds whipping through her long, sun-bleached hair.

Kandler started to wonder why she could ignore the advice she'd given the others to lean low on their mounts, but when she wheeled about in the sky and skated back through the air toward them, the sheer joy in her face told him why. Before he could marvel at it any more, though, she wound her fist in the air over her head and jabbed it forward.

As one, the remaining glidewings waddle-rushed for the edge of the platform, the entire thing shaking like a leaf in the wind as they went, then leaped off into the open air.

As Kandler stifled the urge to scream, a war whoop rang in his ears, a howl of triumph and delight that he later recognized as Burch's voice. At that instant, though, he could think of nothing else but the bright-colored tops of the tents of the Wandering Inn rushing up at him at lethal speed.

Swoop stretched its wings wide, and the rushing wind caught in them and pushed them back from the ground, away from the tents and from certain death. For a frozen moment, Swoop and Kandler seemed to hang there in the air, caught like an insect in amber between two worlds. Then the wind grabbed Swoop's wings and shoved them flying into the sky.

Kandler had flown before on the airship, but the two experiences didn't compare. The airship handled like a boat in the water. It felt like one when you walked over it. If you stood in the center of it, you could imagine that you sailed along through the ocean rather than the sky. He understood that sensation. It made sense.

The glidewing pitched and bucked through the air enough to make Kandler glad he was strapped to it. Racing along on a horse galloping at top speed over rough land, hoping the thing wouldn't find a hole, break a leg, and spill over on top of you as it fell—he would have preferred that.

As the momentum from the dive off the platform played out, Swoop settled into the winds and began a slow, steady climb to the north. Kandler's internal organs all fell back into their places, and he felt like he could breathe again. He looked around to see all of his companions—friends, even, they'd been through so much already—stable atop their own flying beasts.

Burch and Xalt rode the winds to Kandler's left while Sallah and Brendis sailed along at his right. He craned his neck around looking for Monja, who came zooming in from behind on her own glidewing to take the point and lead them all into the great unknown that spread out before them.

"Next stop," the tiny shaman shouted, "Fort Bones!"

CHAPTER

24

The middle of the next day, Burch shouted for Kandler's attention. The justicar saw the shifter signaling toward a gray patch on the horizon, and he sighed with relief as he realized that Burch had spotted Fort Bones where the sky met the plains.

It had been a long, hard trip. At first, Kandler never dreamed he'd tire of flying or even become bored with it, but hour after hour of leaning forward atop Swoop had robbed the experience of any sort of excitement.

They'd made only three stops, each about eight hours apart. They couldn't bring the glidewings in to land on the ground, as they feared they might never get back into the sky on their backs again. Instead, they'd been forced to search out the few small copses that spotted the plains, often near a watering hole or along the edge of a shallow creek or stream.

Perched in the tops of these small trees, they ate and drank what they could fish from their packs. After they finished, they took to the skies again with yet another gut-wrenching takeoff. Kandler swore that his boots had scraped through the tall grasses on the last such embarking, but he preferred not to think about it.

At first, riding Swoop had been exhilarating, but as Kandler's body grew sore from sitting—or leaning—in the strange saddle, the thrill wore off. Eventually, he braved sleeping atop the glidewing as it soared through the skies, trusting the straps around him to hold him in place. He hadn't been sure he'd be able to manage it, but the great beast's rhythmic breathing helped him nod off.

Xalt had tried starting a conversation a few times, but he stopped when Monja pointed out that sound carried far and wide from so high in the air. If they did not want to become a target of some wandering predator, they would do better to keep quiet. The few times Xalt had tossed caution to the winds, Burch had stared him down until he fell silent.

Now, though, their goal called to them from the horizon, growing closer with every passing moment.

From the air, Fort Bones didn't look like much: a set of low wooden buildings surrounded by a high wall fashioned from baked clay. Even from this distance, Kandler could spy armored guards shambling about the crenellated top of the outer wall, forever gazing outward for threats from without—or above.

A hue and cry went up from the walls as a sentry spotted the glidewings. Flying in formation as they were, there could be little doubt that they were headed for the fort. Even if the soldiers in Fort Bones couldn't spot the riders atop the lizards, the arrival of six such large creatures would be enough to rouse every soul—or body, at least—in the place.

"We land here!" Monja shouted back from her place in the lead, turning to be sure the others could hear her. "If we get too much closer, we risk being knocked from the sky."

Kandler pushed down on Swoop's reins, but as had happened every time in the past, the creature seemed to move more according to its own will than his. It followed Monja's beast in a curving dive that came to rest a safe double bowshot from the fort's walls.

Just like before, the landing jarred Kandler to his core, but he was so grateful to find himself on solid ground again that he didn't give it a thought. Instead, he fumbled with the straps around him until they loosened, and he slid off the massive lizard's back and into grasses tall enough to reach up to his chest.

"Everyone all right?" he asked, scanning the relieved faces of the others.

Xalt threw himself to the ground, disappearing in the grass. "I'll never leave you again," he said to the earth beneath him.

Brendis, who'd looked pale and green since the dawn, staggered three steps, then bent over and vomited loudly. The lizards all skittered away from him on their short, folded legs. When he stood up and wiped his chin, he said, "I've been waiting to do that since we left the platform."

"Good thing," Burch said, smirking. "Glidewings don't like the smell. Might have plucked you right off its back."

The young knight smiled, his color already returning to him. "Nothing could have broken the grip I had on that thing's neck."

"Where's Monja?" Kandler asked. The little shaman had disappeared in the grasses, which rose a full foot over her head.

"Just gathering my things," her voice said from off to the left. "You should all do the same. The glidewings will leave us soon."

"Thank goodness," Xalt said as he crept up to his mount to strip it of his supplies.

"They won't wait for us?" Kandler asked.

Monja's head popped up through the grasses, right behind her mount. Kandler guessed she was standing on its tail. "A grounded glidewing is easy prey for larger beasts," she said. "As soon as we let them loose, they'll make their way back to the Wandering Inn."

Kandler said, "How are we going to get into Fort Bones? Just walk up and knock on the gates?"

Sallah, who stood out ahead of the others, shading her eyes with her hand as she stared at the distant fort, answered, "I don't think that's going to be a problem."

Kandler peered out alongside the lady knight. The gates to the fort had been flung open, and a squad of twenty soldiers, each dressed in gleaming, black suits of Karrnathi armor, swarmed out of the place. A trio of what Kandler guessed had to be officers rode out after them astride massive, ebon-coated horses.

"Keep your swords sheathed," Monja said. "We are here to talk, not fight."

"Do they know that?" Burch asked.

As the Karrnathi troops grew nearer, Kandler saw glimpses of thin, white limbs peeking through gaps in the armor of the foot troops. Beneath their high-crested helmets, empty eye sockets stared back at him and the others, merciless and unblinking.

The officers, though, looked out at the newcomers with living eyes as they guided their steeds with their solid, well-muscled frames. Kandler nodded, happy that the Captain of Bones had sent out actual people for him to talk with. It was a good sign. Had there been nothing but skeletons in the greeting party, the only response they would have understood would have been cold steel.

Still, he was prepared to kill them all—every last one—if they stood between him and Esprë.

As the foot soldiers neared, they spread out in a long line that came wrapping around Kandler and the others until the skeletons surrounded them. When the circle of skeletons was complete, it parted on the edge nearest the fort, and the three officers rode their black horses into the gap.

"You have wandered into the lands of the Kingdom of Karrnath, ruled over by his beneficence King Kaius the

Third," the small, stout, broad-faced rider in the center said, her words clipped and efficient. "As his honored representative, the Captain of Bones welcomes you to Karrnath and inquires as to the reason for your visit."

Monja started to reply but then looked to Kandler instead. The justicar stepped forward, reminding himself to keep his hand off the hilt of his sword. The display of Karrnathi force didn't intimidate him as it was meant to, but he needed these people to help rather than hinder him.

"We're pursuing my stepdaughter, a young elf by the name of Esprë. A changeling brought her in this direction aboard a stolen airship."

The dwarf slid down from the side of her horse using an unusual set of double-stepped stirrups. Most dwarves stuck with ponies instead of horses, animals more suited to their stature, but this dwarf wasn't the sort to let her size get in her way. She bounded over to Kandler, her hands stretched out before her in greeting, although she halted a sword's length from the justicar.

"Are you Kandler?" she asked, a smile on her wide lips and a look of astonishment in her eyes.

Kandler froze, staring at the dwarf. He'd never been here before. He'd never met this dwarf. How could she know his name, unless . . . ?

"Tell her, boss," Burch said, slapping the justicar on the shoulder. The gesture snapped Kandler into action again.

"Yes," he said. "That's—I'm Kandler."

The dwarf favored the justicar with an infectious grin. "Have I got some good news for you."

145

CHAPTER

25

Kandler couldn't remember the last time he'd been so happy—perhaps on his wedding day, maybe on the day the Treaty of Thronehold ended the Last War, or not ever.

As he held Esprë in his arms, he felt tears welling up in his eyes. By reflex, he choked them back. He hadn't wept since the Day of Mourning, when he'd realized that Esprina had been caught up in the mysterious massacre, and he wasn't about to start up again now.

Esprë, on the other hand, had been sobbing openly since the moment Kandler and the others had come into the infirmary. Her whole body shook with relief as she let loose all the fears she'd kept bottled up since the changeling had stolen her from her bed in Mardakine. She seemed like she might never stop shaking, but Kandler resolved to hold on to her until she fell still.

After a long while, Burch came around and put a hand on Esprë's shoulder, and she turned and threw her arms around him, leaving her body resting in Kandler's lap.

"Good to see you again, kid," the shifter said. "They feeding you all right here? Looks like the food's so rotten most of the solders are nothing but bones."

Esprë shoved herself back to stare into the shifter's mischievous eyes, then started to laugh between her sobs. Soon the laughter took over the rest. Then it sloughed away too.

The young elf gazed at each of her visitors in turn: Kandler, Burch, Xalt, Sallah, Brendis—even Berre Stonefist. Then she hugged Kandler again.

"I thought I was all alone, that you were all dead." The tears returned but softly this time, for joy.

"You're not getting rid of me that easily," Kandler said, his voice raw with emotion. "I may be only human, but I got a few good years in me yet."

"Decades," Esprë whispered to him. "At least."

Over Esprë's shoulder, Kandler saw Berre smiling at the two of them. He reached out a hand to her, and she took it in a double-fisted grip. "I never thought I'd say this to a Karrnathi officer," he said, "but thanks. I owe you."

"Nonsense," Berre said. "All we did was help a lost child find her parent. What civilized people would not do the same?"

Brendis spoke up. "The creatures who attacked Mardakine when Esprë was kidnapped wore Karrnathi armor. Some were even Karrnathi dead."

Berre's face fell. "I had not heard that." She looked Kandler in the eyes. "I assure you that none of my troops would be involved in such a crime."

Kandler nodded. "They had a lot more meat on them than the creatures you have around here."

"Perhaps they came from Fort Zombie to the west then. If so, it must have been a rogue operation. I know the Captain of Corpses well. He is a good man, and I cannot imagine him perpetrating such an act."

"They wore the symbols of the Blood of Vol," Sallah said.

Berre nodded. "As I suspected. While the Blooded are outlawed in Karrnath, they are still a powerful force. Many

Karrn subscribe to their sanguine beliefs, holding their blood-drenched services in secret. The zombies of which you speak could have come from anywhere in the nation."

"Maybe even from Korth," Kandler said. He did not want to anger his host, nor did he share her apparent trust in her fellow citizens of Karrn.

"I'll grant that," she said, "but I would not tar all of the people of Karrn with the same brush."

"Different brushes it is," Burch said.

"Where is Te'oma?" Esprë asked, cutting off any reply.

Kandler stiffened, his arms still wound around the young elf.

"What do you mean?" he asked.

"She was here when I fell asleep this morning." She blushed. "I'm still a little worn out from all this, but she wasn't here when you came in."

Kandler turned on Berre. "You left her alone with her kidnapper?"

"With a guard outside and one in here."

"Where's that guard?" Sallah asked.

Burch kicked a bleached femur from under a nearby bed, rattling what sounded like a pile of them as he did. "I wondered who handled your housekeeping around here."

Berre cursed. "This is the problem with having to rely on the unliving for everything." She stuck her head out through the curtained doorway of the room and bellowed, "Lieutenant!"

A moment later, a handsome, dark-haired man charged through the door. "Yes, my captain!"

"Where is the changeling?"

The officer glanced at the empty bed across the room from Esprë's. His rock-steady eyes did not blink. Kandler wondered if they ever did.

"Gone," the lieutenant said, no expression marring his face. "I will gather a crew to scour the entire fort for her. If she is still here, I will find her." With that, he turned on his heel and left.

Berre held up her hands in frustration. "Who did I anger to get stationed here among these idiots?" She snarled. "It's an important post, but it's on the backend of nowhere. Do you know why the place is staffed with undead? They can't find anyone else willing to sit here, at least since the war ended. It's too damned dull."

The dwarf glanced at Monja. "It's not that the halflings aren't worthy adversaries, but we haven't seen as much as a hunting party within a league of this place in over a year. The biggest excitement we've had involved a visit from your lathon, and that was eighteen months ago."

Berre stormed over to the bed covering the pile of bones and sat down hard on it. "My apologies," she said. "These are my troubles, not yours. I've added enough to yours as it is."

Monja walked over and put an arm around the dour dwarf's shoulders. "None of that matters. If we never see this changeling again, we would all be happy. Let's hope she took the opportunity to escape and never looks back."

Kandler wanted to believe that too, but his gut told him different. He held Esprë even tighter.

"She likely killed the guard and flew out the window by means of that fantastic cloak of hers," Xalt said. As the words left him, he stopped and cocked his head. "Can you 'kill' something that's already dead?"

"Her cloak?" Berre asked.

"A symbiont," Sallah said. "A living creature attached to her like some unholy parasite."

Berre put her head in her hands and groaned.

"It's not important," Kandler said, trying to believe the words as he said them, finding they offered him little solace. "We have Esprë now. She's safe."

"I'm just so happy to see you!" Esprë said.

"As am I, despite all my errors," said Berre, sighing as she stood up. "I request that you all join me for dinner tonight. We dine at sunset, which should fall in but a few hours. In the meantime, I asked for quarters to be arranged for you. I'll have one of my soldiers bring up your things."

"I can take care of that," said Xalt.

"If you can spare the time," Berre said, "I'd rather chat with you before dinner. It's not often that I get to interview a resident of the Mournland. Living so near to it as we do, I find it fascinating."

Xalt cleared his throat at the request.

"It's fine," Kandler said. "If you don't mind, it's the least we can do to repay her."

"I'll gather our things," Brendis said.

"That's not necessary," Berre said, "I'm sure my . . ." She grimaced at the young knight. "Yes, that might be best."

Kandler nodded his thanks at Brendis, then turned back to talk with Esprë about everything they'd both seen since Construct.

CHAPTER

26

Brendis walked past a dozen skeletons in Karrnathi armor as he found his way to the stables where he and the others had stashed the packs they'd carried with them all the way from the Wandering Inn. The creatures set him on edge. Although they seemed to ignore him, he couldn't read a thing in their empty eye sockets to put his mind at ease.

As a Knight of the Silver Flame, Brendis believed that all undead creatures, be they vampires, skeletons, zombies, ghouls, wraiths, ghosts, or things even worse—were inherently evil. Each of them should be resting peacefully in the ground, their spirits wandering off to their respective rewards. Instead, they were animated by a necromantic power that could only be classified as evil. By the gifts granted him by the Silver Flame, he could feel their evil radiating from them like the dark glow of a lantern that shed naught but chilly death.

By extension, that meant the people who controlled such creatures should be evil too, but Berre seemed as solid and good a dwarf as Brendis had ever met. He fought to reconcile these two ideas in his brain, but it only frustrated him. He ached to call down the power of the Silver Flame to eradicate the skeletons around him or at least to force them to flee from his sight forever, but here they seemed to serve a greater good. He determined to leave them alone for as long as they returned the favor—at least for now.

What, he wondered, would Sir Deothen have done?

He had missed the elder knight's leadership since they had lost him in Construct, crushed to death beneath the mobile city on the orders of the warforged lieutenant Bastard. He knew that Sallah, Deothen's daughter, likely missed him even more. She'd done her best to stand in her father's stead, but with only the shaken Brendis left to lead, the effort sometimes rang hollow. She needed a chance to grieve for her fallen father, and he hoped now that they had finally found Esprë, this time would come to her soon.

As he made his way to the central yard, he spied the battered airship floating there in the middle of the place. When he and the others had entered the fort, he'd stopped in his tracks and stared at the thing. It had been through so much he found it hard to believe it hadn't been destroyed.

The restraining arcs that held the ring of fire in place around the craft bore countless small cracks and a few larger ones. He knew that if the mystically charged arcs ever gave out entirely, the creature of elemental fire trapped in the ring would lash out with explosive, destructive force, possibly consuming every shred of wood in the entire ship, as well as anyone unfortunate enough to be on it at the time.

Brendis had borne all that in mind as he'd rammed the airship straight into the stands of the arena in Construct on Deothen's orders. It had been the bravest thing he'd done in his life, the kind of thing he'd trained for, ever since being accepted as a prospective Knight of the Silver Flame. He'd followed his commander's directions without hesitation or concern for his personal safety, and for that he felt no little pride. That the battle had ended badly reflected more on the unfathomable will of the Silver Flame rather than his own dedication to it.

Now, though, hope leaped in his heart that their whirlwind journey had finally come to an end. With luck, Sallah would be able to convince Kandler that the safest place for Esprë was in Flamekeep, the Thranite capital. There the full force of the worshipers of the Silver Flame could be deployed to keep the girl from the hands of others until they could determine what ultimate fate must befall one who bore the Mark of Death.

Brendis marveled that such a sweet young creature could be burdened with such a dragonmark. As far as he knew, no one else had received such a mixed blessing in well over three millennia, during the closing days of the legendary Dragon-Elf War. That it had reappeared now, after so many centuries, could only mean trouble.

He knew that some in Flamekeep would advocate killing the girl as the only means of being sure of eradicating this dangerous mark once more, but he didn't see how they could prevail. The Church of the Silver Flame respected the fire of life above all else, and to extinguish it as it burned in the soul of an innocent young elf flew in the face of that. Still, people who knew anything of the Mark of Death feared it, and those ruled by fear often made choices they might normally abhor.

Brendis's duty was clear, though: to bring the girl back to Flamekeep to meet Jaela Daran, the Keeper of the Silver Flame. As the voice of the Silver Flame, the youthful Daran would certainly see the proper path for Esprë's life, and Brendis had no doubt it would be good and just.

The young knight walked around the ship one last time, gazing up at it before ducking into the stables nearby. Dozens of skeletons swarmed over the thing, making repairs as they went, shoring up cracks, patching holes, and replacing the large sections of the airship's hull that a pair of twenty-foot-tall warforged titans had ripped away during the battle in Construct.

Brendis breathed a prayer of thanks to the Silver Flame. It had been a miracle that any of them had survived.

The ship looked better already, having been in the care of the Karrn for only a matter of days. The skeletal soldiers worked over it without flagging, despite the fact, Brendis suspected, they'd been at it for days without rest. What was rest to an animated set of remains? In this, at least, Brendis saw how evil could be set to a good purpose.

It had all seemed much simpler when he'd been a child himself during the Last War. The people of Thrane—the followers of the Silver Flame—were good, as were their allies. Those who stood against them were evil. Now, in these strange days of so-called peace, the rules had changed. Alliances forged and shattered overnight. Friendships often only lasted until the job was done, and evil could serve good.

Not for the first time, Brendis wondered if good could not also serve evil.

The horses in the stables whickered as Brendis entered the tall wooden building that served as a home for the dozen or so beasts housed there. He murmured to soothe them, and they calmed down. He suspected the creatures did not leave the gates of the fort too often. Perhaps the skeletons made them nervous, as they did most animals. He would not have been surprised to learn the horses were used to living with such creatures by now, though.

No lights burned in the stable, and the far end of it stood shrouded in shadow, illuminated only by the few lances of light that made their way through random gaps in the walls' wooden boards. Brendis looked around for the gear but didn't spot it anywhere near the doorway. He waited a moment for his eyes to adjust to the dimness after walking outside, unsheltered from the sun.

Brendis had never cared much for direct sunlight. It tended to scorch his fair skin. In the Mournland, though, he had despaired of ever enjoying such bright light again. The thought that Gweir, Levritt, and Deothen—his fellow knights who had perished there—would never have the chance to do so made it somehow seem that much more precious. While riding that glidewing on their insane trip here through the sky, he'd basked in the sun's blazing rays, letting their warmth penetrate him all the way through. He could still feel the burn on the back of his neck as he peered into the shadows here, and the sensation made him smile.

The young knight felt something tickling at the back of his brain. It reminded him of when he'd been in training to become a knight. He always felt that way if he'd forgotten something but couldn't remember what. He'd learned to trust that feeling over the years, his hidden mind trying to tell him something that he couldn't yet put into words. Still, he couldn't understand what nagged at him like that. Perhaps he was confusing it with guilt over surviving when his friends had died.

Gweir had been Brendis's best friend since they'd been squires together, serving the Knights of the Silver Flame in the desperate hope they would someday be called to join their illustrious ranks. To see him die on that corpse-strewn field, a hidden warforged driving a length of steel straight through him, blood coughing up red and warm from his mouth, then his eyes glazing over as the burning flame of his soul left him—something had died in Brendis that day too.

Perhaps staying to give him a proper burial had been a waste of time, especially when Esprë was still in mortal peril, but he couldn't find it in him to leave his friend to lie there under the dead-gray Mournland sky. The traditions of his order forbade it.

A pain stuck in Brendis's heart as he thought of poor Levritt, who'd not been so fortunate. They'd been forced to leave his headless body behind in that warforged camp. Brendis shivered as he remembered the sick, wet sound of the rookie knight's head leaving his neck by means of another warforged's sword.

At that point, Brendis thought he could have been forgiven for thinking of all warforged as soulless beasts, evil creatures no better than the skeletons wandering around the fort. Perhaps they were even worse, for they knew what they were doing. These walking sets of bones only followed orders—and none too well, it seemed.

Xalt put the lie to all that. It would have been all too easy to hate all the warforged, but the artificer had shown them more than kindness. He'd risked his own life to save them from his fellows and had lost one of the three fingers on his hand for his troubles. Brendis flexed his fist at the thought of it.

Then there was Deothen, his leader, his mentor, his friend. Brendis had looked up to the elder knight since his days as a squire. He'd never seen anyone else so—so knightly. He was everything that Brendis aspired to be. When he'd been assigned to Deothen's squad, he'd been thrilled. His parents and sisters had been so proud.

He hadn't seen Deothen die. He thought maybe he'd heard the man's last roars as Bastard ordered the city of Construct to lower itself on him, crushing him to death under only the Flame knew how much wood and steel, but that had probably been his imagination. He'd been only half-conscious, if that, after ramming the airship into the arena's stands. If it hadn't been for Esprë and Xalt, the changeling would have killed him for sure.

Brendis couldn't wait for all this to be over so that he could get back to Flamekeep. Of the five knights who'd left on this mission at the behest of the child-aged Keeper of the Flame, only two of them were left: Sallah and him.

Had it all been worth it? Three good men dead to rescue a dragonmarked elf? He had only his faith to help him answer that question. It said an emphatic "Yes," but the word echoed hollow in his ears.

That shook the young knight more than he cared to admit. He'd grown up in the Church of the Silver Flame. His mother had been a knight too, his father a priest in the church's hierarchy. He had never questioned the wisdom of the Silver Flame, and he wasn't going to start now.

Still, as his father used to tell him, "There are times, my son, that test anyone's faith. If your convictions can weather these moments, then you can take comfort in the strength of your faith and know that it will sustain you throughout your days."

As Brendis made his way to the back of the stable, he spotted the packs he was looking for. While he stooped to shoulder them, he affirmed his faith with a silent prayer to the Silver Flame, petitioning it to help him stay strong.

He felt the leather reins fall around his neck and draw tight as a sharp knee shoved him in the back and knocked him to the ground. The weight of his attacker and his packs kept him down. His tried to bring his arms up to pull the reins away, but they caught in the straps of the packs instead.

Brendis tried to draw in a breath to scream for help, but with the reins twisted tight around his neck he could only cough out a meek protest. His attacker ignored the noise and pulled the reins tighter.

The young knight's eyes locked on a shaft of light filtering into the stables through a thin hole between two boards. In his mind, the soft glow transformed into a silvery flame that beckoned him forward. He struggled to creep toward it as his vision darkened, closing into a tunnel focused on that burning light.

Silver Flame, he prayed with his final thought, may you consume my soul with your light.

Then all went black.

CHAPTER

27

"So Brendis isn't joining us for dinner?" Esprë said as Kandler emerged into the hallway from the men's quarters.

Kandler shook his head at the young elf, who didn't do much of a job of hiding her disappointment. He was still so happy to see her that he didn't mind a bit. He just put his hand on her back and guided her across the fort's open yard toward the private dining room of the Captain of Bones.

"The trip here was hard," he said. "Not everyone's suited for riding a glidewing. Monja thinks he's a bit sunsick too."

"There's also that knock he took when he banged his head in the stables," said Sallah.

With the dust of the flight and the Mournland washed away, she looked more amazing than ever, Kandler noticed. Her skin had a fresh glow to it that he had never seen on her before. It seemed more than just being clean. She looked younger too. Perhaps the relief of catching up with Esprë had erased some of the worry from her face.

"Hurt his head less than his pride," said Burch.

The shifter hadn't bothered with cleaning up. While the others enjoyed their baths, he'd wandered around the fort, getting the lay of the land. He hadn't found much unusual about the place, outside of the skeletons.

"Airship almost looks ready to go," he'd said to Kandler, pointing at the battered craft in the middle of the yard as they walked past it.

Xalt nodded, his exterior plates polished and buffed to a shine. He had found a lanyard and threaded it through the end of his amputated finger. As it rested on his chest, it gleamed in the light as well, and Kandler guessed that if he didn't know better he might think it was an artful piece of warforged jewelry instead of a missing digit.

"The way its ring of fire burns so bright, it seems as if the elemental inside knows how close it came to freedom," Xalt said. "If those restraining arcs ever do give out, the creature is sure to leave a wide trail of scorched earth behind it as it speeds away."

Monja noticed Esprë staring at Xalt's finger necklace and slipped an arm around the young elf's shoulders. Esprë stood a full head taller than the halfling, but she leaned into the embrace with relish.

"He finally let me look at it," the shaman said. "It's a clean cut, but it's beyond my power to reattach it. Things like that take mighty prayers from those who call the gods old friends."

"When we get to Flamekeep, the clerics there should be able to help," Sallah said to Xalt. "Jaela Daran herself may choose to intercede on behalf of a hero such as you."

"Are we going to Thrane?" Esprë asked Kandler, concern etched on her face. "I thought we might go back to Sharn."

Kandler nodded. "Me too, but we can't go back through the Mournland again. It's too dangerous."

"Every warforged in the land will be looking for us," Burch said.

"Better to go north and over the Mournland and then down through Thrane to Breland," Kandler said. "We can even stop in Mardakine if we like."

"You would be welcome to pass through the plains again," Monja said. "I would even travel with you until you reach Valenar."

"The elf-land's not the problem," said Burch. "It's getting through all the goblins in Darguun."

"Right," said Kandler. "We could make for the Thunder Sea and sail up the Dagger River, but that's a long way around."

"Can't you just fly over it?" asked Monja, stabbing a thumb over her shoulder at the airship.

"That," said Kandler, "is one of the first things we need to talk to the captain about."

"Well," Berre said, opening the door to the dining room as Kandler and the others approached, "we are bound to have an interesting conversation tonight then. In the interests of better digestion, though, I suggest we save such details until after the main course."

Kandler acquiesced to the captain's request. He didn't worry about offending her. Most dwarfs were too pragmatic to be bothered by direct talk, but she did have a small army of well-armed skeletons, along with a few well-trained soldiers of the breathing sort, all around them. He could afford to be patient for now.

The meal was simple but tasty, served family-style out of common dishes in the center of the table. It featured more of the typical dark and bitter Karrnathi spices than the justicar preferred, but the sweet, blood-red wine that accompanied it washed it down well.

Kandler noticed that Burch, ever suspicious, refused to eat anything until he saw Berre sample it first. The others weren't so concerned. Sallah ate but without relish. Since Xalt couldn't eat, he didn't bother with the meal at all, although he took part in the small bits of conversation between the others' mouthfuls. The petite Monja devoured everything put in front of her with the appetite of someone four times her size.

A group of six Karrnathi skeletons waited on the table as

attentively as any living servants. They moved according to Berre's exacting orders, performing their duties to the letter and then returning to their corners once again.

Kandler couldn't help but notice that the bony waiters wore their blades and armor still, and that they outnumbered the guests. He knew that with the barest word from their captain they would attack.

"So," Berre said, as the undead waiters cleared the plates away and topped off each diner's goblet of wine, "let us speak of what is to come."

Kandler gazed into the dwarf's dark brown eyes for a minute before he spoke. She had done him many a good turn already today, including reuniting him with Esprë. He knew that he owed her something, and he feared that now the bill would come due.

"Now that we've found Esprë," he said, "Burch and I plan to take her back with us to Sharn. Sallah and Brendis have offered to put us up in Flamekeep for a while on our way."

"So your route will take you north of here through Karrnath before turning south into Thrane? Excellent." An easy smile spread across Berre's lips. "If you will permit me, I will accompany you as far as Korth. If I do not miss my guess, the king himself will long to hear your tale and to entertain such illustrious guests."

Sallah started to speak, but Kandler cut her off with a curt wave. "We wouldn't want to bother your king," he said. "We just want to get Esprë home." He glanced at her and saw concern furrow her brow. "I think she's been through enough without . . . She's been through enough."

"I understand how you feel," Berre said, "but I'd be delinquent in my duties if I didn't bring such a unique person as Esprë to the attention of King Kaius. I just know he'd find the particulars fascinating."

Kandler looked at Esprë, a sick feeling in his stomach. "She's just a child," he said, "my child."

"You are her stepfather, correct?"

Kandler didn't like the direction this conversation was headed. "I'm all she has in the world."

Berre's face turned grim. "I respect that. I would never dream of separating the two of you again, but she must go to Korth. I have been in contact with my superiors in Kaius's court. My orders are clear."

"And if we try to leave?" Kandler felt his anger rising into his throat as he readjusted himself in his chair.

"You are welcome to depart any time you like, you and any of your friends, but a military airship is already on its way here to collect Esprë and take her back to Korth."

Esprë inhaled a single sob, and Kandler felt his heart begin to break. He refused to look at her, though, afraid they would both crack if he did.

"You are welcome to come with her," Berre said. "I would encourage it. Korth is no place for such a gifted young elf to be without the benefit of her guardians."

"Gifted, eh?" Burch said, his voice soaked with suspicion.

Berre put down her goblet and threw up her hands. "She was under our care, and she was near death. We examined her, and we found her dragonmark."

Everyone around the table froze. Berre pretended not to notice and kept talking.

"It is strange, to be sure. None of us could identify it, which is why Korth is so intrigued. We know not if it is some sort of lost mark or a new mark never seen before. Either way, we need to learn everything we can about it. For that reason, Esprë is leaving for Korth on the morrow—with or without the rest of you."

Kandler reached out and put a hand on Esprë's shoulder. She reached up and held it tight. "Well," he said to her, his eyes never leaving Berre's, "it looks like we're about to pay King Kaius a visit."

CHAPTER

28

"We can't let this happen," Sallah said, pacing the floor back in the room assigned to her, Monja, and Esprë. "There must be something we can do."

"There is," Kandler said. He turned to Burch. "How long will it take us to pack?"

"Never unpacked," the shifter said, bouncing on his toes, ready to spring into action. "Get us all ready to travel in ten minutes, less."

"Get started, but take your time. Don't let them see you. We won't try anything until after midnight."

The shifter nodded and bounded out of the room.

"We're going to escape?" Xalt said. He cocked his head at Kandler. "Just leave in the middle of the night?"

"You have a better idea?"

"We're in a Karrnathi fort in the middle of nowhere," Sallah said. "Our foes have over a hundred well-trained skeletons forged from the remains of their former warriors at their disposal."

"Can you handle them?" Kandler asked. "Between you, Brendis, and Monja, can you get rid of them?"

Monja shook her head. "Not that many of them. Not all at

once. I can't speak for these knights, but the gods don't favor my fate that much."

Kandler frowned. "So much for a life of prayer."

"You can't let them take me," Esprë said softly. She hadn't said so many words in a row since they'd finished dinner.

Kandler sat next to the young elf on a fresh-made bed and put his arms around her. "Don't you worry," he said, kissing the top of her head. "You're not going anywhere without us."

Brendis stood up from where he'd sat silently on the other side of the room. "I offer you my sword, Esprë, as your personal protector. None shall harm you while I still draw breath, so I do swear."

The young elf failed to fight back her tears and launched herself into Brendis's arms. "Thank you," she whispered.

"Don't you think Berre expects us to try to escape?" Sallah said. "Every skeleton in the place is sure to be on high alert. They don't sleep. They don't eat. They don't get distracted. This is a fool's errand."

"Do *you* have a better idea?" Kandler said. "Once they put Esprë on that Karrnathi airship, it's over. We're on a one-way trip to Korth."

"Then we go with them," Sallah said.

"No!" Esprë cried.

"Wait," Sallah said, holding up her hands to Kandler as Esprë buried her face in his chest, "hear me out."

Kandler glared at the lady knight but nodded. He'd been through enough with her to give her ideas a fair hearing.

"The court of Kaius is not where I would prefer to be, but they respect the rule of law. Once we reach Korth, I will contact the local prelate of the Church of the Silver Flame and petition for Esprë's release."

Kandler's face fell. If that was the best Sallah could come up with, it wouldn't stop his plans for tonight for a second.

"I know," Sallah said. "Working through the channels

of diplomacy can be a slow and painful process, but there's another option. If we can somehow get Esprë into one of our churches while in Korth, she can then claim sanctuary."

"Sanctuary?" Xalt asked.

"King Kaius respects all established religions in his realm, including the Church of the Silver Flame. Any penitent who enters the doors of one of our churches and petitions for sanctuary is granted protection from the local secular government."

"What's the catch?" Kandler said, still holding Esprë, who'd at least stopped crying long enough to listen to what Sallah had to say.

"Getting to one of the churches may not be easy. There are a number throughout Korth, but getting to one of them would mean waiting for the right time to make our move. Until then, we'd be at the mercy of King Kaius."

"And?" Kandler could tell there was something else Sallah was holding back.

"To be granted sanctuary, you have to be a practicing member of the church. Esprë and anyone else who wanted protection would have to convert."

Kandler shook his head. "The skeletons are looking better all the time."

Sallah growled. "You would rather risk your life—and that of Esprë—rather than consider converting to my faith?"

"Could I lie?" Kandler suspected he knew the answer to this question already.

Sallah grimaced. "The prelate would question you to verify the honesty of your conversion, and he would have the power of the Silver Flame on his side. It would have to be a true conversion."

Kandler hugged Esprë closer. "I don't think I can do that."

"You risk your lives *and* your eternal souls for your defiance."

"The gods haven't been kind to me over the years—if there are any such things. I can't find it in me to worship them. It would be like praying to a general who's been torturing your family for generations. It just wouldn't ring true."

"The Silver Flame is not the sham of the Sovereign Host. It is the one true god, the light of which all other gods are mere reflections."

Monja cleared her throat. "That is the most arrogant thing I've ever heard."

"I meant no offense," Sallah started.

"This is no time for a theological debate," Kandler said. As he spoke, Esprë stood up and walked toward the room's single window. There she gazed out into the night sky.

"Esprë, Burch, and I are leaving tonight. If the rest of you want to come, you're welcome to. Otherwise, just keep quiet."

"You're not getting rid of me that easily," Monja said. "I told my father I'd see you safely through this."

"You did enough just getting us here."

Monja smiled. "Doing just enough is never enough."

Xalt chipped in. "I am with you as well." He rubbed his amputated finger with his damaged hand as he spoke. "I would like to visit Flamekeep someday, but I am prepared for that to never happen."

"Just as long as we don't end up in Korth on the way."

Sallah pursed her lips at Kandler for a moment. She glanced at Brendis before responding, and the young knight nodded at her once.

"Esprë is your stepdaughter," she said. "The choice is yours alone, and we will accompany you no matter if you make the right one or not."

Burch burst back into the room with three packs—his, Brendis's, and Kandler's—ready to go. Startled, Xalt jumped and then fell silent. Kandler saw the way the warforged stared at the floor for a moment, and he wondered if this was his people's way of blushing.

"Get the ladies set, and we're ready to ride," Burch said, ignoring Xalt's reaction.

The shifter started stuffing clothing and other odds and ends into another three packs with practiced ease. He threw some things aside, discarding them as either useless or too heavy or both. Everything else went into the packs until they bulged near bursting.

"All right," Kandler said as Burch kept working, "here's the plan. Sallah and Burch, you head for the stables. We're going to need horses to get out of here. Otherwise, they'll ride us down at first light.

"Brendis and Xalt, you're with me. We need to get the gates open, or we'll just end up riding around the central yard.

"Monja, you stay with Esprë just outside the stables and keep her safe until we're ready to go.

"When we open the gate, you'll all hear the signal. Get on those horses and drive them out of the place—all of them. We don't want to leave any behind for them to chase us with."

"What if we get separated?" Sallah asked.

"Don't." The justicar frowned. "If something happens, just head south as best you can. Burch knows our scents. He can track us down and bring us together if it comes to that."

"I want to help," Esprë said, looking at Monja. "I don't need a bodyguard."

Kandler's frown deepened. "We've all risked our lives to rescue you, and we're risking them again for you tonight. If something happens to you, it's all for nothing."

Esprë glared at Kandler. He knew the look from other times she'd raged at him. He wanted to keep her safe, and she wanted her freedom. They'd gone over it countless times, but this was different.

"I'm not trying to shelter you," he said to her, reaching out to caress her shoulder. As he did, he noticed—not for the first time—how slight she was. Next to Monja, she was huge, but viewed against his battle-scarred hand, his sense of her youth almost undid him.

"This is bigger than you and me now," Kandler said, trying again.

As he spoke, he saw her shoulders tense. He wondered if she could feel the dragonmark itching, burning between her shoulders. Had it grown since he'd last seen it? He wasn't sure he wanted to know.

Esprë looked up at him with red-rimmed eyelids framing sky-blue pupils. She rocked there on the bed for a moment then nodded slowly. She understood.

At that moment, Kandler wished more than anything that he could take the burden of the mark from her. It wasn't fair that such a sweet young elf had to endure such a thing, to be afflicted with it, but nothing in life was ever fair, he guessed. Why should it start now?

"All right," he said, giving her shoulder one last squeeze.

"Get some sleep," he said to everyone. "We move out in just a few hours, and there's no guessing when or where we'll get to rest again."

"Why don't we just steal the airship?" Monja asked. The question leaped from her mouth like it had been burning her tongue since the conversation started.

"It's not ready yet," Kandler said, "or so Berre says."

"It would probably get us out of here," Burch said, "if we could get on it."

Kandler nodded. "The skeletons will work on it all night long, dozens of them. We couldn't get past them. We'd have to destroy them all."

"It's exactly what Berre would expect us to do," said Sallah. "We need to at least make a feint at it."

Kandler licked his lips. "Good point. Xalt, we have a new job for you. While the others sneak into the stables, I need you to go up and try to start a conversation with whoever's on the airship."

"About what?" the warforged asked, his ebony eyes blank as ever.

"Anything—the weather, what it's like to be a stack of walking bones. Whatever. They can't answer you. You just need to distract them for a moment, make them suspicious. That should be all the rest of us need."

"I'll go with him," Monja said.

Kandler shook his head. "I need you with Esprë." He hoped he didn't sound as desperate about that as he felt.

"When the skeletons figure out what's really happening, Xalt may not be able to get away. I can keep them away," she said, fingering the silver, eight-pointed symbol of the Sovereign Host that peeked out from behind the top of her tunic, where it hung around her neck on a colorful strand of woven fibers.

Kandler started to protest, but Brendis cut him off. "I'll stay with Esprë," the still-pale knight said. "I'm still not . . ." he swallowed, and Kandler wondered if he might vomit. "I'd be better in a protective role, I think."

"That leaves me to tackle the gates alone," Kandler said with grim resolve. "If that's how it has to be—"

"I'll go with you," Sallah said.

"No," Kandler tried again.

"She's right, boss," Burch said. "You might need help at the gate. I can wrangle the horses on my own."

Kandler began to say something, then stopped and shut his mouth. "Did I have a say in any of this?"

Esprë reached out and put a hand on his arm. "I know just how you feel."

CHAPTER

29

The crackling fire roared past the window of the room in which Kandler slept, and he awoke. He pried open his eyes to see Xalt's shape silhouetted in the window, a warm, flickering light setting off the edges of his form from the night beyond.

"What is it?" Kandler asked, sure he wouldn't like the answer.

"Sounds like an airship," said Burch.

"Ours?"

Xalt shook his head. "The skeletons are still working on an old ship in the yard. This craft must be the military one Berre referred to."

"It's early," Kandler said. "Damn Karrnathi efficiency."

"Does this change things?" Brendis asked.

The young knight looked as if he'd been sitting on the edge of his bed watching the others the entire time. There were only three beds in the room, and Burch and Kandler had taken the others, as Xalt had insisted that since he didn't need to sleep, the beds were useless to him.

Kandler nodded. "I'm just not sure how." He paused to think for a moment. "We should let them unlimber the new ship, tie it down. The crew will be tired and want to sleep. Once they're settled, we can move. We need to be out of here long before dawn."

A knock at the door made Xalt jump. Kandler and Burch fastened on their weapons as Brendis crept toward the door, his hand on the hilt of his sword. Before he could put his hand on the door, it burst open, and Esprë, Sallah, and Monja spilled into the room.

"Did you see the airship?" Esprë asked.

Kandler nodded as he stood to gather the young elf in his arms for a quick embrace. Then he turned to the others.

"The plan's the same," he said. "We just need to sit tight here for a bit. Then we move."

"Are you sure this is still a good idea?" Xalt said.

Monja looked up at him as the two strolled across the fort's open yard toward the battered airship. "It's a little late for second thoughts," she said. "They've already spotted us."

Xalt stared up at the ship with the black, unblinking stones that served as his eyes. Skeletons still swarmed over the thing like ants across an anthill, building, building, building. The banging of hammers and the high-pitched rhythmic zipping of saws didn't skip a beat as they neared, but an overseer in full Karrnathi armor—black, solid, and covered with burled spikes—standing on the bridge pointed down at them as they approached.

Xalt marveled at how well the repairs had gone so far. He hadn't thought animated skeletons capable of such craftsmanship, and the thought shamed him. Many breathers underestimated warforged in the same way, considering them nothing more than heartless killing machines. He'd spent his entire life—most of it, anyway—proving that notion wrong.

To Xalt's eye, the airship looked almost ready to go. The skeletons had even painted a name across the ship's stern:

Phoenix. Somehow, the gesture made the ship seem much more than just a mode of transportation, and Xalt realized that he would miss it.

He wondered for a moment if they could somehow manage to steal the airship and escape on that instead. He had no idea how to defeat all the skeletons, sever the mooring lines, and then take off into the night, but he thought perhaps Kandler would. Then he remembered that the airship's ring of fire would be like a beacon in the darkness. The other airship would race after them and bring them down long before they could make it to the cover of the Mournland.

He almost laughed at the notion that the Mournland represented safety, but he didn't think Monja would share his feelings. Still, he'd spent almost two years living in the blasted land, sharing space with others of his own kind. For someone who could go without food, drink, and sun, it represented a haven. Most breathers feared to enter the place, which made it safe—at least from them.

Then Xalt noticed that the ship's rudder lay on the earth beneath it. The skeletons had taken it down for repairs. The changeling had nearly torn it to pieces that night she'd plucked Esprë right from the ship's deck. Despite that and all the action it had seen since then, it looked in fine shape now, needing only to be hoisted back into place.

"What's that?" Monja called to the Karrnathi overseer. Her too-innocent tone rang false in Xalt's ears.

"I said," the Karrn called down, "what are you doing out here? You need to return to your quarters. Now!"

"I couldn't sleep," the halfling shaman said. "I decided to go for a stroll. My friend here doesn't need rest, so he agreed to escort me."

"You can't be out here. I have my orders."

"I just wanted to see the airship," Xalt said. "It has many memories for me."

A rope ladder dropped over the side of the ship, and the

overseer slid down it to the ground. "You spent some time on this beauty?"

The overseer didn't seem like a monster, as Xalt might have guessed from the way the others spoke of the Karrn. He was a tall, lanky young man with an easy smile set in a tanned face still battling acne. His dark hair looked as if he'd let one of the less competent skeletons cut it with a rusty knife.

"How many knots do you think she can make?" the Karrn said. "I've never piloted one of these, and I'm looking forward to taking her out for a test soon."

The gates of Fort Bones stood far enough from the airship to be shrouded in darkness but for a pair of large, everburning torches ablaze at the top corners of the gates. There, standing atop two open platforms, they served as signal lights for travelers in the dark as well as light for the pair of living sentries passing the long night hours by playing dice behind the crenellated walls.

Kandler and Sallah crept along the inside of the fort's outer wall until they reached the gates. As they did, they heard the steady trod of iron-shod bones tromping along the walkways overhead, Karrnathi skeletons on their ceaseless patrols.

"What's the plan from here?" Sallah whispered as they stopped for a moment, leaning against a darkened patch of wall.

Her armor made it hard for her to move quietly, but the crackling of the airship's ring of fire, along with the sounds of the repair crew on the other side of the yard, had covered the occasional jangling of the chains in her mail.

"I got us this far," said Kandler as he peered at the gates, only yards away.

A large, heavy bar—a banded log, really—lay across both sides of the gate, resting in a set of iron braces. Moving it would not be easy, but he guessed that the two of them, one on each end, could handle it together. As soon as they did, though, the guards would sound the alarm, and the entire fort would descend on their position.

Kandler pointed to the ladder at the west side of the gate. "We need to get up there," he said.

Sallah glared him. "No," she hissed. "Those men up there are innocents. They've done us no harm. I won't take part in killing them."

Kandler gaped. "You picked a damn poor time to develop a conscience," he said. "You've killed plenty since I met you."

Sallah grimaced. "I fought to defend myself and those around me. Those were just and honorable battles. This," she spat, "this is assassination."

Kandler held his head in his hands. "I knew I should have brought Burch."

The shifter cursed softly as he slipped in a pile of horse apples. He caught himself with an outstretched hand before landing in the mess, but that did little to improve his mood. He scraped the dung from his bare sole as best he could against the inside of the stable's wall and wiped off the rest on some fresh hay.

Burch finished saddling up the black horses they'd need: seven by his count. Then he removed the ropes from across the faces of each of the stalls. There were a dozen horses all told, and he wanted to be able to get them all racing out of the place at the same time. A loud noise from the rear of the last stall should be enough to drive them all out, he hoped. The thought of loosing a howl at the docile creatures made him smile.

As he reached the stall farthest from the door, he smelled something under the standard stable stench. For a moment, he chalked it off to the fact the stalls hadn't been mucked out in far too long, but then he recognized the scent: death.

Burch cursed again. On a tight schedule like this, he couldn't afford to have anything get in the way. Maybe the smell came from a body the Captain of Bones—or some seconded necromancer from the Karrnathi army, more likely—hoped to turn into another of the fleshless soldiers that gave Fort Bones its name, or maybe the cook had just tossed the remains of the freshly butchered pig they'd had for dinner out here.

The shifter wanted nothing more than to just ignore the smell and leave. If any of the others had taken up this assignment instead, they would never have noticed it, he knew.

Instead, Burch reached into one of the packs he'd hung across the saddle horn of a nearby horse. After rummaging around for a moment, he withdrew an everburning torch and uncapped it, exposing its cold, magical flame.

The sudden light stabbed into the shifter's eyes as he tried to stand between it and the stable's outer wall, hoping that he could keep anyone outside from seeing the glare through the unsealed gaps through which the wind sometimes whistled. Burch blinked until his yellow, slit eyes readjusted. Then he followed his nose into the back of the rear stall.

The horse standing there spooked a bit at the proximity of the torch, but Burch calmed it with a quick word and a stroke along its smooth, black neck. It moved aside for him as he pressed further into the back of the stall, seeking the source of the stench.

There, in the far corner, he saw a bare elbow peeking out from under a pile of fresh hay. Perhaps it had once been covered and the horse had brushed the hay over it aside. Either way, there it was.

Burch probed into the hay with the flickering torch, its flames leaving the hay untouched but setting them aglow where its stalks touched the light. He swept the golden stuff aside, exposing the naked body underneath.

The corpse lay face down in the muck, but as soon as Burch saw its short, black hair, he knew who it was. He reached down to draw back the head by that hair, pulling Brendis's face into view. The young knight's neck bore vicious red marks from some kind of rope or strap. His eyes were open, although the pupils had rolled back into his head.

He was as dead as he could be.

Burch closed Brendis's eyes and lowered the young knight's head back into the hay. Then he cursed, cursed, and cursed again.

CHAPTER

30

"Where are we going?" Esprë said as Brendis led her by the hand from the bedchamber in which they had sat waiting for the others. Kandler had instructed them to wait there for fifteen minutes before making their way toward the gate as fast as they could. If they heard any uproar outside, they were to charge toward freedom straight away.

Only ten minutes had passed, and Brendis had taken Esprë by the hand and said, "It's time to go."

At first, the young elf had thought perhaps her nervousness about the escape had made the time they'd spent alone, in wordless contemplation of the chaos to come, seem shorter than it had been. Maybe the time had passed, and she just hadn't noticed it. There hadn't been a clock in the room, not like the ones perched atop some of the shining towers of far-off Sharn. She just couldn't tell.

Then, when they left the room, Brendis took her to the right instead of to the left, which would have brought them closer to the gate.

"This isn't the way," she said to him. "The gate is back in that direction."

Brendis's grip tightened on Esprë's hand. "That way isn't safe," he said.

"But that's the way everyone else went." Esprë felt her heart freeze in her chest.

"I know."

The young elf yanked her hand from the knight's grasp. "I'm not going a step further until . . . Oh, my holy ancestors."

The knight stopped and turned to stare at Esprë, a secret little smirk on his face. "You didn't think I'd leave you behind just like that," he said, "did you?"

Esprë drew back a breath to scream, and a firm hand clamped down across her lips. She tried to spin away from it, but another strong arm wrapped around her, pinning her arms to her sides.

"You are my captive," a low voice said in her ear. "I'd like you alive, but you will do dead. Be silent."

Esprë nodded against the hand across her face, but it stayed in place. She recognized Ibrido's voice and manner, and she knew that he would not hesitate to break her neck given half a reason.

She had to defend herself. She felt the dragonmark on the back of her neck start to burn, and the sensation sluiced down the backs of her arms to pool in her hands. Even here in the darkness, they seemed to glow black, their unnatural absence of color standing out against even the night.

Now, if she could just raise her hands enough to touch him—or the changeling. She lunged forward at the false Brendis, but Ibrido's embrace held her fast.

"Stop her," the Karrn said. "Or I'll kill her now."

A bolt of pain stabbed into Esprë's mind. It felt as if her brain had shrunk to the size of an apple and now rattled around in a skull that was far too large.

Then the hand around her mouth slipped down to her neck and squeezed. The arteries there closed off, and the world went black before the young elf could shout a word of protest.

"That was close," Te'oma said in her own voice, although she maintained Brendis's form. "Did you see her hands?"

"What of it?" Ibrido asked as he slung the unconscious Esprë over his shoulder. "She is but a child—a valuable child, but too young to hurt one such as me."

"Think what you like," Te'oma said as she shifted into a new shape. "She almost killed me with but a touch." She glanced down at herself, trying out a new voice. "How do I look?"

Ibrido parted his lips and exposed his teeth in what Te'oma could only guess was meant to be a smile. "Just like our esteemed Captain of Bones," he said, scanning her from head to toe, "if you can ignore the fact you're dressed as a Knight of the Silver Flame and stand at least foot taller still. Wear this, and slouch over." He tossed her a black cloak, which she flung over her shoulders and draped over Brendis's armor.

"Much better," he said. "In the darkness, the guards should not be able to ascertain any differences. Assuming we don't stumble across Berre herself, your disguise should be impenetrable."

Ibrido turned and stalked down the hallway until he reached a ladder that led to a hatchway in the ceiling. Toting the young elf along as if she weighed as much as a feather pillow, he shoved the hatch back and launched himself up through it into the well-lit night beyond.

Te'oma followed close on his heels, struggling just a little with mimicking Berre's shorter gait. The changeling preferred her own long legs, and those of a dwarf seemed cramped and bothersome.

When she popped her head up through the hatch, Te'oma saw the Karrnathi airship hovering above her. It stretched longer and wider than the one the justicar and his friends had stolen from Majeeda, the mad elf trapped in her own tower in the Mournland, and the ring of fire that encircled it like a ring around a finger crackled even louder.

The Karrnathi airship hung moored over the northwest corner of the fort, as far away from the fort's front gate as possible. Several ropes held it in place, and a wooden gangplank led from the crenellated rear wall up and over to the ship's main deck. The name of the ship—*Keeper's Claw,* named for the icy grasp of the god of the dead—sprawled across the bow in blood-red letters, just beneath the masthead hanging under the bowsprit. The massive wooden carving depicted a monstrous skeleton with a demon's horns and a werewolf's teeth flying along as if it held the entire rest of the ship on its tremendous back. Painted a gleaming white, it looked like it might somehow detach itself from the rest of the ship and go on a deadly rampage at the slightest provocation.

Ibrido stopped halfway up the gangplank and beckoned for Te'oma to hurry up. She doubled her pace and reached his side in seconds. As she approached, she gazed at the unconscious Esprë on his back. For someone in such mortal peril, she slept blissfully unaware, and Te'oma smiled at that.

"You are in charge of this fort," Ibrido said. "Remember that."

Te'oma nodded, irritated that the Karrn felt he had to tell her about her business. She'd been impersonating people her entire life, so often that she sometimes wondered who she was. She recalled a moment as a teenager when she'd been unable to tell if she'd returned to her own form or just something that looked a great deal like it. She'd cried herself to sleep that night, only confident about her own self when she awoke the next morning, comfortable in her own skin.

She suspected that was why the natural form of a changeling was so plain, almost blank. It was too much effort to try to know every inch of a complex physique—far simpler to be a simple person in the first place.

It seemed that no living creatures stood on the ship, that they had all gone to the guest barracks in the fort below, leaving their crew of Karrnathi skeletons behind. These were not so well armored as the ones working in the fort, who served as guards full time. Instead, they had little clothing at all, making it easier for them to move about the ship at speed. Each of them wore a black vest lined with crimson silk and many pockets to give them someplace to store tools and the like. Each also had a long knife in a leather sheath strapped to its right femur. Some of them had a brightly colored bandanna either tied around their neck or wrapped around their naked skulls. Te'oma couldn't be sure, but they seemed to be some indicator of either rank or position. She supposed you might need such a thing to tell the creatures apart if you were trapped on a ship with dozens of them for a week or more at a time.

None of the creatures moved a single bone as they waited for their visitors to board their ship. The silence among so many creatures made Berre's skin crawl over the changeling's flesh. She expected them to burst into lethal action at any moment and wasn't sure she could stand waiting for that any longer.

Te'oma brushed past Ibrido on the gangplank and stepped onto the ship's wide, polished deck. This seemed even more like a boat than the other airship, wide enough that she could ignore for a moment the fact that the craft hung floating high in the air rather than in an open sea.

A gaunt, sunken-eyed man wearing a black, silk bandanna tied around the crown of his head stepped forward as she boarded the ship. Some of the skeletons aboard the ship seemed to have more mass than this lean figure, who stepped forward and saluted Te'oma. "Bosun Meesh, at your service," he said in a dry, unused voice.

"I am Berre Stonefist, Captain of Bones, in charge of this fortress and all who come within its bounds. I am taking command of this ship. Prepare to cast off."

The bosun stared at Te'oma with his cavernous eyes, his lips frozen for the moment. The changeling felt like she might vomit. She had no idea how the Karrn maintained a chain of command over these soulless creatures, and she feared that they were as likely to tear her to shreds and feast on her flesh as accept her orders.

Ibrido reached around Te'oma's chest and pulled a fold in the cloak open to expose a silver wolf's head embroidered in profile there. A set of three knucklebones rested beneath these, stitched fast to the cloak's fabric in a triangular pattern.

At the sight of these, the black-capped man developed a thin-lipped smile and said, "Aye, aye." Then he turned and made a complex signal to the ship's skeletons, each of which had been gazing at him with an empty stare. They launched into a burst of chaotic activity, working fast to remove the moorings and pull the gangplank up behind Ibrido.

"Soon we will be on our way," the Karrn said as he carried Esprë's body to the captain's quarters in the ship's forecastle. "Then no one will be able to stop us."

Te'oma smiled at those words as she followed Ibrido, hoping they were true.

CHAPTER

31

We need to open that gate," Kandler said. "If we do that without removing that guard, he'll bring the entire fort down on our heads. It's him or us."

Sallah nodded, then shouldered past the justicar. "Wait here," she said.

Flummoxed, Kandler watched as the lady knight strode straight up to the ladder. She climbed up into the guard's post in a small niche along the narrow walkway that lined the upper edge of the wall just high enough to let a man peek his head out over the crenellations.

"Hello," he heard her say. "I think I'm lost."

"True enough," the guard said, amused. "You're a long way from Thrane."

Kandler crept over to the barred gates, still listening.

"It's been a long, lonely trip," she said. "I was hoping to find some civilized company here."

The guard laughed. "There's little of anything civilized out here on the edge of nowhere, but I'd be pleased to do what I can to please you."

Kandler heard Sallah try a girly giggle, but it fell flat.

"Are you all right?" the guard said. "Something caught in your throat?"

The lady knight coughed. "I'm fine," she said. "It must be the night air."

A pair of skeletal guards converged on the post from opposite directions. Kandler could hear their booted feet stomping along the wooden walkway above, and he pressed himself harder against the gates. He put his hand on the pommel of his sword, ready to draw it at a moment's notice, but fearful that the sound of it clearing its scabbard would give him away.

"Just let me put these two at ease," the guard said. "They don't talk much, but they listen to orders."

A moment later, Kandler heard the skeletal guards pacing back off in the directions from which they'd come. He breathed a silent sigh of relief.

"Now," the guard said to Sallah, moving closer to her, "let's see what I can do for you."

"Why don't you join me down below?" Sallah said. "I feel a bit too exposed up here. Anyone could see us."

"An excellent idea," the guard said. "Ladies first."

Sallah came down through the hole in the flooring, picking her way carefully down the ladder to the ground. As she cleared the decking, she waved Kandler into a nearby patch of shadow to wait.

The lady knight stood at the foot of the ladder until the guard joined her. "Now," he said with a leer, "just what was it you were hoping I could do for you, my pretty lass?"

Sallah sidled closer to the guard, running her hands up his chest until they rested on the front of his breastplate. "I just have one simple request," she whispered in his ear. "Keep quiet."

She shoved the man back into Kandler's arms, where he put a knife to the man's throat. The guard's eyes grew wide, but he pressed his lips shut as if he feared some sound might accidentally escape.

Sallah tore off the guard's tunic and used strips of it to gag and bind him. He didn't struggle a bit. Just before she stuffed a ball of fabric in his mouth, he whispered, "My thanks to you. This job's not worth dying over."

"See," Sallah whispered with a smile as she and Kandler each grabbed an end of the bar holding the gates shut, "there can be a better way."

"Hey," said Trisfo, the Karrn who hoped to fly *Phoenix* to Fort Zombie and back the next day, "do you see that?"

Xalt froze stiff. These were some of the words he dreaded to hear most in what had been a pleasant conversation so far, covering subjects ranging from the vegetation of the Mournland to the airworthiness of ships like *Phoenix*.

Monja smiled. "I can't hear much of anything standing this close to the ring of fire."

Trisfo stepped between the halfling and the warforged to peer toward the fort's gates. "I said, 'Do you *see* that?' Puakel's gone from his post again." He pointed up at the guard post above and to one side of the gates. "He's going to spend a year in Khyber for that if Berre catches him again."

"He's probably just gone to relieve himself," Xalt said. When Monja stared at him, he added, "I understand humans have to do that all the time."

"Warforged don't?" Trisfo asked, intrigued.

"No," said Xalt. "Compared to breathers, we have a tremendous amount of control over our bodies."

"If you don't eat, how do you stay alive?" Trisfo asked, still keeping one eye on the gates.

"It's complicated," Xalt said, warming to the subject, happy to be talking about anything but guards and gates—especially guards near gates. "Mostly we are motivated by a complicated system of magical means, much like a golem. We don't need any more sustenance than that. However, the wizardly researchers who designed us wanted us to have some measure of free will—as much as any other self-aware creatures, it seems. To that end, the running theory is that they decided to make us as much like breathing people as possible."

"Fascinating," Trisfo said, now completely engaged by the conversation again. "You mean to say that you have a heart, lungs, a brain?"

"In some sense, yes," Xalt said. "You might even recognize them as such if you were to dissect one of us. They have the same form, even if they are not constructed from the same substances."

"Then there is no flesh to you nor bone?"

"Not, again, in the traditional sense. I have an underlying framework that is just as strong as bone, and I have fibers that move in much the same way as your muscles, but they do so without need for food, drink, or even—"

A heart-stopping howl rang out in the night, and for a moment Xalt forgot from where such a horrible sound could have come. Monja reached up and grabbed the warforged's hand and started pulling him toward the gates. As he turned, he saw them start to creak open.

"What's going on here?" Trisfo said, stunned. Then he shouted at the top of his lungs, "The gates! Puakel! The gates!"

Burch came charging out of the stables, still howling as he rushed up behind Xalt and Monja. "Stay here!" he snarled at them as he bounded past, faster than either of them could move.

Xalt halted in midstride and nearly tripped over his own feet. He turned to face Monja, who stared at him with horrified eyes.

At the same time, Trisfo kept shouting for help, screaming for Berre and anyone else to come to his aid. Skeletons came slipping down from the deck of *Phoenix* on mooring lines, landing all around the pair, weapons drawn.

"The gates!" Trisfo roared at them. They sprinted off toward the tall, wide, iron-banded doors as they peeled open inch by inch, foot by foot. They ran with what Xalt would have thought was bone-breaking speed, like death chasing after the fleeing shifter.

"This," Xalt said, "cannot be good."

"What?" Kandler yelled as Burch came sprinting toward him across the open yard, letting everyone in the place see that he and Sallah stood in front of the now-open gates. "What is it?"

With anyone else, Kandler might have been angry. He'd been in tense situations like this time and again, and he'd seen a lot of people crack under the strain. More than one perfectly good plan had gone all to pieces when someone decided to panic at the exact wrong moment.

The justicar knew that Burch, though, was as solid as they came. If he came screaming and howling at him in the middle of a delicate operation, he knew something had to be horribly wrong.

"Brendis is dead," the shifter said as he came panting up to Kandler and Sallah and crashed into the justicar's arms.

"No," Sallah breathed. Kandler could feel the horror strike her. She'd lost three of her fellow knights already. With Brendis gone, she alone bore the responsibility of completing the mission with which five Knights of the Silver Flame—including her father—had been charged.

He had problems of his own though.

"Is Esprë all right?" He dreaded the answer. Although he suspected that Burch would have brought him bad news about his daughter first, he didn't see any way that a story that began with "Brendis is dead" could end well.

"Don't know," Burch said. "Found his body in the stables. It was cold."

"But . . ." Kandler's voice trailed off, unable to keep up with the thoughts whirring through his head.

If Brendis's body was cold, that meant he'd been dead for hours, but he'd seen the young knight with Esprë only minutes ago. That meant . . .

"The changeling!"

Burch nodded. "She can't be too far."

Kandler grimaced. "So much for a clean escape. We need to rouse Berre and sound the alarm. Maybe we can still stop her, whatever her plan is."

At that moment, the new airship, the one with the grotesque masthead, caught his eye from across the whole of the fort. "That's it," he said. "She has to be going for it."

As he spoke, he thought he could make out two figures walking up the gangplank and on to the ship. The larger of them carried something slung over its shoulder.

"They're on the—"

Before Kandler could finish his sentence, a voice rang out. "Hold! If you move a muscle, you will die!"

Kandler spotted Berre dashing toward them from across the yard. As he glanced around, he saw at least two score Karrnathi skeletons leveling crossbows at them. It seemed that the Captain of Bones didn't make idle threats.

CHAPTER

32

Te'oma heard the howl just as she opened the door to the captain's quarters. It ran icicles through her veins. She shivered as she froze in the doorway. Indecision transfixed her as she tried to determine what she should do.

Ibrido pulled her into the cabin and slammed the door behind her. She heard the latch fall shut as she picked herself up off the crimson rug that covered most of the floor. She noticed Esprë laid out on the red-velvet couch in front of her. The young elf slept there peacefully oblivious, not a mark on her pale skin. The fort infirmary had been good to her, unnaturally so. Te'oma suspected that the Captain of Bones had slipped a healing potion of some sort into Esprë's drink, something she was equally sure hadn't been wasted on herself.

"What do you think you're doing?" Te'oma said as she spun to face Ibrido. "We need to cast off."

The soldier stared at her with his unblinking eyes. "The crew is set to that task already. We will be off as soon as we can."

"Is there a good reason, then, for locking us all in here?"

Ibrido bared his teeth. "There are a few details I need to take care of before we go. As an added bonus, they may help delay any pursuit for a vital few minutes."

"What in the Dark Six's most damned names are you blathering about?"

Ibrido smiled as he rubbed a ring he wore on the pinky of his left hand. "I am afraid I have let you labor under a misconception," he said, his voice as even as if he were describing the weather.

Te'oma narrowed her eyes at the creature. "What do you mean?" she said. As she spoke, she reached out with her mind, probing Ibrido's thoughts, hoping to determine the truth behind his mysterious comments. Something frustrated her efforts though. When she reached out for him, it was as if he wasn't there at all.

"Do you think I would be so indiscreet as to allow you unrestricted access to my innermost thoughts?" he asked, a soft snigger in his voice. "That would not make me much of a spy, now would it?"

Te'oma's hand went to the sword hanging from Brendis's weapon belt, the sacred, burning blade of a Knight of the Silver Flame. Before she could get it clear of the scabbard, though, Ibrido was on her.

The soldier smacked her to the floor with the back of his hand. She reached up to feel her face and brought her hand away slicked with blood trickling from her nose.

"Are you mad?" she asked, more shocked by the betrayal than the injury. "The Lich Queen will skin you alive for that. I'm to bring this child to her in Illmarrow Castle. There is no more important mission."

"The Lich Queen?" Ibrido laughed. "You think I fear that fragile bag of bones? There are greater things in this world than long-dead elves who refuse to relinquish their hold on it."

Te'oma stared at the Karrn, unable to make herself understand what he meant.

"Even if I cared about her, what makes you think I need you anymore?" Ibrido said as he delivered a vicious kick to Te'oma's ribs. She felt her ribs crack as she tried to scramble away. "The Lich Queen wants the child who bears the Mark of Death. I doubt she'll mind it if there's one less changeling thief in the world."

Te'oma mentally unfurled her cloak, commanding the symbiont to transform itself into a set of batlike wings that could carry her to safety. When the tips of the wings rapped against the ceiling, though, she understood why Ibrido had hauled her into the captain's cramped quarters before confronting her.

The Karrn slammed into the changeling from below, smashing her wings flat against the cabin ceiling above her. She felt something in them snap, and pain stabbed into her through the nerves she shared with the parasitic creature. She closed her eyes as she flinched in pain, and when she opened them something terrible stood in Ibrido's place.

The creature holding Te'oma against the ceiling looked something like the Ibrido she knew but different. Shimmering green scales covered him from head to toe. His crimson eyes were slit like those of a serpent, and his thin, black tongue flicked about the rim of his slash of a mouth when he wasn't using it to speak. His scale-covered ears were pointed like an elf's. He was taller than before and stronger too, and when he drew back his lips all Te'oma could see were rows of vicious, knifelike teeth.

Under any other circumstances, this revelation—that Ibrido was a half-breed that bore the blood of both dragons and elves—might have made Te'oma fall to pieces. To have Esprë stolen from her by such a creature, just as she was about to make off with her for good, would have been enough to drive her mad. As it was, though, her every thought was consumed with keeping herself alive instead. She had killed enough people in her time to know when someone was ready to commit murder, and Ibrido bore all the signs.

Te'oma reached down with her mouth and bit the hand that Ibrido was using to hold her against the ceiling. The dragon-elf shouted in surprise and pulled back his injured fist, letting the changeling drop to the floor in front of him. He steeled himself for a follow-up attack from Te'oma, but it never came.

Instead, the changeling turned and made a mad dash for the set of windows that lined the back of the room, designed to give the captain of the ship a panoramic view of the lands before them. The frames of the windows formed from the ribs of the airship's monstrous masthead, pale and thick as a giant's bones. She smashed into the windows at full speed, hoping to burst through into the open air beyond. If she could get free, if she could survive, she could lick her wounds and come back to take Esprë from Ibrido when the time was ripe. She'd managed to take her from Kandler and his friends. She could do it again.

The wooden ribs cracked but held, and Te'oma bounced back into the room, reeling from the impact. Before she could utter a moan, Ibrido scooped her up off the floor and wrapped his hands around her neck.

"Impressive," he said as he started to strangle her. "Your drive for survival suits you well. Perhaps in other circumstances we could be true allies. You would be an asset." He squeezed even harder, and the changeling felt her world start to go black. "As it is, though, you are far too competent a foe to be allowed to live."

Desperate, Te'oma lashed out blindly with her fists. The dragon-elf's arms were half again as long as hers, though, and she only found purchase on his biceps. She tried digging into them with her nails, but she could not penetrate his scales. She morphed back into her natural form, but her arms still weren't long enough. She considered duplicating Ibrido's form, but a better idea struck her.

The changeling brought her knees up to her chest, and Ibrido laughed at her. "You cannot escape me by rolling into a ball," he said, just before she lashed out with a two-footed kick that crushed his snoutlike nose.

The dragon-elf dropped Te'oma to the floor. She hit it hard then rolled away, hacking hard, trying to cough away the impressions his fingers had left on her throat. She crawled toward the door as best she could, not bothering to look back. How badly she might have hurt her foe didn't matter. The only thing she could think about was getting out of that room.

"You bastard bitch!" Ibrido roared.

Te'oma still didn't glance back, but she heard the dragon-elf suck in a deep breath then exhale it in her direction. A thick, cloying gas enveloped her before she could blink, its acidic fumes eating away at her, stinging her eyes and burning her skin. She screamed in horror, and as she drew in her next breath she sucked the stuff into her lungs. This set her coughing hard enough to snap one of her already cracked ribs.

Te'oma was still wincing in pain as Ibrido snatched her up by the collar of her stolen armor and hauled her to her feet. She coughed blood into his face.

"Having a hard time breathing, are we?" he said. "That is a problem I can help you solve."

Ibrido reached out with his other hand and grabbed Te'oma by the chin. Then, with relentless force, he began forcing her head around, away from the direction in which he held her shoulders.

Te'oma struggled against the dragon-elf's incredible strength with what was left of her might. Still coughing that horrible gas from her lungs, she beat at him with her arms and legs, but he just hauled her in closer, drawing her into a terrible embrace she could not resist. She tried to bite the web of his hand, between his index finger and thumb, but she couldn't do more than scratch his scales as his talons dug deep into her cheeks, drawing blood that flowed down his fingers and into her mouth, threatening to drown her in her own hot fluids.

When her neck twisted to the farthest point she thought it could, Te'oma unleashed a horrid, desperate scream.

Ibrido gave her head one final push and snapped her neck like a dry piece of kindling.

Te'oma felt her body go limp and numb beneath her. Helpless, unable to even raise her arms to defend herself, she did the only thing she could.

She wept. She cried for herself, for her long-dead daughter, and for the rest of her life, which it seemed she would never have.

CHAPTER

33

"We caught you red-handed trying to escape," Berre said. "For that, there will be consequences."

Kandler bit back a snarl.

"That's doesn't matter right now," he said, pointing his sword over the dwarf's shoulder at the airship beyond. "You have to listen to me."

A bolt whizzed past Kandler's outstretched arm, and he dropped his blade like a hot iron.

"The rest of you, drop your weapons," Berre said.

She didn't need to raise her voice for everyone to hear the menace in it. Her time living with so many skeletons had made her used to having her orders followed without question, Kandler realized. He knew that she would not brook any disobedience, however pleasant she might have been to him and the others before.

Sallah sheathed her sword, and Burch slung his crossbow back across his shoulders. Kandler stepped forward, putting up his hands to show that he wasn't a threat.

"We're not your problem here," he said, struggling to keep the desperation from his voice. He had to make her listen to him, and if she thought he was lying, there was little chance of that.

"Stand back." Berre shoved her battle-axe into Kandler's face, and he stuttered two steps away.

"You don't want us," he said. "You want Esprë."

The Captain of Bones fidgeted a moment as she weighed the truth in the justicar's words. "Where is she?" she asked. "What have you done with her?"

"We were trying to escape," Kandler said. "That much is true, but we were tricked, betrayed. We don't have her any more."

Berre scowled at the justicar. "Where is she?"

Exasperated, Kandler pointed at the Karrnathi airship again, this time with his finger. "Why don't you ask whoever's in charge of that ship?"

Berre turned to gaze out at *Keeper's Claw* and gasped. The skeletons crewing the airship had tossed off all of the mooring ropes and drawn in the gangplank, cutting off access to the ship from the top of the fort's rear wall. All it waited for was for someone to take the wheel and fly it away.

"Who would dare?" the dwarf asked.

"It's the changeling," Burch said. "She never left the fort."

The windows framed by the ribs of the ship's horrific masthead shattered, sending broken bits of wood and shattered glass cascading down to the ground behind the fort. A body followed along with them, spilled toward the ground. Whitish but covered with blood, it fluttered down slowly on tattered, black wings that could not keep it aloft.

As the body disappeared behind the back wall of the fort, Burch looked at Kandler. "All right," the shifter said, "I could be wrong about that too."

The door to the captain's quarters in the lower part of the forecastle opened, and a tall, powerful creature covered with green scales strode forth. He wore a black cloak that seemed to have some sort of insignia of rank embroidered across a fold near the wearer's chest. The green-scaled creature stopped for a moment to stare down at the crowd assembled near the fort's open gates. Then he sprinted toward the rear of the airship.

"Sailors of *Keeper's Claw*," Berre shouted. "Halt!"

The skeletons on the airship ignored the captain and kept about their work, preparing the ship to leave.

Berre cursed. "The bastard has one of our command cloaks," she said, "one with a rank at least as high as mine." She cupped her hands around her lips.

"Soldiers of Fort Bones," Berre called in her loudest voice, "stop that ship!"

The skeletons inside the fort turned as one to face the airship. Those armed with crossbows loosed their bolts at the craft, several of which bounced off their fellows on the deck of the ship. One or two caught in an eye socket or between a couple ribs, but they did no real hurt. None of them found the stranger.

"The half-dragon!" Berre said. "Kill the half-dragon!"

As the skeletons loaded another round of bolts into their crossbows, Kandler launched himself forward, with Sallah and Burch following close in his wake. Berre started to protest but cut herself off before she distracted any of her soldiers from the more vital target of the half-dragon.

As Kandler raced past Monja and Xalt, they joined the others chasing after him. He charged for a ladder near the fort's rear wall and hauled himself up it as fast as his arms would take him. He knew that Esprë had to still be on that ship, and he was determined not to let it leave without him. He hadn't come so far, gone through so much, to lose her again.

By the time he popped through the walkway floor and hurled himself to the top of the wall, though, he was already too late. Ibrido stood on the bridge, the wheel in his hands, and the ship was scudding away. The justicar could do nothing to prevent it.

He leaped atop the crenellated wall and gauged the distance to one of the ship's mooring lines. It hung far out of his reach, but a desperate leap might put it within grasp. He crouched low to jump and shoved out with all his might, stretching his fingers as far as they would go in the vain hope that they might catch on one of the fast-moving ropes and give him one last chance at saving his daughter.

As his feet cleared the fort's wall, though, a pair of hands reached out from behind and snatched him back by his sword belt. The nearest rope skated by his fingers, just out of his reach.

Kandler fell back to the walkway behind the wall, tangled in the arms of whoever it was who had robbed him of his—of Esprë's—final chance. "No!" he raged. "No!"

The justicar drew back his fist to smash into the face of the person who had stopped him in mid-leap, but his eyes fell on Sallah's beautiful features. His hand froze behind him. "You?"

"It was too far," she said as she panted for breath. "You could have been killed."

Kandler punched his fist into the floor behind the lady knight's head, then stood up to stare after the airship as it sped away into the night. Already, all he could see of it was the ring of fire and some of the rear parts of the ship silhouetted against it.

He swore he could hear something else over the crackling of that massive wheel of flames though, something dry and painful, something that sounded like laughter.

The justicar turned on the lady knight, who now stood behind him, watching the airship over his shoulder. Her emerald eyes shone with pain but showed no regret. He knew she'd have made the same choice over and over again, no matter what it might cost her. He didn't care.

"That was *my* call to make," he said as he shouldered past her and slid down the ladder to the fort's open yard.

"Explain yourself," Berre said, stepping square into Kandler's face, although she was at least two feet shorter than him.

"We were trying to escape," he said. He didn't care what she thought of that or what she might do to him. He only knew he had to get after Esprë fast. "It went wrong."

He stormed past her, heading for the stables. Three of the horses, saddled up and ready to go, had wandered out of their stalls after Burch went sprinting past them. Kandler strode up to one and mounted it. As he grabbed the reins, he saw that the gates to the fort were closed and a handful of Karrnathi skeletons stood dropping the gates' ironbound bar back into place.

"Get that out of my way," Kandler said to Berre as she stalked after him.

"I'll do no such thing," she said. "You are my guest here, but you are not permitted to come and go as you please."

Kandler put his hand on the pommel of his sword. "It wasn't a request. I'll kill you and everyone else in this backwater pit."

"You are not in charge here," she said, drawing her battle-axe.

A hand reached up and held Kandler's sword arm in place before he could bring forth his blade. The justicar looked down to see Xalt staring up at him.

"Don't try to stop me," Kandler said.

"I want Esprë safe too," the warforged said, keeping his hand—the one missing the finger he'd lost standing up to his cruel superior—on Kandler's, "but you are no good to her dead. The ship is gone. This horse cannot catch it."

Kandler slapped Xalt's hand away and kicked the horse into a trot toward the gates. As he reached them, he dismounted and strode up to the bar holding them shut. With a mighty shove, he pushed up on the bar, dislodging it from its home.

"Guards," Berre said, "bar the gate."

A half-dozen skeletons leaped forward to obey the order, pressing the heavy bar back into its brackets. Kandler bent his knees and shoved up against them, struggling with his every muscle. He knew he couldn't win. There were too many of them. Even if he drew his sword and beat them all into a pile of broken bones, scores more stood ready to take their place. And with every moment Esprë grew farther away.

Someone pounded on the gates then, a desperate, hammering knocking that rattled them from end to end. It took Kandler a moment to realize the sound had originated outside the fort's walls.

"Open up!" a strained voice called over the top of the gates. Kandler would have recognized it anywhere. It belonged to Burch.

"Didn't you hear him?" Kandler said, not caring for an instant how the shifter had wound up outside the fort. Perhaps he'd tried a jump for the mooring lines himself—without Sallah to stop him—and had come up short. At least he'd tried. At least he'd had the chance.

Berre nodded. "Open the gates," she said.

The skeletons who had been pushing down on the massive bar reversed themselves and pulled the heavy, banded log out of its brackets with one practiced move. Then they moved as one to push the gates outward into the night.

As soon as the gates cracked open wide enough, Burch sidled through into the yard, bearing someone's slack body in his arms. At first, hope leaped in Kandler's heart that it might be Esprë, that the shifter, his closest friend, had somehow found a way to rescue his little girl.

Then Kandler saw the clothing and armor that had belonged to Brendis, the chain mail, the breastplate, the red tabard embroidered with the silver flame. He wondered if Burch had gone outside to recover the young knight's corpse.

But then he saw the long, blond hair and bone-pale skin of the changeling poking out above the tabard's collar. Blood the same color as the tabard covered her face, even running into her eyes. Her neck hung at an unnatural angle.

"She's still alive," Burch said.

CHAPTER

34

Is there anything you can do for her?" Kandler asked Monja as they followed Burch into the fort's infirmary. The shifter carried the changeling to the nearest bed and set her down on it, arranging her neck in a position that looked less painful. Although she had stopped bleeding, she still left crimson streaks on the bleached white sheets where the shifter moved her across them.

The halfling shrugged. "It's in the hands of Olladra now," she said. "I can only offer up my prayers and see if the fickle goddess of fortune smiles on our wayward changeling."

"I thought you'd want to kill her," Sallah said, trooping in after Kandler and Monja, with Xalt and Berre on her tail.

Kandler looked down at the battered changeling, her breath rattling in and out of her in shallow, ragged bursts. He felt a mix of pity and wrath that he could not reconcile. Part of him felt that no one deserved to suffer like this, but another part said that if anyone did have such agony coming to her, it was this changeling.

He shook his head at Sallah's question. "No," he said. "She's the only link we have to Esprë now."

"Then step aside and let me work," Monja said.

The halfling stepped up to Te'oma's bedside and placed her hands on each of the changeling's ears, cradling her head in a gentle grasp. Te'oma's breath came shorter and shorter now. Without the shaman's intervention, Kandler knew she wouldn't have long. From the fear he read in her blank, white eyes—the tears which ran pale, pink streaks through the blood on her cheeks—he could see she knew it too.

Monja chanted a short series of words in a language that Kandler could not understand, at least not in his head. He felt their warmth and comfort in his heart.

The little shaman's hands began to glow with a golden light. As she spoke, the light ran down through her palms and fingers and crawled along Te'oma's flesh. Where it passed, blood stopped flowing, skin knitted back into shape, and bones healed as strong as they'd ever been.

Kandler heard the sound of the changeling's neck healing. The bones popped clear and sharp as they meshed back together into their original form. The golden light effused Te'oma's entire body, washing over her in benevolent color before finally fading away to nothing.

The changeling's breathing returned to normal, and a healthy hue filled her cheeks once again. She relaxed back into the bloodstained bed sheets, the pain that had wracked her body now gone. She slept peacefully now, even in the armor and tabard she'd stolen from Brendis.

"It's all right," Monja said softly, as if not wanting to disturb Te'oma's rest. "She will live."

"Good," said Sallah, who stepped forward and slapped the unconscious changeling with all her might.

Te'oma's wide, white eyes flew open, and she half sat up in bed. Her eyes wandered for a bit before focusing on the furious, red-haired knight standing over her. Then, perhaps out of some kind of confused reflex, she morphed into Brendis's form.

Sallah froze as she looked down into her dead compatriot's

eyes. The wrongness of it appalled her in many ways, Kandler could tell. The lady knight had only learned of her friend's murder moments ago, and now with the changeling seeming to mock her grief she lost the tenuous control she had on her temper.

Sallah's fist smashed into Te'oma's jaw, knocking her back into the bed. The changeling's head landed on the pillow as blood spattered on the wall behind her from her split lip.

Monja leaped on top of the changeling, interposing herself between the two ladies. "Stop!" the shaman said, holding up her hands in Sallah's face. "I just fixed her up!"

"I'm not going to kill her," Sallah snarled, "just make her wish she was dead." Then she leaned over the halfling's shoulder and shouted down at the changeling, who tried to squirm away from her across the bed.

"You had to kill him, didn't you?" she said. "You couldn't just tie him up. You had to choke the life out of him and then leave him naked and alone in that Flame-damned horse stall. You—"

Kandler reached out, grabbed Sallah around the waist and pulled her back from Te'oma's bed. "We haven't got time for this right now," he hissed into her ear. "She's an evil, awful bitch, but we need to ask her about Esprë."

"Let me go!" Sallah said. "You can have her when I'm through softening her up."

"That's not you talking," Kandler said. "That's your grief. Think for a moment. Think about who you are. Think about the morals you uphold. Cold-blooded murder doesn't fit with any of that. Would Brendis want you to betray your vows as a knight like this?"

He could feel the lady knight start to calm down, to hear his words and consider them. He knew he had her on her last legs. He pushed her right back off them.

"What would your father say if he could see you now?"

Sallah spun around, ready to slap the words out of Kandler's mouth. He caught her hand as she brought it back to strike him, and he frowned into her face.

The knight looked up into Kandler's eyes for a moment, and then the pain, the grief, the agony all melted away into despair. She collapsed forward into his arms, sobbing, "Why?"

Kandler held her in his arms until her body stopped shaking and she could push herself away from him of her own accord. "Thanks," she said in a raw voice, unable to meet his eyes. She refused to glance back at the changeling as she gave Kandler a small kiss on the cheek and then staggered out of the room.

"I have a burial to attend to," she said as she passed through the curtain covering the empty doorway.

"I have matters of my own to deal with," Berre said catching Sallah by the elbow. "Stick with me, and I'll bring you to him first."

The two walked out of the room arm in arm. Kandler noticed that the dwarf somehow seemed as tall as the knight as they went.

Sallah gone, Monja leaped off of Te'oma as if the changeling might bite her.

"Thank you," Te'oma said to the shaman.

"Thank the big human," Monja said. "If he didn't need you, I'd have finished you off with my knife." She slipped toward the door. "I'll go see if I can help Sallah with the last rites. You can't be too careful about such things in a fort full of skeletons."

As the curtain flapped behind the halfling, Kandler turned his full attention to Te'oma. She stared back at him with wide eyes.

"You don't have to hurt me," she said. "I'll tell you what you want."

"I don't doubt it." Kandler cracked his knuckles for emphasis. Burch sat on the edge of the room's lone windowsill, blocking that avenue of retreat as he checked the action on his crossbow and slipped a steel-tipped bolt into its home.

Te'oma's eyes grew wide, and she edged back on the bed. As she did, Kandler cracked his neck. Her hands flew up to her own neck as if to hold her head in place.

"Where's he headed?" Kandler asked.

"I don't know."

A bolt stabbed into the wall next to Te'oma's head. She screamed in surprise.

"Wrong answer." Kandler grimaced at the changeling. "Don't think you're lucky that Burch missed there. Burch never misses, not at this range. That was your warning."

As the justicar spoke, the shifter slipped another bolt into its home and cranked back the crossbow's handle. He worked the action slowly, and every click on the weapon's wheel sounded like a breaking bone.

"The dragon-elf betrayed me," Te'oma said. "We were supposed to get away with Esprë together, but he betrayed me. He serves another master than mine."

"Who?"

"I don't know," Te'oma said.

Kandler clenched his fists in frustration. "Where is he taking her?"

"I don't—wait!" the changeling shouted at Burch, throwing up her arms to protect herself as he leveled his crossbow at her. Kandler waved him off, and the shifter rested the weapon back on his lap.

"I don't know," she said. "He didn't tell me."

Burch raised his weapon again, and Te'oma winced at the gesture.

"I can find out!" she said. "After I caught up with Esprë on the airship, I forged a mindlink with her while she was still unconscious."

Kandler stared at her with a mixture of hope and horror.

Te'oma shrugged. "She's a slippery young elf. I wanted to

make sure I could find her if I lost her again. I can contact her telepathically no matter where she might be."

Kandler's heart started to crawl its way out of his heels.

"Can you do that now?"

Te'oma nodded, then closed her eyes for a moment. Her forehead knit with concentration, as Kandler imagined her reaching out to his daughter with her mind. The fact that the changeling had managed to establish such a link with Esprë appalled him, but that warred with his gratitude that they might be able to use it to find her again.

After a long moment, the changeling frowned and opened her eyes. "She's still unconscious," she said. "I can't reach her."

"How was she when you last saw her?"

"Asleep. I knocked her out psionically." She put her hands up in supplication. "At worst, she'll wake up with a slight headache."

"You're sure she's not dead?" Kandler dreaded the answer, but he had to ask.

Te'oma nodded. "The mindlink severs if she's dead."

"Do you think he'll keep her alive?"

She nodded again. "She's worth much more if she's breathing."

"I suppose you could say the same about yourself."

CHAPTER

35

Alone in the stables, Sallah knelt down in front of Brendis's body and wept. The corpse lay there still half covered in hay, the top half twisted back at an awkward angle to expose its face. It wore only a thin set of undergarments worn to gray after repeated washings in open streams.

It comforted Sallah to think of the body as an "it." Brendis's spirit had long since fled, she knew—or been forced out at the hands of that changeling bitch. Perhaps it had already joined in eternal communion with the Silver Flame, yet another in the infinite number of burning tongues of argent fire merged with the great god to whom she had dedicated her life. It dulled the edge of the pain that lanced through her soul, but not by much.

Sallah had known loss in her life. Her mother had died when she was but a girl. With her extended family off fighting the Last War for Thrane, she'd lived with the threat of bereavement hanging over her head like a sword on a slender thread for years.

To her, it had always seemed that the only way to deal with this ever-present threat was to confront it, so she had petitioned to be admitted to the Knights of the Silver Flame as soon as she could. As one of the youngest squires in the church, she had served as both swordbearer and mascot, but as the years passed she grew to be one of the order's most promising young knights.

Living in the shadow of her father, Deothen, had never been easy. As a father, he'd made a great commander. From as early as she could remember, he'd always treated her like a little soldier. Was it any wonder that she'd grown up into one?

As a Knight of the Silver Flame, Deothen had become a legend in his own time. No one in Thrane could not know who he was, and that fame extended to his daughter by proximity, whether she deserved it or not. Everyone had always had high expectations of Sallah, and she'd done her best to live up to them, never questioning why. She saw it as her duty.

Sallah pulled the body that had once housed Brendis's soul from under the hay. She pulled one of its arms over her shoulder and carried it that way out of the stables. When she emerged with the corpse in her arms, Berre stood there waiting for her.

"I've already set a detail to digging a grave," the dwarf said. "Do you have any special instructions we need to know of?"

Sallah shook her head. "Just show me where to bring the body. I'll take care of the rest."

Berre stepped up under Brendis's other arm and offered the corpse what support she could. Then she pointed toward a patch of open ground along the fort's western wall, and the two dragged the body to it.

The patch already featured a handful of headstones, low, stone markers on each of which a name had been chiseled. The ground here was the only section of the fort's yard in which grass of any kind grew, the rest of the well-trodden ground nothing but hard-packed dirt. The grass grew thick under the headstones. Only the section where two men worked was broken. It had been a long time since someone else had died here—or at least someone who warranted a burial.

Sallah noticed that the two soldiers digging the grave bore flesh on their bones. "I'm surprised," she said as she and Berre lowered the corpse to the ground beside the deepening grave. "I thought you'd have put some of your skeletons to such a task."

One of the men in the hole, a red-faced fellow with dark, receding hair, snorted at that. "This is hallowed ground, miss," he said. "Those clothes racks can't come near here."

Sallah sighed in relief. She'd feared having to leave her friend in an unprotected grave. With all the undead creatures running around this place, she worried that some Karrnathi necromancer might see Brendis's body as fodder for King Kaius's forces. While Brendis's spirit might be beyond insult, his earthly form deserved a better, more peaceful fate than that.

The lady knight looked down at both of the men in the hole and said, "You have my thanks."

As Sallah gazed down at the corpse of her friend, her brother in arms, she realized that something was missing. "I'll be right back," she said to no one in particular, then stalked back toward the infirmary.

When she entered the room, Kandler was on his way out. Without a word, he took her in his arms again. She held him tight for a moment, thankful to have someone she could look to in this terrible time. He may not have been a Knight of the Silver Flame or even a member of her church, but she knew he was a good man. She could feel herself falling for him, but she stayed wary of such things. Alone, hundreds of miles from home, grieving for both friends and her father, she knew she was vulnerable.

She surprised herself by not crying another drop. She had wept enough for today, it seemed. She had a job to do—burying Brendis—and she refused to let her emotions get in the way of that.

"Don't kill her," Kandler said. "We need her."

"Where are you headed?"

"To find some chains." He kissed her once on the forehead and strode off.

The lady knight took a moment to compose herself then walked into the infirmary. Burch still sat there, perched in the windowsill. Sallah couldn't help but remember when she'd first met the shifter, how he'd sat the same way in the front window of Kandler's house. She was tempted to smile.

Then she spied Te'oma lying in a bed on the other side of the room, and the temptation faded away. She crossed over to the changeling, who cringed as she neared. The temptation returned, stronger than ever.

Sallah reached down and plucked up Brendis's sword, which lay on the bed nearest to Te'oma. It felt warm and comforting in her hands, as if she somehow had managed to recover a vital part of her lost compatriot.

Then she glared over at the changeling. "Take off his things," she said. "Now."

Te'oma opened her mouth to protest but no words came out. She climbed out on the other side of the bed from Sallah and stripped off Brendis's tabard and armor, leaving herself in nothing more than a pitch-colored shift so black her skin glowed white in contrast. She lay them on the bed before her and then backed off so that Sallah could snatch them away.

"I didn't kill him," the changeling said. "Ibrido was just supposed to . . ." The look on Sallah's face made her falter.

"I don't care whose hands held the straps that strangled him," the lady knight said. "You're responsible just the same."

She turned and left before the changeling could respond, before she let her see again how much she hurt.

Kandler met her at the door. "Hold on," he said, hefting a set of manacles and a collar connected with thick chains.

Sallah waited while the justicar went into the room and put the changeling in irons while Burch stood guard. No one said a word.

Kandler emerged from the room, looking grim.

"Do you think that will hold her?" Sallah asked.

He shrugged. "It's the best we can do for now."

With that, he took Brendis's things from her, except for his sword, which she cradled in her arms like a lost child. She led him down the stairs toward the fresh-dug grave.

One of the Karrnathi soldiers waved to them as they approached. "Just about finished," he said, leaning on his dirt-crusted shovel. "It's always slow going at the end. When you get so deep, only one man can work the hole."

Clods of broken earth arced up out of the grave at a steady rhythm, falling near the first soldier's feet. The sound and scent comforted Sallah somehow, as part of the ritual to acknowledge the end of a friend's life. She'd been to too many funerals, she knew, but it didn't seem like that would end any time soon.

As she and Kandler stood there, Berre strode over from where dozens of skeletons seemed to have redoubled their efforts to get *Phoenix* ready to fly. Sallah watched as a crew used a giant block and tackle to hoist the airship's repaired rudder back into place.

"She should be set to go by dawn," Berre said. "Any idea where you're taking her?"

"She's ours to take?" Kandler asked.

The Captain of Bones nodded. "When we found it, Esprë was at the wheel. You're her next-of-kin, right? It's yours to return to her."

Berre sighed. "I'd send some troops with you, but I'm bound to have enough trouble here without wasting resources on what Korth could only see as a wild goose chase."

"Wouldn't Kaius want his airship back?"

"It's gone. Even were I to commandeer *Phoenix* to go after

her, I wouldn't know where she's fled." She narrowed her eyes and lowered her voice. "So don't you tell me."

Kandler lowered his head for a moment. "Thank you."

The chunks of earth stopped coming, and a shovel followed them, landing atop the mound of fresh dirt. A hand came reaching up after that, and the soldier above helped pull his friend from the hole. As he dusted himself off, the soldier gave Sallah and Kandler a solemn nod.

The soldiers had already laid Brendis's body out on a tarpaulin nearby, with ropes slid under it so they could lower the corpse into the ground. Sallah knelt down and spread the young knight's armor over him, then laid his tabard over that. Kandler helped her wrap the body in the canvas sheet.

When only Brendis's head was left exposed, Sallah leaned over and kissed him on his pale forehead. Then she covered his face and stepped back so the soldiers could put him in his grave.

As Brendis's body went into its final resting place, Sallah spoke. "By the grace of the Silver Flame, my brother, may you find peace in its warmth and illumination in its eternal presence."

"Amen," Kandler murmured, reaching for her. She turned in his strong arms and let him hold her as she wept what she promised herself would be the last tears for her fallen friends—at least until she completed their quest. Tomorrow, there would be no time for grief.

Chapter

36

Esprë awoke to the sound of someone screaming. It took her a moment before she realized it was her.

She stared around with wide, terrified eyes. She was in a cabin of some sort, a room made entirely of wood stained mahogany-dark and polished to a glistening finish. She sat up on an overstuffed couch of crimson velvet, clutching at its back and arm.

A stiff wind blew in from the windows at the front of the room, which had been smashed through. The back of the couch had shielded her from the night chill. She stared out into the darkness beyond and could see nothing but a black, featureless void.

Several everburning torches lit the cabin, their magical lights guttering in the wind but never going out. A four-poster bed crouched in one corner, a paper-cluttered desk in the other. The wind had strewn the papers all about the room, most of them ending up near the door opposite the windows.

Esprë swung her feet off the couch and on to a carpet the same shade of red as the couch. She felt something wet on her hand as it brushed along the couch. She brought it to her face and saw blood on her fingers.

She inventoried her body, checking for pain or wounds but found nothing. Her head ached a bit, and she remembered the last thing she'd seen before falling asleep had been Te'oma's face. The changeling had mentally battered her into unconsciousness as a pair of hands held her in place, hands that could only have belonged to Ibrido.

The cabin door opened, and a pair of Karrnathi skeletons stalked into the low-ceilinged room. An elf with dragonish features crept in behind them, keeping them between himself and the young elf. He wore a black cloak with the Karrnathi wolf embroidered on one breast. A triangle of knucklebones hung just below that, white and pure against the cloak's dark fabric.

"Welcome to *Keeper's Claw*," the dragon-elf said. "Make yourself comfortable. You will be with us for some time."

"I–Ibrido?" Esprë said. "Is that you?"

The dragon-elf nodded. "The time for masks is over. I have captured you, and no one can stop me from disposing with you as I please."

At first, Esprë had wanted to scream again. Now, noticing how carefully the dragon-elf treated her, she had to struggle to keep a wry smile from her face. Ibrido knew of her dragonmark, and he feared her. She enjoyed knowing that.

"It's hard to be comfortable with the wind blowing in like that," Esprë said, pointing at the windows.

Ibrido grimaced. "I will have a detail assigned to repairing that right away. In the meantime, please keep yourself far from the windows. Come daylight, you'll find that it's a long, fatal drop to the ground."

"Where are we going?" Esprë asked. She surprised herself by how calm she felt. Perhaps the growing power of her dragonmark came with a bit of maturity, or maybe she was just used to getting kidnapped by now.

"To visit an old friend. Someone I've not seen in many years but who is very eager to meet you."

"Kandler will come after me. They all will."

"How? In that battered airship you crashed to the earth? By the time they get that rowboat in the air, we will be leagues from Fort Bones, and they will have no idea which way we went."

Esprë steeled herself as she felt her confidence waning. "They found me before. They'll never give up."

Ibrido bared his teeth. "If they somehow do manage to catch us, I will knock them from the sky. This is a warship on which we travel, not some enchanted pleasure boat."

Esprë stood up, and the dragon-elf took one step back. The skeletons closed ranks in front of him, keeping him far from the young elf's reach.

"Perhaps I'll kill you myself," she said, trying to inject some menace into her voice. The dragonmark on her back began to itch, and the tips of her fingers began to numb with cold.

"Take her," Ibrido said.

For an instant, Esprë wondered whom he spoke to. Then the twin skeletons darted forward and grabbed her by her elbows. They shoved her back into the overstuffed couch and pinned her there.

Esprë struggled against the skeletons' grasp, but they held her fast as steel. She kicked out at them, but they just draped their leg bones over her and pressed her feet to the floor too. She grabbed at them with her grave-chilled fingers, wishing them to die, to fall over at her feet into a pile of shuffled bones, but they ignored her.

"Your dragonmark has no power over those already dead," Ibrido said. "Of all the creatures on this ship, only you, I, and the terrified bosun flying this ship still draw breath. They exist to help maintain this ship and to protect me. If I die, they have their orders."

"Which are?" A ball of ice formed in Esprë's gut.

"To kill you. To rend your corpse to pieces. To scatter it across open leagues of land."

One thought speared through Esprë's mind, and she gave voice to it. "What happened to Te'oma?"

The dragon-elf let loose a low, rumbling sound that Esprë guessed was meant to be a laugh.

"We had a parting of the ways," Ibrido said. "She became a loose end, and I tied her off."

"Where is she?" Esprë whispered, barely audible over the whistling wind.

Ibrido pointed a taloned finger over the young elf's shoulder. She turned to gaze out the window and saw that something had been thrown through it from this side: something—or someone—who had probably fallen to her death.

Esprë bowed her head, her shoulders shaking. After a moment, she realized she was crying. How could she mourn for this twisted creature who had brought so much misery into her life? She didn't know. She couldn't explain her sadness to anyone, not even herself. All she could do was give herself over to it or fight it away.

She wept openly and unashamed.

"How ironic," Ibrido said. "If she were here still, you'd be threatening her life as well. Now that she's gone, though, you mourn her passing."

The dragon-elf shook his head. "I do not understand the cruel tricks that fate plays on us all. That one such as you should have a gift like the Mark of Death bestowed upon you is beyond my ability to fathom. Is this a random world in which little makes sense, or is there some higher purpose to this choice that only the gods could possibly understand?"

Anger flared in Esprë's heart. It was one thing for Ibrido to threaten her, but she could not abide being mocked. She kicked and struggled with the skeletons pinning her in place, but she made no headway against them.

As she tired, she glared up at the dragon-elf and said, "Why don't you come a little closer and find out?"

Ibrido snorted at the young elf. Then he spoke to the skeletons. "Release her."

The two creatures let Esprë go and stood up flanking her, ready to move against her again at Ibrido's word. She rubbed the spots on her arms where they had pressed their thin, hard finger bones into her flesh, leaving livid marks. She wondered what the dragon-elf's game might be, but she was willing to let him keep talking while she tried to figure a way out of this trouble.

Ibrido stepped forward until he was only a few feet from Esprë. She gauged the distance, wondering if she could reach out and touch him with her deadly power before he could dodge out of the way. It would be close, she was sure, and she was not ready to take that chance yet.

Then Ibrido leaned down until his snoutlike nose rested only inches from Esprë's face. "Go ahead and give it a try," he hissed through his long, sharp teeth. "You can kill me right here, right now. You can put an end to all of this. It will only cost you your life."

The dragonmark started to burn on Esprë's back. She wondered how it could get so hot and not scorch her shirt. She brought up her right hand, which felt as if she'd plunged it into a snow bank. She raised it toward Ibrido's scaly face but stopped just before touching it.

The dragon-elf bared his teeth again. Esprë could smell old meat and fresh wine on his breath. "You may have something of the killer in you after all," he said. "The changeling doubted it, but I can see it in your eyes. Still, you value life too much to risk tossing away your own, don't you?"

Esprë growled in frustration as she threw herself back against the couch again. The icy sensation in her hand and the fiery one between her shoulder blades ebbed, each seeming to wash away the other.

Ibrido snorted as he stretched to his full height and glared down at Esprë with his unblinking, reptilian eyes.

"I want you to remember this moment," he said. "Etch it in your mind. Think back to it when you are brave enough to consider raising your hand against me again.

"I gave you your chance. I put myself almost literally in your hands. My life could have been yours to devour like an overripe fruit, but you were too cowardly to pluck it."

With that, he spun on his heel and strode out the door. The two skeletons stayed there, standing at either end of the couch, undead escorts who gazed past her with nonexistent eyes.

CHAPTER

37

"Who is your master?" Kandler asked.

Te'oma sat up in the bloodstained bed, the chains hanging from her collar and manacles rattling as she did. "You don't want to know," she said. "It's not important any more."

"Whoever you serve sent you along with a pack of bloodthirsty vampires and Karrnathi skeletons to destroy my town and kidnap my daughter from her own bed. It's important to me."

Kandler had chased this changeling across the whole of the Mournland and through the Talenta Plains into Karrnath. As long as he had her, he was determined to pump as much information out of her as he could.

Te'oma considered his words for a moment, staring up at the justicar with her blank, white eyes. Then she nodded. "I work for the Lich Queen."

She paused for a moment, as if waiting for a bolt of lightning to come crashing out of the clear night sky and strike her down. When it failed to happen, she continued. "Does that mean anything to you?"

"She's a powerful, undead wizard who lives among the pirate nations in the islands to the northeast of here."

Te'oma shook her head. "That's accurate but insufficient. It's like calling a dragon a large lizard. It sells the creature short and illustrates your own ignorance."

In the corner, Burch—who still sat perched in the room's lone window, as he had for hours—lifted his crossbow off his lap and sighted down the length of its loaded bolt. The changeling eyed the tip of that bolt for a moment before turning her attention back to Kandler.

The justicar leaned forward. "Enlighten me," he said.

"The Lich Queen lives in Illmarrow Castle, high in the Fingerbone Mountains, which rise out of the Bitter Sea as the island called Farlnen."

"That's on the northwest side of the Lhazaar Principalities?"

"You're not as ignorant as you seem."

Kandler gave her a mirthless smile. Let her underestimate him. Let her tell him things he already knew. He wasn't here to impress her.

"What does the Lich Queen want with Esprë?" Kandler asked. "Mardakine is a long way from the Bitter Sea."

"The lich queen wasn't always a lich. In her breathing days, she was a powerful wizard by the name of Vol. This was back in the years of the Elf-Dragon War, which pitted the continents of Aerenal and Argonnessen against each other in a bitter conflict.

"Vol's parents were the daughter of the leader of the House of Vol and the most powerful of the green dragons in all of Argonnessen. Their own parents arranged the marriage in an effort to bring the two factions together and perhaps put an end to the war. It did unify the elves and dragons, but not in the way the House of Vol had hoped.

"If love between a dragon and an elf was forbidden in both societies, then an offspring from such a match was an abomination. When news of Vol's birth spread, the leaders of the other elf houses met with the dragon kings and agreed that they must put aside their differences to destroy this abomination and all who had spawned it.

"The resulting battles nearly tore Aerenal apart. The House of Vol had long been one of the most respected and powerful of the elf lines. This was, after all, the house that carried the Mark of Death, the thirteenth and most dangerous of all the dragonmarks. Vol herself bore this mark, which gave the elves and dragons yet another reason to fear her and her power.

"Within a matter of months, the House of Vol was destroyed. According to recorded histories from the time, no one survived. The name of Vol was stripped from the elf libraries and expunged from their conversations. It was as if no one from the house had ever lived."

Kandler had heard some of this before, in bits and pieces, in his travels. His wife Esprina had mentioned the House of Vol, but only as an example of how pride went before the fall. Like most elves, she had a long memory, and she had family members who'd been alive at the time of the crusade against House Vol. According to her, the members of the House of Vol had been involved in some kind of horrible breeding program designed to drive up the numbers of the rare dragonmarks that showed up among elves.

"But the Lich Queen survived," he prompted.

Te'oma nodded, warming to her tale. "Exactly. While the rest of the House of Vol fought for their lives, Vol's parents had her smuggled away to Khorvaire where she could live in safe obscurity. The other houses searched in vain for the young elf for years. Eventually they gave up, declaring that she must have died in one of their many offenses and been lost.

"Vol dedicated herself to revenge. She took to the study of magic, becoming one of the most powerful wizards on the planet. When her life neared its end, she took the next step, something no smaller-minded elf would have ever considered, with their worship of their ascendant councilors. She didn't wait for their Priests of Transition to grant her immortality.

The Undying Court would never have allowed it. She took it for herself.

"She transformed herself into a lich."

Kandler watched the changeling as she spoke. She betrayed a range of emotions about this Vol, which he found curious.

"You admire her," he said.

"Why not?" The thought seemed to surprise Te'oma even as she agreed with it. "Despite the persecution of two of the most powerful groups in the entire world, she not only survives but thrives. She lives on her own terms and has everything she could ever want—but for one thing."

"A digestive system?" Burch said.

Te'oma ignored the shifter. Kandler thought perhaps she rolled her eyes at him, but since they were white throughout he couldn't be sure.

"The Mark of Death."

Kandler shook his head. "You said she bore the mark."

"She did. She does, but there's one problem with dragonmarks, at least from a lich's perspective: You have to be alive to use them.

"To survive forever, Vol had to give up her most personal and incredible powers."

"She literally traded death for immortality."

Te'oma smiled. "Exactly."

"Why does she want Esprë? It's not like she can just steal the dragonmark from her." Kandler paused, a sick feeling in his stomach. "Can she?"

Te'oma frowned and shook her head. "No, but you won't believe the real reason."

"Try me."

Te'oma gazed up at Kandler from her bed and said, "She wants to protect her."

Burch burst into howling laughter from the windowsill. Kandler snapped his head around to glare at the shifter, and he clammed up.

"Tell me how that makes sense," Kandler said to Te'oma. He didn't know what to believe, but his instincts told him that this was too outlandish to be a lie.

"The Lich Queen knew that if she had escaped the purge of the House of Vol, others may have too. The bloodlines in elf society are long and tangled. It was one thing to murder every named member of the House of Vol. It would be another to kill everyone related to them as well. It would have torn Aerenal in half.

"If some of her distant cousins had survived, then the Mark of Death might someday resurface. If it did, it would cause an uproar within Aereni society again, perhaps resulting in another purge, and the bearer would be murdered for sure.

"Vol devoted a portion of her time and magic to searching for any sign of the return of the Mark of Death. Over the centuries, she found a few false clues, but she always remained wary of these lulling her into a false sense of hopelessness. She tracked down every lead, sure that one of them would finally prove true."

"That's how you and those vampires came to Mardakine."

Te'oma nodded. "We lurked around the edges of the town for a few days, until we were sure we'd located the right person. Then the knights showed up, forcing our hand. We struck."

Kandler put a fist up to his mouth for a moment. He put it back down when he noticed the knuckles were white. "Tell me again how this is supposed to be for Esprë's protection."

"Vol wants to bring Esprë to live with her in Illmarrow Castle. There she can train her in the use of the Mark of Death in a way that no one else possibly could. Every other bearer of the mark is long since dead."

"Including Vol."

"She can also hide her there from others who would seek her out, either to kill her or to use her for their own ends." Te'oma spread her arms wide, her chains rattling with the gesture. "Think about it. If the Silver Flame could detect the appearance of the Mark of Death—the first in over three millennia—do you think others don't know about it as well? The Undying Court in Aerenal? The dragon kings of Argonnessen? The Finders Guild? The Lords of Dust? The Deathguard? The Dreaming Dark?"

Kandler nodded.

"Can you protect her from all of them?" Te'oma said in a whisper. "You couldn't even keep her safe from me."

Kandler fought the urge to reach out and strangle the changeling, to twist her neck back into the shape in which Ibrido had left it. Instead, he stood up and walked toward the doorway. Before he left, he shot back over his shoulder.

"Tomorrow's another day."

CHAPTER

38

I t's time," Kandler said as he entered the infirmary. Three human guards stood watching over the changeling, one at the window, one at the door, and a third standing a sword's length away from Te'oma's bed. Berre had sent them in shortly after Kandler left the room last night, with orders to make Burch leave and get some sleep.

Kandler had bumped into the Captain of Bones this morning already, and she'd told him about the switch. He'd thanked her for it. He needed Burch fresh and ready for their trip, no matter where it took him. Berre looked like she'd been on her feet for the entire night, but that was fine. Once *Phoenix* took off, her part in all this would be done.

The changeling sat bolt upright in bed at the sound of Kandler's voice. He wondered if she'd slept at all herself. She looked horrible. Since she was a changeling, the justicar knew that either she'd made herself look like that on purpose or she was too distracted to bother with her appearance at the moment. Her red eyes and puffy face told him she'd been crying.

"All right," she said in a defeated voice, rubbing her eyes.

"Try to contact Esprë," Kandler said.

The changeling closed her eyes and concentrated. She remained silent for a long moment, until Kandler cleared his throat.

"I have her," Te'oma said. "She's unharmed. She's in the captain's cabin on *Keeper's Claw*."

"Where are they headed?"

"She can't tell. From the direction of the sun, they're heading east by northeast, but that's all she knows right now."

"Tell her to stay safe and keep her head down."

Te'oma looked up at the justicar and nodded.

"And tell her I love her. We'll contact her again once we're in the air."

Te'oma smiled. "She knows."

Kandler waited for a moment until he thought the changeling had broken her psionic connection with his daughter. "How is she?" he said. "Is she frightened?"

"No more than you'd expect. That's one tough elf you've raised."

"Living with him will do that to you," Burch said as he walked in through the curtained doorway. "I used to be a gnome."

Kandler ignored the shifter. A thought about the changeling had struck him, and he needed to know the answer now.

"Do you have a mindlink set up with anyone else?" he asked Te'oma.

The changeling froze, then lay back down in the bed. She closed her eyes and nodded without a word.

"With whom?" Kandler asked. "The Lich Queen?"

Te'oma nodded again.

"Have you contacted her recently?"

The changeling didn't move. A growing dread filled Kandler's heart.

"Is that why you've been crying?"

Te'oma's body shook so hard it rattled her chains. She rolled forward into a ball, unable to hold back her tears any longer.

"It looks like I'm not the only one who's failed at his job around here," Kandler said.

"She's dead," Te'oma said softly.

"For centuries," Burch said.

"Not the Lich Queen," Te'oma said, her voice rising to a hysterical note. "My daughter!"

The words shocked Kandler. He couldn't help but feel pity for the changeling, although he didn't imagine she deserved it.

"What happened to her?" he asked.

As the words left his mouth, he regretted saying them. He glanced at Burch, who shot him an insane look. He shrugged at the shifter, not understanding his actions any better than his old friend.

"An angry mob stoned her to death after catching her impersonating their justicar." The changeling wiped the tears from her face with the heels of her hands.

"The Lich Queen couldn't stop that?" The more Kandler knew, the less it seemed he understood.

"She died three years ago," Te'oma said, her voice as raw as her face. "The Lich Queen promised to restore her to life in exchange for my services."

"But now that you failed her, the deal's off."

The changeling nodded, fighting back another round of tears.

"Who's not protecting her family now?" Burch asked, back in his spot on the windowsill.

The changeling leaped off the bed, ready to attack the shifter, but Kandler shoved her back down before she got two steps away.

"Try that again, and I'll break your ankles," he said. "As it is, you're lucky I don't rip those wings off your back."

"They could die," she said, angling her back as far from Kandler and Burch as possible.

"I wouldn't be bothered by that."

"Do you have any other insults you'd like to heap on me, or can we get going now?" Te'oma said.

The wind whipped through Kandler's hair as he stood on the bow of *Phoenix*, shading his eyes with his hand and staring out toward the horizon in some vain hope of spotting a ring of fire floating there. As he brought his gaze back around to focus on the airship, he had to admit that Berre's skeletons had done a fantastic job getting the ship back into shape. Besides being whole once again, it looked better than he'd ever seen it, polished and coated with fresh varnish and paint.

Burch waved at him from where he watched over Te'oma, and the justicar nodded back. They'd chained the changeling in front of the bridge, between it and the hatch that led to the hold, by means of a length of links that led from her collar to a large, solid eyelet bolted through the deck.

Despite her bonds, Te'oma seemed relaxed, almost cheerful. She'd been happy to put Fort Bones far behind her, and her joy put the justicar's suspicions on edge. He still wasn't convinced she wasn't pulling some horrible scam on them, designed to send the heroes in the wrong direction while Ibrido got away. He'd had Monja petition the gods to confirm the truth in the changeling's words, though, and Te'oma had passed that test. Despite that, he knew he could never trust her.

Monja stood atop the railing where the raised bridge overlooked the main deck below, balanced on it with the confidence of a tightrope walker. She grinned into the rising sun, and her attitude infected the justicar enough to bring a tight smile to his lips.

The ring of fire crackled overhead, driving the airship forward at top speed. Kandler imagined that the elemental trapped inside enjoyed moving again, although it might have preferred its freedom. The Karrns' reinforcement of the mystical restraining arcs put that worry to rest for now. They ran from the stern and arced over and under the main part of the ship. At their ends, they held fast opposite sides of the fiery band that encircled the ship like a ring on a finger.

If that ring ever managed to get loose of its restraints, the resultant explosion would consume the entire ship, he'd been told. Kandler preferred not to think about it.

It felt good to be back on the road again, so to speak, even if that path took them a mile into the air. Kandler had always enjoyed traveling, sometimes more than arriving at his destination. The open road called to him in the way seas beckoned sailors.

That was at least part of the reason he'd become an agent of the Citadel back in Sharn. As much as he loved the City of Towers, he couldn't bear to stay in the place for more than a few weeks at a time. That job gave him a chance to serve his country and still not be confined to it.

"Crown for your thoughts," Sallah said as she appeared behind him, wrapping her arms around his chest.

"Who's flying the ship?"

"Monja."

"Is that wise?"

Sallah pursed her lips. "Flying an airship requires a strong personality more than anything else. You have to be able to get the ship's elemental to listen to you and follow your lead. Despite her size, Monja has one of the largest personalities I've ever encountered."

Kandler nodded, satisfied.

"About those thoughts?"

The justicar lowered his head for a moment before he gazed out past the prow and spoke. "All of us, we're on this road together," he said, "each of us with our own past and our own futures. Do any of us know where we're going? Where does it all end?"

"There's an old Thranite proverb," Sallah said, " 'All roads lead to death.' "

Kandler laughed.

"It means," she continued, "that there's no escaping our eventual fate. All of us are doomed to someday die. In the meantime, it's our duty to make the best of the journey that we can."

"I think we can do that," Kandler said, turning in Sallah's arms and tenderly, tentatively kissing her full, pink lips. "As long as we're on that road together."

CHAPTER

39

Esprë stared at the cabin door for a long time. Violent dreams had disturbed her sleep enough that she felt as if she'd never shut her eyes. She might still be trying to rest if a skeleton hadn't brought her a bland bowl of steaming gruel and a skin full of water sometime after dawn. She'd forced herself to eat it, all of it, not knowing how long it might be to her next meal.

Then she sat on the couch and stared at the door. It was thin but solid, polished with a mahogany finish, just like the wood in the rest of the room. A shiny, brass doorknob stuck out of the right side of the door, and matching hinges lined the left side. It opened inward, and a brass sliding bolt and catch sat high on the door's right side to give the captain his privacy.

Esprë considered locking herself in the room and refusing to come out, but that would mean getting rid of her two skeleton guards first. They watched her without pause, their blank eye sockets following her wherever she went. At first, it made her skin crawl, but by the time she woke up this morning, she could ignore it.

The young elf stood up, and the skeletons shifted in

anticipation of accompanying her. Their bones rattled in their ill-fitting armor.

Esprë strode to the door and flung it open. The wind that swirled through the room now had a way to go, and it blew past her, shoving her out on to the airship's main deck.

She gazed out over the deck and into the blue sky beyond. Karrnathi skeletons moved about the place like termites on an old log, busy and silent, performing the dozens of jobs necessary to keep such a massive craft in perfect shape. Some of them swabbed the deck, while others checked the actions on the ballistae mounts that lined the gunwales, keeping them in top condition. Another team of skeletons inspected the restraining arcs that held in place a massive, roaring ring of fire that spanned at least twice as wide as that around *Phoenix*.

Esprë wondered about the creature trapped in that ring, how powerful it must be, and how angry. She hoped to take the ship's wheel sometime and learn more about it. She'd come to enjoy working with the elemental that drove *Phoenix*, coaxing it to move the ship as she wished because it had decided it liked her. She took pride in the fact she'd been able to forge that kind of friendship with the thing. Trapped elementals rarely cared for their masters and often refused to serve those who could not somehow massage their massive egos.

She wondered how Ibrido flew the ship. None of the skeletons could manage it, she knew. It required a forceful personality, which they didn't have.

She spied the dragon-elf standing on the bridge and decided to satisfy her curiosity. She strode across the deck, the winds whipping through her clothes, snapping her long hair around her like a golden banner in a storm.

Ibrido spotted her crossing the ship and waited for her on the deck. As she neared, she saw his hands gripped the ship's wheel like it was a weapon. She thought he might tear the thing off and hurl it into the ring if it disobeyed him.

She wondered, for a moment, what might have happened to the bosun, but she put such thoughts out of her head. If the man was dead, she could do nothing for him. If he was alive, then all the better.

"Good," Ibrido said as Esprë climbed the stairs to the bridge. "I feared you might spend the entire trip in the cabin. This is a view that no one should miss."

Esprë turned to look in the direction the airship charged, and her breath caught in her chest. There, on the horizon, a range of high, snow-capped mountains stretched before her. Below the pure, white peaks, the steep slopes turned a rusty red before tumbling down into leagues of rolling foothills covered with green grasses and the occasional stand of trees. Feathery wisps of clouds, lit a glowing gold by the sun rising behind them, spiraled high in the sky over the mountain-tops, which seemed to stretch from one side of the world to the other.

"Where are we?" she said when she could speak again. She clutched her arms around her for warmth. While the sun promised to heat the land later in the day, standing on the deck reminded her how cool the sky could be.

"We are flying over Karrnath still," Ibrido said. He seemed almost careless about her presence, and his confidence irritated Esprë. She wished she could detect even a hint of fear about him, fear of her nascent powers.

"What are those?" she said, pointing out at the mountains. "I mean, what are they called?"

"The Ironroot Mountains. They mark where Karrnath ends and the lands of the dwarf clans begin. They call the region the Mror Holds, and for the most part their word is law there."

"Is that where we're going?" Esprë held her breath as she waited for the dragon-elf's answer. Would he keep his plans a secret, or would his arrogance loosen his tongue, she wondered.

"It is but the first step on our journey," he said. "We must report in to my superior here in Khorvaire."

"Who is that?"

"Does it matter?"

Esprë looked up at the dragon-elf, who stood a good two feet taller than her. He stared down at her with suspicious eyes.

"Just curious about my fate," she said.

"You could say the same of any of us."

Ibrido returned his attention to the horizon again. Esprë noticed that he hadn't any hair for the wind to ruffle, although it wobbled through the small ridges of horns that ran back from between his eyes and over his wide, batlike ears. They seemed like eyebrows, and their slant gave him an evil, savage look even when he was in a good mood. They fit him well.

"What does your superior want with me?" she asked.

"The last time the Mark of Death appeared, it triggered a crusade that ended with the death of an entire house of elves."

"Why?" Esprë said, horrified.

"To make sure it would never arise again." He looked askance at her. "It seems they missed at least one of your ancestors."

"Wouldn't it be simpler just to kill me?" she asked. She knew she wouldn't like the answer to this, whatever it was, but she had to know why she still lived.

"If they were only interested in picking the Mark of Death like a weed any time it appeared. They want to tear it out by the roots. To do that, they need to learn everything they can about you and your elf family."

"I don't have any family," Esprë said, "just Kandler, and he's no elf. My blood parents are dead."

"They had parents and aunts and uncles and cousins. Any of them might also be able to produce an offspring with the Mark of Death, just like you. They must all be exterminated."

Esprë felt the need to vomit. The thought that her drag-onmark could bring doom to anyone related to her in any way—everyone! She couldn't bear it.

"I don't know any of my relatives," she said, "not even their names. We moved to Khorvaire when I was too young to remember."

"Even if that's true, it matters not. My masters have powerful spells they can weave to learn your history and that of your line. Once they have you in their clutches, they can begin their inquest. This time, they will not make the same mistake. No one will be missed."

"The Undying Court will never let you get away with it," Esprë said. "This will mean war."

Ibrido snorted at that. "You are an amusing child," he said. "How unfortunate that you know so little about the forces that whirl around you."

"What do you mean?" Esprë said.

"Who do you think helped destroy the Mark of Death the last time?"

CHAPTER

40

*E*sprë, are you there?

The changeling's voice rang in the young elf's mind. She'd returned to the captain's cabin and locked the door behind her. She knew that Ibrido could break the door down if he wanted to get to her, but she didn't want him to see her cry.

She'd thought long and hard about everything the dragonelf had told her. Deep down, she knew it all made sense. She didn't want to believe any of it, but the fact that he had stolen her from another kidnapper to whisk her off to the Ironroot Mountains—and then beyond—meant there had to be something to it.

Esprë?

For a long time after she'd left the bridge, Esprë had considered killing herself. It wouldn't be easy. She guessed that Ibrido had given the skeletons orders to protect her if they could. They wouldn't just let her dive through the shattered windows in the front of the captain's cabin. Would they?

Esprë had been working up the courage to try when the changeling contacted her again. Would the girl's death put an end to the plans to destroy everyone who shared any kind

of blood with her, or would it be some kind of pointless gesture? She'd heard that powerful priests could raise even the
ancient dead back to life. Her persecutors no doubt had access
to such power.

Esprë?

"Yes," the young elf said aloud, "I'm here. She glanced at
her skeletal jailors, but they remained as impassive as ever.

Thank the Host. Where are you?

"I'm back in the captain's cabin." Esprë wondered if the
changeling could hear the rawness in her voice. She didn't
want her to know she'd been crying either.

You got out onto the deck?

"Yes, and the bridge."

Can you tell where you're going?

"I've never been to this part of the world before. I don't
recognize anything."

Of course. What direction are you heading?

"Still east by northeast, I think."

Do you see any landmarks around you? Anything we could use to steer by?

"We're heading for the Ironroot Mountains. At least
that's what Ibrido says."

Ibrido? You spoke with him?

Esprë looked up at the skeletons. They hadn't moved since
she started talking to Te'oma over their mindlink. Could they
hear her? Even if so, could they report what she said to their
master? They couldn't speak for sure. Could they write? Use
hand signals?

She didn't think so.

"Yes. He's flying the ship."

Do you think there's a way you could get free?

Esprë shook her head, even though she knew Te'oma
couldn't see her. "No. He's ordered the skeletons to kill me if
anything happens to him."

Damn.

Esprë waited for a moment. "Are you still there?"

Yes. I'm sorry. I was relating things to Kandler.

"Tell him I love him."

He knows.

"Tell him anyhow."

I will.

"Ibrido says he's taking me away."

We won't let that happen.

"How are you going to stop it?"

We're—we're working on that.

"We're going to visit someone living in the Mror Holds first."

A dwarf? This doesn't seem like the work of the Iron Council.

Esprë shrugged, even though she knew Te'oma couldn't see it. "How far behind me are you?"

We have no way of knowing. We're coming after you as fast as we can.

"We should reach the mountains soon."

Do what you can to delay Ibrido. The longer you stay in the mountains, the better our chance to catch up with you.

"I think *Phoenix* moves faster than this airship. Ibrido is mean to the elemental. Maybe it doesn't move so quickly for him, or maybe it's because the ship is so big."

Just keep alert. Do you think Ibrido suspects I'm talking to you?

"I don't see how he could." Esprë looked up at the skeletons. They still hadn't moved. "I've been careful."

Be sure you keep it that way. We need you alive.

"You mean *you* need me alive. Isn't that why you're helping Kandler now? Once you rescue me from Ibrido, aren't you just going to try to kidnap me yourself again?"

Don't be silly.

"I'm not being silly. I'm not a little girl. I'm older than you."

I'm sorry. I—I don't have any plans to kidnap you again. Once we get you back, I'll sit down with Kandler, and we'll figure out what's best for you.

"Don't you mean what's best for *you*? What about your daughter?"

For a long moment, the only thoughts in Esprë's head were her own.

"Well?"

I failed the Lich Queen. She put an end to our agreement.

"Even if you manage to get me back and deliver me to her anyhow?"

She doesn't think that's possible.

"You do. Don't think I trust you for a minute. Be sure to tell Kandler that too."

You don't need to worry about that. If you could see me right now, you'd know he doesn't trust me either. He has me chained to the deck by a collar, and that shifter friend of his watches me constantly.

Esprë laughed at the image that leaped into her mind. "Good."

A fist hammered at the door. Esprë stayed locked to her seat, but one of the skeletons got up and slid the bolt aside.

"I have to go," she whispered.

I'll try to contact you again later then. Keep yourself safe.

The door opened, and a third skeleton entered the room. It pointed at Esprë with a long, thin finger bone. She stood up and followed it from the cabin without a word, the wind pushing her from the place once again.

Ibrido waited for her on the bridge, his green scales glinting in the midday sun. The bosun, a reedy man who looked to have been left out to dry too long in the sun, stood at the wheel this time. He eyed the girl carefully, without a trace of hope in his eyes, only the desperate glare of a cornered animal that knew it had been outmatched. Esprë decided that this one would be no help to her.

The dragon-elf bared his teeth at her as she stepped up on to the bridge and walked over next to him. "There it is," he said, indicating a tall, snowy peak that towered over everything else for miles around, "Mount Darumkrak."

Esprë stared at the mountain from top to bottom as they scudded near it, already slowing down. She thought she detected a plume of smoke escaping from somewhere near the peak. "Does your superior live at the top?"

Ibrido shook his head. "That smoke comes from the forge fires of the clan of misfit dwarves who live like sparrows tucked into the eaves of his roof. They believe they have walled him into his lair, but there is nothing the pathetic creatures of Clan Drakyager could do to keep him trapped."

"He lives with them?"

"His home is an underground lake deep beneath the mountain's roots, a swamp of sorts in which he lets his food fester before he devours it."

Esprë craned her neck around. "How do we get to it then?"

"We will moor the ship over there," he said, pointing toward a tall stand of pines. "Then we will descend via a rope ladder, along with a skeletal escort. Once we reach the lair, only you and I will enter though. He has a taste for bones, and he would devour the first skeleton he saw."

Keeper's Claw inched closer to its mooring point. A few skeletons stood along the port gunwale, twirling loose ropes and looking for a tree to tie the ship to.

"Do we both have to go?" Esprë said. "It sounds dangerous."

"It can be," Ibrido said, "but those are my orders. I'm to present you to him right away. He will then decide exactly what's to be done with you. He might eat you on the spot."

Esprë's stomach flipped over on her. She'd hoped to figure out a way to stay behind on the ship until *Phoenix* caught up with them. She wondered if she could make herself vomit. The dragon-elf might not push her for a bit if he figured she was sick.

"I don't feel—"

She never got to finish her sentence. A loud explosion rocked the airship and sent her reeling toward the rear rail of the bridge.

CHAPTER

41

Duro Darumnakt saw the airship coming from leagues away. "In all my years," he said to his younger cousin Wolph as they watched the craft, "I've never seen an invader show himself so plainly."

The ring of fire stood out strong and bright, even in the midday sun. At first Duro had thought it was the sunlight glinting off something hard and metal in the distance, but it never once twinkled the way you'd expect a reflected light to do as it moved through the air, unless it targeted you on purpose.

Soon he had realized the light burned with its own energy. He thought it might be a bit of glowing gases emerging from the swamp near the foothills of the mountain, right where the streams that spilled down from the melting snowpack melded together into a shallow delta before gathering themselves into the headwaters of a creek that wound its way toward lower lands. Perhaps it was a will-o-the-wisp playing around those murky waters, hoping to lure unwary prey to its doom.

The light grew too steadily and came at him in too straight a line. When he saw it was not a ball of light but a ring, he knew it could only be trouble. He sounded the alarm and brought his kin to gather around him near the secret gate he'd been charged with watching that afternoon.

At first, not all of them had believed him. Many of the stragglers had heard too many false alarms over the years to give such sounds much credence, but they came anyhow. Even if it wasn't the emergency it should have been—and turned out to be—they figured they wouldn't want to miss the chance to mock whoever had set the alarm off.

"It's an airship," Duro had told them.

By the time he had an audience worth talking to, he was sure. "I saw these things during the Last War. The Karrn used them as troop transports and sometimes in battle too. They move faster than any mount, and they can carry an entire platoon of troops into a fight before their foes can react."

"What can we do about such a thing?" Kallo had asked. The young dwarf liked to play at being a great warrior, but he had yet to be blooded, and everyone knew it.

"We should retreat into the caves and wait for them to come to us," had said Medd Karaktrok. "We can make our stand there in our element, where none can hope to prevail against us."

"Where they can trap us like rats in a blind hole," Duro had said, shaking his head. He thanked the Sovereign Host that the Clan Drakyager elders had seen fit to give him this command and not entrusted it to one of his slow-witted friends. "We make our stand out here on the mountain's face. If things turn against us, we will retreat into the caves where we can rally a counterattack."

"Who could hope to 'turn things against' the sons of the Ironroot Mountains?" Shano had said, a broad grin across his wide, white-bearded face as he hefted his battle-notched axe.

Duro had often wondered how Shano had survived to such a ripe old age with such ill-considered notions rattling around in his head. Perhaps the Host did smile on drunks and fools, for Shano qualified as both. Duro thought he might even have been intoxicated at that moment, perhaps along with a few of his younger brothers. He knew they had secreted a still somewhere on the mountainside, despite the way their last such efforts had brought down a section of the caves on their heads when it exploded.

"Get the shockbolts ready," Duro said. "With luck, we can use them to blow the thing out of the air before anyone has the chance to disembark."

Medd gasped at the plan. "You know those are only to be used in the direst circumstances. We only have five of the magical bolts, and each is worth a year's wages for any of us. You risk much."

Duro handed Medd his spyglass at that point so the rock-brained dwarf could see for himself. "I'd say that a Karrnathi airship crafted to look like a giant, hungry skeleton might just qualify as a 'dire circumstance.'"

Medd stared through the spyglass for a long moment before handing it back to Duro. "Host preserve us," he said, "I fear you are correct."

From there, the others scrambled into their designated positions, ready to launch themselves into battle as soon as Duro fired the first of the shockbolts. Standing alone on the rocky lookout point, Duro cradled the shockbolts in his hands before slipping one of them home into his crossbow. It was the same shape as a regular bolt, but it felt heavier in his hand, dense like gold or lead. He could not read most of the runic letters carved into its steely surface, except for the few along one edge that stated in clear, simple Dwarvish, "Use with utmost caution."

He waited for the airship to come closer and closer. He treated it as a test of his nerves, to see if he'd loose the bolt before the airship came into range. He wouldn't have more than one or two chances before the Karrns aboard the craft retaliated. He had to make sure his first attack found its mark.

The air itself seemed to warp as the airship neared, its ring of fire devouring the atmosphere all around it as it passed. It crackled louder in Duro's ears than any bonfire, and it was all he could do to sight along the shockbolt in his crossbow and aim it square at the craft's hull. As he waited for it to come closer, it seemed to grow larger and larger until it blotted out most of the sky.

He heard Wolph shouting at him over the noise. "Loose!" the young dwarf yelled. "Loose!"

He held off a moment longer, just another moment longer, until it seemed that the heat of the ring of fire might singe the ends of his forked and braided beard. Then he pulled the trigger and stared after the shockbolt as it sped toward its monstrous target, the gaping mouth of the skeletal masthead that promised a swift and painful death to all that crossed its path.

The shockbolt slammed into the masthead and exploded with such force that Duro wondered that the mountain didn't come crashing down on his head in response. The airship rocked backward like it had struck a reef. A number of bodies catapulted over the gunwales and crashed toward the rocky slope below.

Even before the smoke had cleared, Duro loaded the next shockbolt into his crossbow. He hoped that the first bolt would be enough to scare off the ship, perhaps even disable it, but he wasn't willing to bet his life on it.

When the smoke around the airship cleared, Duro's ears still rang louder than the cave bells announcing the Winter Feast. He ignored the fact he couldn't hear anything else and peered up through the vanishing smoke to see that he'd blasted the masthead's carved face clean off the craft.

Wolph came up from behind Duro and smacked him on the back, letting loose a war cry neither of them could hear. Duro grinned back at his cousin, pleased—despite his pessimistic nature—at how much damage he'd done.

Then a bolt fired from the ship took Wolph through the neck.

The younger dwarf fell over backward, clutching at his throat. He smashed his head against the rocks behind him, denting his helmet and cracking his skull.

Not knowing if Wolph lived yet or not, Duro brought up his crossbow and loosed the second of the shockbolts at the airship. This one sailed wide of its mark and skittered off the hull at an oblique angle. It sailed straight into the ring of fire, which set it off.

The explosion shoved the airship up as if it had run aground. The break in the ring of fire, though, brought it slamming down toward the mountainside. It righted itself only a dozen feet shy of crashing into splinters.

Duro turned to check on Wolph and saw blood trickling from under his cousin's helmet. He knelt next to the young dwarf and saw by the blank roll to his eyes that he was dead.

"May Dol Arrah guide your spirit home," he whispered as he closed Wolph's eyes. He wondered how he would explain this to his aunt and uncle, to his parents. Then another bolt ricocheted off his own helmet, knocking it from his head.

"Retreat!" he bellowed at the top of his lungs as he picked up Wolph's corpse and tossed it over his back. "Fall back!" he yelled, hoping the others could hear him over the angry crackling of the ring of fire and the ringing that might sound in their ears too.

He'd made it only a handful of steps before the first Karr-nathi skeleton landed on the rocky slope behind him.

CHAPTER

42

"Get down!" Ibrido shouted, shoving Esprë to the bridge's deck. The ship rocked back from the force of the explosion, throwing her toward the rear railing. She came up hard against it instead of going over it as some of the less fortunate skeletons did.

Ibrido crashed into the railing next to her, and it flashed through Esprë's mind that she should try to shove him up and over it. He righted himself before she could act on the thought though.

If the bosun hadn't been strapped to the console—or perhaps chained, it now seemed—Esprë was sure he'd have been knocked away from it too. As it was, his white-knuckled grasp never left the wheel, and the ship started to weave back and forth in an insane effort to avoid another blast.

"Crossbows!" the dragon-elf shouted. "Find your targets, and loose your bolts!"

A group of skeletons gathering near the front of the ship each snatched up a crossbow off a rack of them near the bow, loaded the weapons, and peered down over the prow, hunting for whatever it was that had attacked the ship. Ibrido glanced down at Esprë, who still huddled against the rail, and said, "Stay down!"

With that, the dragon-elf sprinted toward the bow. Esprë scrambled to her feet and peered out over the bridge to watch him run. She noticed he had the strange loping gait of a large lizard.

Before Ibrido could reach the bow, though, the Karrnathi skeletons seemed to find a target. A handful of them loosed their crossbows toward the ground, and the sound of someone's dying wail rewarded them.

Esprë looked over at the bosun, who seemed to be smiling, or perhaps he bore a grimace of pain. She wondered if he might help her if she freed him.

Before that could happen, though, another explosion went off. This time, it came from underneath the ship, to the starboard side. It lifted the airship up several feet in the air, knocking Esprë to her knees.

Then, before she could recover, the ship fell toward the ground as if someone had shoved it off the edge of a cliff. Esprë clung to the railing around the bridge as she felt her feet lift up off the bridge, and she screamed right along with the bosun's wordless voice.

Esprë was sure that this was her death. The airship would smash into the mountain's face and then tumble down the quarter mile to the foothills. If she was lucky, she'd be thrown clear before the restraining arcs holding the elemental ring of fire in place broke. When that happened, the explosion would make whatever had knocked the airship from the sky seem like a distant thunderclap. It would consume the entire ship and anything near it.

"No!" Esprë shouted at the bosun as the ship plummeted to the rocks below. "Up! Up! Up!"

Just before the ship smashed into the mountainside, the ring of fire managed to reconstitute itself, and the craft came to a bouncing stop. Esprë didn't know how near they were to the ground, but she suspected it was far too close.

The hard stop hurled Esprë to the deck. She landed flat on her chest, knocking the air from her lungs. It took her a moment before she could reach her feet again.

When she did, she saw Ibrido standing at the ship's bow, shouting for a skeleton landing party to disembark. "Go!" he said to them. "Get those dwarves! Kill them all! Make them pay!"

The skeletons slipped over the gunwales on thin ropes, sliding down faster than any flesh-covered hands could manage. Some of them carried crossbows, but all of them bore long, curved scimitars as well. A few of them clamped the blades in their teeth before taking the rope in their hands and diving overboard to the ground below.

Esprë heard shouts from below and the clash of metal on metal. She rushed to the railing on the starboard side of the bridge and looked down to see what was happening. There, on the mountainside, she saw a pair of skeletons pull a screaming dwarf from his hiding place and start carving him into pieces. Another dwarf—this one with a long, silver beard he kept tucked into his wide, leather belt—leaped into the fray with a double-handed grip on his heavy warhammer. With a single, mighty swing, he shattered the helmet of one skeleton and the skull hiding beneath it.

The other turned and stabbed the dwarf right through the thigh. He fell backward, clutching his injured leg and tumbling down the mountainside. Esprë thought perhaps he was the lucky one. A third skeleton came up to join the other, and together they made quick work of the cowardly dwarf, who'd gone from screaming to simple whimpering as he tried to hide behind his shield. The skeletons systematically tore the dwarf's defense to pieces and then continued to do the same to him without a pause.

Esprë gasped in horror but found herself unable to turn away. Ever since she'd realized that her dragonmark was the Mark of Death, she'd become more and more interested in how people died, and she'd rarely seen a battle like this. She'd witnessed the conflict in Construct, but that had been Kandler and the others fighting for their lives against those two warforged titans and the juggernaut known as Bastard.

Somehow, the struggle going on below her seemed much more personal and real. Perhaps it was her gods'-eye perspective on the battlefield. From her vantage point, she could see no fewer than five different hard-fought conflicts pitting dwarf against skeleton, the desperate living against the implacable undead.

The dwarves grunted, cursed, spit, and bled as they fought. They panted loudly as they swung their hammers and axes. They cried out in pain when injured, and they roared in victory when they struck a solid blow against their foes.

In contrast, the skeletons uttered not a word. The only sound they made was the rattling of their bones in their armor and the clash of their blades on the shields, the weapons, and even the flesh of their foes. The dead dealt death and misery wherever they went, but they took no joy in it, and their compatriots shed no tears when they fell. They were only tools made of bone, emotionless contraptions forged from the violated remains of the dead and turned into killing machines.

Esprë watched as one dwarf tossed another over his shoulder—wounded or dead, she couldn't tell—and shouted for a retreat. His words came too late for many of his fellows. Some of them already lay dead, and others could not break away from their foes for fear of being struck down as they fled.

One dwarf faced with a pair of skeletons decided to give running a try. Even though he had been born to this rugged land and could climb the slopes better than a mountain ram, the longer-legged skeletons chased him down within only a few yards. One of them slashed him across the back of his legs, hamstringing him, and he fell to his knees with a bitter roar. He struck back with his warhammer, smashing his attacker's rib cage and spine to tiny bits.

The creature's entire structure gave way, and it collapsed on top of the dwarf, showering him with bones. As it fell, its compatriot hacked into the terrified dwarf's arm, cutting through sinew to the bone. His weapon fell away from his useless hand and tumbled back down the slope, far out of his reach.

The dwarf roared in frustration and hurled himself at the skeleton with his one good arm, blood trailing behind him from his other arm and legs. He fell upon the creature, and the two rolled down the slope in an uncontrollable double cartwheel. The spectacular fall ended only when the pair cascaded off a small ridge and came smashing down onto the rocks below. The dwarf landed atop the skeleton, smashing it to pieces, but he smacked his own head open on a pointed rock as he went, dashing his brains behind him.

Esprë screamed as a rough, scaly hand landed on her shoulder. She spun about, terrified, to find Ibrido staring down at her with his unblinking eyes. He bared his teeth at her, and she cringed.

"It is beautiful, is it not?" he said to her. "The ballet of battle, the dance of death. It is poetry at its most savage and desperate, each stanza featuring a victor and a vanquished."

"It's horrible," Esprë said. "Disgusting."

Ibrido nodded. "It is all that and more, but somehow you can't bring yourself to stop watching it, can you?"

The dragon-elf's words rang true, but Esprë refused to admit it, even to herself. The sight of the battle had frozen her with fear, she told herself. She wasn't some kind of voyeur of death. Right?

Esprë curled up on the deck, hugging her knees to her chest and closing her eyes. The dragonmark between her shoulder blades began to burn. She wondered if it had some kind of a mind of its own. Would it start talking to her someday, if it grew large or powerful enough? Or would that just be her mind cracking if that happened?

With all that pounded at her these days, she sometimes

feared for her sanity. She didn't think she could be blamed if it somehow gave way. She was far too young to be expected to carry such a burden as her dragonmark, and the series of kidnappings, and the fact that a continent—or perhaps two—full of the most dangerous creatures in the world wanted her, and everyone who could possibly be related to her dead.

Esprë threw back her head and screamed. The earpiercing blast forced Ibrido to step back and cover his ears. The sound hurt Esprë's head, which made her scream even louder and longer, as she channeled every bit of her frustration and fear into it.

At that moment, Esprë was sure that Kandler, Te'oma, Burch, Xalt, and Sallah would never catch up with her. She was on her own, and she was doomed to be torn to pieces—physically, mentally, and spiritually—by the most ancient and evil inhabitants of Eberron.

The dark powers of the Mark of Death surged into Esprë's hands, freezing them into the shapes of claws. They glowed black with her unimpeded wrath, and the color—or absence of it—snaked up around her arms and danced across her shoulders.

Ibrido stepped back at the sight of the vengeful young elf, and for the first time she saw fear in his reptilian eyes. A laugh leaped to her lips and burst from her mouth in savage delight as she jumped to her feet and reached for the dragon-elf.

"You do not know the powers you toy with," she told Ibrido as she stretched toward him, determined to put an end to him, no matter what the skeletons might do to her afterward. They would be too late to save him, and at the moment that seemed it would be enough.

Ibrido's fist flashed out and caught Esprë squarely on the chin. She went sprawling back onto the bridge's railing, blood spiraling out from her face. Before she could recover, the dragon-elf waded in under her defenses and beat her senseless.

Esprë felt her power fading, waning from her under Ibrido's relentless battery. She tried to grab at him again, but he knocked her to the ground with a blow to her temple, and all the fight ran out of her.

"Neither," Ibrido said, as she collapsed to the deck, "do you."

CHAPTER

43

Chains rattled in Esprë's ears as she regained her senses. They hung from manacles on her wrists, and a set of walking bones dressed in battered Karrnathi armor held their other ends.

"No more time for sleeping," she heard Ibrido's voice say. "We have an engagement to keep."

She shaded her eyes against the afternoon sun, which stabbed lances of pain into her brain, and stared up at the dragon-elf, who towered nearby but out of reach. She cursed herself for her foolishness. She should have known better than to attack a trained warrior barehanded, even with hands flowing with the deadly energy of her dragonmark. If she was going to kill him, she should have bided her time, waited for the right moment, and struck. Only when his guard was down would he be vulnerable, and now she had guaranteed that he would not be so incautious around her perhaps ever.

A pair of skeletons escorted her to the starboard gunwale. She couldn't say if they were the same two that had watched over her in the captain's cabin, but she supposed it didn't matter. One dead body was the same as another.

The skeletons made the perfect soldiers. They obeyed

their orders without question. Being already dead, they had no fear of death. Since they all seemed equal in skill and talent, they could be swapped in and out of positions at will.

Best of all—from Ibrido's point of view, at least—Esprë's powers were useless against them. You couldn't make the dead any deader.

The young elf followed along after the skeleton that held her chains and peered over the edge of the ship. A rope ladder hung there, leading down to a level spot on the mountain's slope. She rubbed her aching temple and turned to glare at Ibrido.

"I don't think I can climb down there with these chains on," she said.

The dragon-elf bared his teeth, though whether in amusement or frustration, Esprë could not tell. "I suggest you hold onto them tightly," he said.

Then he pointed to the skeleton paired with the one holding her chains. "Put her on the ground," he said.

The skeleton reached out with its bony hands and grabbed Esprë under the arms. She shrieked and kicked at the creature with all her terrified might, but her blows glanced off its armor. She grabbed on to her chains above her manacles, just before the skeleton heaved her over the side of the ship.

Esprë screamed as she tumbled toward the rocks below and then again as the chains caught short, the other ends held firm in the grasp of the skeleton above. The manacles scraped against her wrists, biting into the skin there and drawing blood. Her arms felt like they might pull from their sockets, but they held. She looked down to see her feet swinging a mere yard from the hard, unforgiving ground.

The skeleton above played out the chains, lowering Esprë to the ground. When her feet rested on the rocks, she sighed in relief and rubbed the blood from her injured arms. After her last outburst, she wondered if Ibrido hoped to anger her again or put her in her place. Either way, she refused to give him the satisfaction. She mastered her temper, and she stuck out her chin, determined to see this through with the grace her mother had always shown.

Esprë's outburst had frightened her as much as anyone, probably more than Ibrido. She had never felt the power of her dragonmark course through her like that. She had been sure that nothing could stand against her—right up until the dragon-elf smacked her to the deck. The humiliation of her miscalculation burned in her more than the scrapes along her wrists.

A pair of skeletons escorted her away from the rope ladder, and Ibrido crept down in their wake. He shouldered past her and followed a path in the stone that she hadn't seen until he started down it. The skeletons grabbed her by the elbows and pulled her along after him.

The path narrowed, and one skeleton walked in front of Esprë while the other followed close behind. The slope dropped away dozens of feet onto stunted trees and sharp rocks to her right, and to her left the cliff face became so steep as to be unscalable. She held her breath and focused on looking straight ahead of her as she walked, concentrating on the solid breastplate of the skeleton in front of her, grateful that it wore some kind of armor so she couldn't just see straight through it. The path continued up for a while before it turned into a small hole secreted behind a thick clump of gnarled bushes rooted in the side of the cliff.

Esprë balked outside the hole, but the skeleton in front of her gave a firm tug on her chains, and she followed it into the darkness beyond. As her eyes adjusted to the dimness, she saw that she was inside a small, dry cave no larger than the main room in the house she'd shared with Kandler in Mardakine.

Ibrido uncapped an everburning torch and handed it to the skeleton standing between him and Esprë. The creature passed it back to the young elf, who held it up before her.

"The rest of us do not need the light," Ibrido explained, "but I'd prefer that you didn't slip into a bottomless shaft by some sick twist of fate."

As an elf, Esprë's eyes were better than Kandler's in the dark, but the pitch black of an unlit cave would have blinded her as well. She nodded at the dragon-elf, not in thanks but for him to proceed.

They crept through the caves for some time, always working their way lower and lower. Most of the passages were natural, but some had been carved by skilled hands and reinforced to keep them from collapsing. Esprë had never been in such a place, but she recognized the handiwork of dwarves. Temmah, one of Kandler's deputies back in Mardakine, had often spun tales of such glories for her, locked deep away in his ancestral home in the Mror Holds. These were no crude tunnels but clean passageways cut from the living rock by skilled hands.

Even so, the passages seemed long unused. Dust kicked up around Esprë's feet as she walked, and a stale smell permeated the place. Underneath it lay a subtle stench of rot that grew as they worked their way deeper into the mountain.

At one point, the passage emerged into a large chamber, so expansive that the light from Esprë's torch could not reach the ceiling or the opposite wall. Tall pillars of stone stabbed high into the vaulted darkness, each carved with intricate statuary that depicted ancient tales of the dwarf clans that Esprë hadn't the time to study or comprehend. Graffiti marred some of these, scrawled in some sub-literate hand, pictograms that seemed to speak of violence, blood, and death. In other places, rubble from the carvings littered the floor where they'd been torn down or broken to pieces with hammers and axes.

Esprë gawked as she moved through the chamber, and several times the skeleton leading her had to yank on her chains to bring her along. As an elf, Esprë knew that she would—could, at least—live for many centuries. If the Undying Court somehow allowed her to ascend into its ranks, she might walk this world for millennia untold. As young as she was now, though, she had only the barest idea of what this entailed, and the thought of things as old and full of history as this chamber standing abandoned and unused filled her with sadness.

"This was once the Great Hall of Clan Drakyager," Ibrido said. His voice echoed in the empty darkness, bouncing from distant walls at which Esprë could only guess. "They were a wealthy and powerful line in those bygone days, but they fell into decadence and could not stand against the Jhorash'tar orcs who overran this part of the mountains a hundred years ago."

Esprë stopped and gaped at what little of the hall she could see at once. To her delight, Ibrido halted as well, and the skeleton leading her by her chains stopped next to him. The other skeletons that walked with them clustered about them for a moment, an earless audience of the dead.

"Who were those dwarves who attacked us as we approached then?" she asked.

The dragon-elf snorted. "The remnants of that once-proud clan. The Iron Council in Krona Peak granted them the right to attempt to return here in exchange for accepting a solemn duty, a responsibility with which none of the other clans cared to be charged."

"What was that?" Esprë brought her torch closer to one of the pillars and saw a carving of a great dwarf king sitting atop a mound of gold and jewels. Its head was missing, and several empty spots stared back at her from the carving, possibly where real jewels had once rested before being pried out by trespassers and thieves.

"Guarding the home of my superior, of course." Esprë could see Ibrido's bared teeth glowing softly in the torchlight. "Come now," he said. "Our host will be waiting."

CHAPTER

44

From the Great Hall, the procession turned left and down, even deeper into the mountain's roots. The passages became rougher and rougher as they went, until the smoothness of the floor was the only sign that anyone had ever been here before.

The walls turned blacker here too. Esprë reached out with her hand and felt the wetness on them, as if they were soaked through with untold millennia of water that had run through them since shortly after the world had been born. The air became humid, nothing like the clean, dry stuff from the caverns' upper reaches, and the stench of rot grew stronger, filling her nostrils until her lungs ached for a taste of the untainted sky.

After what seemed like an endless series of twists and turns, the procession came to a halt. Esprë followed her skeletal keeper into a large room filled with other skeletons. Some of these were of the Karrnathi variety, standing tall and dressed in various pieces of armor, waving about the swords that seemed to be forever grasped in their bony hands. Others lay scattered on the floor in pieces, bare of flesh but held together by rotted bits of clothing and the occasional mail shirt. Most of these were short—no taller than Esprë, she guessed—but broad. Others stood taller but even wider and had long, savage tusks spearing out of aggressive underbites.

The room bore carvings like those in the Grand Hall, but they seemed fresher and less polished, the fruit of less-skilled hands. Whereas the others had depicted legends of all sorts, these showed only images of war, pitched battles between the dwarves of Clan Drakyager—their shields bore an icon of a sparkling diamond, just as Esprë had seen on the statuary above—and their orc foes.

A slab of cast iron comprised the wall opposite of where Esprë and the others had come in. It had once been smooth and polished, the young elf guessed, but the constant exposure to the damp had rusted the surface a cracked and burnt red. Some of the pictographs she'd seen above appeared here too, splashed across the iron wall in some crude attempt at a mural that only served to horrify with both its subjects and its style.

Ibrido stood before the rusted iron wall. His boots disappeared into inches of black, unwholesome water that covered the floor. His hands rubbed at the center of the wall, removing flakes of rust as large as the leaves of the maples that Esprë had climbed in during her early childhood in Cyre.

The skeleton holding Esprë's chains gave them a tug, and she followed him into the frigid water, which swallowed her shoes and soaked her up past her ankles. She splashed after him as close as she could, not wanting to stumble into the water and be dragged through it to where Ibrido waited.

The dragon-elf nodded at her as she came up. Then he took a hammer from one of the nearby skeletons—a dwarf that had probably died defending this chamber many years ago—and smashed it into the iron wall in the center of the spot at which he'd been peeling the rust away.

A dent appeared where the hammer struck. Ibrido

grunted and swung the weapon again and again. After three blows, an outline appeared around the dents, a series of cracks that defined a square about a foot wide.

Ibrido set to the square with a flurry of blows that echoed throughout the skeleton-packed chamber like rolling thunder. The sounds from beyond the iron slab came back a spilt-second later but no less loud.

The dragon-elf puffed with the effort, and the blows came less frequently and powerfully than before. Soon he gave up, his arms hanging like the branches of a willow at his sides, limp and useless. He cursed between panting breaths and dropped the hammer. It disappeared into the black waters around his feet.

The skeletons stood like statues throughout this, never twitching a single knucklebone. It seemed that they were part of the decorations here and that only Esprë bore witness to Ibrido's efforts and his failure.

The young elf laughed. The first giggle escaped from her throat before she could stop it. When Ibrido's yellow reptilian eyes narrowed at her, the giggle grew to a guffaw, and she soon found herself howling uncontrollably, tears flowing down her reddened face.

"Do not mock me!" Ibrido said, showing the first emotion Esprë had ever seen in the creature. He reached out with his taloned hand and wrapped it around her throat. With it, he lifted her inches off the ground and snarled in his face.

"*Never* mock me," he hissed into her face.

For a moment, Esprë feared the dragon-elf would sink his vicious teeth into her face. She felt the dragonmark itching, begging for her to scratch it by letting it loose. Before she could act on that impulse, though, something on the inside of the iron slab banged back.

Ibrido hurled the young elf into the arms of the skeleton that held her chains and spun to glare at the door. The furious look of defeat on his face turned to one of triumph.

The banging sounded again and again, and Esprë noticed that a new set of cracks had formed in the rusted wall. These were set in a square at least twice as tall as her and just as wide, right in the middle of the slab.

"Back," Ibrido ordered her and the skeletons. The creatures pressed against the walls to either side of the iron slab. The skeleton holding Esprë dragged her into the corner to the right of the slab and kept itself between her and the noise.

A horrifying roar sounded on the other side of the slab. Esprë had never heard anything like it, but it chilled her to the bone. Had she not been chained to the skeleton shoving her into the corner, she would have broken and run straight back up the twisting hallways that had led them here, until she reached the sun and fresh air again.

Then the cracked section of the iron slab smashed inward, blasting past Esprë, Ibrido, and the Karrnathi skeletons. Some of the other remains, the ones that were lying against the slab, shattered from the impact, smashing to tiny pieces. The sound of the section of the iron wall clanging against the opposite wall deafened the young elf for a moment, and she closed her eyes and ears, pleading for it to stop.

When she opened her eyes again, Esprë saw Ibrido beckoning her skeletal escort to bring her along after him through the new-made hole in the slab, which now seemed like a perfectly cut doorway. As the skeleton tugged at her chains, she pulled back against it and screamed.

A trio of skeletons broke off from the others and grabbed at her from all angles. Their sharp fingers, uncushioned by flesh, snatched at her and pulled her up off her feet. As she struggled, caught in their many grasps like a fly in a spider's web, they hauled her over to the doorway and followed Ibrido through.

Once beyond the iron slab, Esprë fell silent. The air in the massive cavern felt oppressive, thick and cloying, stinking with the rot of the swamp, the grave. It filled her lungs and quieted her voice with a paralyzing sense of menace.

The young elf stopped struggling against the skeletons that carried her, and at a signal from Ibrido they set her back down on her feet. She landed in more of the frigid, pitch-black water, this time reaching up past her knees. She shivered, but not from the cold.

She realized she still clutched the everburning torch, and she held it up high in the air over her, peering out into the distance, looking for some sign of whatever it was that had made that terrifying roar.

The torch seemed small and insignificant against the darkness surrounding her. Esprë had never wanted her mother more in her life than at that moment. If she couldn't have her—and she knew, in the deepest recesses of her heart, that it was impossible—then Kandler would do. Where was he? she wondered.

Te'oma had told her that they pursued her in the refurbished *Phoenix*, but could she trust a thing the changeling told her? For all she knew, Te'oma was still in league with Ibrido, off someplace else on another mission of evil, just using her telepathy to give the young elf enough hope that she wouldn't take her own life in a brave attempt to put an end to all the horrible plots that swirled around her.

Something foul, like the stench of a latrine, assaulted Esprë's nostrils. Staring out across the water to the limits of the torch's light, she saw bubbles bursting on the black surface. She wrinkled her nose at the swamp gases that something below had stirred up.

Then the waters in front of her erupted, splashing forward and drenching her from head to toe. Standing there, shuddering in the icy waters, she looked up and saw a pair of orangish eyes glowing down at her from the darkness, each of them larger than a pumpkin. Then a set of teeth, each of which was half as long as Esprë and set in a monstrous, black-scaled snout, slipped forward from the gloom. From behind them, a low, loud laugh rumbled, and somewhere in the darkness she heard the flapping of wet, leathery wings.

The sounds shattered Esprë's trance of fear. She threw back her head and screamed.

CHAPTER

45

Kandler knew Burch would be the first to spot *Keeper's Claw*. The shifter had been peering out at the horizon for hours, scanning every spot in the distance in the hopes of somehow finding the airship. With his keen vision, he had the best chance of spying it of anyone, so he kept at it no matter how tired his eyes might get from staring into the midday sun.

From what Te'oma had relayed from Esprë, they knew it would be somewhere along the front range of the Ironroot Mountains, in a portion traditionally occupied by Clan Drakyager. This meant little to Kandler, who couldn't keep track of the various clans of the Mror Holds without a diagram, but Burch knew who they were. Monja did too, although she'd never met any of them in person before.

From what Burch and Monja had said, the Drakyager dwarves were a solitary lot, bitter about their fall from power so many centuries ago. Still, they were determined to live up to their hereditary duties, which included trying to reclaim their ancient homeland deep within the mountains and to protect the rest of the clans of the Iron Council from an ancient and evil dragon that had set up housekeeping far beneath their homes so long ago.

"Yeah," Burch had said, "they made some kind of deal with the dragon, believe it or not—a black one, scales darker than its soul. They kept him fed and protected, and he left them alone. Course, that didn't stop the orcs from killing most of them a while back."

"No one cried a tear for them," Monja had said. "A dragon like that doesn't get by on munching potatoes and carrots, after all."

"What happened to the dragon after Clan Drakyager got run off, then?" Kandler had asked.

Burch had shrugged. "Dragons can go a long time without eating much," he'd said. "They just get hungrier and hungrier."

"And when they can't take it any more?" Sallah had asked.

Monja had frowned. "I've never heard of a dragon dying from starvation."

When Burch spotted the *Keeper's Claw* right along the mountains under which the dragon supposedly lived, Kandler's heart pumped with a mixture of hope and dread. His daughter had to be around here somewhere, but a hungry dragon might be there too.

"There it is, boss," Burch said, pointing at a twinkling bit of orange glowing partway up a mountain. "Ready and waiting for us."

Kandler slapped his friend on the back in thanks and jogged back along the deck to talk with Sallah on the bridge. The lady knight had done most of the flying since they'd left Fort Bones. *Phoenix* seemed to respond to her well. She was a natural pilot, almost as talented as Esprë, who'd surprised Kandler with her easy command of the airship.

"Found something?" Sallah asked, a tentative smile on her lips.

Kandler nodded and pointed at the tiny light that Burch had found. "That's either the airship or the biggest bonfire

I've ever seen. Either way, we need to check it out. Take her up high. Try to mask our approach by keeping the sun directly behind us."

"Aye, captain," Sallah said with a grin. Although the wheel in her hands didn't move—couldn't move, in fact—the ship tilted in the direction Kandler had pointed, and it picked up momentum. "Full speed ahead."

Kandler squinted at her. " 'Aye, captain?' "

"I've always wanted to say that. Thrane doesn't border any seas—we have rivers, lakes, and sounds, but mostly I stayed off them, so I never really had a chance."

"Ever?"

"Not before now."

Kandler leaned in and kissed the lady knight on the cheek. He could have sworn she blushed at the attention, but it could have just been the wind on her face.

He wondered why Sallah had pulled away from him when they were in the Mournland but was willing to accept his affections now. Did she think he'd finally gotten over his love for Esprina?

As much as Kandler felt himself starting to care for Sallah, he didn't think he'd ever be able to ignore his feelings about Esprina, no matter how long gone she might be. He and Burch had buried her in that grave in the Mournland, but his love for her couldn't be covered up so easily. He didn't think he could ever give it all up. It was too much a part of who he was.

"What are we going to do when we catch up to *Keeper's Claw*?" Xalt asked.

The warforged had stood at the back of the bridge so quietly that Kandler had forgotten he was there. He wondered if warforged could shut themselves off and turn themselves back on at will. He'd never seen another living creature stay so still for so long.

"We'll attack and bring them down," he said.

"A Karrnathi warship with a full contingent of skeletal soldiers? Do you think that's possible?"

"Do you have another plan?"

"Suicide is not a plan."

The fact that Xalt valued his artificial life just as much as anyone else—perhaps more, it seemed—struck Kandler hard. The warforged had a point. Dying in the attempt to rescue Esprë wouldn't help her.

Kandler knew from the start of all this that he'd be willing to do anything for his daughter, even die for her, if it meant she would be safe and free. The others, though, might not have that blind, unconditional love for the young elf. Burch did, Kandler thought. The shifter had been his best friend for so long—before he'd met Esprina, even. Since the beautiful elf's death, Burch had been even more than just a friend. He'd become a part of Kandler and Esprë's family, sometimes as much of a father to the young elf as he'd been, especially in those early months after Esprë's mother's death. Kandler hadn't been much use to anyone in those days, and Burch had watched over Esprë until the justicar could stand to get back into the world again.

Sallah had her orders. The Keeper of the Flame herself had charged the lady knight with finding the bearer of the Lost Mark. She'd lost so much on this journey already that she could never turn back now. The ghosts of her father and her other fellow knights pushed her on, more than any growing affection for Kandler could, he knew.

Xalt and Monja, though, didn't have the pressing need of the others to be here. Kandler didn't know why they'd follow him into what could be a quick but terrifying death. What drove them on?

Kandler put his hand on the warforged's shoulder. "If you don't want to go through with this, I understand," he said. "You've already done more for us than you had to."

He looked over at Monja, who climbed up on to the bridge

at that moment to learn the news Kandler had brought from Burch. She'd been watching the changeling, but her curiosity seemed to have gotten the better of her.

Xalt stepped back, forcing Kandler's hand from his shoulder, and the warforged's jaw dropped. "You think I want out of this now?" he asked. "You think I am a coward who would abandon friends in the time of their greatest need? I didn't *have* to do any of this."

Kandler flushed. "I'm sorry," he said. "I—I don't want to force you into risking your life for my daughter." He looked down at the halfling shaman. "The same goes for you. If you like, we'll drop you off here. If we survive, we'll come back for you. Otherwise, I'm sure you can find your way home."

The halfling shaman furrowed her brow at the justicar, then crooked her finger for him to come lower so she could speak to him directly. He knelt in front of her, and she reached out and took his face in her small, childlike hands—smaller, even, than Esprë's.

"Don't be a fool," she said. She glanced up at Xalt and then stared long and hard into Kandler's eyes. "You insult us both with your offer."

She smiled at him then. "I'm not here for you," she said. "I'm here for your daughter. It's more than repaying my debt to Burch. He saved my life once, but not because he owed me anything—just because it was the right thing to do."

Kandler felt a hand on his shoulder. He looked to see it belonged to Xalt—the one missing the thick finger the warforged had lost saving Kandler and his friends once before.

"This . . ." Xalt said. "Saving Esprë is the right thing to do."

Kandler nodded and stood, a grim look on his face as he stared at them both.

"Damn you two for being right."

Burch stepped up on to the bridge then. "I don't think she's on the ship, boss," he said.

Kandler spun on the shifter. "How's that?"

Burch pointed back at *Keeper's Claw*, toward which they zoomed with amazing speed. "There's only a few skeletons left there, and they're not moving. They're waiting for something."

"Like for Ibrido to return," Kandler said.

He leaped over the bridge's railing and landed next to Te'oma. The changeling stood there, still chained to the deck by her neck and wrists, staring out at the ship they approached.

"She's in danger," Te'oma said.

"How long have you known?" Kandler grabbed the chain that led to her collar and rattled it. "How long?"

"Does it matter?" she said, her head bowed. "She's beyond our help now."

Kandler reached up and yanked back the changeling's head by the back of her collar. He snarled at her, his face close enough to hers that he could have bitten her nose off. "What does that mean?"

He noticed then that Te'oma had been crying. His heart fell down past his toes and tumbled through the airship toward the ground far below.

"What does that mean?" he hissed.

"She's still . . . alive," the changeling said, choking on the collar as she spoke.

Kandler released her, and she fell forward on her knees, tugging the collar from around her throat. "She's in the mountain. Ibrido is taking her down to present her to his master."

"Why?" Kandler asked. Stories of dragons devouring young virgins roiled through his head.

"I don't know," Te'oma said, glaring up at him. "If Esprë can't figure it out, how should I?"

Kandler growled down at the changeling. "You're the telepath around here."

"All I know is what Esprë tells me," she said, tears streaming down her face again. Kandler couldn't tell if they were in rage against him or for some more horrible reason.

Kandler tried to calm himself. "What does she tell you now?" he asked. "What's happening to her?"

Te'oma stared up at the justicar, weeping openly now, her mouth twisted into a grimace of grief and fear. " 'It's coming,' is all she can say right now. 'It's coming! It's coming! It's coming!' "

The changeling let loose a skull-rattling shriek. "Oh, no!" she said. "No, no, no, no, no." Her voice was barely more than a murmur now, and Kandler had to strain to hear her words.

"No," Te'oma said, her voice as raw as an open wound. "It's here."

CHAPTER

46

The skeletons crewing *Keeper's Claw* never had a chance. One moment they were scattered about the deck of the Karrnathi airship like macabre statues, waiting for their master to return to activate them once more, and the next instant three warriors dropped into their midst from the sky.

Duro Darumnakt had been watching the airship with a few of his fellows when they saw the *Phoenix* soar down from out of the sun—which the undead creatures seemed to hate looking anywhere near—plummeting like a ship of that size should, instead of being suspended in the air by an unholy ring of fire. It managed to catch itself scant yards above *Keeper's Claw*, and that's when the three slid down at them on ropes cast over the smaller airship's gunwales.

The first of them bore a longsword that sliced through the Karrnathi armor as easily as parted the air. A tall man—human, for sure, Duro decided—with short, brown hair, he carved his way through the creatures with a trained soldier's ease. This was a man who had seen many a battle and walked away triumphant from them all.

The second one down was a woman, another human, but like none that Duro had ever seen. She wore a crimson tabard embroidered with a blazing silver flame over a gleaming breastplate and mail made of polished chains, thin but tough, worked together in the manner Duro's ancestors had perfected centuries ago. Her sword burned with tongues of fire the same unnatural silver color of the emblem on her tabard.

The fire-haired woman struck left and right at first, then presented her sword before her and shouted, "By the light of the Silver Flame, you shall not stand!"

The skeletons nearest her turned and fled, spilling over the gunwales of the ship and shattering on the rocks below. One of them tried to get up and flee on its splintered leg bones, but it gave up after a moment and fell into its component parts.

The third warrior, a shifter from the look of him, slid only halfway down the rope hanging from the second airship. Wrapping himself in the rope, he then started loosing bolts from his crossbow at the rest of the skeletons chasing about after the other two invaders. Some of his bolts clanged off the Karrnathi armor, but one knocked a helmeted skull right off its owner's shoulders. Another smashed apart a skeleton's elbow just as it was about to bring its scimitar down on the man's back.

"What's happening?" Kallo asked from behind him as he peered over Duro's shoulder.

"Get down," Duro said, shoving the young dwarf back.

Though he had barely come of age, Kallo itched to get his axe involved in a real fight. He'd notched it on one of the Karrnathi skeletons they'd fought earlier that day, but since such creatures didn't bleed he'd technically not yet been blooded. Duro knew the difference was small but that it gnawed at the eager, young dwarf, making him less cautious than he perhaps should be.

"I don't know what's happening yet," Duro said, scolding Kallo. "If you'd keep your trap shut, I might be able to figure it out."

"Seems obvious to me," Kallo said, thumbing the edge of his axe. "Big people who hate the skeletons are kicking them to pieces. We wait until the fight is over and then kill the survivors."

Duro smacked Kallo on the back of the head, then grinned at him. "You are an idiot," he said, "but sometimes even you come up with a fine idea. Spread the word to the others. As soon as the big people come down off that airship, we strike."

"What makes you think they'll come down?" Kallo asked, rubbing the back of his head.

"They're here for the same reason the others came," Duro said. "Why else would we see two airships in a place that hasn't had a visitor in over a decade?

"Now do as I order. Go!"

"Everyone all right?" Kandler asked after he hacked the last of the Karrnathi skeletons to bits. It had been cowering behind the bridge, unable to bring itself to face Sallah's blade. The justicar had made quick work of it, putting an end to its troubles.

A man—someone Kandler had never seen before—stood slumped over the ship's wheel, his arms still chained to it. The justicar poked the emaciated sailor with the tip of his sword and provoked no reaction.

"I'm fine," Sallah said, calling over from the gunwale, where she'd been making sure that the creatures she'd chased overboard weren't somehow crawling back up to greet them.

"Fine, boss." Burch slid down the rest of the way on the rope and went about collecting any unbroken bolts he could find. Kandler admired the shifter's economy. Here, a long way from the nearest village, getting your hands on a decent supply of bolts would be tricky. Better to keep hold of the ones you had as long as you could.

Kandler inspected a small cut on his left forearm. One of the skeletons had slashed at him there, and he'd been too busy defending himself against another to move out of the way. The wound bled freely between the fingers he used to grasp it. He cursed himself for being so careless. They could ill afford for him to be injured right now. Esprë was depending on him.

"Let me help you with that," Sallah said. The lady knight sheathed her blade and walked over to put her hands on the cut. She chanted a few words to the Silver Flame, and Kandler watched as a golden light suffused her hands then spilled off them to soak into the justicar's injured flesh.

When Sallah removed her hands, she wiped the blood on the arm away with her fingers. The skin beneath was unmarred, healed as if it had never been cut open. She smiled up at Kandler as she cleaned her hands on the edge of her tabard. He noticed that the fabric was the same color as his blood, and he wondered if the Knights of the Silver Flame had chosen that hue on purpose.

"We've got two airships," Burch said. "Now what?"

Kandler grimaced at his friend as he thanked Sallah. "This is just the first step. We've cut Ibrido off from his escape. There's no way he can get away from us. Now all we have to do is find him."

"When we find him, we find Esprë," Sallah said.

"Exactly." The justicar looked around. "We don't have enough hands to fly both ships at the moment, but we need to make sure that Ibrido can't get his hands back on this one."

Kandler walked over to the gunwales and started hauling up the mooring ropes hanging over the edge of the ship. Sallah and Burch joined in as well.

When they were done, they had one rope left. Kandler slid down it first, drawing his sword as soon as his feet touched the small, flat shelf on the rocky slope. Sallah came down after him, with Burch coming last.

"What about this rope?" Burch said.

Sallah drew her sword, which burst into silvery flames. She touched it to the rope and ran it up and down the fibers as far as her blade would reach. It caught fire quickly, and the flames began to work their way up the length, toward the ship above.

"Good thing these airships are fireproof," Burch said. The ring of fire surrounding *Keeper's Claw* seemed to grow louder to punctuate his words, as if the elemental within wished it could find a way to consume the craft to which it was bound.

"Which way?" Kandler said.

Burch stretched and growled, drawing upon the blood of the werecreatures that ran through his veins. Those ancient ancestors might be long dead, but they still lived on in the way the shifter could call on their legendary powers.

As long as Kandler had known Burch, this still made him a bit uncomfortable. When the shifter called on his animalistic side, he became less like the justicar's friend and more of the kind of savage beast some of the "civilized" folk from Sharn assumed all of his kind to be. In any case, it was part and parcel of who Burch was, and Kandler had to admit it came in handy at times like this.

Burch knelt down toward the rocky ground and sniffed about like a bloodhound hunting for a scent. He wrinkled his nose more than once, then performed a crouching walk in a circle around the entire shelf. His search complete, he stood up once more and pointed off to the south, along the mountain's slope.

"Follow me," he growled.

Kandler trotted along straight after Burch, with Sallah falling in behind him, her sword still out and ready. Kandler drew his own blade, wanting to be prepared for anything that might happen. They had no idea where Ibrido and Esprë were, after all. The last they knew from Te'oma, the pair had somehow entered the mountain to find his master, but anything could have happened since then. They had to expect that the dragon-elf might be cautious about people following after him. Around any corner, there might be another pack of skeletons waiting to—

"Halt!" a low voice shouted in a thick-accented version of the common tongue of the Five Kingdoms of Khorvaire.

Burch looked up from where he'd been bent over the narrow trail that cut along the mountain's slope, still sniffing out Esprë's path. They'd reached a small shelf where the trail switched back, and a dark hole appeared in the face of the rock before them.

Kandler swung his neck around and spotted a pair of dwarves coming up the path behind them. They were stunted creatures, even for dwarves, and their pasty skin and squinty eyes told Kandler that they rarely saw the light of day. They wore light suits of armor and metallic helmets covered with dirt and dust the same color as the mountain itself, allowing them to blend in. They each bore an axe or hammer and carried a loaded crossbow that was pointed straight at Kandler, Burch, and Sallah.

"Surrender or die!" one of the dwarves on the lower trail called up at them.

Kandler glanced at Burch and Sallah. "I don't like the looks of that hole much," he whispered.

"Esprë went in there," the shifter said.

Kandler grinned. "All of a sudden, I like it a lot more. On my mark, we charge into it. Ready?"

Before the justicar could get to "set," another handful of dwarves emerged from the blackness, their double-sided axes out and ready to taste blood.

CHAPTER

47

The dragon waited for Esprë to stop screaming before it spoke. Its low, rumbling voice sounded like a pair of giant millstones being ground against each other, and its breath smelled like a charnel house on a hot day.

"Finally," it said. "The Mark of Death returns."

Esprë wanted to scream again, but she'd already run herself hoarse. Instead, she stood there mute, with the swirling waters bubbling around her knees, and stared in horror at the massive beast.

She had heard stories about dragons before, but they were nothing like meeting one in the scale-decked flesh. She felt grateful that she could not see the entire thing at once. The light from the everburning torch she held didn't stretch far enough to encompass the entirety of the beast in its glow. She could only see its long, horned head, its sinuous, snakelike neck, and the broad expanse of its chest.

Black scales covered all of these, ebon-colored bits of mail that could turn aside the mightiest sword. They fitted seamlessly over the beast, stopping only at its mouth, nose, ears, and eyes. Its toothy mouth dripped with some disgusting green fluid that reminded her of nothing more than distilled stomach bile. Its nostrils flared at her as the stale atmosphere of the cave hacked its way in and out of its phlegm-coated lungs. Its batlike ears waved at her independently of each other, as if batting at tiny creatures that lived inside their tattered flaps. Its orange eyes seemed to glow with a fire that threatened to devour her body if not also her soul.

Every bit of Esprë wanted to run, but something in her brain kept it from happening, some instinct that told her to freeze when confronted with something so large. Despite her fear, she listened to that instinct and held her ground.

"You have done well, half-breed," the dragon said to Ibrido. "Capturing the bearer of the Mark of Death is not something done lightly. Is she . . . ?"

It reached out with a taloned claw that stretched as long as Esprë's arm. Its breath wrapped around her, and she struggled not to gag on the stench. Her eyes began to water, and she couldn't say if it was entirely from the smell or not.

"Unharmed?" the dragon finished. The green fluid spilled from between its long, sharp rows of teeth as it spoke. Where it landed, the blackened waters fizzed and foamed in protest.

Ibrido stepped forward, a half pace in front of Esprë. "For the most part, Nithkorrh. The journey here was not an easy one for her. Before she came into my care, she was in an airship crash."

Two, Esprë thought, but she didn't wish to correct the dragon-elf at that moment.

"Yet she survived?" the dragon said.

It bared all its teeth in a way that Esprë could only guess was a dragon's means of smiling, just as she'd seen on Ibrido's face. On such a massive scale, though, it scared her all the more.

"Fate would not have placed the Lost Mark on a creature unblessed with a certain amount of luck," the dragon said, "or so the prophecies would have us believe."

"I . . ." Esprë started to speak and then thought better of it and let her voice trail off.

"Yes?" The dragon craned its neck back around toward her, inching its face closer to her as it did.

Esprë remained mute. She'd brought the creature's full attention to her, and it had addressed her directly for the first time. She knew it expected an answer, but that was the last thing she wanted to give it.

"Answer the great Nithkorrh," Ibrido asked. "Dragons do not like to be kept waiting."

Esprë tried to keep her lips sealed, but this meant breathing through her nose, and the scent of the dragon and the place in which it lived soon made her nauseous. She parted her lips so that she could breathe without smelling the stench, and the dragon leaned in even closer. She could feel the chill from its cold-blooded breath. It stank like a sodden garbage pit.

Esprë looked up into the dragon's eyes—twinned orange lanterns floating in the darkness before her—and found it difficult to tear her gaze away. Still, she managed to glance over at the dragon-elf and down at the remains of several flesh-bare skeletons staring up at her from under a thin veil of water. Then she looked back up into Nithkorrh's eyes.

"This doesn't seem very lucky to me," she said.

Esprë felt Ibrido freeze next to her, unsure as to how the dragon would react to such impudence. She discovered that she didn't care any more. If the creature killed her, then at least this ordeal would be over.

Robbed of an elf's centuries-long life, she could still expect to be reunited with her mother in the afterlife, the limbo reserved for those elves who died before ascending to the Undying Court. Such a dark and dreary place was meant to be torture for those who aspired to a more meaningful existence, but Esprë could only think that it might be a wonderful respite for those who had grown tired or terrified of this capricious life.

The dragon snorted down at her, and the cloud of green mist that it expelled burned at her face and eyes.

"Elfling," Nithkorrh said, "you may be too young to know better. There are far worse fates than this. You shall learn this soon enough. Some of them lie in your future."

Esprë heard Ibrido breathe a sigh of relief. Perhaps he worried that Nithkorrh would kill her on the spot. Dragons had a reputation for acting impulsively. How would the dragon-elf explain the results to any other dragons interested in her fate? Chances were that Nithkorrh would kill him as well to remove any witnesses to his crime.

No, Esprë corrected herself. To a creature such as Nithkorrh, there were no crimes, only errors.

"The dragon kings will be thrilled to meet such a creature," the dragon said, more to Ibrido than her. "We have been waiting a long time. I was barely a hatchling myself when we launched our crusade to destroy the House of Vol."

The dragon leaned closer to Esprë, so much that it had to turn its head and focus just one of its burning orange eyes on the young elf. "You have no idea of the carnage your emergence shall beget."

Esprë trembled despite her newfound resolve. It was one thing to decide that death wouldn't be so bad. It was another to die.

"Turn around," Nithkorrh said. "I must see it."

CHAPTER

48

Esprë remained as still as a statue.

"He is speaking to you," Ibrido said. "You must obey."

Esprë shook her head. This dragon didn't have any hold over her, or so she told herself. She just stared ahead, remaining mute.

Ibrido reached over and grabbed Esprë by the arm. He swung her about so her back faced Nithkorrh, and he presented her to the dragon.

"The mark is on her back," he said, "between her shoulder blades."

"How do you know that?" Esprë asked. "You've never seen it."

She could feel the mark start to itch around its edges. In her mind, she could see the pattern it cast on her skin, although she'd only seen the mark once herself, in a mirror in her home back in Mardakine. The black lines that made up the mark seemed more solid than those of any tattoo. It had looked angry and red around the edges, even then when it didn't itch at all. From the way it felt right now, she wouldn't have been surprised to learn her skin was blistering there, with large pustules of burnt skin ready to pop and ooze down her back.

As the itching turned to scraping and then to burning, Esprë ached for that kind of release. She didn't know what was happening with her dragonmark. She knew only that something had to give, and soon.

She heard the dragon creeping closer to her, sloshing through the black waters in which they all stood. She felt it reach out with a serrated talon, caked with mud and other unclean things. She could smell the rot in its own flesh, sitting there underneath scales that spent most of their time immersed in the stale waters in this frigid, underground lake.

Then the talon hooked in the back of her shirt collar and pulled it back. Nithkorrh's touch was gentler than Esprë would have thought possible. She never would have guessed that such a large creature could have such delicate control. It dragged the collar of the shirt back until the front of it pressed against her throat, choking her.

She could tell, though, that the dragonmark was exposed to the air, as it began to burn even warmer, so hot that she was surprised her shirt didn't catch fire. She leaned forward, gasping in pain, and Nithkorrh let her go.

"Yes," the dragon said. Esprë looked back and saw that it had bared its teeth again, showing more of them than ever before. "That is it. I saw it once on Vol herself before she disappeared. Hers was larger, of course, but she was full grown, and she had mastered its use."

Esprë's mind reeled at this. The thought that the mark could be larger than it already was seemed ludicrous. It felt as if it could consume her right now.

Nithkorrh's talon fell on Esprë again, this time across her shoulder. The dragon pulled on it, spinning the young elf around to face it.

"Do you have any dragon blood running in your veins, I wonder?" Nithkorrh said.

"I'm told her mother was a sorcerer of some repute,"

Ibrido said. "Many scholars have long theorized that the talent for sorcery is inherited by those honored to include dragons in their ancestry."

Esprë frowned at that. "We are elves, pure-blooded, through and through."

Ibrido chuckled. "You should be honored to have even a dash of such regal parentage."

Esprë shook her head. "I'd rather have nothing to do with dragons at all. I wish they would stay in my childhood stories and never come to life."

Nithkorrh snorted, and an acrid green mist engulfed the young girl, burning at her eyes and lungs like bitter smoke. "My kind predates your stories, elfling. We were here before your kind could even speak, and we will be here long after. Eberron is our world. The word 'Eberron' means 'the dragon between.' All of your other so-called 'races' are just visitors here, transients who will fade away with the cycles of time like the bothersome insects you are."

Esprë couldn't hold back her disgust and anger any longer. If the Mark of Death wanted to be free, if it wanted to kill, then she would let it. She had never found any creature more deserving of an untimely death than Nithkorrh, and she was ready to hand it to it.

She had to get the dragon closer to her, though. She'd learned her lesson with Ibrido. While she had the power to kill, she needed to get close enough to use it. Otherwise, she would fail for sure.

She had to make sure that Ibrido and Nithkorrh could not see the blackness snaking along her arms and glowing from her hands. She wasn't sure if their eyes could see such things in total darkness, but she knew they could see them in the light.

"Whoops!" she said. She bobbled the everburning torch in front of her, finally smacking it away from her as she dropped it, knocking it to the right of the dragon.

Ibrido snickered at what Esprë hoped he thought was her misfortune. "Now," he said, "you will have to make your way out of here in the darkness."

The cave wasn't entirely dark though. Esprë could see the torch still glowing as it sank through the black waters to the muck-covered bottom of the lake. There wasn't much light from it now, but just enough for her to detect the silhouette of the dragon and the dragon-elf, and she could see the dragon's glowing eyes as well.

"I think Nithkorrh should make you go get it," Esprë said, taunting Ibrido. "After all, I'm worth more to him than you are."

"Do not think yourself so valued," the dragon rumbled. "The dragon kings don't need much of you to work with. If you somehow die before you get there, it just makes transporting you that much easier for the half-breed here."

Esprë spat out into the darkness. "Which of you has the guts to try it?" she shouted, letting her anger loose now, feeling the dark, cold energy snake along her arms and envelope her hands in its bone-freezing blackness. "You live down here in the darkness, thinking you're something important, some kind of king. You're just a coward, hiding here from the 'insects' who could sting you to death."

"Check your tongue, elfling," the dragon said, frustration edging into its voice. "You do not know of what you speak."

"Dragons are magnificent, powerful creatures who fly through the sky and command respect from all who see them. You're no dragon," Esprë said. "You're a catfish, a bottom-feeder who swims in the coldest, deepest parts of the river where no self-respecting creature would go, living on the rotted refuse of the insects who outnumber you ten thousand to one. You're no better than a maggot chewing on a year-old corpse!"

"I have heard enough!"

The dragon's eyes, still glowing in the dark, lunged

forward. Its snout shoved Esprë back, and she fell into the water, which closed over her head. She thrashed about in the freezing lake for a moment, wondering why she hadn't realized until now that she could no longer feel her feet.

Then a set of what felt like long, serrated knives closed on the front of Esprë's tunic and hauled her back to the surface, sputtering and gasping for air. As she came up, she reached forward with both hands and grasped the dragon's hard, scaly snout. She focused all her anger and all of the power from her dragonmark—which burned so hot now she was surprised it hadn't boiled the lake when she fell—into her hands and channeled it out of her fingertips and into Nithkorrh's face.

"Die!" she screamed with all her might. "Die! Die! Die!"

CHAPTER

49

Nithkorrh hurled itself backward, away from Esprë's necrotizing touch. She held on to its face as hard as she could, determined to kill the creature or die trying. Her hands found purchase on the inner edges of its nostrils, and she refused to let go.

Esprë kept concentrating on her dragonmark, on forcing the chill power through her hands and into the dragon's face. She guessed that with such a powerful creature it would take some time for the iciness to reach its heart. If she could stop that from beating any further, though, she—she couldn't think any further than that. She just gritted her teeth and clenched her fingers tighter, shoving more and more freezing energy into the beast.

Esprë was glad she couldn't see the dragon's face or anything but its glowing orange eyes. She knew it would terrify her, maybe to the point where she would lose her grip.

The dragon roared, and the expulsion of its breath blasted Esprë's body away from its mouth. She held on, her legs flapping behind her like a banner in a storm. The noise stabbed like needles into the young elf's ears, and it left her deafened by their ringing. Tears flowed from her eyes, not in sadness or even pain but from the horrible stench that sprang from the dragon's maw.

Nithkorrh drew in another breath, and Esprë steeled herself for it to roar again. Instead, it drove her backward with its mighty neck and plunged her bodily into the black waters of its home lake. The impact forced the air from her lungs. Now she held on not out of murderous intent but for her life. If she let go, she feared she might never find her way back to the surface. In the endless blackness, she might swim too far in the wrong direction and run out of air before she had any hope of finding it again.

Esprë realized that her only hope was to hurt the dragon as much as possible before her lungs and her will gave out. She prodded her dragonmark like she was stirring the embers of a dying fire, and at her command it sprang back to life. The burning returned as hot as ever, and the ice flowed down her arms and out through her hands so fast she was amazed that the waters around her didn't freeze solid on the spot.

The dragon hauled its neck out of the water and roared again. This time, the timbre seemed rooted more in fear than rage.

Esprë's heart soared as she gulped the stale air of the cave as if it were from a rain-swept sky. She had frightened a dragon. She had hurt it. That meant she could kill it. She prepared to draw on her deepest reserves to put an end to the dragon's life.

Nithkorrh took that moment to shake its head so hard that Esprë felt her arms might break. Despite her desperate efforts, her grip on the creature's nostrils came loose, and she went sailing through the air to splash into some distant part of the underground lake.

As Esprë plunged into the water, her only hope was that it was deep. She thanked her mother for teaching her to swim at an early age. She had loved kicking her way around Lake Cyre in those days, so much so her mother had called her "my little fish." One of the things she'd missed most in Mardakine was the lack of any water deeper than a bathtub. She'd often sat on the front porch of her house on a hot summer day and dreamed of a cool pool to take a dip in.

She'd never imagined it to be anything like this.

When Esprë hit the water, she spread out her arms and legs to slow herself down. Even so, the force of the dragon's toss shoved her through the water until she smacked into the bottom of the underground lake. She'd expected to smash into bare, hard rock, but instead landed in a thick layer of loamy muck. It cushioned her abrupt stop enough that she managed to keep the air in her lungs.

Esprë swung her legs beneath her, feeling for the bottom, then kicked off against it. It felt soft and sticky, like it would suck her down if she hung on to it too long. She didn't want to thick about what it might be made of. She swam for the unseen surface as hard as she could.

When Esprë's head broke the water, she heard the dragon still roaring in pain and rage.

"Where are you, cockroach?" Nithkorrh said, spitting each word. "I will tear out your brain with my tongue and use your bones to pick my teeth!"

In the darkness, Esprë couldn't see a thing, not even the dragon's glowing eyes. It must have been facing away from her, at least at first.

Then, treading water in this black cave—the water so cold it seemed to freeze even the heat from her dragonmark—trapped and lost in a dragon's home, Esprë realized she had failed. Nithkorrh would kill her, just as she had expected. That didn't bother her—although she knew she would much rather live. The fact that the dragon had survived her best effort crushed what little spirit she had left.

"I will find you, elfling," the dragon said, still thrashing about, its voice filled with menace. "I will skin you alive and fashion your dragonmark into a glove."

Esprë shuddered at the thought and held her breath, trying to keep afloat as quietly as possible.

"The dragon kings will take your skin and learn of your family. We will hunt them down and devour them all!"

The thought of all those dead elves chilled Esprë's heart. She hadn't lived among other elves for decades, but she remembered Aerenal from her youth. It was a place filled with history that the people of the land lived every day. To leave it behind to move to Khorvaire had felt like leaving part of herself behind. She remembered her mother had wept about it bitterly, but they had gone just the same.

"Sometimes," Esprina had said, "history is not a platform on which you stand but a cage in which you live."

Those words had followed them to Valenar and then up through Cyre until they reached Metrol, where they had settled. Esprë had thought then that this would be forever, but Esprina had said, "Elves live too long to think of forever."

"If we cannot figure out who you are, from what line you hail, we will invade your precious Aerenal and destroy it. We will kill every elf we find there, and then we will go to the other lands and kill their elves too!"

"Stop!" Ibrido shouted. Esprë realized he'd been trying to make himself heard over the dragon's ranting for a while, but his voice finally managed to find a break in which it could ring out.

Nithkorrh came to a sloshing halt. From where Esprë was, she could see the dragon's lantern-like eyes bear down on the dragon-elf, picking him out of the darkness in their golden-orange glow.

"An elf's blood runs through your veins too, half-breed," the dragon said. "Do not think I shall forget it."

"You have let your anger master you," Ibrido said. "If the youth is dead, railing at her won't help. If she is alive, then you should take care you do not kill her in your rage."

"What do you suggest I do?" Nithkorrh hissed each word

at the dragon-elf as if any one of them could spell Ibrido's death.

"Just stop for a moment and listen."

Esprë cursed silently. She knew they would hear her as soon as the waves from the dragon's rage quit sloshing through the lake. Even the barest sounds of her breath would echo loud enough in the cavern for Nithkorrh's ears to catch them.

For a moment, she thought she should scream at the dragon, dare him to come and get her, to tangle with her once more. She found she could not bring herself to do it. Nithkorrh's tossing her about had tired her out. She could barely tread water any longer, but she didn't dare give up.

"There!" Nithkorrh said. Its glowing orange eyes spun about and focused on her, catching her in their light like a fly in amber.

Esprë grabbed one last breath and let her arms and legs go limp. She dropped away from the surface as fast as her weight, and that of her sodden clothes, would take her, but it wasn't fast enough.

She saw the twin orange orbs follow her into the water, and then, before she could try to swim away, a taloned claw caught her around the waist and pulled her screaming to the surface.

The dragon dragged Esprë through the water and deposited her at Ibrido's feet. "Keep control of her this time," it said to the dragon-elf. "Your life is not worth as much to me as hers."

CHAPTER

50

"Give them your swords," Kandler said.

"What?" Sallah brandished her blazing blade before her. "This is a sacred symbol of my office. I cannot give it away lightly."

"Forget it, boss," Burch said, waving his crossbow around and around at the three groups of dwarves that surrounded them. "Let's just kill them all and be on our way."

Kandler lowered his own blade. "These people aren't our enemies," he said. "They're just trying to protect their home."

The justicar stabbed the tip of his blade into a small patch of dirt in front of him. "Besides, who knows what's down in those caves?"

Burch snorted. "They do."

"Right," Kandler said, motioning again for the others to put down their weapons, and they did. "We could use their help."

The dwarf who'd called upon them to surrender rushed up to them to kick their weapons away. "A wise decision," he said, keeping his crossbow leveled at them. Kandler could see the runes carved along the bolt's length, and he wondered if maybe he'd made a mistake. "Much wiser than your friends from before."

"Those aren't our friends," Kandler said. "We're here to rescue my daughter, a young elf who was with them."

The dwarf sized up Kandler. "Your ears are awfully round for an elf."

"She's my stepdaughter."

"Ah," said the dwarf. He glanced nervously at the other dwarves around him. "About your bony friends there—"

"They're not our friends," Kandler said.

"Didn't you see us on that airship?" Burch said. "Some lookouts."

Sallah pointed at the embroidery on the front of her tabard. "I am a Knight of the Silver Flame," she said. "The only truck I have with such creatures is their destruction."

The dwarf frowned for a moment and bowed his head. "Those skeletons killed a number of my crew here, good dwarves." He raised his eyes. "If your quarrel is with them, then we share a foe, and we are short of allies. Pick up your weapons, and join the dwarves of Clan Drakyager if you will."

Sallah and Burch gathered their sword and crossbow. Kandler pulled his blade from where he'd stuck it in the ground. Then he stuck out his hand and introduced himself.

"Duro Darumnakt," the dwarf said with a tentative grin as his many fellows gathered around behind him. They were a dour sort but happy to let their leader talk with the strangers for them. "Do you know why those skeletons came here? Most of them and their half-dragon leader entered the caves through that hole not long ago."

Kandler shook his head. "They are looking for the dragon-elf's master. It seems he lives here." A few of the dwarves gasped. Others muttered a quick prayer to the Sovereign Host.

"Nithkorrh," Duro said, his face as white as a ghost.

"You're looking for the dragon Nithkorrh."

Kandler grimaced. "That could be."

"Well," Duro said, "I knew this day would come. I'd just hoped it wouldn't be in my lifetime." He swallowed hard before continuing. "This dragon of which you speak is a black-hearted beast my people have kept trapped in its lair for centuries. This is the first visitor it's ever gotten."

"That you know of," Burch said, checking the action on his crossbow. Kandler noticed the shifter eyeing the bolt in Duro's weapon too.

"Are you impugning our ability to fulfill our duties?"

Kandler stepped between Burch and the dwarf. "We don't have time for this. Can you take us to the dragon's lair?"

Duro started to nod but then thought better of it. "That may not be wise."

"Forget them, boss," Burch said. "We don't need them. I can follow Esprë's trail myself."

"We don't know what we'll find in there though," Sallah said. "It would seem prudent to engage a native guide."

Kandler gazed down at the dwarf. "If Ibrido has entered your caves already with a contingent of skeletons, I think we're the least of your troubles. Can you take us to the dragon's lair?"

Duro narrowed his eyes at Kandler for a moment, then nodded. "If you can't take foolish chances in desperate times, when can you?"

Kandler nodded his agreement then followed Duro into the mountain, with Burch and Sallah hot in his wake. A dozen well-armed dwarves followed after them.

They made good time through the mountain. As they jogged down various narrow and twisting passages and across expansive chambers, Kandler realized that they could easily have gotten lost on their own. Despite Burch's legendary tracking skills, there were so many different ways to go that even a map would have been only a small help.

After a long while, they emerged into a massive chamber supported by tall, thick pillars that seemed to be in the business of holding up the night sky. As Kandler gazed up toward where he hoped a ceiling would be, he did notice a faint bit of light filtering down from above.

"We are in the Great Hall of Clan Drakyager," Duro said. "Where you look, great louvered windows once hung, bringing sunlight into the most massive chamber under the mountain.

"We're not far from the surface here then?" Kandler asked. "It seemed like we were heading down the entire time."

"That matters not," said Duro. "The mountain above follows its own mind. An avalanche covered those windows many years ago. Sadly, we have not had the resources or the need to clear them again. If we lived in this part of the caves again, that would be one thing, but the clan makes its home under peaks to the north of here, closer to the seat of the Iron Council."

"Where to from here?" Sallah asked.

"We cross the Great Hall, then we find passages to lead us into the mountain's very bowels. Once there, we'll look for the Iron Door. It is a stunning piece of craftwork that legend says cannot fall while Clan Drakyager still stands. Beyond that lies the dragon, the monstrous beast itself."

"What will we find when we get there?"

"Only the gods know that for sure. With luck, we'll beat the half-breed and his friends there and be able to make a last defensive stand before the doors."

Then, a rhythmic beating began echoing from all around. It sounded like a giant banging on a gong the size of a house's roof, and it rattled the floor on which Kandler walked and shook dust from the stone pillars and the unseen ceiling.

"What in the name of the Flame is that?" Sallah said, the

dust catching and sparking in the tongues of fire licking her raised sword.

"The dragon!" Duro said over the frightened words his friends murmured among each other in their own guttural tongue. "It's trying to break free."

CHAPTER

51

An inhuman scream of frustration echoed throughout the Great Hall, and Kandler nearly dropped his sword to clutch his hands to his ears. A howl of monstrous determination chased straight after it.

"Is it trying to shake down the mountain with its roars?" Kandler shouted over the din.

Duro shook his head. "The dragon has not tested the wards we put in place around its lair for over a century. Our finest artificers laid these while the great beast slept."

"Now that it found them, it's furious," Sallah said. "Will they hold?"

Duro shrugged. "It is impossible to tell. As I said, they've never been tested this way before."

A large chunk of rubble crashed to the stone floor next to Kandler's feet. "We need to put a stop to this now," he said.

"The only way to do that is to slay the dragon." Duro's eyes grew wide as another blow shook the chamber, and he stared up into the darkness, looking for another piece of the ceiling to fall loose.

"Funny," the justicar said, hefting his blade, "that's just what I had in mind."

With a gentle shove from Kandler, the dwarf leader regained his composure and bounded off across the Great Hall. When he reached a portal, he waved the others down the stairways beyond. The other dwarves led the way, with Kandler, Sallah, and Burch bringing up the rear.

"It's not too far from here," Duro said, following after Burch. "It's mostly straight down, then it opens up into a large room. We should be there shortly."

In the narrow passageway, the dwarves proved far faster than their visitors and raced ahead of them. It was all Kandler could do to keep the last of them in sight without banging his head on the ceiling.

The noise only got worse as they worked their way lower. They switched their way back and forth through a number of intertwined passages in a bewildering route. Kandler thought that even Burch would have had a hard time following anyone through this place, and he was glad—for the moment, at least—that they'd decided to talk with the dwarves instead of fighting their way through them.

As Kandler turned a corner, rubble cascaded down from the low ceiling and fell across his shoulders. Sallah dragged him back from the collapse, and he watched as a few hundred pounds of stone landed where he'd been standing. Before the dust even cleared, though, he stumbled his way over the rocks and through the danger zone. He reached back to help Sallah through and then continued on his way after the dwarves, confident that Burch would find his way through with Duro's help.

"Prideful fools!" a horrible voice roared from below in words so loud that Kandler could barely make them out. "You dare to try to cage me? I will bring this mountain down around your stunted ears!"

The stench assaulted Kandler then. It smelled like they had stumbled across the repository of the dwarves' sewer system. The rot in the air was so thick he thought he might choke on it. He paused only a second, though, before charging down the last tunnel.

"Ready, Drakyager!" a dwarf called out from somewhere ahead. A chorus of voices joined in a wordless cry of approval.

"No!" Duro shouted from behind. "Hold back! Wait, damn you! Wait!"

Kandler heard something wet gush forth and splash out below, and acrid fumes chased up past him, stinging his eyes. He heard a strange sizzling noise and then a dozen screams.

Some of them lasted longer than others. A few gurgled into silence right away. Others wailed on for long seconds until Kandler reached the death chamber.

In the entryway, the justicar paused and peered into the room beyond. It was large, carved out of the living rock of the mountain, but barely worked, other than a floor that sat covered under inches of water bubbling and releasing a greenish mist. A door-sized hole appeared in a rust-colored wall opposite him. It looked like much of the rust had been removed recently, perhaps by the thunderous force of the dragon's rage, and Kandler could see ancient dwarven runes carved into the wall's iron surface.

Dwarf skeletons lay scattered about the room, some obviously decades or more old, their bones long since picked clean by whatever creatures prowled these darkened depths. Others, though, bunched closer to the portal in the iron wall, were fresh. The flesh had been melted off the front of them. The backs of their heads still bore skin and hair, although these boiled away from their skulls in a greenish paste as Kandler watched.

"Acid!" Duro shouted as he tried to push his way past the others. "The dragon spits acid!"

Kandler stepped into the room and felt the heat in the water as it combined with the acid, bubbling away into the acrid steam that burned at his skin and eyes. He coughed once, and a glowing orange ball appeared at the doorway, seemingly floating there in the darkness beyond. It bore a slit that ran straight up and down on its surface, and the slit contracted as Sallah pushed into the room as well, her blade blazing with light.

"They send knights to foil me now, do they?" a voice outside the doorway rumbled. "Knights? As if I were some hatchling to be dispatched with a magic blade? The world above has lived too long without my presence! They have forgotten how to fear me. It is a lesson I shall relish teaching again!"

With that, the globe in the portal disappeared, only to be replaced by a humongous scale-covered snout. A wet black tongue flickered from between rows of swordlike teeth framed in the rust-coated rectangle.

"Prepare to join your precious Flame," the dragon said. Its noxious breath almost made Kandler gag, but he was able to choke out a few words as he shoved Sallah and the others back the way they'd come.

"Move it!" he said. "Get back! Now!"

The others turned and fled before him, and Kandler followed right behind them. As he reached the dry part of the stairs leading down into the room, he heard the dragon inhale a breath so ferocious, it seemed to suck all of the air from the room.

"Go! Go! Go!" he shouted.

The blast of acid sprayed into the room behind him, but Kandler didn't dare look back. He felt tiny drops of the stuff fall on to the back of his arms and legs, burning their way through his clothes and skin. They stung like a cloud of red-hot embers, but he ignored the pain and kept running until they managed to turn a corner at the top of a long flight of stairs.

"How in the Host's hallowed names are we supposed to fight *that*?" Duro asked. The shaken dwarf stood shivering in the corner of the niche at the end of the stairs.

"Got a point, boss," Burch said, his own eyes wider than Kandler had ever seen them. "That's one angry dragon in there."

"You're not afraid of it, are you?" Kandler tried to keep the fear from his own voice and hoped his sharp-eared friend didn't notice.

Burch shook his head, denying his emotions, even to himself. "It's not fear to know we can't take that critter toe to toe."

Kandler grimaced. "We need an edge, something to balance the scales in our favor." He glanced at Sallah's sword.

"I'm ready to give my life to rescue Esprë," the lady knight said, no trace of irony in her voice. "I pledge this sword and my arm to that cause, but . . ."

"But?"

"It won't be enough."

"What about that?" Burch said, pointing at the rune-covered bolt in Duro's crossbow. "What's that do?"

The dwarf's hands shook so hard that he had trouble prying the bolt from his weapon. Once he managed it, he handed it to Burch. "It's a shockbolt," he said. "Release it at something, and it blows up. The dwarves of Clan Drakyager have made them for centuries. My whole patrol here had only five. Up until today, I'd never seen one fired."

Duro reached into a case of bolts slung under his shoulder and pulled out two more of the rune-crusted bolts. He handed them to Burch. "These are all that's left."

"What happened to the others?" Kandler asked.

"We used them on the Karrnathi airship."

"Knight!" the dragon's voice bellowed from below. "Have you run off with your tail between your legs? Have you realized the extent of your folly?"

Burch slotted the shockbolt into his own crossbow.

"I will charge into his maw and cut him open from

301

within," Sallah said, raising her flaming sword and preparing for a charge down the stairs, "or die trying."

Kandler put a hand on her shoulder, holding her back. "We're not quite ready for that," he said. He looked into his old friend's eyes. "You ready?"

The shifter blew out a long breath as he sighted down the length of his crossbow. "Never more."

When Burch looked up, Kandler saw that he had put his fear behind him. All business now, he pulled back the winch on his crossbow and started down the stairs.

CHAPTER

52

As Kandler watched Burch creep back down the stairs toward the angry dragon below, he felt Sallah lay a hand on his arm. "That is a true friend you have there," she said to him.

"None better," Kandler said.

He held his breath as he saw the shifter reach the bottom of the stairs, poking the tip of his crossbow out in front of him.

"Is that you, knight?" the dragon said in a low, mean rumble. "Did you drop your burning sword in the water as you ran?"

Kandler saw Burch crouch down and creep forward until his feet touched the edge of the bubbling pool on the floor of the entry chamber.

"Ah," the dragon said, "a shifter sent to do a knight's job." It laughed, a low horrible rumble. "Have the others all died? Are you all alone? If you leave now, it might amuse me to let you live."

"Burch!" Esprë's voice screamed from somewhere beyond the dragon.

Kandler launched himself down the stairs before Sallah could stop him.

"Let the kid go," Burch said as Kandler reached his side. He heard the lady knight come down right behind him.

"You are here for the elfling?" The dragon snorted, and Kandler felt the room tremble. "You waste your breath and my time if you think I will relinquish the bearer of the Mark of Death. She is mine forevermore."

Burch stepped forward and leveled his crossbow at the dragon's glowing eye, still framed in the portal.

"You think you can hurt me with your weapons?" A transparent eyelid flicked down over the dragon's eye, protecting the soft tissue beneath. "The temerity of mortals . . ."

Burch smiled at the dragon, showing all his sharp teeth. "Watch this," he said, as he loosed the shockbolt at the creature's eye.

The magic bolt struck right in the center of the slit that ran vertically down the center of the dragon's eye. It exploded with such force that it knocked Kandler and Burch back off their feet and splattered acidic water on every wall in the room. The noise deafened Kandler, and it took him a moment before he realized Sallah was trying to talk to him.

He ignored her for the moment to stare back at the portal in the iron wall. In the flash from the explosion, the dragon's eye had disappeared.

"You got him!" he shouted to Burch, clapping him on the back. The justicar could barely hear his own voice from the ringing in his ears, and he suspected the shifter was deaf as well. Still, he wrapped his old friend in a bear hug and whooped for joy.

Sallah slapped him on the back of the head then, hard. He turned around and glared at her, bothered that anyone could interrupt such an amazing moment. She jerked her thumb back over her shoulder as she grabbed him by the collar, mouthing something he couldn't yet make out. All he could catch was the word "go."

Then the stairwell shuddered, and Kandler could hear

something that seemed as loud as the explosion had been, although a bit farther away. Some wounded beast screeched at the top of its capacious lungs for bitter revenge, and the justicar knew.

The dragon was hurt but not dead.

"What about Esprë?" Kandler shouted, trying to stagger toward the portal. He shrugged off Sallah's efforts to haul him back up the stairs. He knew she was only trying to save him, but he wasn't about to leave there without his daughter.

He stumbled across the shaking ground toward the portal. As he reached it, he saw a crowd of skeletons standing in front of the doorway, cutting him off from what lay within. Somewhere in the darkness, the dragon trashed and crashed his way against every bit of the cavern, bringing large chunks of it crashing down into the churning waters of an underground lake.

Ibrido stood to one side, shouting at the dragon, trying to calm it down, but without success. The dragon-elf was near hysterics, but the black-scaled dragon paid him little heed.

Two skeletons stood near Ibrido, just opposite him from Kandler. In the darkness, the justicar couldn't be sure, but he thought they held someone between them, someone about Esprë's size.

Just then, Kandler's hearing cleared a bit, and he heard Esprë screaming at him at the top of her lungs. "Kandler! Kandler, I'm right here!"

The justicar leaped forward, but a pair of Karrnathi skeletons rattled into his way. He reared back to charge at them when the roof came tumbling down upon them, burying them under tons of rock.

Burch's firm hands snatched Kandler back into the entry chamber, keeping him from sharing the skeletons' fate. The falling rocks sealed off the doorway, though, separating Kandler from his daughter once again.

The justicar charged forward and threw himself against

the rocks. They were too many and too heavy, though, and he knew after a moment's effort that there was no way he could move them on his own.

Kandler cast about desperately, looking for some means of removing the rocks. His eyes fell on Burch's crossbow.

"Use one of those shockbolts," he said, pointing at the wall. "You can blast those rocks out of the way."

"Not a very good idea," Duro said as he ran his hand along the tumbled rocks. "This entire area is unstable now. Even if you blast these out of the way, more will just fall in to take their place, and you could bring the roof down on us here too." He looked up at the ceiling of the entry chamber and took in a faceful of dust for his efforts.

"We have to try something!"

"After a cave-in like that, you don't even know if she's alive," Duro said. Kandler saw the concern etched on the dwarf's face was real. "It could take days to dig her out safely even then."

"We know someone who can tell us if Esprë's alive," Sallah said, pointing her sword back up the stairwell.

"The changeling," Kandler said. He nodded at the lady knight. "She's our only hope now. Let's move!"

The trip back through the mountain seemed to take twice as long, even though Kandler knew they were moving faster than before. The way the entire place kept shaking kept him on his toes. It was hard to tell when a large chunk of the ceiling might decide to break loose, and Duro saved him and the others more than once by steering them away from unsafe regions just before they gave way.

When they reached the exit, Kandler couldn't remember a time he'd been so thrilled to see the sun. It was low in the west now, heading toward a handsome sunset over the plains of Karrnath.

Leading the way, he charged down the narrow path until he reached the wide shelf underneath *Keeper's Claw*. As he ran, he shouted out, "Monja! Monja!"

He spied the halfling's head popping up over the gunwale of *Phoenix*. She didn't bother to shout anything back. Instead, she ran over and found the ship's rope ladder and pitched it over the railing. It tumbled out, falling toward the shelf and landing directly in Kandler's path.

The justicar held the end of the ladder down and waved the others on to it. Burch went first, slinging his crossbow over his shoulder and scrambling up so fast he reached the top before Sallah grabbed hold of the bottom. The lady knight hustled up next, climbing steadily, hand over hand.

When Duro reached the ladder, he stopped. "Where are you going with this contraption?" he asked.

"What's holding you back?" Kandler asked. "Everyone else is dead."

Duro considered this for a moment, then reached out and started up the ladder. "Good point," he said, as he passed Kandler by.

Once Duro was aboard the ship, Kandler launched himself up the ladder too, the bottom end swaying wildly underneath him. When he cleared the gunwale, he glanced around. The first thing he noticed was that Te'oma was missing. The changeling's chains lay empty on the deck.

CHAPTER

53

"Where is she?" Kandler asked Monja as she greeted him at the top of the ladder.

"I'm glad to see you're all right," the halfling shaman said. "The mountain shook so hard we thought it was an earthquake."

"The changeling," Kandler said. "Where is she?"

Monja pointed up at the bridge, and Kandler spun about to stare at Te'oma waving at him from behind the wheel.

"It turns out I'm not as good at flying this airship as I'd hoped," Monja said. "I decided to release Te'oma in case we needed some fancy flying."

Kandler stared down at the halfling. "Are you insane?" he asked. "Wait." He knelt down in front of her and peered into her eyes. "Did she use her psionic powers on you? She's a telepath, you know."

Monja beamed at the justicar. "My mind is stronger and sounder than yours," she said. "Have you spoken with her? She's a charmer."

Kandler shook his head. "For a kidnapper and a killer."

"Have you not killed plenty of people?" Xalt asked from Kandler's other side.

Kandler did not want to have this conversation. "She kidnapped *my* daughter. She tried to kill *me*. I don't think I'll forgive that soon—especially since Esprë's still in danger."

"She's alive!" Sallah shouted as she sprinted over to where Kandler stood to greet her. "Te'oma says she's in contact with Esprë, and she's alive. Ibrido still has her, and he's protecting her while Nithkorrh—that's the dragon's name—tries to batter his way out of the mountain."

A muffled bit of thunder sounded from the middle of the mountain to punctuate Sallah's report.

"I want that changeling back in her chains," Kandler said as he strode up to the bridge. "We can't trust her. She's not safe." He turned to glare up at the changeling behind the wheel, his hand on the hilt of his sword. "You're dangerous."

Te'oma frowned down at Kandler. "Right now, I want what you want: Esprë out of that dragon's hands, safe and sound. Isn't that enough?"

Kandler considered this for a moment. "I can't concentrate on saving my daughter if I'm worried you're going to stick a knife in my back."

"I got a solution to that, boss." Burch stepped up from where he was holding his crossbow trained on the changeling's back. "We got two airships here. Sallah's the only other decent pilot we got. Let the chameleon here take the other."

Kandler goggled at his friend, sure that Te'oma had somehow altered his brain. "That can't be you talking, Burch. You'd give her a Karrnathi warship to pilot all by herself? What if she grabs Esprë and runs off again? What if she decides to ram our ship?" He frowned. "This is a bad idea all around."

Burch patted the side of his crossbow and said, "I'll go with her."

Kandler climbed up on to the bridge and stared into his friend's deep, black eyes. The shifter met his gaze without flinching.

"It's me in here, boss."

Kandler stared a moment longer, then broke into a grin and clapped the shifter on the back. "All right," he said, throwing his arm around Burch's shoulders. "All right," he called to the others. "This is what we're going to do.

"Sallah, come up here and take the wheel."

The changeling stepped aside as the lady knight made her way on to the bridge and took hold of the wheel. Sallah showed Te'oma what she thought of her by putting her back to her.

"Bring us over the Karrnathi airship. We're going to drop off a couple of passengers." He nodded at Burch, and the shifter took the changeling by the arm and escorted her over to the rope ladder. Kandler followed them as *Phoenix* moved into place.

As they reached the gunwale, Kandler pulled Te'oma around by the shoulder and looked into her blank white eyes. "Keep in contact with Esprë. If something happens to her, I want to know right away." He paused for a moment. "How is she right now?"

"Still terrified, still in Ibrido's care."

"And the dragon?"

"He's making progress. Esprë thinks he'll break free soon."

Kandler nodded. "I want you two on point for this," he said. "Your ship is expendable. If the dragon tries to fly off, I want *Phoenix* ready for pursuit." He looked to Burch.

"How many of those things do you have left?"

The shifter held up two fingers.

"Make them count."

Te'oma went down the ladder first, with Burch sliding down right after her. Kandler watched as the changeling strode over to the Karrnathi bridge and took the wheel. The shifter prowled around the bow of the ship, scouting out the best spots from which to loose his crossbow.

For not the first time in the past week, Kandler wished he

was a praying man. He looked up at Sallah as he strode back toward the bridge, and he hoped she could do enough of it for all of them.

"Monja," he said, "I need you ready to heal my daughter as soon as we get her aboard."

"Of course," the halfling shaman nodded.

"Duro," Kandler said, "how good are you with that crossbow?"

"I'll hit the dragon," the dwarf said, unslinging his weapon. "It's a big target."

Kandler clapped Duro on the back. Although he'd known the warrior only a short time, he'd already decided he liked him.

"Good," the justicar said. "I want you back here covering the bridge. Sallah will be too busy with the wheel.

"Sallah," Kandler said, "keep on the changeling's tail. They're to engage with the dragon first. We'll try hit and run attacks until we can get a good angle on snatching Esprë away."

The knight stuck out her chin and nodded. "We'll get her back."

"What about me?" Xalt said.

Kandler hadn't forgotten the warforged. "How are you with acid?" he asked.

Xalt stared at Kandler with his ebony eyes for a moment. "My metal plates would provide some protection against it, but it would eat my fibers away as quickly as your skin."

Kandler frowned. "Can you fire a bow?"

Xalt nodded. "Every warforged was built to be a soldier, no matter what path we followed after that."

"Excellent. The lathon stocked our weapons stores at the Wandering Inn. Go into the hold and grab a bow for me, one for you, and as many arrows as you can find."

Soon after Xalt disappeared into the hold, *Keeper's Claw* took off, climbing higher into the sky. Under Sallah's hand,

Phoenix followed. Kandler strode up to the ship's bow and soon found he had an excellent view of most of the mountain.

The air was cold and thin up here. After the close, foul atmosphere of the dragon's lair, it made Kandler feel lighter. It gave him a focus he needed, something he'd been unable to find when facing down the dragon through that doorway in the iron wall.

He knew that this was his best chance to rescue Esprë. He'd had enough of this chase that had led him across three nations and into a fourth. He was prepared to kill whoever or whatever he had to so that he could put an end to it. He was ready to die so that she might be free. One way or another, this pursuit would end today.

Below him, a plume of smoke erupted from the mountain. It took a moment before he realized it wasn't smoke at all but a tower of dust thrown up from the rocks below.

"Take us down," he called back at Sallah. As he spoke, he saw *Keeper's Claw* moving into position to one side of the plume near its base.

Another plume went up inside the first, piercing it as it surpassed it. A terrible boom sounded out, and the mountaintop shook with it. Rocks tumbled down from the mountain's tallest heights. Off to the west, an avalanche started, the snow shaking from the top of the mountain in waves and roaring down until it passed the snowline and became part of a rockslide instead.

The noise drowned out all else for a moment. Kandler thought he could still hear a steady pounding coming from somewhere inside the mountain, but he couldn't be sure.

As the avalanche ground itself out somewhere near the base of the mountain, another plume went up near where it had before. Te'oma and Sallah adjusted the positions of their ships to accommodate it, for a moment coming perilously close to the plume. Kandler could smell the dry, metallic scent of shattered rock in the chilly air.

Then a part of the side of the mountain exploded outward, showering *Phoenix* in gravel and rocks. Kandler ducked his head under his arms to protect himself and found himself coughing on the fine dust that seemed to blow onto and through everything.

He looked up to see something had blotted out the sun. At first, he thought it was the cloud of dust and dirt still settling out of the air.

Then he heard the dragon's mighty roar.

CHAPTER

54

Kandler leaned back and shaded his eyes against the rain of dust and gravel as the dragon burst into the sky not a hundred feet off the bow. He struggled to peer through the sun-flecked haze as the dragon spiraled high above him, climbing toward the clouds.

He still searched the sky when Xalt tapped him on the shoulder with the end of an already strung bow. The justicar took the weapon from the warforged, along with a quiver full of arrows, which he slung over his back. He nocked an arrow fletched with white feathers and pulled back on the bowstring, sighting along the shaft as he scanned the sky again.

Nithkorrh roared again. Finding the dragon wouldn't be the problem, Kandler knew. Getting a clear angle at some part of him that an arrow could pierce, that would be the trick. He knew that he had little chance of hurting such a beast with a thin piece of wood, no matter how sharp it was or how far back he drew the bow. Even if it punctured the dragon's ebony scales, it would be little more than a bee's sting to it.

But then he wasn't here to kill the dragon. He just wanted his daughter back.

He heard Esprë scream as the echoes of the dragon's

roar finally faded away. He spotted her then, hanging in the dragon's clutches as its wings beat a path to the open sky.

No, he corrected himself. The dragon held Ibrido in its claws, and the dragon-elf had Esprë slumped over in his arms. Kandler couldn't tell if she was alive or dead, but she seemed to be in one piece at least.

Keeper's Claw raced toward the dragon, its ring of fire crackling loudly as the changeling pushed its elemental to its limits. Nithkorrh spotted the ship coming and rumbled out a horrid, phlegm-caked laugh. It hovered in the air for a moment, then dove away to the east, over the mountains and toward the darkening sky.

Sallah brought *Phoenix* to bear on the dragon, which ended up following in the creature's turbulent draft. Nithkorrh might be more nimble in the open than an airship, but he was no faster. Kandler suspected that all those years spent trapped within the mountain had atrophied the creature's wings. Soon *Phoenix* was gaining on it.

"Ready?" Kandler said to Xalt. Out of the corner of his eye, he saw the warforged nod.

"Fire!"

The two released their bowstrings as one, and the shafts raced toward the beast before them. Kandler's struck the dragon in the back, while Xalt's hit its leg. Both arrows pierced the dragon's scales but did not bite deep. With the next flap of Nithkorrh's wings, they both fell away in the breeze.

As the dragon glanced back over its wings, Kandler smiled. The arrows had done their job: getting the dragon's attention.

Xalt cursed as he nocked another arrow to his bow. When Kandler looked over at him, the artificer laughed. "What? I am a warforged, not a priest. Swearing is part of our training."

Kandler would have replied to that, but the dragon in front of them decided to roll up and over until it hovered above them, cackling and preparing to spit.

This was the first good look Kandler had gotten at the beast. He'd seen a great many things in his life. A career as an agent for the Citadel in Sharn took him to a number of strange and distant lands. Even so, he'd never been this close to a dragon before.

If Nithkorrh had been frightening in its lair, out here in the sunlight its presence numbed the mind. Its wings spanned nearly as long as the whole of *Phoenix*, and its mouth burst with dozens of serrated teeth, some as long as a sword. It bore a pair of horns atop its head, the points of which swung out over its leathery batlike ears and toward its toothy jaws. Its ebony scales each looked as solid as a pikeman's shield. Its hands and feet terminated in long, sharp talons that Kandler guessed could pry apart a suit of armor in seconds.

A flaw leaped out of the dragon's menacing majesty though. Where its right eye should have been, a blackened hole peered out instead. Burch's shockbolt had half blinded the beast. If it could be hurt, it could be killed, Kandler thought, although faced with the entire dragon, he had no idea how.

Sallah hauled back *Phoenix* as hard as she could, shoving Kandler and Xalt against the bow. Nithkorrh's burning green spittle tumbled past the front of the ship, right where the craft would have been if the lady knight had maintained her speed. Instead of landing on the deck, though, it fell through the air to the rocks far below.

Duro let loose a bolt from his crossbow, but it sailed through the gap between the dragon and its wings. The dwarf cursed as he reloaded his weapon.

The dragon snorted in glee. "Well played," it growled down at *Phoenix*. "I appreciate foes who make the fight interesting."

The ship leaped forward again, leaving the dragon hovering as *Phoenix* zipped away. Kandler and Xalt managed to hold on to the bow rather than tumble back down the length of the ship.

"Where is it?" Kandler shouted as he scanned the sky behind the ship. The dragon was gone.

Xalt tapped the justicar on the shoulder and pointed up. Kandler craned his neck back and saw the dragon climbing higher and higher into the air on its leathery wings.

"What is it doing?" Xalt asked. "Trying to escape into the sky?"

The ship slowed down, and Kandler spotted Sallah gazing up at the dragon high above and behind them. Just as the dragon reached the top of its climb and started its downward dive, he understood its plan.

"Full speed!" he shouted back at Sallah. "Full speed!"

The lady knight grabbed the wheel with both hands, and *Phoenix* leaped forward, but it was too late. The dragon's power dive gave it far too much speed for them to outrun it.

Kandler and Xalt stood shoulder to shoulder and nocked their arrows. "Fire low," Kandler said. "We don't want to hit Esprë, just shove the dragon off his mark."

They fired their shafts as one, speeding toward Nithkorrh's legs. The creature ignored them, letting them stab into one clawed foot and the bottom of its snaking tail.

"Duck!" Monja yelled from her spot next to Sallah on the bridge. It took a moment before Kandler realized the halfling's warning was meant for Xalt and him.

Xalt pushed Kandler aside at the last moment, just as the dragon charged in for its attack. It lashed out with its tail, which smashed into the ship's deck, right where Kandler had been. The tip of it caught Xalt in the shoulder and spun the warforged about, sending him hurtling toward the bow.

Kandler reached out and grabbed Xalt by the wrist as he went by, but the justicar hadn't managed to anchor himself. The warforged's momentum pulled them both toward the gunwale and the empty space beyond.

As he slammed into the railing across the bow, Kandler scrabbled for a good, strong hold and found one, just as Xalt tumbled over the edge. The sudden shift in the warforged's momentum from outward to downward felt like it might shatter Kandler's elbow, but he managed to keep hold of both the ship and Xalt too.

The airship slowed down and Kandler fought against gravity to haul the warforged back on to the ship. As he hung over the railing, his arm stretched almost to the breaking point, he looked past Xalt's dangling feet to the ground far below. From this high up, it didn't seem real, more like a painting than anything else. The amber glow of the dying sunlight gave the landscape a surreal cast that Kandler wished he had more time to appreciate. If he didn't let go of the heavy warforged soon, he thought it might be the last thing he ever got to see.

"Release me!" Xalt shouted.

"Pull yourself up!"

"I'm too heavy. I'll bring us both down," the warforged said. "Release me now!"

Kandler didn't bother to respond. He gritted his teeth and locked his knees under the railing along the gunwale. Then he swung his other arm out to grab the warforged too.

It was a calculated risk, and Kandler instantly regretted it. He felt the wood digging into his knees and then starting to slip. Sweat broke out on his brow as he strove to hold on to both Xalt and the ship, and he felt both getting away.

Then a set of hands grabbed him by his sword belt and pulled him back and up hard. He shoved his legs under the railing and pushed with all his might, hauling up with his arms at the same time. He thought the strain might tear the muscles in his back, but as he straightened his legs with the help from behind, he saw Xalt's head and arms clear the railing and clamp on.

Kandler grabbed the warforged's shoulders and hauled him bodily on to the airship's deck. As he did, he fell back against Sallah, who held him in her arms.

"Thank the Flame," she said.

"Thank you," said Kandler.

"Wait," Xalt said, "if you are here, who is flying the ship?"

Kandler scrambled off Sallah to spy Monja standing at the wheel, waving at them. The halfling stood on the spokes in the middle of the wheel, just so she could see over it, but she seemed to be handling the ship well enough. Duro stood behind her, waving his crossbow about as he tried to cover the sky.

"As long as we don't need any fancy maneuvers, she should be fine," Sallah said.

The dragon didn't roar as it approached this time. The first Kandler saw of it, its claws had already touched down on the deck between him and the bridge, its reptilian, orange eye glaring out at him. As the justicar bounded to his feet, the creature set Ibrido and Esprë down on the deck in front of it and started to laugh.

CHAPTER

55

Kandler stood and drew his blade as Ibrido leaped from the dragon's claws and landed on the deck of the airship, the unconscious Esprë in his arms. Beside him, Sallah did the same, silvery flames crawling up and down the length of her sacred sword. Xalt drew a short knife from a sheath on his side, and the three stood ready to face the dragon together.

As Nithkorrh rested his weight on *Phoenix*, the entire ship dipped in the air, and Kandler lost his footing. Sallah and Xalt went down too.

"Here you are, half-breed," the dragon rumbled as it flapped its wings to take the bulk of its mass off the sinking airship, which then stopped falling again. "Time to earn your keep. I do not intend to carry you and the elfling all the way to Argonnessen."

The dragon-elf lay Esprë down on the deck, then drew his blade, a length of what looked like ivory fashioned into a long, curved blade, serrated along its cutting edge. He held it as if it weighed nothing in his hands, swinging it about in tight loops, weaving a deadly defense around him.

The dragon growled with delight, baring its many teeth. It crouched back on its massive haunches, clutching at the airship with its massive claws as its beating wings kept it partially in the air, ready to savor the upcoming battle. Kandler had no doubt it would make quick work of him if he somehow managed to defeat Ibrido. First, though, he had to keep the dragon-elf from killing him.

Kandler glanced up in the sky and had to stifle a smile. He snapped his eyes back down to Ibrido and stalked toward him, making sure he and the dragon kept their eyes focused on him. Sallah strode up on his left and Xalt on his right, each of them keeping pace with him, forming a line across the ship that Ibrido would not be able to dodge past.

The dragon-elf leaped forward, over Esprë's sleeping body, and swung his sword down at Kandler. The justicar brought up his sword to parry the blow, catching Ibrido's strange blade on the tip of his own. A strange clang sounded in Kandler's ears, and when he brought his sword back he saw that Ibrido had notched it nearly in half at its tip.

"You face no sell-sword here," the dragon-elf said. "No mindless skeleton, no careless vampire."

Kandler glanced at his weapon again. "There's more to your blade than to you," he said, taunting Ibrido. "It's easy to boast with a dragon at your back."

"Nithkorrh is only here as an audience. I don't need his help to deal with trash like you."

"Well," Kandler said, "here's your chance to prove it."

With that, Kandler, Sallah, and Xalt all turned and threw themselves against the railing that ran along the bow of the ship. Confused, Ibrido stood where he was for a moment, his sword held out before him.

"Cowards!" he shouted at them. "Face me, or I will kill you where you are!"

Kandler kept crouched against the railing and made sure that Sallah and Xalt were pressed in tight there too. He didn't want anyone going over the edge again. "Hold on tight," he whispered to them.

Ibrido turned to Nithkorrh for guidance. "What am I to do with such—" Right then, he spotted *Keeper's Claw* soaring in behind the dragon. "Master!" he cried.

Startled, the dragon beat its wings harder and lifted a few feet off the deck of *Phoenix*. The claws that it had dug into the ship, though, didn't come free so easily. As the dragon tried to free itself, Burch's shockbolt slammed into it, right between the bases of its wings.

The explosion hurtled the dragon into the air. It knocked down Ibrido as it went cartwheeling over the bow, howling in pain and rage. It disappeared over *Phoenix's* gunwale and went plummeting toward the mountains below, smoke trailing from its back.

A cheer went up from the bridge, and Kandler stood up to see Monja leaping up and down on the wheel. As he rose, he grabbed Xalt by the shoulder and said to him, "Protect Esprë. That's your job. Leave Ibrido to Sallah and me."

The warforged nodded and circumnavigated the dragon-elf to the right, hoping to work around him to reach the young elf. Ibrido scoffed and stepped to the left, leaving the way wide open.

"If you wish to care for her while I carve up your friends, please do," the dragon-elf said. "With luck, I'll finish them off before my master returns."

Kandler ignored Ibrido and said to Sallah, "Get to the bridge and fly the ship."

The lady knight froze. "Monja can handle it," she said.

"We need Monja to check out Esprë," he said. "We don't know how badly she's hurt."

Sallah stared at Kandler for a moment, locking him in her beautiful green eyes. "All right," she said. "Just don't get yourself killed."

Brandishing her blade before her, Sallah followed in Xalt's path then sprinted by him toward the bridge. As she went, the warforged picked up Esprë and started to carry her aft.

"How foolish—I mean, 'brave'—of you," Ibrido said. "With three of you working together against me, you might have stood a chance. Sequentially, I shall dissect each of you with my blade and leave you for the carrion fowl to testify to my handiwork."

"Shut up and fight," Kandler said, readying his notched blade. He wanted to make this quick, to kill Ibrido before the dragon came back, while he still had a chance. Esprë came first, of course, but faced with the dragon-elf and his mysterious sword, he felt as alone as he ever had.

Ibrido stepped forward and slashed out at Kandler with his blade. The justicar sidestepped the blow and returned it with a quick stab to the dragon-elf's ribs. The point of his sword skittered off Ibrido's hide, slicing open the creature's shirt but little else. He realized to hurt Ibrido he would have to land a much more solid blow.

The dragon-elf swung his sword back, and Kandler had to hurl himself to the side to avoid the blade. It slid off the edge of his sword, just missing slicing off a bit of his ear.

"First blood!" Ibrido said.

Kandler rolled back to his feet and saw that red fluid covered the tip of Ibrido's bone-colored sword. He brought his hand to the side of his head, and it came away the same color. The dragon-elf's blade was so sharp, his strike so fast, that the justicar had not even felt it.

Kandler wanted nothing more than to wipe the smug look from Ibrido's face. Instead of pointing out, though, that his own touch would have brought blood on anyone not covered with scales, he gripped the hilt of his sword even tighter and launched his next attack.

The ferocity of Kandler's assault drove the dragon-elf a few steps back. Try as he might, though, the justicar could not penetrate Ibrido's defenses. Every time he tried a new angle, Ibrido's blade leaped out to protect him, almost as if it had a mind of its own.

Eager to put an end to this fight, Kandler shifted to a two-handed grip on his sword's hilt and brought it down in a sweeping overhand motion designed to smash the dragon-elf's blade aside. A mighty clang sounded as the two blades met, and Kandler smiled as his sword met little resistance past that. As he pulled back from the fight, hoping to find that he'd sliced into Ibrido's scaled flesh, he realized he held only half a blade in his hand. The upper portion had gone sailing off after smashing into Ibrido's amazing sword.

The dragon-elf cackled with glee.

"My blade is superior to yours in every way," he said. "It was a gift from the dragon kings, forged in furnaces stoked with their own fiery breath, from an ancient dragon's own fang. No weapon can stand against it. No armor can hope to stop it."

As Ibrido launched his own counterattack, Kandler raised what was left of his blade and swore.

"Is she all right?" Sallah asked, glancing down to where Monja and Xalt huddled over Esprë's body. Duro gave her a thumbs-up sign and then went back to peering over the aft railing, looking for any signs of the dragon's return.

"She's still breathing," Monja said, "but just barely."

Xalt cradled the young elf in his arms as the halfling shaman began to pray, a warm, golden glow washing over her arms.

As a member of the Church of the Silver Flame, Sallah believed that there was only one true god, the Silver Flame itself. All others were mere pretenders, unwitting reflections of the Flame viewed through a cracked prism. Watching the shaman work her prayers to the Sovereign Host, though, she felt a moment of doubt. Monja connected to her gods so effortlessly that it seemed churlish to think that her relationship with them was somehow less than that of Sallah or the elders in her church.

Now was not the time to worry about such things though, Sallah told herself. Her main concern was keeping the ship away from Nithkorrh. An enraged roar from somewhere below told her that Burch's shockbolt hadn't put the great beast down for good. Since she couldn't see the creature from that angle, she figured the best thing she could do was push the airship to its top speed and hope the dragon would never catch up.

The elemental in the ship didn't like the idea much though. It fought against Sallah's control, perhaps sensing that the dragon in pursuit could damage the ship enough to finally free it.

Sallah shoved the elemental along as hard as she could. She sensed that if she relinquished the wheel it would go back to slacking, but for the moment it obeyed her as well as she could hope.

She peered down the deck and saw Kandler facing off against Ibrido. Over their short time together, she'd come to respect the justicar as a top swordsman. When she'd first met him working as the justicar for Mardakine, that tiny little town in a crater on the edge of nowhere, she'd thought he'd just been the only man in town crazy enough to take on the job.

Kandler carried his skill with a blade so quietly that few would ever guess its extent. He never went for flashy or showy moves, preferring to get the job done with as few strokes of his sword as possible. "The longer the fight, the more chances for something to go wrong," he'd once told her.

Ibrido, though, seemed to be pushing the justicar to his limits. At first, Sallah couldn't understand it. The only reason she'd agreed to leave Kandler with the dragon-elf was that she figured he'd make quick work of the dragon's minion. As the fight wore on, though, she knew something was wrong, and she began to regret her choice.

"No!" she said when she saw Kandler's blade part on

Ibrido's. It looked like the dragon-elf's blade had cut right through the justicar's, leaving him armed with only its remnant.

Sallah looked down and saw Xalt helping Esprë to her feet. Monja's prayers had been answered, and the young elf looked fit if yet a little dazed.

"Take the wheel," Sallah said, not caring if Monja or Esprë complied with the order, as long as someone did. She drew her blade and leaped off the bridge, shouting, "I have to go save your father!"

CHAPTER

56

As the dragon spun away from *Phoenix*, Burch bared his teeth in a wide, toothy grin. Somewhere behind him on the bridge of *Keeper's Claw*, the changeling cheered as they watched the winged beast tumble down through the sky.

"That won't be it," Burch called back. "Let's take the fight to him!"

The shifter slapped another shockbolt into his crossbow. It was the last of the ones Duro had given him, and he knew he had to make it count. He raced up the ladder to the airship's bridge and stood next to the changeling, who had her hands wrapped around the ship's wheel. She'd shoved aside the body of the bosun, who still hung from the bridge's console by a set of manacles.

"Nice hit," Te'oma said, no trace of a grudge in her admiration.

"Two nice hits," Burch said, checking the crossbow over again to make sure it was in top working order. "With magic, exploding bolts, and it's still alive."

"What does that tell you?" the changeling asked.

Burch stared at her for a moment. He didn't want to

trust her, but he'd put himself in a situation where he had no choice.

"That we're in real trouble."

He strode to the back of the bridge and gazed down over the gunwale. He listened hard as he did, hoping he wouldn't hear the changeling's footsteps coming toward him. He knew it would take only a little shove to push him out into the open air. Unless he could sprout wings, he'd be dead for sure.

"There he is," Burch said, pointing down below and behind them. "Six o' clock low."

"Six o' what?"

Burch scowled at the changeling. "Ever seen a clock?"

"Of course," Te'oma said. "What does that have to do—?"

"Six is behind us," Burch said, pointing aft. "Noon is ahead. High is above. Low is below."

The changeling nodded. "You've spent a lot of time on an airship before."

Burch shook his head. "Many pints drinking with pilots."

He glanced back over the aft rail. The dragon had arrested its fall and was beating its wings once more.

"It's heading straight for *Phoenix*," Burch said, pointing off to the starboard. "It'll come up through three o'clock and keep right for them."

"What should I do?" Te'oma asked. She gripped the airship's wheel so tight that her knuckles seemed whiter than ever, almost the same shade as her eyes.

"Get in its way," Burch said. "If I get a chance, I'll do the rest."

Te'oma nodded and the ship swung starboard and downward on a rough course to intercept the oncoming dragon.

From Burch's point of view, the trouble was that the dragon was now below the ship. He couldn't see down there—the ship was in the way—and he couldn't attack something he couldn't see. This meant he had to wait for the dragon to rise above the ship and give him a clear angle. From which direction the creature would pop up, though, was anyone's guess.

Burch expected Nithkorrh to swing around the hull of *Keeper's Claw* and head straight for *Phoenix*. Instead, something large and unseen smashed into the hull and sent him flying from the bridge, to land in a heap on the deck.

Burch glanced back and saw that Te'oma had managed to keep her feet, but only because of her death-grip on the wheel. Something hit the bottom of the ship again, and this time she screamed.

"It's going to tear us apart!"

Burch didn't see how the changeling was wrong. The dragon had the right idea. If they couldn't see it from above, then it was safe below. It could rip the airship to splinters, and they couldn't do a damned thing to stop it.

The shifter ran over to the gunwale, grabbed an end of the rope ladder, and tossed it overboard. If he could just get into position, he might be able to get a clear look at the beast and knock it from the sky.

Then he realized that "if" was way too big. To pull it off, he'd have to get off a clean release while bouncing along like a minnow on the end of a fishing pole. The image reminded him he'd be the bait in that scenario. He wondered if the dragon would be able to resist it, and if it didn't, where would that leave him?

A splintering sound below told him he'd better come up with a good idea soon. He charged up to the bridge, shouting to Te'oma, "Take us down! Down, as fast as you can!"

A moment later, *Keeper's Claw* plunged toward the rocky slopes of the mountain below. The dragon bellowed in surprise and then distress.

"He's trapped beneath the ship," Burch said. "Keep going, and we'll smash him into the rocks."

"Are you insane?" Te'oma yelled. "That'll kill us too."

"What's your point?"

The changeling goggled at the shifter with her wide, white eyes. "I don't want to die!" she said.

Burch raised his bushy eyebrows. "He keeps tearing at the ship, we're dead anyhow. This way, we kill him too."

Te'oma glared at the shifter for a moment then reached out to hold his hand. "All right," she said. "Let's do it."

The airship plummeted toward the ground, the dragon screeching in protest now. The ship's ring of fire tried to drown it out with a crackling roar of its own. If the ship was destroyed, the elemental inside the ring would be free, Burch knew, and it seemed happy to do everything it could—within its orders—to help make that happen.

A terrible tearing sound came from beneath the ship, and Burch saw the dragon break free, flapping away off the port side.

"Pull up," he told Te'oma. "He got away."

The ship kept falling. "Pull up, I said."

Sweat beaded on the changeling's snowy brow. "I can't!" she said. "The ship's not responding."

Burch cursed. "The dragon must have damaged the lower restraining arc. The wheel's useless."

"What are we going to do?"

Burch peered down at the ground hurtling up toward them.

"Die a messy way."

CHAPTER

57

Kandler cursed as Ibrido's sword hacked off another section of his blade. At this rate, he'd soon be left with nothing but his hilt.

The dragon-elf smirked as he aimed another blow at Kandler's head. "Give up, human," he said. "You can't win."

Kandler said nothing as he retreated in a wide circle, trying not to let Ibrido back him into a corner. As soon as that happened, the dragon-elf would have him at his mercy. The justicar's sword wasn't doing much to protect him. The only thing he had going for him was space.

He tried to work his way past Ibrido, to make a break for the bridge. There, he'd have Sallah and Duro to help him, but the Karrn always managed to step into his way.

Kandler saw Sallah break free from the bridge and come dashing toward him. He just needed to hold Ibrido off for a few more moments, and she'd be at his side.

The dragon-elf heard the knight's footfalls pounding up behind him, though, and redoubled his efforts to bring Kandler down. His dragon-fang sword flashed about like a hummingbird, picking away at Kandler's defenses until he could barely see from the sweat pouring down into his eyes.

The justicar gave up all conscious thought about the swordplay and let his training take over. The only things left to him were the sound of Ibrido's sword clanging against his own, the impact of the clashing blades jarring his arm, and the thought that he had to kill this creature to save his daughter.

Just as Kandler thought his will to keep his defenses up might falter, Ibrido cried out and fell backward, clutching at his back with his free arm. A moment later, he drew a crossbow bolt out of his shoulder, the end of it dripping with his fresh, red blood.

Kandler spotted Duro standing on the bridge, reloading his weapon. He breathed a word of thanks to the dwarf, then watched as Sallah raced up to the dragon-elf, her blazing sword held over her head, ready for a two-handed blow.

Still howling in pain from the bolt, Ibrido spun and met Sallah's attack, parrying her mighty chop with his fangblade. As the swords met, Kandler held his breath. Sallah's sword was a sacred icon, holy to her and her church. That didn't mean, though, that it could stand against the amazing edge of the dragon-elf's weapon.

Sparks flew as the blades clashed off each other, and both blades held. The magic in Sallah's blade made it stronger than Kandler's, the justicar realized. While his had been the finest sword in Mardakine, it was just steel, forged by his friend Rislinto and given its razor edge by hours of sharpening during the dull hours working the town watch. It could not hope to stand against something as marvelous as the fangblade.

Kandler wondered the same thing about himself. Here he stood, only a man, nothing to aid him but his own skill and determination. He was no knight, no shaman, no wizard, and he had to face monstrous creatures like Ibrido and his magical sword. What hope did he have against such power, much less that of a full-fledged dragon?

Still, Kandler had never been one to worry about the odds. If there was a way to defeat Ibrido, he would find it, then he'd kill the dragon too.

It wasn't for himself that he'd do it. He'd had a full life, seen many things, fought many a foe for all sorts of good causes. He'd loved and been loved more than he'd had any right to expect. If the Keeper came for his soul now, he'd let that dark god take his hand, but to give up on himself meant giving up on Esprë too, and that he refused to do.

Kandler reversed his grip on the hilt-shard of his sword and hurled himself at Ibrido as the dragon-elf turned to face Sallah full on. He plunged the bit into the dragon-elf's shoulder, but the weapon turned on the creature's scaly green hide.

While parrying yet another blow from the lady knight, Ibrido turned and slammed his elbow into Kandler's face, knocking the justicar to the deck. As he fell to his knees, Kandler spun toward the dragon-elf, trying to catch him in the back of his legs and take him to the deck along with him.

Ibrido leaped backward over Kandler instead, and Sallah nearly ran the justicar through. To keep from doing so, she threw herself to the side, away from both him and the dragon-elf.

This left Kandler on his knees before Ibrido. The dragon-elf wasn't one to ignore such an opportunity, the justicar knew. He fought the instinct to raise his hands to protect himself. If the fangblade could cut through steel, it would slice through his bones like warm butter.

Instead of trying to scramble away, he launched himself at the dragon-elf again, this time aiming for Ibrido's middle. If he could get in under the blade's reach, he reasoned, he might have a chance.

Kandler's tackle knocked Ibrido back, but he couldn't manage to wrap his arms around the creature's slippery scales. For a moment, he thought he had a chance, but the dragon-elf stiff-armed him in the jaw and shoved him back again.

Still trying for a tackle, Kandler stepped forward, but this time Ibrido managed to get his blade up in time, and he ran it right through the justicar's guts.

Kandler felt the point of the fangblade stab into the wall of his abdomen and pass through his coiled intestines before passing out his back, just nicking his spine. The pain was incredible, like nothing he'd ever felt before, and he knew right then that he was dead. The only question left was how long it would take for him to draw his last breath.

Desperate to sell his life dearly, Kandler grasped at the hilt of the fangblade. His fingers clasped over those of Ibrido's, and the dragon-elf bared its teeth at him.

"You were a fine foe," Ibrido said. "Give my regards to the Keeper."

With that, the dragon-elf put a boot to Kandler's belly and shoved him off his blade. The justicar's hot, thick blood poured out after the withdrawn sword, drenching his clothes as he fell to the deck in a heap.

He heard voices screaming: Sallah's and—somewhere far away—Esprë's too.

CHAPTER

58

Burch could barely hear himself think, Te'oma was screaming so loud. He couldn't understand how she could make so much noise when he felt like he could barely breathe. He saw her black cloak flapping around her, the living tissue it was really made out of trying to deploy its wings. He reached out and wrapped his arms around them and her, putting an end to that.

"You'll kill us both!" the changeling cried, struggling in Burch's grasp. She let go of the airship's useless wheel and tried to shove him away.

"I don't plan to die alone."

"You bastard!" Te'oma screeched. "Let me go!"

"Would you just *listen* to me?" he shouted in her face, his nose less than an inch from hers. "Try one more thing for me," he said, trying not to sound like he was begging. "Do that, and I'll let you go."

"We don't have time," she started. "What is it?" she continued, not waiting for him to press his argument.

"Can you reach it with your mind?" Burch shouted.

"What?"

"The elemental," he said, jerking his head at the ring of

335

fire. "You're a telepath. Forget about the wheel. See if you can get its attention on your own."

Te'oma stared at the shifter for a moment, her hair blowing straight up at the sky as the ship raced toward the ground. He released her and she blinked her white eyes at him once before saying, "All right."

The changeling closed her eyes and furrowed her brow. For a long moment, nothing happened, and Burch wondered how it would feel to be crushed to death from a fall from such a great height. Would he have any sensation at all of bouncing off the ground after he smacked into it, or would he lose consciousness at that point? Curious as he was to find out, he knew he'd be happy to put off the answers until another day.

The first clue Burch had that the ship was stopping was when he felt heavier. The unexpected change in momentum drove him to his knees. It felt like the ship was swinging from the end of a long rope. Now that it had reached the end of its length, it slowed its descent, hovered where it was for a split-second, and then began its long climb back up again.

Te'oma screamed in delight as the airship zoomed back into the open sky, hot on the trail of *Phoenix*, which was now moving off to the south. She reached out and embraced Burch, hopping up and down the entire time. The shifter allowed himself a smile and gave her a one-armed hug back. With his other arm, though, he pointed up at the dragon coming down at them again.

"Just won't give up, will it?" Burch said, pulling himself out of Te'oma's arms. He picked up his crossbow from where he'd let it fall, thankful that he hadn't accidentally set off the shockbolt, and he placed it on the bridge's front railing. Then he got down on one knee and sighted along the shockbolt's shaft.

The dragon swung back and forth in its flight path as it sped toward *Keeper's Claw*, making it impossible for Burch to get a perfect angle at it. With only the one shockbolt left, he was determined to wait for the right moment to loose it. He didn't miss often, but this attack had to be perfect. He wouldn't get another chance.

Even if the shockbolt smacked the dragon square in its good eye, though, Burch wasn't sure it would do a lick of good. He'd already loosed two of these amazing bolts into the beast, and it had still disabled the airship. If it hadn't been for Te'oma's psionics, right now he'd be dead.

Still, he didn't have any better ideas at the moment. The only thing he could think of was to wait until the dragon opened its mouth to devour him before loosing the shockbolt down its rotting gullet. With luck, that would do it. The only trick was that it involved getting close enough to the dragon to be eaten, and Burch wasn't all too comfortable with that.

"Let him have it!" Te'oma shouted at the shifter. "Now!"

Burch ignored her. The angle was either there or it wasn't. Some people marveled at his skill with the crossbow. They asked him who'd blessed his crossbow or what kind of magic infused it. He always smiled at them and told them the truth. Most of them never believed him.

You just line up the angle. Don't loose your bolt until it's there.

Lots of things got in the way of an angle. People screaming in your ear never helped. Riding a bouncing ship driven by a sullen elemental creature of fire didn't come up often, but it made things harder. Firing at a moving target, even one as large as a dragon, that was more common.

The trick, if there was one, was to let those other things go, to focus on the task at hand, and to wait for the angle to present itself. When ready met chance, you pulled the trigger.

Sometimes it never did.

The dragon spun in a swashing roll right over the ship and disappeared behind the airship's rudder.

Te'oma slapped Burch on the back of the head. "Why

didn't you loose? What good does that bolt do stuck in your crossbow?"

Burch snarled at the changeling, and she backed off. That was one distraction taken care of, at least for now.

He hefted his crossbow again and scanned the sky for the dragon. The sun rode low and red in the west now, making it harder to pick out the black-scaled creature against the encroaching night sky.

He was peering out at the bow when the beast appeared over the rudder, having doubled back instead of following the momentum of its loop out to the front of the ship. Burch started to swing his crossbow back to find the angle, but he was too slow.

Nithkorrh whipped its arched neck forward and spat something green and viscous down at the ship.

Te'oma screamed and dove over the bridge's front railing, trying to avoid the burning acid, but the dragon hadn't aimed it at her. Instead, it sloshed into the airship's upper restraining arc and began eating away at the rune-crusted wood.

Burch swore as he sprinted toward the changeling, the dragon's monstrous laugh echoing in his ears. The ship's deck jangled beneath his feet, but he kept his legs pumping, the long, dark nails at the ends of his bare toes digging into the wood.

As the restraining arc melted, the ring of fire flared up and out, the elemental straining against its magical bonds. The first burst slashed out and caught Nithkorrh through one of its wings, setting it ablaze. The dragon roared in pain and surprise, and then it was gone, falling away behind the ship again.

When Burch reached the tremulous Te'oma, the ring of fire flared again. The heat singed his mane of hair.

"We have to leave!" the changeling shouted, trying to push the shifter away. "This thing is falling apart!"

"Not yet," Burch growled in her face. "Not yet."

CHAPTER

59

Kandler smiled as he felt his life's blood leaving him by the hole the dragon-elf had speared through his middle. He struggled to his knees, the world around him seeming colder by the minute. It wasn't the chill of the high, thin air, he knew. His blood was his heat, the magic fire that kept him going, and it was leaking out between his fingers.

"You cannot have him!" Sallah said, slashing at Ibrido with her flaming sword, the sacred symbol of her office.

It was not her own blade, the one she'd been given when she'd been knighted. She'd left the fragments of that in Construct, having shattered it trying to avenge the death of Sir Deothen—her mentor, her commander, and her father.

This blade had belonged to her friend Brendis, a fellow knight who'd died at Ibrido's hand. She'd taken it from the hands of the changeling who—at the dragon-elf's behest—had impersonated him long enough to spirit Esprë away once again. Now she was ready to plunge it into the heart of the beast who had caused her so much grief.

Kandler staggered back against the railing along the airship's bow. If not for the gunwale to rest against, his knees would have given out for sure. Instead, as his blood dripped down on to the deck between his feet, he watched the woman he loved fight for his life and hers.

Ibrido stood his ground against the lady knight's onslaught, weaving his fangblade into a defense that shielded him from all her blows. The blade's light heft and incredible strength combined to let him equal Sallah's efforts and surpass them.

After the dragon-elf parried yet another of her mighty blows, Sallah fell back panting, brandishing her burning sword before her. The sweat on her brow glistened in the silvery light, giving her skin a metallic sheen, except for her fiery curls and her emerald eyes, the same color as the tight-fitted scales covering her foe's skin.

"You cannot stand before the light of the Silver Flame," Sallah said, a snarl curling her lips. "Righteousness will prevail."

Ibrido stared at the knight with his unblinking, yellow eyes for a moment, then laughed. "You think your little cult can withstand the full power of the dragons of Argonnessen? Nithkorrh alone is older than the candle you worship. He could snuff it out with the beating of his wings."

Sallah narrowed her eyes at the dragon-elf as she caught her breath. "The Silver Flame burns in the heart of us all. It is the spark of goodness that melds us together like tongues of fire joining to form a mighty blaze."

"Goodness?" Ibrido scoffed, stepping forward and slashing at Sallah with his blade, testing her, seeing how tired she was. "That's a concept for fur-bearing beasts. Those with scales know better. There is no good or evil, only triumph and loss!"

The ferocity of Ibrido's assault caught Sallah off guard. Still exhausted, she fell back before the dragon-elf's flurry of blows, managing to bring her sword up just in time, over and over again. As she went, Kandler could see that she strove to keep her foe from getting past her to the justicar, protecting him from the beast too.

Still holding his middle together with one hand, Kandler slipped his knife into the other. He knew he'd never get close enough to stab into between the dragon-elf's scales. Instead, he reversed it and grabbed it by its gleaming blade, smearing it with his blood. Then he hurled it at Ibrido's head.

The dragon-elf never saw the knife coming. Kandler's feeble throw lacked the force it needed to hurt Ibrido, but when it smacked the dragon-elf in the nose it stopped him in mid-slash.

Sallah saw her chance and stabbed at the dragon-elf with her sword. Its vicious point rammed right through the scales in Ibrido's chest and stuck there between his upper ribs. She tried to wrench it back, but Ibrido's free hand reached up and held the blade in place.

The dragon-elf bared his teeth at the lady knight. "Time to end this," he said, slashing out at her with his blade.

Defenseless without her sword, Sallah flung herself backward, trying to avoid the whizzing arc of Ibrido's fangblade. She almost made it, the tip of the blade slicing through her breastplate and across her chest.

"No!" Kandler shouted as Sallah backpedaled. He couldn't tell how badly she'd been hurt, but he refused to let her stand alone against the dragon-elf's sword.

The justicar shoved himself off the gunwale so he could be at Sallah's side. As he did, she stepped in the pool of blood he'd left behind when he'd been run through. Her booted heel slipped in the slick, red fluid, and she tumbled back on to the deck.

Kandler reached out to catch Sallah and wrapped his arms around her. Too weak to support both his weight and her, he fell backward to the deck too, cushioning her landing.

"So now you see how history shall record this," Ibrido said as he tossed Sallah's sword aside. "My triumph. Your loss."

The emerald-scaled dragon-elf stalked toward Kandler

and Sallah, tangled together on the deck.

"Go ahead," Ibrido said, waving his sword over them, ready to plunge it through their hearts or their heads. "Beg for your lives. I love it when they beg."

Kandler snarled at the dragon-elf, trying to find something to say, when Sallah turned her head and kissed him full on the mouth. Too startled to respond, he stared down at her as their lips parted.

She looked up at him with her emerald eyes, blood on her ruby lips. He realized he could taste it on his own. "I love you," she said.

He squeezed her in his arms as he glanced up at Ibrido gazing down at them in disgust. "I love you too," he whispered.

CHAPTER

60

Esprë tried to run after Sallah to come to Kandler's aid too, but Xalt and Duro wouldn't let her.

"They are fighting to protect you," Xalt said, holding her by the arm. "If you put yourself in harm's way, you can only distract them."

"But he's killing them!" she said.

"Have some faith in them," Monja said from the ship's wheel. "I've never met warriors so fine."

"Look at Kandler," Esprë said. "He's dying! I have to help them."

"Hold still, little elf," Duro said as he leveled his crossbow at Ibrido. "You'll spoil my aim."

The dwarf pulled the weapon's trigger and loosed a bolt at the dragon-elf. It stabbed into Ibrido's shoulder, causing him to howl in pain. Duro cheered his success as he hunted for another bolt and slapped it into his crossbow.

"See?" Xalt said, his hand still on Esprë's arm. "Sallah is there now. She will protect him."

The young elf, the dwarf, the halfling, and the war-forged watched the lady knight and the dragon-elf square off in a dazzling display of swordplay. Esprë held her breath through most of it, only letting it out to squeal with delight or dismay.

Duro cursed as his crossbow wavered toward the fight. "I can't get a clear angle," he said, "not on a moving airship."

"Burch could do it," Esprë said.

"He is occupied," Xalt said, pointing down and to the starboard, where Nithkorrh assaulted *Keeper's Claw*.

The young elf heard Monja praying at the wheel. "Can you do anything for them from here?" she asked the shaman.

The halfling shook her head. "When I pray to the Host every morning, I don't ask for the power to hurt others, only to help and heal."

Esprë looked down the length of the ship to see Kandler struggling to stand against the railing along the bow. Blood trickled through the fingers he held over his stomach.

"I think we're going to need some of that," the young elf said.

Hope leaped in Esprë's heart as she watched Sallah launch a furious attack at Ibrido. She couldn't hear the words they traded over the sounds of their clanging blades and the crackling roar of the airship's ring of fire, so she crept down from the bridge, trying to get closer.

"I do not see the wisdom in this," Xalt said as he escorted the girl on to the deck. "I do not believe Kandler would approve."

"He's too hurt to object right now." She took a few more steps forward along the ship's starboard side, trying to get a better view of what was going on. She noticed Duro creeping forward along the port gunwale, looking for a clear angle with his crossbow, too.

If Ibrido defeated Sallah, Esprë didn't know what she would do. She'd been sure that Kandler could handle the dragon-elf. Everyone she knew always said he was the best swordsman they'd ever known, but that damned sword of Ibrido's more than evened the odds. How could Kandler have hoped to win a swordfight in which his foe destroyed his sword?

Esprë was grateful that Sallah's sacred sword had held up better against Ibrido's fangblade. Otherwise, she knew the lady knight would already be dead. Right now, she was Kandler's only hope—and by extension, Esprë's too.

The young elf knew that the others would be no match for Ibrido should he beat Sallah. Xalt was next to useless with a weapon. Duro's crossbow bolt had barely broken the dragon-elf's hide, and she guessed the fangblade would slice his axe apart in seconds. That left only Monja and her, and the shaman had already declared herself a healer, not a fighter.

It would be up to Esprë then. As the thought struck her, the dragonmark on her back began to burn.

When Ibrido lay open Sallah's breastplate, the young elf gasped in horror. The lady knight seemed to hang there in the air for a moment, shocked at the ease with which the dragon-elf had sliced through her armor. Then she stepped backward and slipped in a pool of Kandler's cooling blood.

Esprë stifled a scream as she watched Sallah fall into Kandler's arms. She knew she had to act, and fast, or Ibrido would kill them both.

The Mark of Death on her back felt like it might sizzle through her tunic. She felt icy fingers of glowing black run down her arms and envelop her hands, which she flexed as she slipped up behind the dragon-elf. Xalt tried to pull her back by her elbow, but the warforged flinched away at her freezing touch. She turned and shushed him with a finger to her lips. The ebon glow didn't bother her at all.

Esprë remembered what had happened the last time she'd tried to kill Ibrido, and she refused to make the same mistake again. This time, she would strike before he could react. On one level, it seemed an act of cowardice to her to ambush someone like that, but she knew it was a matter of survival. If she took on the dragon-elf toe to toe, he would cut her to

pieces. The only chance she and everyone else on the ship had
was if she could catch Ibrido by surprise.

Esprë reached out with her glowing hands to grasp at the
dragon-elf as he prepared to finish off Kandler and Sallah.
She struggled to be as silent as she could, but just before she
could grasp Ibrido from behind, Kandler spotted her, and
his eyes grew large with surprise.

The justicar bit his tongue, trying not to give the young
elf away, but the look on his face was enough to arouse the
dragon-elf's suspicions. Ibrido snapped his head around to
look over his shoulder, and his crimson, reptilian eyes caught
Esprë in their unblinking gaze.

As if Ibrido were a walking basilisk, Esprë froze.

"So," the dragon-elf sneered, "you think to kill me with
your deadly touch? A good try, elfling, but—"

A crossbow bolt smashed into Ibrido's snout and ricocheted
off into the open air. Stunned, the dragon-elf tottered
backward and lowered the tip of his fangblade.

Before he could recover, Esprë leaped up and wrapped
her hands around his throat. As she did, she let go every bit
of power she had pent up in her dragonmark.

The night-colored glow flowed out through her hands and
swallowed Ibrido whole. The dragon-elf dropped his sword
as he toppled backward, frozen stiff as if rigor mortis had
already set into his joints.

"No!" Ibrido screamed through clenched teeth as the
heat of his life was forced from him. "Please, stop. I beg of
you. Please!"

Esprë didn't respond, not with a single word. She fed the
fire of all her frustrations and anger into her dragonmark
and let the grave chill of death ripple down her arms and into
her victim.

"Please," Ibrido whispered as the light left his eyes, as they
froze wide open, staring at the sky.

Esprë never uttered a word as she pulled her hands from

the dragon-elf's neck. The glow around him vanished, and what was left funneled back up her arms and disappeared. The dragonmark on her back that had itched for so long finally felt like it had been scratched.

Esprë looked down at the body beneath her and collapsed on top of it, sobbing. She wept for herself, for her lost innocence, and she wept for Ibrido as well. Sad as she was, she knew she wouldn't have done anything differently. She'd had to kill the dragon-elf, whether she wanted to or not. Now that it was done, so permanently, she cried—she knew that not even her hot tears could thaw him back to life.

Chapter

61

Burch heard Ibrido's final scream and smiled. "One more bastard down," he said. As he spoke, the dragon—one of its wings still smoking from its encounter with the ring of fire—soared past the ship's bow and beat its wings toward *Phoenix*.

"One more to go."

"We're not going anywhere but down," Te'oma said. "This airship is ready to explode!"

"We're not leaving them," Burch said, stabbing a finger at *Phoenix* as it scudded through the sky above. "Get this ship after that dragon, now!"

Te'oma shuddered, shaking her head. "We'll never make it," she said. "We'll blow up in midair."

Burch considered drawing his knife and threatening to kill the changeling. It would be a bad bluff though. If she could get a hold of herself long enough to think, she'd realize he couldn't fly the ship himself.

Instead, he reached out and steadied her by the shoulders. "They need us," he said. "If we don't get up there, they're all dead."

The changeling refused to meet his gaze. "They're dead either way," she said. "There's no way to stop that dragon. What good is it for us to toss our bodies onto the same pyre?"

Burch pulled Te'oma's chin around so that he could look into her round white eyes. Gazing back into his black eyes seemed to calm her. She stopped shivering, she swallowed hard, and she took a deep breath.

"Don't count us out yet," Burch said, patting the crossbow hanging from its sling around his shoulder. "We still have one angle left."

Te'oma exhaled through her nose and nodded. "All right," she said, staring up at the dragon and the airship above them. "What do you need me to do?"

Even before Burch could speak, the ring of fire around the airship crackled louder than ever, and *Keeper's Claw* leaped upward after its prey. The shifter grinned at the changeling as he took his crossbow in his hands again. "Just get me as close to that flying lizard as you can."

Te'oma nodded, then furrowed her brow with concentration. To Burch, the resultant roar sounded as if the elemental creature in the ring of fire laughed with glee. Whether with them or at them, he couldn't tell. He decided he didn't care to know.

The ship soared up after the dragon, devouring the distance between them. Burch couldn't tell for sure if they would catch up with Nithkorrh before it reached *Phoenix*, but the race would be close enough for him to hope.

Burch put an arm around Te'oma and escorted her to the ship's bow. Out here, as far from the airship's roaring ring as he could get, he had a much clearer field of fire. He knelt down and rested his crossbow against the gunwale and did his best to wait.

❦

"Monja!" Xalt shouted back toward the bridge. "We need you here now!"

"This ship won't pilot itself," the halfling called back.

Esprë cursed and raced back toward the bridge. "Can you save them?" Esprë asked in a raw voice as she raced toward the wheel.

"With luck and a prayer," Monja said, already halfway off the bridge. Her normally affable manner had turned dead serious. "Or two."

The warforged knelt down next to Kandler and Sallah, staining his knees with their blood. He couldn't tell whom all the crimson had spilled from, and at this point he didn't guess it mattered. Both the justicar and the knight required aid, more than he could give. Only the shaman's healing powers could save them now.

While Monja's tiny feet padded toward him, Xalt helped Duro separate the two. Kandler's skin had turned as white as the changeling's, and he looked like he might pass out at any moment. Sallah's complexion was not much better.

Xalt removed Sallah's breastplate to inspect the damage. Ibrido's sword had cut through her skin and bones. From the crimson dripping from her lips and the way she hacked out every breath, the warforged guessed she was bleeding into her lungs.

Xalt glanced at both of the humans as they raced toward death. He couldn't tell who would cross the finish line first.

"Is there anything I can do?" Esprë shouted from the bridge, near hysterics.

Xalt felt bad for the young elf. For all her power, her dragonmark could only destroy life, the opposite of what they needed right now.

Monja glanced back and shook her head at Esprë's request as she knelt down and began to pray. The halfling's lips moved so fast that Xalt could only guess at the words, but he could see the golden glow granted to her by her gods begin to form around her hands.

Then the warforged heard the roar of a furious dragon

coming fast off the starboard stern.

"I don't suppose you can do something about that?" Duro yelled to the young elf.

Esprë stared back at the dragon as it came rushing up toward them. "I don't think so," she shouted.

"Keep pushing," Burch said to Te'oma. "We're gaining on him."

The shifter glanced over his shoulder at the changeling, her eyes still closed, and saw the sweat beaded on her brow despite the chilly dusk air. He decided not to risk distracting her, and he went back to lining up an angle at Nithkorrh.

The dragon had dispensed with dodging about like it had before. Instead it put every bit of its effort into flying toward *Phoenix* as fast as its wings would take it. So far, the strategy had worked well. While *Keeper's Claw* was gaining on the dragon, they still weren't close enough that Burch felt he could risk a bolt.

As they neared the dragon, the gunwale started to tremble. For a moment, Burch thought he could compensate for it by lifting his crossbow up into his arms, but soon the entire airship began to shake as if every one of the boards that made it up might fly apart from each other at any second.

"What's going on?" Burch said, standing up into a wide stance.

"The ship can't take the speed!"

"Then slow it down. I can't loose a bolt like this."

The changeling grimaced for a moment. Burch noticed tears running down her cheeks. "I can't!" she said. "The elemental won't let me." She opened her eyes. "It wants to destroy the ship."

Burch cursed. He stared up at the dragon, wondering

what to do next. Then he turned to Te'oma and said, "Quit fighting it then. Give it what it wants."

The changeling's jaw dropped.

Burch pointed up at Nithkorrh. "Tell it to ram the dragon."

CHAPTER

62

Kandler opened his eyes to see Monja looking down at him. Her smile faded instantly, though, as a dragon's roar rattled the airship. "Welcome back to the land of the living," she said glancing up, "at least for now."

Kandler coughed out his thanks as he turned to look for Sallah, reaching out for her with his arm. She lay next to him, her chin and chest covered with blood.

"Is she—?" he started, thinking she was dead, wishing he could trade his life for hers.

The lady knight opened her emerald eyes and smiled at him. His heart leaped in his chest.

"Are you . . . ?"

"Stiff and sore?" she said as she struggled to sit up. She nodded. "You?"

"Happier than I have any right to be." He reached out and hugged her. As he did, he glanced around, searching for his daughter. He spied Esprë gazing down at him from behind the ship's wheel.

"I saw what you did, kid," he called. "You were great. If your mother—"

Esprë cut Kandler off with a scream. He whipped his head

about to see Nithkorrh hovering over the ship. The dragon turned to glare down at the group of people gathered there at the ship's bow.

"How thoughtful," the dragon said. "Now I can kill you all at once."

"Scatter!" Kandler yelled.

Xalt helped Sallah to her feet and pulled her to the port side of the ship, away from the others. Duro pushed Kandler in the other direction. Monja raced back toward the bridge.

Nithkorrh roared, then whipped back its neck in the way that Kandler now knew meant the beast was about to spit down at the ship. The justicar sprinted for the bridge, hoping to protect Esprë from the worst of the green acid. As he glared up defiantly at the dragon, *Keeper's Claw* barreled into the beast and knocked it from its spot in the sky.

Kandler threw back his head and cheered louder than he had since the end of the Last War.

"Let's get to the bridge!" Burch said. "When we smack that beast, we'll want to be as far from it as we can."

Te'oma raced ahead of the shifter along the length of the ship. He had to give her credit. He didn't think she'd be brave enough to push the elemental in the right direction—or trust him enough to do what he asked.

When they reached the bridge, Burch pulled her down to hunker behind the wooden console where the now-useless wheel hung. The ship shook so violently that the shifter wondered if they'd make it to the dragon before coming apart.

Burch peeked out over the console and spotted the dragon hanging in the air in front of *Keeper's Claw*, terrorizing the other airship below it. Nithkorrh's roaring at *Phoenix*'s passengers drowned out the mad crackling of *Keeper*'s ring of fire. The airship rocketed straight at the dragon, its prow aiming for its heart like a massive lance.

Glancing a hair lower, Burch saw his friends scattering from the dragon, heading in all directions across *Phoenix*'s deck. They all seemed to be alive, although some were soaked in blood. He didn't see Ibrido anywhere, which he hoped was a good sign.

As *Keeper's Claw* neared, the dragon finally heard it coming and turned to face it. Burch swore, knowing this could not be good. Then an idea struck him cold and clear.

"Come on," the shifter said, pulling Te'oma to her feet. "Spread those wings of yours. We're leaving."

"You're insane," the changeling said as he hauled her toward the ship's stern, her cloak already morphing from black cloth into a set of batlike wings. "These aren't strong enough to keep us both in the air."

"They just need to slow us down," Burch said, wrapping an arm around Te'oma's waist as he leaped off the back of the airship.

The changeling screamed.

Just as they left *Keeper's Claw*, she slammed into the dragon. The canny beast managed to avoid the ship's prow, slipping up over her to smash into the upper restraining arc instead. Its furious roar rang throughout the mountains as it found its wings too tangled in the ship for it to fly, and it crashed into the bridge, right where Burch and Te'oma had been. The airship's ring of fire flared again, like a bonfire fed a cartload of dry tinder, and the ship ground to a halt less than fifty yards past *Phoenix*.

The changeling's wings beat madly to keep the two of them in the sky, but gravity was sure to win that battle. Holding on to Te'oma by her belt, Burch arched out and around and leveled his crossbow back at the ship. Drifting lower in the sky like a wounded bird wasn't the best way to loose a bolt, but it beat riding an airship quaking like a toddler in a graveyard, and this time, the target stayed still.

Burch held the crossbow out in front of him at the end of

his arm for a moment, waiting for the angle to appear. Then he pulled its trigger and loosed the bolt.

The shockbolt sailed straight toward *Keeper's Claw* and smashed into its upper restraining arc, exploding against the curved length of rune-carved wood.

The dragon's head poked up from the bridge on its long, sinuous neck, and it unleashed a low, evil laugh.

"You missed!" Te'oma cried.

Burch grinned to himself.

"I wasn't aiming for the dragon."

The upper restraining arc of *Keeper's Claw* toppled forward over the bridge, trapping the dragon beneath it. As it fell, the magic inside it spilled out, and it released the monstrous elemental that had been trapped within its ring of fire for years.

The explosion engulfed the entire airship from stem to stern, including Nithkorrh. The dragon howled an unholy screech as the fire burned through its scales and flash-fried the flesh from its bones. Then it and the remains of the ship began a long, blazing descent to crash into the mountain far below, inscribing an arc across the heavens like a falling star.

The concussion from the blast knocked Te'oma and Burch senseless for a moment, but the changeling's cloak-wings kept beating. When the shifter managed to clear his head, he saw the deck of *Phoenix* rising to meet him, and he heard a cheer go up from his friends.

CHAPTER

63

Sitting on the deck of *Phoenix*, Kandler couldn't believe he was still alive. He held Esprë on his lap and kissed the back of her head, not sure he could ever bring himself to let her go. Sallah sat next to him, leaning into him. Every now and then, he heard her whisper, "Thank the Flame."

He looked at the people arranged around him and marveled at what they'd all been through. Burch paced back and forth at the bow, scouting the sky, making sure no other threats were coming their way. It seemed unlikely, but the shifter wasn't willing to take anything for granted.

Monja stood on the spokes of the ship's wheel again, pushing the ship gently toward the southwest, back in the direction of her homeland. The Talenta Plains stretched out before them, holding the promise of a respite if not an actual haven. Could anything protect them from the dangers that still threatened them? Certainly not the tribes of halfling barbarians over which Monja's father ruled—if it could be said that anyone did.

Xalt sat in front of him, fawning over Esprë. The two had formed a quick bond back in Construct when Kandler had entrusted the warforged with his daughter's welfare. That link had been cemented when Te'oma had stabbed Xalt in the back and kidnapped the young elf once again.

Kandler guessed that Esprë enjoyed the simplicity of the warforged's outlook. Here was a creature with little or no history, no twisting lines of family politics full of intrigue. He was about as unlike an elf as you could get.

As for Xalt, perhaps he was just interested in children, having never been one himself. Like all warforged, he had come into the world fully grown, and to discover a person who was not only a child but had been one for longer than Xalt had been alive must have piqued his curiosity to no end.

Duro prowled the deck, reflecting on moments that left him thrilled and then dour. The dwarf grieved for all the good friends he'd lost today, but the thought that he'd helped rid his ancient homeland of the creature that had plagued it for so long pleased him more than he could express. Kandler wondered what the dwarf would do now. Was there anyone waiting for him back home? Or was he now without any ties at all?

Te'oma lay sprawled on her back in the middle of the deck. She hadn't said much of anything since she and Burch had landed on *Phoenix*. Kandler was grateful to her for everything she'd done—he didn't know if they'd have prevailed without her help—but he still wasn't sure he could trust her. She'd been a strong ally when they'd faced a common foe, but now that the dragon was dead, he couldn't tell what she might try next.

"Where to now, boss?" Burch said as he came up behind the justicar. "Monja needs a direction."

Kandler nodded. "Back to the Talenta Plains is fine for now," he said. "If we can find the Wandering Inn again, we can lay in some more supplies and take a short break, get healthy before we head out again."

"How about after that?"

That was the real question, wasn't it? He'd not had long

to think about this. Before, he'd thought maybe they'd go back to Sharn. He still had friends there, family even. In a place like the City of Towers, they could blend in, disappear, at least for a while.

He knew it wouldn't last though. Eventually someone would find them: servants of Vol, agents of the dragon kings, even missionaries from the Undying Court.

"I'm tired," he said, giving Esprë a squeeze, "tired of running, of hiding. It's time we went on the offensive."

"What do you mean?" Sallah asked, pushing herself up to sit on her own.

"These forces after Esprë, they're never going to stop until they get their hands on her, right?"

"She could come to Thrane. She'd be welcome in Flamekeep, and the full complement of the Knights of the Silver Flame would work to protect her."

Kandler shook his head. "That would only bring the dragons down on your heads." He put up his hand to silence her objections. "I respect you and your friends, but can you believe they'd be able to withstand a full-out dragon assault? I'd rather not see all of Flamekeep burn on Esprë's behalf."

Sallah grimaced at the thought. "Where else do you suggest?" she asked. "Should we return to Mardakine? Or Metrol? Perhaps flee north across the Thunder Sea?"

Kandler shook his head. "There's only one choice for us. We'll find the Wandering Inn and outfit ourselves for a long voyage. Then we'll head for Valenar."

"The elf colony?" Esprë said. "I haven't been there for decades. I don't think I know anyone there any more."

Kandler ruffled her hair. "That's all right. That's not our final stop."

"Where to from there?" Te'oma asked, implying that she would accompany them wherever they might go—perhaps whether Kandler liked it or not.

"To Aerenal, of course."

"To a whole continent full of those pointy-eared elitists?" Duro said. "Sounds like a slice of damnation."

"That's where the Undying Court sits," Sallah said. "Aren't those some of the people who would want Esprë dead?"

"Some of them, sure, but not all of them, I don't think, not if it's going to mean exterminating a good chunk of their population. With luck, we can get them to side with us."

"Side with us against who, boss?"

Kandler looked up at Burch and then around into the eyes of each of the others, all of them waiting for him to speak.

"Against the dragons of Argonnessen," he said. "They want a war, and we're going to give it to them."

Glossary

Aerenal: An island nation off the southeastern coast of Khorvaire. Aerenal is known as the homeland of the elves.

Argonnessen: A large continent to the southeast of Eberron, said to be the home of dragons.

Argonth: A floating town designed as a mobile fortress to help defend Breland during the Last War.

Ascendant councilor: One of the revered undead of the elves of Aerenal.

Balinor: One of the Sovereign Host, god of beasts and the hunt.

Baronet Walsley: A halfling leader of House Ghallanda, in charge of the Wandering Inn.

Barrakas: The largest of Eberron's twelve moons.

Bastard: A warforged lieutenant of the Lord of Blades and commander of Construct.

Berlun: The lath (chief) of a band of nomadic halflings living in the Talenta Plains.

Bitter Sea: The sea to the north of Khorvaire.

blackscale lizardfolk: The largest and strongest of the lizardfolk of Khorvaire. They live in the jungles around Haka'torvhak and serve the dragon Rhashaak.

Blade Desert: A barren landscape at the western foot of the Endworld and Ironroot Mountains that forms the eastern border of the Talenta Plains.

Blood of Vol: Those who worship the Blood of Vol refuse to bow to the power of death. Drawn from the traditions of an ancient line of elven necromancers, the Blood of Vol seeks to abolish death. They revere vampires and other undead creatures as champions in this struggle. This tradition is especially strong in the nation of Karrnath, and while it is not inherently evil, there are subsects—notably the infamous Order of the Emerald Claw—that have turned the battle against death into a struggle to dominate the living. As a result, throughout most of the Five Nations the common image of a follower of the Blood is that of a crazed necromancer leading an army of zombies as part of some mad scheme. The Church of the Silver Flame takes a particularly hard stand against followers of the Blood, and knights of the Flame may assume the worst when dealing with acolytes of Vol.

bloodwing: A fibrous, living symbiont, possessed of its own intelligence, which can sometimes bond to another creature. When dormant, the bloodwing's fibrous body shrinks to a very small size, but when aroused, the creature expands to large batlike wings, enabling its host the power of flight.

"breather": A derogatory term used by the warforged to describe non-construct creatures, e.g., elves, humans, dwarves, shifters, etc.

Breland: The largest of the original Five Nations of Galifar, Breland is a center of heavy industry. The current ruler of Breland is King Boranel ir'Wyrnarn.

Brendis: A young Knight of the Silver Flame.

Burch: A shifter and deputy justicar of Mardakine.

Captain of Bones: Commander of Fort Bones, currently Berre Stonefist.

changeling: Members of the changeling race possess a limited ability to change face and form, allowing a changeling to disguise itself as a member of another race or to impersonate an individual. Changelings are said to be the offspring of humans and doppelgangers. They are relatively few in number and have no lands or culture of their own but are scattered across Khorvaire.

clawfoot: A human-sized predator of the Talenta Plains. This lizard is often used as a war-mount by the Halfling nomadic tribes. (A velociraptor.)

cold fire: Magical flame that produces no heat and does not burn. Cold fire is used to provide light in most cities of Khorvaire.

Construct: A mobile city of the warforged in the Mournland.

Council of Cardinals: Along with the Keeper of the Flame, the ruling council of the Church of the Silver Flame.

Cyre: One of the original Five Nations of Galifar, known for its fine arts and crafts. The governor of Cyre was traditionally raised to the throne of Galifar, but in 894 YK, Kaius of Karrnath, Wroann of Breland, and Thalin of Thrane rebelled against Mishann of Cyre. During the war, Cyre lost significant amounts of territory to elf and goblin mercenaries, creating the nations of Valenar and Darguun. In 994 YK, Cyre was devastated by a disaster of unknown origin that transformed the nation into a hostile wasteland populated by deadly monsters. Breland offered sanctuary to the survivors of the Mourning, and most of the Cyran refugees have taken advantage of this amnesty.

Dagger River: One of the largest rivers in Khorvaire, the Dagger runs south through Breland and into the Thunder Sea.

Dal Quor: Another plane of existence. Mortal spirits are said to travel to Dal Quor when they dream.

Darguul: Common name for someone or something from Darguun.

Darguun: A nation of goblinoids founded in 969 YK when a hobgoblin leader named Haruuc formed an alliance among the goblinoid mercenaries and annexed a section of southern Cyre. Breland recognized this new nation in exchange for a peaceful border and an ally against Cyre. Few people trust the people of Darguun, but their soldiers remain a force to be reckoned with.

Dark Six: The six malevolent deities of the Sovereign Host, whose true names are not known.

Darumnakt, Duro: A dwarf of Clan Drakyager of the Mror Holds, leader of the patrols through Mount Darumkrak.

Darumnakt, Wolph: The younger cousin of Duro Darumnakt, who works the patrols with him.

Day of Mourning, the: A disaster that occurred on Olarune 20, 994 YK. The origin and precise nature of the Mourning are unknown. On Ollarune 20, gray mists spread across Cyre, and anything caught within the mists was transformed or destroyed. See the Mournland.

Deathguard: An elite order of Aereni knights and priests, dedicated to the utter eradication of evil undead and the necromancers who defile the souls and bodies of the dead. The Deathguard played a critical role in the destruction of the line of Vol.

Deothen: A senior Knight of the Silver Flame.

Dol Arrah: The Sovereign of Sun and Sacrifice. She is a patron of war, but she fights her battles with words and cunning strategy as well as steel. She is a god of light and honor, and her holy paladins seek to bring her sunlight to the darkest places of the world.

Dol Dorn: The Sovereign of Strength and Steel. He is the lord of war and patron to all who raise their arms in battle. He is the patron of physical arts, and the greatest sporting events of the year are held to mark his holy days. His followers are not held to the same standards of nobility and sacrifice as those of his sister, Dol Arrah, but he still encourages honorable conduct.

Dolurrh: The plane of the dead. When mortals die, their spirits are said to travel to Dolurrh and then slowly fade away, passing to whatever final fate awaits the dead.

dragonmark: 1) A mystical mark that appears on the surface of the skin and grants mystical powers to its bearer. 2) A slang term for the bearer of a dragonmark.

Dragonmarked Houses: One of the thirteen families whose bloodlines carry the potential to manifest a dragonmark. Many of the dragonmarked houses existed before the kingdom of Galifar, and they have used their mystical powers to gain considerable political and economic influence.

Drakyager: A clan of dwarves who once lived under Mount Darumkrak in the Mror Holds.

Dreaming Dark: A secret order of psionic spies and assassins that serves as the eyes and hands of the quori in Dal Quor, the Region of Dreams.

Eberron: 1) The world. 2) A mythical dragon said to have formed the world from her body in primordial times and to have given birth to natural life. Also known as "The Dragon Between."

Endworld Mountains: A large chain of mountains that separates the southeastern Talenta Plains from the land of Q'barra.

Eternal Fire: See cold fire.

Esprë: Kandler's elven stepdaughter.

Esprina: Kandler's elven wife, now deceased.

Everbright Lantern: A lantern infused with cold fire, creating a permanent light source. These items are used to provide illumination in most of the cities and larger communities of Khorvaire. An everbright lantern usually has a shutter allowing the light to be sealed off when darkness is desirable.

Farlnen: One of the largest and northernmost islands that make up the Lhazaar Principalities.

Finders Guild: A guild controlled by House Tharashk, made up of those carrying the Mark of Finding, as well as freelance inquisitives, law enforcement agents, bounty hunters, and explorers.

Fingerbone Mountains: A range of mountains on the isle of Farlnen.

Five Nations: The five provinces of the Kingdom of Galifar: Aundair, Breland, Cyre, Karrnath, and Thrane.

Flamekeep: The capital of Thrane.

'forged: A slang term for the warforged.

Fort Bones: A Karrnathi outpost that guards the border between Karrnath and the Talenta Plains. It is manned primarily by human and dwarf mercenaries, bolstered by a large force of almost one hundred Karrnathi skeletons.

Fort Zombie: A Karrnathi outpost that guards the border between Karrnath and the Mournland.

Galifar: 1) A cunning warrior and skilled diplomat who forged five nations into a single kingdom that came to dominate the continent of Khorvaire. 2) The kingdom of Galifar I, which came to an end in 894 YK with the start of the Last War. 3) A golden coin minted by the kingdom, bearing the image of the first king. The golden galifar is still in use today and is worth ten sovereigns.

Gatherhold: A large town built into the rocky outcroppings and hills along the eastern shore of Lake Cyre. It is considered the capital of the Talenta Plains.

ghostbeast: An aggressive, glowing creature found in Metrol.

Ginty's: A Brelish pub in the heart of Metrol.

glidewing: A large, birdlike reptile with a long, toothy beak, a thin headcrest, sharp talons, and small claws at the joints of its leathery wings. It is often used as a mount by Talenta Plains halflings. (A pterosaur.)

Gweir: A young Knight of the Silver Flame.

Haka'torvhak: An ancient city in Q'barra, carved into the side of an enormous volcano. The name literally means "the throne of the holy dragons," and the city serves as the center of the Q'barran lizardfolk religion.

Halpum: Lathon (high chief) of one of the largest nomadic tribes of the Talenta Plains halflings.

House Cannith: The Dragonmarked House that carries the Mark of Making. The artificers and magewrights of House Cannith are responsible for most of the magical innovations of the past millennia. The house made tremendous profits during the Last War through sales of arms and armor, including warforged soldiers.

House Ghallanda: The halfling House of Hospitality and bearer of the Mark of Hospitality.

Ibrido: A lieutenant of the Captain of Bones.

Ikar the Black: The leader of a band of outlaws who often ventures into the Mournland in search of treasure and artifacts.

Illmarrow Castle: Home of Vol on the island of Farlnen.

Iron Council: The governing council of the Mror Holds, made up of a conclave of the major clans.

Ironroot Mountains: The large mountain chain that makes up the western border of the Mror Holds.

ir'Ranek, Alain: Captain of the city of Argonth.

ir'Wyrnarn, Boranel: King of Breland.

Jaela Daran: The young Keeper of the Flame, head of the Church of the Silver Flame.

Jhorash'tar: A loose confederation of orcs that haunts the darkest, least hospitable parts of the Ironroot Mountains.

justicar: An official chosen to enforce the law and keep the peace. Justicars have little legal authority beyond their local jurisdiction.

Kaius III: King of Karrnath.

Kallo: A young dwarf of Clan Drakyager of the Mror Holds, who works under Duro Darumnakt.

Kandler: Justicar of Mardakine.

Karaktrok, Medd: A slow-witted dwarf of Clan Drakyager of the Mror Holds, who works under Duro Darumnakt.

Karrnath: One of the original Five Nations of Galifar. Karrnath is a cold, grim land whose people are renowned for their martial prowess. The current ruler of Karrnath is King Kaius ir'Wyrnarn III.

Keeper of the Flame, the: The head of the Church of the Silver Flame.

Keeper's Claw: A Karrnathi airship currently stationed at Fort Bones.

Khorvaire: One of the continents of Eberron, home of the Five Nations of Galifar as well as many other regions.

Khyber: 1) The underworld. 2) A mythical dragon, also known as "The Dragon Below." After killing Siberys, Khyber was imprisoned by Eberron and transformed into the underworld. Khyber is said to have given birth to a host of demons and other unnatural creatures. See Eberron, Siberys.

Korth: Capital city of Karrnath.

Krezent: An ancient ruin in the Talenta Plains. It is home to a tribe of benevolent yuan-ti who revere the Silver Flame.

Krona Peak: Capital city of the Mror Holds.

Lake Cyre: A large lake between the Talenta Plains and the Mournland.

Last War, The: This conflict began in 894 YK with the death of King Jarot ir'Wyrnarn, the last king of Galifar. Following Jarot's death, three of his five children refused to follow the ancient traditions of succession, and the kingdom split. The war lasted over a hundred years, and it took the utter destruction of Cyre to bring the other nations to the negotiating table. No one has admitted defeat, but no one wants to risk being the next victim of the Mourning. The chronicles are calling the conflict "the Last War," hoping that the bloodshed might have finally slaked humanity's thirst for battle. Only time will tell if this hope is in vain.

lath: The tribal chief among Talenta Plains halflings.

lathon: The "chief of chiefs," i.e., a leader of several tribes among the Talenta Plains halflings.

Levritt: A young Knight of the Silver Flame.

Lhazaar Principalities: A collection of small island nations that run along the northeastern coast of Khorvaire. The people of the Lhazaar Principalities are renowned seafarers, and there is a strong tradition of piracy in the region.

lightning rail: A means of transportation by which a coach propelled by an air elemental travels along a rail system of conductor stones, which hold the craft aloft.

Llesh Haruuc: A Darguul hobgoblin leader in the Last War.

Lord of Blades: A warforged leader reputed to be gathering a substantial following of other warforged somewhere in the Mournland.

Lords of Dust: An evil cabal, plotting to free their ancient masters from the depths of Khyber.

Lost Mark: Common term for the Mark of Death.

lupallo: A breed of horse noted for its distinctive white-and-brown patched coloring.

Majeeda: An ancient elf wizard.

Mardakine: A small settlement on the border between Breland and the Mournland.

Mark of Death: Believed extinct for hundreds of years, this dragonmark holds powers of death.

Mark of Hospitality: The dragonmark that holds powers of food and shelter.

Mark of Shadow: The dragonmark that holds powers of illusion, deception, and scrying.

Meesh: Karrnathi bosun of *Keeper's Claw*.

Metrol: Capital city of the doomed nation of Cyre.

Monja: Halfling shaman of the Talenta Plains, daughter of Lathon Halpum.

Mount Darumkrak: A large peak in the Ironroot Mountains.

Mourning, The: A disaster that occurred on Olarune 20, 994 YK. The origin and precise nature of the Mourning are unknown. On Ollarune 20, gray mists spread across Cyre, and anything caught within the mists was transformed or destroyed. See the Mournland.

Mournland, The: A common name for the wasteland left behind in the wake of the Mourning. A wall of dead-gray mist surrounds the borders of the land that once was Cyre. Behind this mist, the land has been transformed into something dark and twisted. Most creatures that weren't killed were transformed into horrific monsters. Stories speak of storms of blood, corpses that do not decompose, ghostly soldiers fighting endless battles, and far worse things.

Mror Holds: A nation of dwarves and gnomes located in the Ironroot Mountains.

New Cyre: A large town in Breland that began as a refugee settlement but has since grown into a sizeable community.

Nithkorrh: A black dragon.

Norra: A resident of Mardakine and friend of Kandler. She often watches Esprë when Kandler is out.

Oargev ir'Wynarn: The last surviving son of Cyre's ruling family, who has since become the unofficial leader of the Cyran refugees scattered throughout Khorvaire.

Olladra: One of the Sovereign Host, goddess of feast and fortune, bringer of luck and joy.

Phoenix: An old airship that Kandler and the others found in the Mournland. At Fort Bones, she was repaired and renamed *Phoenix*.

Puakel: Karrnathi soldier at Fort Bones.

Pylas Maradal: A port city on the southern coast of Valenar.

Q'barra: A young nation hidden within the jungles of southeastern Khorvaire.

Rhashaak: Draconic overlord of Haka'torvhak.

Rings of Siberys: A ring of dragonshards that encircles the world high above Eberron's equator.

Rislinto: Mardakine's resident blacksmith.

Sallah: A Knight of the Silver Flame.

Seawall Mountains: A mountain chain in southern Breland. The Seawall separates Darguun and Zilargo, and many kobolds and goblinoids still lurk in its shadows.

Shano: An old dwarf of Clan Drakyager of the Mror Holds, who works under Duro Darumnakt and who likes his drink.

Sharn: Also known as the City of Towers, Sharn is the largest city in Khorvaire.

shifter: A humanoid race said to be descended from humans and lycanthropes. Shifters have a feral, bestial appearance and can briefly call on their lycanthropic heritage to draw animalistic characteristics to the fore. While they are most comfortable in natural environs, shifters can be found in most of the major cities of Khorvaire.

shockbolt: Magical crossbow bolts that explode on contact.

Siberys: 1) The ring of stones that circles the world. 2) A mythical dragon, also called "The Dragon Above." Siberys is said to have been destroyed by Khyber. Some believe that the ring of Siberys is the source of all magic.

Silver Flame, the: A powerful spiritual force dedicated to cleaning evil influences from the world. Over the last five hundred years, a powerful church has been established around the Silver Flame.

Sovereign: 1) A silver coin depicting a current or recent monarch. A sovereign is worth ten crowns. 2) One of the deities of the Sovereign Host.

Sovereign Host, the: A pantheistic religion with a strong following across Khorvaire.

sprayship: A watercraft propelled by a water elemental.

Spurbin: A halfling hunter of the Talenta Plains.

Ss'lange: A lycanthropic yuan-ti (lizardman) from Q'barra.

Stonefist, Berre: Currently Captain of Bones, commander of the Fort of Bones in southern Karrnath.

swordtooth: A large predator of the Talenta Plains. (A tyrannosaur.)

Talenta Plains: A vast stretch of grassland to the east of Khorvaire, the Talenta Plains are home to a proud halfling culture. The people of the Talenta Plains live a nomadic lifestyle that has remained more or less unchanged for thousands of years, though over the centuries a number of tribes have left the grasslands to settle in the Five Nations. A wide variety of large reptiles are found in the Talenta Plains, and the halfling warriors are known for their fearsome clawfoot mounts.

Tan Du: A vampire.

Temmah: A dwarf resident of Mardakine, currently serving as one of the deputy justicars.

Te'oma: A changeling.

Thrane: One of the original Five Nations of Galifar, Thrane is the seat of power for the Church of the Silver Flame. During the Last War, the people of Thrane chose to give the church power above that of the throne. Queen Diani ir'Wynarn serves as a figurehead, but true power rests in the hands of the Church, which is governed by the council of cardinals and Jaela Daeran, the young Keeper of the Flame.

threehorn: A large herbivorous lizard of the Talenta Plains. (A triceratops.)

Thunder Sea: The large sea separating Khorvaire from the continent of Xen'drik.

Treaty of Thronehold: The treaty that ended the Last War.

Trisfo: A Karrnathi soldier at Fort Bones.

Undying Court: The council of deathless elders that advises and empowers the rulers of Aerenal.

Valenar: A realm of southeastern Khorvaire populated primarily by elves who came to Khorvaire to fight in the Last War and later founded their own nation.

Vol: The Lich Queen, founder of the Blood of Vol.

Wandering Inn: A traveling fair run by House Ghallanda that moves throughout the Talenta Plains. It provides a place for rest and trade for the tribes and other travelers that range far from Gatherhold.

warforged: A race of humanoid constructs crafted from wood, leather, metal, and stone, and given life and sentience through magic. The warforged were created by House Cannith, which sought to produce tireless, expendable soldiers capable of adapting to any tactical situation. Cannith developed a wide range of military automatons, but the spark of true sentience eluded them until 965 YK, when Aaren d'Cannith perfected the first of the modern warforged. A warforged soldier is roughly the same shape as an adult male human, though typically slightly taller and heavier. There are many different styles of warforged, each crafted for a specific military function: heavily-armored infantry troops, faster scouts and skirmishers, and many more. While warforged are brought into existence with the knowledge required to fulfill their function, they have the capacity to learn, and with the war coming to a close, many are searching their souls and wondering what place they might have in a world at peace.

Whitecliff: A small town in Q'barra. It rests in the foothills of the Endworld Mountains.

Wodager: The halfling shaman who trained Monja.

Xalt: A warforged artificer.

yuan-ti: One of the minor races of Eberron, yuan-ti are descended from humans who mingled their bloodlines with serpentine creatures.

Zilargo: Located on the southern coast of Khorvaire, Zilargo is the homeland of the gnomes. Known for its vast universities and libraries, Zilargo also possesses considerable mineral wealth in the form of gemstones and Khyber dragonshards. The gnomes themselves are masterful diplomats, shipwrights, and alchemists, renowned for their cunning and inquisitive nature.

ENTER THE NEW WORLD OF

THE
DREAMING DARK
TRILOGY

Written by Keith Baker
The winning voice of the DUNGEONS & DRAGONS® setting search

CITY OF TOWERS
Volume One

Hardened by the Last War, four soldiers have come to Sharn,
fabled City of Towers, capital of adventure. In a time of uneasy
peace, these hardened warriors must struggle to survive. And
then people start turning up dead. The heroes find themselves
in an adventure that will take them from the highest reaches of
power to the most sordid depths of the city of wonder, shadow,
and adventure.

THE SHATTERED LAND
Volume Two

The epic adventure continues as Daine and the remnants of
his company travel to the dark continent of Xen'drik on an
adventure that may kill them all.

AVAILABLE IN 2005!

ENTER THE EXCITING, NEW DUNGEONS AND DRAGONS® SETTING... THE WORLD OF

THE
WAR~TORN
TRILOGY

THE CRIMSON TALISMAN
Book One

Adrian Cole

Erethindel, the fabled Crimson Talisman. Long sought by the forces of darkness. Long guarded in secret by one family. But now the secret has been revealed, and only one young man can keep it safe. As the talisman's powers awaken within him, Erethindel tears at his soul.

THE ORB OF XORIAT
Book Two

Edward Bolme

The Last War is over, and it took all that Teron ever had. A monk trained for war, he is the last of his Order. Now he is on a quest to find a powerful weapon that might set the world at war again.

AVAILABLE IN 2005!

THIS IS WHERE YOUR STORY BEGINS

Create your own heroes and embark on epic tales of adventure filled with monsters, magic, trouble, and treasure with the **Dungeons & Dragons**® roleplaying game. You'll find everything you need to get started in the **D&D**® *Basic Game* and can take your game to the next level with the **D&D** *Player's Handbook*™.

Pick them up at your favorite bookstore.

wizards.com/dnd